INTO THE DEEP

OTHER TITLES BY BRITTNEY SAHIN

Stand-Alones

Until You Can't

The Story of Us

Falcon Falls Security

The Hunted One

The Broken One

The Guarded One

The Taken One

The Lost Letters: A Novella

The Wanted One

The Fallen One

The Wrecked One

Dublin Nights Series

On the Edge

On the Line

The Real Deal

The Inside Man

The Final Hour

Becoming Us

Someone Like You

My Every Breath

Hidden Truths Series

The Safe Bet

Beyond the Chase

The Hard Truth

Surviving the Fall

The Final Goodbye

Stealth Ops Series

Finding His Mark

Finding Justice

Finding the Fight

Finding Her Chance

Finding the Way Back

Chasing the Knight

Chasing Daylight

Chasing Fortune

Chasing Shadows

Chasing the Storm

Costa Family

Let Me Love You

Not Mine to Keep

The Art of You

The Best of Us

Delta Shield Security

Against All Odds

INTO THE DEEP

BRITTNEY SAHIN

This is a work of fiction. Names, characters, organizations, places, events, and incidents are either products of the author's imagination or are used fictitiously. Otherwise, any resemblance to actual persons, living or dead, is purely coincidental.

Published by Montlake, Seattle

www.apub.com

EU product safety contact:
Amazon Media EU S. à r.l.
38, avenue John F. Kennedy, L-1855 Luxembourg
amazonpublishing-gpsr@amazon.com

ISBN-13: 9781662526725 (paperback)
ISBN-13: 9781662526732 (digital)

Cover design by Caroline Johnson
Cover image: © Wander Aguiar Photography; © TravelCouples / Getty

Printed in the United States of America

INTO THE DEEP

PROLOGUE

Alejandro

Queenstown, New Zealand; February 2027

I scanned the crowded event, my heart pounding at the fact I'd lost sight of her. I knew Ryder would have eyes on her if I didn't, but still—she was *my* wife.

Well, not really mine. Not legally. But try telling that to my heart, soul, and brain. They'd teamed up and bought the lie around my finger like it was the gospel truth.

There you are. My entire body relaxed the second I found her.

Of course she'd drifted closer to the orchestra. The sax solo had lured Audrey in, her hand at her side, fingers moving as if she were playing along on some invisible piano. She was locked in and completely mesmerized by the music, just like I was with her.

I lifted my bourbon for a sip, needing to steady my pulse, but the band on my finger caught my eye. Clinging to me like it belonged there, representing a false sense of forever with my best friend's sister.

And here I am, trying to remind myself we didn't actually exchange vows. While in truth, I was already in so deep with her, I might as well have been standing at the earth's core.

Then she turned. Swept the skirt of her dress aside to find me. And I rose. Not just to the surface, but to the top of the entire damn world.

Her blonde hair was pinned up, a few loose strands framing her face the same way my hands had not too long ago. Her hair softened the line of her jaw, pulling my attention to the delicate curve of her neck. Then down to the perfect slope of her shoulders, and to the black dress that looked like it'd been painted on her body. The memory of where my hands had been earlier hit me all over again.

Not really my wife. That reminder ghosted over my skin, tightening the collar of my shirt, crawling across my shoulders, slipping down my spine.

I lowered my tumbler to my side, letting it rest against the leg of my tailored Italian slacks as I remembered what had happened in the honeymoon suite tonight.

She finally looked away, but I didn't. I *couldn't.*

I only wished I could make everyone vanish, right along with our problems.

At the feeling of being watched by someone else, I pivoted. Delta One's eyes were on me. Audrey's brother. My friend of fifteen years.

I made love to your sister tonight. Broke my promise.

I wished I could blame it on walking in on her half dressed, standing there in wedding-white lace. It wasn't the first time I'd seen her naked, but tonight had been different.

Tonight, after I'd slid the wedding band on her finger, she didn't just feel like my wife. She felt like my forever. And when she'd whispered orders to herself to stop touching me, given what was at stake, her fingers kept moving. Kept unbuttoning my white dress shirt. Mine didn't follow my own commands to shut it down, either.

At Ryder's continued stare, I cleared my throat, forcing my head back into the game. I gave him a subtle nod, one I hoped he'd read as *I'm fine.*

That was far from the truth. And he'd know it. No way was he fine, not with what was about to go down any minute.

But it would be over soon.

So would this role as Audrey's husband.

After all, we were here because Audrey's reality shattered a year ago, when her son's stepfather's plane went down.

But in this world, nothing stayed buried.

Not lies.

Not the truth.

And apparently, not even the dead.

CHAPTER ONE

Audrey

Evergreen, Colorado; one week earlier

Six months, fourteen days, and three hours. Give or take. That was how long I'd been trying to turn this house into a home. But I knew my fresh start couldn't happen until I dealt with this box.

With my bedroom feeling far too quiet, I set my half-empty glass of red wine on the dresser and went over to the old record player I hadn't touched since the move. It'd belonged to my dad. The man who'd raised me as his own, never letting me know I wasn't biologically his—not even on his deathbed.

I opened the lid. The last vinyl I'd played back in Virginia still rested on the turntable.

"Not sure I can handle you tonight. Not with that box glaring at me." Against my better judgment, I moved the arm in place and dropped the needle, letting Ella Fitzgerald's "The Man I Love" play.

The first crackle of sound ran up my spine. Each note unfurled like a memory I wasn't ready for, curling into the air.

I turned toward the unopened box in the corner of my room.

My hands settled on my hips, fingers aching for piano keys instead of scissors to cut through packing tape to get to the emotional land mines.

Just do it. This was why I'd asked Trevor to take Chase out in the first place, to be alone with this box and finally deal with it.

After two and a half hours, all I'd done was scroll job listings, cry into half a bottle of red, and avoid it.

I knelt in front of the box, the same way Mitch had dropped to both knees when he proposed, and I picked up the scissors I'd left on the floor.

With my free hand, I traced the tape's seam, exhaling a shaky breath as I remembered the day I packed the items inside shortly after Mitch died a year ago.

I sliced the tape down the center, peeling it back like an old wound. One flap. Then the other.

A yellow envelope sat on top of the neatly folded remnants of a life that didn't belong to me anymore. Inside were divorce papers. Mine signed, his untouched. Because Mitch never had the chance. He'd never come home.

His death had changed me from a woman secretly enduring the collapse of her marriage to a widow.

People had mourned his loss, hugged me, cried at my side, and whispered about the tragedy. But no one had asked what our final months had really been like. No one saw me as someone grieving two different kinds of loss. And why would they? The only person aside from Mitch who had known our marriage was over was my lawyer.

But to lose him like that? To really lose him meant I wasn't allowed to be mad anymore.

I wasn't allowed to feel bitter or broken, because what kind of person hates the dead?

I set aside the envelope and reached for his ring box, which was sitting on top of a folded-up flag in a glass case.

He'd had no family besides me to take his belongings, so I was stuck with everything.

Each piece was a painful reminder of promises he'd stopped trying to keep long before his uniform made it into the box.

Died serving our country. Died as my husband. And died having broken my heart before his plane went down.

As the record slowed to its final, haunting notes, a chill crept up my arms and silence reclaimed the room.

I opened the ring box, and something shifted. I didn't believe in ghosts, but . . .

"Mitch?" I glanced over my shoulder.

The air felt wrong. There was a painful, biting sting to it.

I'm not ready for this.

I had a decent excuse to leave the box untouched for another day. Chase would be overtired if he wasn't home and in bed soon. I'd be the one dealing with our cranky son in the morning, not Trevor. But that was me, always worrying about tomorrow, even though tomorrow seemed to take care of itself.

The *tick-tick-tick*ing of the grandfather clock sliced through the quiet, alerting me to the fact that it was officially ten o'clock.

I put the ring box away and pushed off the floor to grab my phone to text Trevor, my ex-husband.

Yes, I'd been married twice. Of course people judged me. And as my son wisely liked to say, *Sometimes people just suck.*

Me: Almost back? It's late.

Trevor: Be there in 5. We went for ice cream after the movie.

I relaxed for a second, relieved that he'd answered, only to tense again at his response.

Me: He's lactose intolerant.

Trevor: A little dairy won't hurt him.

Me: The nausea he'll have all night will. And why are you texting while driving? Especially at night while it's snowing.

Trevor: Why are you texting me while knowing I'm driving with such precious cargo, then?

Trevor: And I'm voice-texting. Relax.

Trevor: And I got him that vegan crap. Even if I think that dairy intolerance stuff is nonsense. So, relax there too.

Me: Maybe one day he'll thank you for toughening up his gut. Today's not that day.

Trevor: Roger that.

Trevor was an excellent father, and even a good friend now, but we were total opposites, and sometimes he could be such a pain in the butt.

I tossed my phone onto the bed and went to my dresser for the wine. I needed to kill five minutes, and it wouldn't be with that box.

Instead of picking up my glass, I lifted the framed picture beside it. It was a photo of Chase mid–snowball fight with his uncle, Ryder, along with Ryder's two teammates. Three elite Delta operators had lost—and lost quite comically—to my son.

We'd taken hundreds of photos during those few days at Christmas, trying to make up for lost time.

Trevor had spent the holiday with his parents in Michigan, so I'd used the quiet to introduce myself to my brother. The brother I'd only found out existed at Thanksgiving, when I learned the man who'd raised me as his daughter my whole life wasn't my biological dad.

Talk about an eye-opening family dinner. Something told me it wasn't the wine that'd loosened my mother's lips that evening; it was the guilt she'd been living with for thirty-three years.

The ink on the paperwork for this house had barely been dry when I had to survive two curveballs: I had another dad and a half brother. One sent me packing, and the other welcomed me with open arms.

I was seconds from rethinking every bad decision I'd ever made when my neighbor's dog started barking. I set down the photo, the barking drowning out the clock but not the other sound. Had the floorboards creaked downstairs?

I tried to listen closely, but Peter Pan, the Labradoodle next door, wouldn't quiet down long enough for me to focus.

Still, that noise hadn't come from the pipes . . . and I *had* heard something, hadn't I?

Feet flat to the floor, I crept toward the door, intending to shut and lock it. I was *not* going to be like the girl in a horror movie who investigated strange noises in the dark.

Of course, even Chase knew how to pick the lock with a butter knife, which was why step two would be to grab my phone. Step three was under my bed.

Trevor had insisted I keep a gun in the house—a 9mm in a biometric lockbox. I'd humored him, never thinking I'd need it.

Please, God, don't let tonight be the exception.

Chills burst up my back and goose bumps covered my skin as I softly turned the lock. That sense of unease spread into something sharp and distinct. Something *real.* No, my mind wasn't playing tricks on me. *Someone's here.*

Peter Pan finally went quiet, and I heard the unmistakable sound of someone walking around my house.

My heart pounded, terror tightening in my chest. My lungs begged to scream, but fear and common sense held me in silence.

I backed away from the door, grabbed my phone, and called Trevor. I fell to my knees by the bed with plans to reach for the lockbox.

"Hey, we're pulling in to the driveway now," Trevor answered as the doorknob rattled, officially triggering my panic.

"Someone's in the—"

I never finished. Never made it to the gun, either, because the lock gave easily.

The door flung open, and I let out the scream I'd been holding in so Trevor would know to keep Chase away from the danger.

A man in dark clothing, face hidden behind a ski mask, stepped inside. His gaze snapped to my phone, to Trevor shouting through the speaker.

"We've got company," a deep voice called from the hallway.

The man shifted slightly, reaching behind him for something.

I prayed the self-defense lessons Trevor had drilled into me would kick in, and lunged for him.

The guy was faster. He wrangled me in one arm and took me down, then climbed on top of me.

I turned my head, peering under the bed to that tease of a lockbox just out of reach, terror choking me up, mangling my insides.

"Mommy!" Chase crying out over the line was the last thing I heard before I was hit on the side of the head and knocked out.

CHAPTER TWO

Alejandro

Just outside Jackson, Wyoming

"Like hell you won that round." Recruit Two brushed the snow off his pants, scowling. "You fell on your ass in a snowbank and pretended it was a strategy."

"It *was* a strategy." Our other recruit's breath fogged the air between the two of them as he scoffed, "It was a tactical retreat."

I listened to the two candidates continue their back-and-forth nonsense as Ryder stepped forward to shut it down.

He barked out a gruff noise of annoyance. "A retreat into what, exactly? Hypothermia?" He waved them off, motioning for another lap through the course.

The two candidates groaned, held back the curses I knew they wanted to sling our way, then started for the reset point.

"Were we such pains in the ass when we were recruits?" I asked, my breaths coming out in steady white puffs, the cold air managing to bite through my layers.

Ryder slid his sunglasses down his nose just far enough to give me his classic *shut the hell up* look.

"I'll take that as a no," I responded, following his gesture toward the ranch.

The light reflected off the snow like a spotlight, turning everything into a white wasteland. Even my shades didn't offer a reprieve. I bowed my head, eyes to the ground, as we walked, with only the sounds of the recruits arguing in the distance and the crunch of snow beneath our boots.

For whatever reason, the white blanket covering the field sent me back into the past—to Christmas, which was less than two months ago. I'd helped Ryder's nephew roll a snowball bigger than his head while Audrey had watched on from the deck with Ryder's fiancée, Seraphina.

While the air burned my lungs today, the same as it had then, it didn't carry the laughter from that day, and I couldn't help but miss that sound.

Shit. Why was I thinking about that? Or remembering her smile, and the way her blue-green eyes lit up when I said something funny?

I did my best to try to shatter those thoughts and force them through the cracks of the steps as I climbed up to the porch.

Our third teammate, Reed, was there, in a rocking chair like an old man, sipping his black coffee and silently judging the world. I was one step behind him in losing my faith in people. The only thing that gave me hope was knowing there were kids like Chase out there, growing up to be better than us.

"Good news," I muttered, resting against the porch rail and glancing at Reed. "The recruits can't possibly get worse."

"A three-man team is the sweet spot. No need to add more people," Reed remarked.

That was the original agreement when we'd let go of our fourth man last fall, but things had changed. Hence, the current recruitment-weekend disaster.

"You hate people." I laughed, my breath ghosting before me. "But I agree with you." I folded my arms, watching the candidates I knew we'd be cutting. Just like the other six we'd already axed in the last few days.

"So, who's telling the White House?" Ryder asked, arms crossed like mine.

We all respected President Bennett, but we were irritated that he kept pushing us to expand. Now that we were working directly for him, running covert missions, we didn't exactly have veto power.

"They're sending someone here who will *convince* us they're right and we're wrong," Ryder gritted out in an agitated voice.

"Gotta love when life-and-death decisions are made by guys in loafers who've never had a gun pointed at their head," I said, on the same page of annoyance as our team leader.

"Tell me about it." Ryder removed his glove to go for his buzzing phone. "It's my sister."

Was Audrey a mind reader? Did she know I'd been thinking about her not even a minute ago? I shifted my jacket sleeve up to check the time. "Is it normal for her to call you this early on a Saturday?"

"No, it's not." He set his glove aside and answered. "Hey, you okay?"

The uneasy, gut-sinking feeling that hit me—and Ryder, more than likely—must have also slammed into Reed, because he abruptly stood.

"But she's fine? Chase?" Ryder dropped his forehead into his palm and exhaled. "They got away?"

Someone else had to be using Audrey's phone. What the hell had happened?

Reed and I exchanged a quick look as that chill settled in deeper.

"No, of course. You did the right thing." Another pause. "I'll be there as soon as I can. Just don't let her or—" Ryder was cut off. "No, I'm not telling you what to do, but I—" He let out a frustrated grunt, lifting his head. "Yeah, okay. Have her reach out when she wakes up." He ended the call. "That was Trevor Sloane."

Chase's dad, right. He was a veteran, and he and Audrey had divorced seven or eight years ago. Audrey had mentioned back at Christmas that she'd moved from Virginia to Colorado so Chase could be closer to his dad. Other than that? I knew nothing about the man. I figured Ryder had done his homework, but he hadn't shared his findings, so I had to assume there weren't any red flags.

"Someone broke into Audrey's place last night," Ryder said, finally revealing why Trevor had called, then lifted a hand like it might dismantle the nerves between us all.

I stood tall and at attention, ready for marching orders.

"Who's our target?" Reed asked, beating me to it.

"No one yet." Ryder pocketed his phone, his fingers dragging through his hair before he slipped his hand back into his glove. "Trevor was on his way over to Audrey's to drop Chase off after the movies when it happened. He arrived just in time. Scared off whoever was there before they could . . ."

He didn't need to finish that sentence. I couldn't stomach thinking about what someone might've done to a woman alone in her home. All that mattered was that it didn't happen. She was okay.

"Trevor couldn't chase after them without leaving her and my nephew alone," Ryder added after a heavy pause. "The sheriff's calling it a burglary."

"But . . . ?" Reed cut in again before I could.

"Maybe it's random. Maybe not. We've got to keep in mind who her ex is. Well . . . both her exes. Trevor was a SEAL for twenty years. Maybe he racked up a few enemies in that time. And while Audrey doesn't like to talk about Mitch, I went ahead and looked him up." His mouth twisted, guilt tugging at the fact he'd gone behind her back.

I did my best to water down his worries over doing what any good brother would have done—not that I had a sibling. "Of course you checked. It's what any of us would do." I cleared my throat, waiting for his eyes. "What'd you find out?"

"Naval pilot for twenty-one years. Highly decorated. His files were heavily redacted, though, so something tells me he was doing a lot more than a routine supply run when his plane went down a year ago." Ryder's jaw flexed. "I hate that I wasn't there for her at the funeral."

"You didn't know you had a sister," I reminded him. The man loved to carry the weight of the world on his shoulders, even when the weight didn't belong to him.

"Anyway, uh, I'm hoping it really was just a break-in—and the assholes thought no one was home. So they took off the second they heard Trevor coming." The side of his mouth hitched. "She didn't even want me to know. Didn't want me worrying. Thankfully, Trevor disagreed with her."

"Stubborn, huh? Must run in the family." I swallowed down the knot rising in my throat. "Where's she staying now?"

"At his lodge. He owns a bed-and-breakfast with his sister. It's why he moved out to Colorado after he retired. Their parents gave it to them after they retired. She tried running it by herself for a few years, but Audrey said she was struggling, and Trevor offered to step in under one condition."

"He'd only move if his son came too?" I guessed.

Ryder nodded. "He thought it'd be good for Audrey to start over somewhere new after everything that happened as well."

"Start new with *him*?" The jealousy in my tone bled straight through, and I didn't know where that'd come from. That feeling had no business being anywhere near me.

Ryder read my expression correctly, and I knew I needed to immediately backpedal.

"I'm sure she's not a fan of being under the same roof with her ex." I'd run the wrong direction I was supposed to go with that. Like, straight into the truth. I was the one who was uncomfortable with the idea. What the hell was wrong with me?

"I don't know," he grumbled. "Better with him than at a hotel, I suppose." He shook his head. "This whole brother thing might be new to me, but I know I need to be there for her. Not just work the case from a distance."

"What about the White House?" Reed pointed toward the recruits, who were younger than us but limping through the final obstacle. "The president's man today won't listen to us; it has to be you that tells him we don't need to expand."

Ryder hung his head, sighing. "Seraphina's flying here from Charleston tonight too."

"Then let one of us go ahead. We can get a room at the lodge and stay close until you're free tomorrow," I suggested. "And if her ex gets territorial, we'll remind him Delta guys make SEALs look like weekend warriors."

"I'll go," Reed offered.

I arched my brow. "You? You hate people. You're going to play nice with Audrey's ex?"

"I can be civil when I have to." Shockingly, Reed sounded offended.

"Sure you can. Your idea of being nice is using cyanide to kill a guy instead of putting one in his head," I deadpanned.

Reed smirked. "And that is more humane."

"Watching someone choke on his own vomit, hmm?" Ryder cracked a smile. "Alex is right. He should go. He's better with kids." He winced as a form of apology to Reed.

Reed sat again, resuming his rocking. "Animals like me."

"And that's your lane; stay in it. Nothing wrong with that." I winked, then turned back to Ryder. "She's going to be fine. We'll figure out who broke in and deal with them. It's what we do. Don't lose sleep over this." I nodded. "I've got this."

"This big-brother thing . . ." He rubbed his chest like something heavy sat there. Probably the weight of that moral compass we all did our best to follow. "Should've come with a damn manual. I got a late start."

"Yeah, well, better late than never." I stepped back. "I'll go pack."

Ryder frowned. "We'll meet you there tomorrow morning."

"Roger that." I turned to go, but he caught my arm.

"Alex?"

"Yeah?"

"She's my sister."

I blinked. "I'm aware."

He dragged his sunglasses down his nose and locked on to me. *"Sis. Ter."*

Ah. I heard the subtext loud and clear that time.

"You don't have to worry. Falling for anyone is the last thing on my mind. My ex-wife tried to kill me, remember?" I pointed to the spot where Beth had shot me just last fall. Physically, I was fine. Emotionally? Probably still teetering on the edge of being wrecked.

Thanks to that woman, I had zero plans to date or get married again.

Ryder didn't respond. Didn't even crack a smile. He just stared.

"I'm serious," I said, holding his gaze. "I promise."

And really, why would Audrey want anything to do with me? She had to still be mourning the loss of her husband.

After everything she'd been through, the last thing she needed was another man with a military past full of baggage blowing up her life.

"But for what it's worth . . ." I half turned with a grin. "This brother thing? You're a natural."

CHAPTER THREE

Audrey

Being placed in one of the two honeymoon suites at Silver Ridge Retreat, which my ex-husband owned, was probably the epitome of irony. Nothing like spending the night alone in a room designed for romance, especially after a break-in at my home where my ex had to come to my rescue.

Thank God for him being there in the nick of time. Thank God for a lot of things. Including the fact I had a safe place to stay and could be near my son, even if *safe* also meant a little awkward thanks to sharing a roof with Trevor.

The guest rooms were tucked in one wing of the house and away from Trevor's living quarters, so I wasn't sleeping right next to him, at least.

His sister, Eden, had a cute cabin at the back of the property, where their parents had lived when they ran the place. Her boyfriend often bunked with her. He was the sheriff and the first to arrive at the scene of the crime last night when Trevor had called him.

I took a seat on the edge of the four-poster bed, which would remain unused for its intended lovemaking purpose, and clutched my phone to check my last text.

Trevor had unlocked my cell using Face ID while I was asleep. He'd warned me to switch to a numerical password, and I'd dismissed his advice. I should have listened. He'd contacted my brother despite my wishes.

Ryder had enough on his plate. The last thing I wanted was to add to his burdens.

I pressed my free hand to the side of my head where that bastard last night had clocked me with his gun, sending me into unconscious no-*woman*'s-land for a few minutes, only to wake up with Trevor shaking me and no bad guys in sight.

The ibuprofen the doctor had insisted I take after Trevor forced me to see him to rule out a concussion hadn't done much to help. The dull, pulsing ache was even worse this morning.

But I'm alive. I wasn't seriously hurt and hadn't been taken. Chase was safe and hadn't lost his mother. And my home wasn't haunted. That eerie sensation I'd felt hadn't been a ghost. More like my instincts warning me of real danger.

Ryder: I'll be there tomorrow with Seraphina and Reed.

Ryder: In the meantime, Alex will watch you until then. I'm sorry I won't be able to come today myself.

I stared at the screen, fingers hovering, unsure how to respond. How to convince him not to come.

Me: Someone broke in. Burglary gone wrong. Just bad luck. Story of my life.

I wanted to believe that, at least.

The nagging chill crawling up my spine from knowing those men had bypassed Trevor's advanced security measures told me otherwise.

I decided to delete the *story of my life* line before hitting send. No need to give Ryder more fuel for questions I didn't want to answer. He barely knew my story. Just bits and blurry pieces.

We'd only seen each other a few brief times since Christmas, and my baggage wasn't something to unload over a short weekend or a phone call.

I kept telling myself I was waiting for the right moment to share more, but maybe I was afraid to open up.

Me: All that matters is Chase is fine.

His reply came instantly.

Ryder: AND THAT YOU ARE FINE, YES?

I snorted softly.

Me: Easy with the caps. I can hear you from . . . wherever you currently are.

Ryder: Unfortunately, I'm in Wyoming freezing my ass off. And sorry, this brother thing is new to me.

Me: Same, but as a sister.

Me: Also, I think we both inherited the worry gene. That's a thing, right? I'm an overthinker and worrier. You too?

Ryder: 100%

The corner of my mouth tugged into a near smile. It felt strange, even a little wrong, to smile after last night.

Ryder: Are you okay? I should have already asked that. Like I said, I'm still learning.

Ryder had a grounding effect on me. No pressure. No drama. Just this quiet presence—even with the caps lock.

I supposed we'd get the chance to learn more about each other now that he'd be coming. Of course, the idea of my brother and Chase's father together sounded more like a Navy SEAL versus Delta Force showdown than anything cozy or comforting.

Who was stealthier? Who had the bigger ego? Who could shoot tighter groupings at two hundred yards? I more than likely had those discussions to look forward to.

I shook my head, rubbing my temple again. That only made it worse.

Me: Doctor wasn't too worried about the bump on my head. So, yeah, I'm fine.

Ryder: And how is Chase? I should have also asked that. Fuck, I suck.

I laughed. Actually laughed. That hurt to do, but still.

Me: You're a great uncle. Chase adores you. But yes, he's okay. Thanks to Trevor. He calmed him down last night. Made him feel better. Safe. He'll still need to talk to someone since he did hear me scream, but . . .

Ryder: I'm going to find who did this. They'll pay, I promise.

Me: Great. Now, my brother and ex are vying for who gets dibs on the burglar.

Me: Teamwork makes the dream work.

Ryder: You're hilarious.

Ryder: Please read that with a sarcastic tone.

Ryder: But I'll try to get along with Trevor.

Ryder: As long as he's never hurt you, then I have no reason to hurt him.

Me: You might be a natural at this whole brother thing.

Ryder: Funny enough, Alex said the same thing this morning, right before he caught a flight out your way.

Alejandro, not Alex. That was how he'd introduced himself at Christmas. Alejandro Rodriguez. Even his name had swagger.

I sighed. Heaven help me. All the sighs from thinking about him.

Shitttt. I was *not* allowed to feel warm and fuzzy about men. I wanted cold, sterile, and avoid-at-all-costs reactions. It wasn't just that I felt it'd be too soon to feel anything for anyone as a widow (even if I'd been trying to get divorced)—it was that I never wanted to have romantic *anything* again. Period. End of story. No questions asked (pretty please).

Yet there I was, about to crawl under the covers and hide at the fact I *had* noticed another man. More than that, I may have exchanged a few embarrassing texts with my best friend, Hollis, about him, including how funny and hot he was.

Her great advice, which I'd actually taken, had been: *Since you never plan to date again, at least have him star in your fantasies on lonely nights.*

And now he was on his way, at my brother's orders, and planned to share a roof with us. *Kill me now.* I needed to do damage control to prevent him from coming without raising the alarm as to why.

Me: How about Jason Reed instead?

Ryder: Too late. Alex is already on his way. Should be there any minute. But why don't you want Alex there?

Oh, I could think of a hundred reasons, but I made up a lame excuse.

Me: I just figured Alex has a girlfriend at home he should be with instead of spending time babysitting me.

Ryder:

Ryder: Are you okay? You got hit on the head, right?

You know what? I was absolutely going to run with that excuse as to why my brother's best friend did something strange to my pulse. Like elevate it.

Me: You're right. I'm a little off. Don't mind me.

More than a little, since Alejandro "Alex" Rodriguez kept infiltrating the part of my brain reserved for "do not think about that" outside of what was supposed to be a few innocent fantasies here and there.

Me: Just focus on whatever it is you're doing. We'll talk when you get here tomorrow. Chase will be happy to see you. We'll tell him you were planning a visit with Seraphina anyway, so he doesn't worry about why you're really coming.

Ryder: Okay. Stay safe. Get some rest. Later.

I tossed the phone onto the bed and went out into the hallway, nearly colliding with a couple heading to the second honeymoon suite. *How nice for them.*

After apologizing, I continued toward the stairs to the first floor.

The house's centerpiece was a beautiful stone fireplace. It crackled with flames and cast a warm light across the wood-beamed ceilings of the main living room. A small kid was off to the side, playing with superhero figures while his parents chatted and sipped mimosas. Being surrounded by so much life after having my home broken into was somewhat comforting, I supposed.

I followed the aroma of cinnamon and cocoa down the hall and stopped outside the kitchen at the sound of Eden's voice rising.

"Are you sure you can handle this? I know you said you're over her, but I'm just worried that her being here might be confusing. For everyone."

I backed up against the wall, hoping no one would see me lurking.

"It's temporary." Trevor's tone was low and tired. "But what was I supposed to do? Send her to a hotel? She's the mother of my child. I need to keep her safe, plus Chase needs to be near her. And I . . ."

"You what?" Eden asked him, speaking on my behalf as well, especially since he hadn't answered her original question.

Did he think now that I was single, my move to Colorado might amount to a second chance for us?

"We can't be together. She knows that. I know that. And you do too." I could hear the gruff, measured breath he took afterward all the way in the hall. "But I'm never gonna stop lovin' her as family, and if something had happened to her last night, I'd never be able to live with myself."

I couldn't hear her response, just a murmur passing in the air, as if she was hugging him, trying to erase his worries.

"Mom?" Chase called out, exposing the fact I was creeping outside the kitchen.

Shit.

Trevor stepped into the hall almost immediately, his gaze volleying between Chase approaching and me standing awkwardly, a statue of red embarrassment.

"I was just coming to find you. Everything okay?" I lifted one shoulder, attempting to pull off innocent, but based on Trevor's tight mouth and pinched brows, he called bullshit.

Trevor's blue eyes cut to our son's, and with a tip of his head, he motioned for Chase to give us a moment.

"Cocoa in the kitchen. Go ahead," Trevor encouraged when Chase looked him up and down, holding his ground in a firm, protective stance in front of me. My little guardian.

"It's okay," I told him, knowing he needed both of us to agree before following any kind of order.

Chase shifted around so I could see his face. His lips rolled inward, his eyes still suspiciously darting between us, assessing the uncomfortable situation. Smart beyond his years.

Once he hesitantly took off for the cocoa he didn't care about, Trevor gently took me by the arm, a silent order to have that moment in private.

I quietly allowed him to guide me down the hall to his office. Books lined the walls, and as the door softly clicked shut, I sought them out as a refuge while waiting for what would probably be a lecture.

"How much did you hear?" His words projected low and deep as I removed a book from the shelf.

Silence of the Lambs. I thumbed through it until I landed on a dog-eared page. "Really? No bookmark?" I faced him, holding up the evidence of his crime.

"Audrey." He let my name stretch, a plea for me to focus on his question.

I turned away, returning the book to its place, curious how many months or years it'd been since page fifty was folded over and those words were left to live their fictional lives without him.

"Does Eden not want me here?"

"Of course she does," he shot back without hesitation.

I could feel him closing in behind me. "Please don't lie to me. You were never good at it."

"I unfortunately tried to lie to you quite a lot, didn't I?" Regret seeped into his voice and had me guilt-turning around.

"You just had trouble talking about everything you went through. White-lied your way through your struggles. There's a difference."

"Shut one too many doors in your face." That solemn tone hurt to hear as he hung his head, tearing a hand through his hair. "I'm trying to be the man I should have been before . . ." He looked up, meeting my eyes. "For our son," he said steadily, as if worried I might misread his intentions, and I was thankful for the clarification.

I reached for his forearm and gave him a gentle squeeze. "You have to stop beating yourself up. The war . . . it just . . ." What could I possibly say that he didn't already know? I'd only ever imagined walking that mile in his shoes (well, combat boots) to try to understand. He'd been the one to wear them every day.

"I know, I know. I'm here now. We all are. Fresh start for us as co-parents." He forced a smile. "I'm trying to make this work, I promise."

"And you're really happy not jumping from planes anymore?" I frowned, worried about him all over again, especially with that hesitant look.

All he did was nod.

I knew him well enough to know that was a yes and a no. Yes, he was happy to be fully present in Chase's life. Attend his hockey practices and never miss a game. Be there for his sister at the lodge to help her out too.

But *also*, I heard the unspoken *no*. He was miserable no longer being part of a team and saving the world.

Wasn't there a happy medium somehow? There had to be.

I'd tried to have that conversation with him a hundred times before he turned in his official papers and left the navy. I had to assume Eden had, too, but when the man made up his mind, there was no turning back.

"I'm going to find out who broke into your place and handle it," he said, steering the conversation back into territory he could control. His jaw tightened, blue eyes sharp on mine as he ground out, "You have my word."

I let go of his arm and stepped back. I recognized that look, and I didn't like it being aimed at me. "What are you keeping from me?"

"Nothing."

"Trevor."

He rubbed his temple as if he'd been the one hit instead. "You know me."

"And that's supposed to mean . . . ?"

His hand fell to his side. "That I won't rest until whoever's responsible for Friday's break-in is taken out, that's all."

"Fine," I huffed out, nowhere near satisfied with his answer, but I'd let it go for now. I pointed up, a silent message he'd understand. "But are you really okay with me staying until then? Same roof and all."

His head tilted. "Would you like me to build a second one?"

I sighed. "Something tells me you would."

"I'm fine, I swear. Haven't thought about you naked in at least five years." He winked, and I swatted his arm, letting go of a laugh.

"Smart-ass."

A grin cut across his face; then he lifted his chin as a directive. "Change. Eat. Relax. And get used to being here until I know it's safe for you to go home. Got it?"

I rolled my eyes at his punctuated commands, though he probably didn't realize they'd come out so order-like. "What? No cocoa for me, too?"

"Take that up with the boss. Maybe she'll give you a cup." He turned to the side. "Now, scram. I have shit to do."

A soft chuckle broke the last of the wall between us. "Fine, fine." I glanced down at my clothes, pondering throwing a shower somewhere in that chain of commands he'd given me. "Did my brother tell you that—"

"That he plans on showing up to mark his territory? Show who's boss?"

"Guess he'll soon find out it's Eden, not you." I smothered my smile with the back of my hand. "Oh, and, um, do me a favor and be nice to his friend coming here today. He should be here any second."

"And who is this 'friend'?" he asked, air quotes in full force. "He going to be a problem?"

"Why in the world would Ryder's friend be a problem?"

"Because you have . . ." He squeezed one eye closed like he regretted starting that sentence. "You have the tendency to see the good in people where there isn't any."

"Is that such a bad thing?"

A steady, gruff breath escaped his lips. "You never gave up on me even after I did, even after you should have. And as for Mitch, well . . . you know how I feel about him. Never liked the guy. And as much as I hate speaking ill of the dead, we both know he didn't deserve you."

I had no idea how to answer that, so I didn't respond. Instead, I gave him a nod, then went to open the door.

The fresh smell of pine hit me as I halted when he remarked, "Just so I'm clear: Nothing will stop me from making sure no one ever hurts you again."

I shivered as if an icy hand had touched my bare skin. "I have no plans to get my heart broken, so you don't have to worry about that." I peeked back at him over my shoulder. "Okay?"

"And how can you guarantee you'll keep that from happening?"

"I think you know," I said somberly.

He grimaced and rested his hands on his hips while whispering, "That's what I was afraid of."

CHAPTER FOUR

Alejandro

"You're her brother's friend?" The guy's tall, built frame filled out one of the two large front doors of the lodge. His blue gaze swept over me. Assessing me—not as competition, but as a threat to the safety of those inside.

I dropped my duffel bag alongside my boots. "You're the ex?" I shot back, using the same tone he had.

The tension crackled between us like an exposed wire. What was that all about?

"Trevor Sloane." He hesitantly offered his hand.

"Alex Rodriguez."

He squeezed my hand, and I was thankful he didn't turn it into some kind of pissing contest over whose grip was stronger.

"You're late." The grunt filled the cold air between us, and I could feel the heat radiating out from behind him as he released my hand.

I was eager to get inside out of the cold, hating this weather as much as I hated dry-firing my rifle. I may have *also* been anxious to see Audrey. "The mountain roads, snow, ice, and life-threatening curves might've had something to do with that."

I picked up my bag, waiting for the invite inside his lodge.

"Audrey's upstairs. Had a rough night."

"You don't say?" *Shit.* That wasn't the attitude that'd win this guy over. Ryder would kick my ass if Trevor booted me for mouthing off when I was there to protect Audrey.

His eyes tightened. Scanning again. Assessment 2.0. Searching for weaknesses.

"Any update on the break-in?" I shifted gears, worried I was two seconds away from having to check in to the B-grade motel that probably had bedbugs I'd spotted on the drive up here.

"No." His posture stiffened, attention locking beyond me.

I followed his gaze to the parking lot and to my rented four-door sedan, which looked like it belonged in a nursing home.

Jump into enemy fire? Easy fucking day.

But drive that death trap up icy mountains? Different story.

My prayer hands had worked overtime on that last curve. I'd drawn a shaky cross over my heart on the road I'd nicknamed *Where Old Souls Go to Die*. (Don't ask why, I couldn't tell you if I tried.)

I'd rather jump off a cliff with a chute strapped to my ass than drive that fossil again. That'd been all that was available, but I had every intention of getting it towed and swapped out for something with a little more kick and stability once there was another option.

"What is it?" I asked, not seeing anything but the heap of junk I'd driven.

Trevor's eyes narrowed. "Thought I saw something."

"And?"

"And I didn't." The edge in his voice didn't cease and desist.

I'm not a threat. We're on the same side. I kept those thoughts to myself for now. "Based on your guarded stance, I'm guessing you don't think the break-in was some random B and E."

Trevor's icy stare cut through me, but this time I knew it wasn't meant for me. "They had to be pros to take out every security measure I had in place. They never should have been able to get into her home undetected."

"What in the hell would they want from Audrey?"

"I don't know, but I've made some calls. I have people outside the locals here checking things out for me."

"What kind of people?" I tipped my head, wondering who else was working my case—and it was *my* case. Because Audrey was Ryder's sister, and that made her family.

"Your kind of people." He lifted his head, making it clear he knew what I did for a living. Doubt he knew who I now worked for, though, and it was no longer DHS.

"Private security?"

"Yeah." He shifted to the side, hopefully preparing to let me in. "I'll figure this out, don't worry."

The "I" in that sentence was about as subtle as a shotgun round, but I'd save that battle for later.

Step one: get my ass out of the cold and see the reason for my being here herself.

Once inside the lodge, the cedar walls and ceiling beams greeted me, making me feel like I'd walked into a giant whiskey barrel. Or maybe I was the whiskey. After my confrontation with Trevor, I could use a glass.

Not a bad place, all things considered. Definitely better than freezing outside.

Trevor dug into his pocket and handed over an antique-looking key stamped with the number six. "Your room's upstairs, three doors down from Audrey's." He said it like three doors was two too close for comfort, ex or not.

I cleared my throat, channeling my manners. "Thanks for letting me stay here—well, all of us. We'll need two more rooms tomorrow. They available?"

He parked a hand on my shoulder and gave it two solid pats. "As long as someone's paying the bill, yeah."

"I'm going to check on her." I stepped back, and he wisely withdrew his hand.

"We'll talk about the case and how involved your team will be later. Just do me a favor and don't tell Audrey what I shared with you for now. She doesn't need the stress, not until I know more." The polite tone didn't soften the command. Message received.

I nodded once, then took the stairs.

I reached the door marked 6, then slid the key into the small hole, only to realize the door was already unlocked.

Nice security. Maybe it *had* just been a random break-in, if this was the tight ship the SEAL kept at his own lodge.

I pushed open the door and went inside, expecting more cedar and the smell of pine, not to see Audrey there.

The door thudded shut behind me, and she froze. Yeah, well, so did I. Like a damn deer in headlights.

She became a still-life portrait of a beautiful and very *naked* woman.

Full lips parted. Blue-green eyes wide. One hand outstretched where, presumably, that towel now on the floor had been before I walked in.

Wet, light-blonde hair clung to her shoulders, and I did my best to blur and censor the rest of her.

I waited for her to realize she was *naked* naked, not towel-wrapped naked. Full-on, kill-me-now naked.

I looked away. Looked back.

At least my gaze landed north of her breasts that time, at the curve of her collarbone, then on to her flushed cheeks.

But my brain? It was already filing this under RYDER'S GOING TO KILL ME. Something told me Trevor would too.

"You're here," she whispered.

"And you're naked," I blurted out.

I waited for her to register the draft in the air. My eyes burned from the effort it took not to blink my way south again.

"I, um . . ." She dropped down, then popped back up, this time with the towel around her body. A modest improvement. Better for my sanity. "Why are you in my room?" Her skin went from shock pale to a deep embarrassed red real fast. Much faster than the towel had made it back on.

"*Your* room?" I finally connected the dots to what she'd asked, my bag slipping from my hand like I was about to move in.

I held up the key and flipped it. A nine. It was a damn nine, not a six. Fate, always playing games. The cold must've frozen my brain downstairs for me to have made such a rookie mistake.

When our eyes met again, it was clear she was only just realizing the full impact of the moment.

I barked out, a little harsher than I intended, "Why didn't you lock the door, especially while in the shower?"

"I thought I did." She paused, letting the truth sink in. Her careless mistake mirrored my own. The *oops* was written all over her face, right down to the tension bracketing her full mouth. "This place is safe. Trust me, no one would dare cross Trevor or Eden's boyfriend."

Eden's boyfriend? No clue who he was, but her protest still felt as weak as she was now making my pulse. Borderline lifeless at her cavalier attitude toward her safety.

"People around here, even the guests, are friendly." There it was again. A casual disregard for the whole being-caught-naked thing.

My eyebrow arched, an automatic response. "Right," I said dryly. "Your home was broken into. Kind of kills that vibe."

"This place is different. And an important FYI . . . when my son is around, I *quadruple*-check locks."

Her collarbone was still beaded with water droplets, and she dragged the pad of her thumb along the bone right where my gaze had gone.

"Why didn't you knock?" she asked instead, before I could respond, a hint of sass in her voice. "Something tells me your mother taught you manners. You forget them?"

Her challenge jolted my gaze up to hers.

Bold and unapologetic. Daring me to answer.

"I thought this was my room." That memory clicked into place a few seconds too late. "Later," I demanded roughly, "we're going to have a conversation about locks, safety, and stranger danger. Because your life matters. Not just your son's." After that, I finally did the smart thing and turned my ass around.

"Now you sound like Ryder." A little *harumph* noise followed her grunty—albeit cute—tone.

I braced for the mini war I knew was coming.

She surprised me with a quick "Despite the circumstances, it's good to see you."

"Good to see you, too." *Saw more than I should have.*

I squeezed my eyes shut for a few seconds, needing to ground myself and think of Audrey as a client to protect. As Ryder's sister. As a widow to a man who died wearing the uniform.

That last thought had my stomach turning. Guilt, thick and hot, coursed through my veins at that reminder.

When I opened my eyes, the first thing I saw was the carved cross on the door. Twined in vines, it glowed at me like a message. A 3D warning to behave. As if on cue, a phantom sting from the bullet wound where my ex-wife had shot me had me pressing the hand holding the key to the scar.

Yeah, yeah, I know. I get it, I get it. Don't fall for anyone ever again—especially not her, of all people. My brain and body were collaborating to signal that message as clearly as possible.

"You didn't have to come, you know," she spoke up, closer now. "Trevor's good at this stuff. Has lots of friends and family who are good at it, too."

So he said. I almost turned around. Almost risked welcoming death-by-Ryder. "I know. But Ryder's better at giving orders than taking them, so here I am." I smirked, wasting that smile on the door. "So it was me or Reed, and Reed's better with dogs than people. Consider yourself lucky."

I could feel her presence behind me. Her heat. The faint scent of whatever she'd used to lather her very, very naked—

Nope.

Not going there.

I needed to Houdini myself from there and go gouge out my eyes. I still couldn't believe this had happened. *Damn my luck.* "Glad you're okay. I'll be in my room. You know, not going anywhere. Staying here whether anyone wants me to or not. Ensuring you're safe and locking your door from now on."

"Figured as much. Didn't take you as a quitter." That teasing tone lit a fire under me.

I grabbed my bag and left her room before I could change my mind.

Door shut, I tested the handle, waiting for her to do what she should have done the first time to avoid our awkward encounter.

Satisfied at the sound of her lock being turned, I finally took off.

After shutting myself in Room 9, I chucked my bag by the bed and went over to the dresser.

Hands down, eyes on the mirror, my dark gaze stared back at me like a stranger. Well, like someone I hadn't seen in forever.

The me before I married Beth.

The me before my ex-wife tried to kill me.

The me before I'd made up my mind to never fall in love again.

And that was enough to scare my ass back two steps, send my hands through my black hair and my eyes away from the mirror to the cedar beam overhead.

Jaw tight, body strung up, I cursed in Spanish, then hissed in English, "I'm so fucked."

CHAPTER FIVE

Audrey

"Move to Colorado. Sure, why not?" I muttered to myself. "Start over like I'm the title to a Chris Stapleton song expecting better luck? Who wouldn't want that?"

I knocked my forehead against the door twice, forgetting I'd been hit on the head only last night and the pain still lingered.

"House broken into. Forced to move in with my ex. Brother's best friend down the hall just saw me naked." I pressed my hands next to my head by the door, trying to get a grip. "Yup, everything's going perfect. Luck has for sure changed moving here."

Why, God, why? I lifted my eyes to the ceiling, waiting for a response. After I was met with only silence, I remembered I still needed to dry my hair and get dressed.

But I couldn't stop replaying our exchange, including how long it'd taken me to cover up with that towel. That was *not* how my fantasies ever went. The part where he stared into my eyes, though? Maybe that was.

His gaze had been as deep and as complex as my favorite piano notes that always hit the right spot. I could write a solo based on his eyes alone and how they made me feel as he looked into mine.

Of course, from his point of view, I'd probably gawked at him like he'd been the one in his birthday suit. All six-two of that man standing in my room, in all black like a groom who belonged with me in the honeymoon suite.

"And I really gotta stop talking to myself . . . *she says to herself.*" I laughed. At this point, why not? Why not just box this whole thing up as one funny *ha ha* thing, then never think about it again. *Perfect. Time to move on.*

Now that I was dressed and my hair mostly dry, I picked up my phone to text my best friend and give her an update.

Me: I'm still alive. But kinda wanna be dead?

Hollis: Umm, whyyyy? P.S. - Don't say the word dead in the same sentence with yourself. The world needs you. I mean, I for sure do. You already moved to the other side of the country. Don't leave the world too.

I plopped down on my bed and sighed.

Hollis: By the way, you tell your mom yet you're bunking with Trevor and the reason for it?

Me: Nope. I'm not ready to talk to her. You know why.

Me: And as for the other thing, welllllll, you'll never believe who is three doors down from me and just saw my ass. Wait, actually, he only saw my front. But saw me naked, so, you know . . . that's great.

Hollis: Guessing you're not talking about Chase's dad. So it must be Romeo.

Me: I hate that name you gave him, but yeah, he's here.

At the unexpected notification popping up, I nearly dropped my phone.

Me: "Romeo's" texting me. I gotta go.

Hollis: Wait.

Me: Yeah?

Hollis: Be a little flirty (it won't kill you, I promise). Try it. You might like it. 😈

Me: Byeeee 😇

I took a second to pull myself together, as I was feeling as though I was about to perform on *American Idol* instead of reading a man's texts.

Unknown: Thought you should have my number.

Unknown: It's Alex, by the way. Ryder gave me your digits.

I stared at his name, allowing it to unfold in my mind to his given one, Alejandro. I let it roll off my tongue, loving it far too much. Went so far as to program his number that way, too.

Me: Thank you.

This is not happening. Absolutely not. Zero feelings of any kind allowed outside the comfort and safety of my fantasies.

Alejandro: I apologize for walking into the wrong room. I can't remember if I said that to you yet. I was a little thrown off.

Yeah, so was I.

Me: Things happen, whatcha gonna do? lol

Me: Sorry, that's the millennial urge in me to end every uncomfortable statement with a haha or lol. You do that?

Alejandro: I identify as Gen X. Feel older than 37. I'm more of a thumbs-up kind of guy. I heard that it drives millennials crazy, though.

Me: Just a smidge. Almost as bad as a plain K for a response.

Alejandro: I'll be sure to remember that 👍

I smirked. *Now I'm smiling at a man's text. Not good.*

Alejandro: Maybe we shouldn't tell your brother about what happened?

Me: And if I already did? 🙈

Alejandro: I'd be dead. Ryder's an excellent shot.

Me: All the way from Wyoming, you don't say?

Me: I've already forgotten about what happened. In fact, what are you even talking about? What should I not tell Ryder? 🤷

Alejandro: I like you.

I stared at the bouncing dots as he typed, my pulse rate jumping just as much.

Alejandro: I meant you're cool.

Me: And maybe you are Gen X. Borderline Boomer with that response. haha

Alejandro: 😎 Guilty as charged.

Alejandro: I should probably shower. After, I plan on heading to your place to have a look. I need to borrow a ride, though. My rental might do what my ex-wife tried but actually succeed.

I reread his message as those bubbles appeared again, even more furiously this time. *Your ex-wife?*

Alejandro: No idea why I felt you needed a play-by-play of what I'm doing . . .

Me: Probably so I wouldn't accidentally walk in on you too. 😉

Me: And do you really think you're going to just blow past that rental car comment on me like that?

Alejandro: The rental's dangerous. It'll kill me.

I stood and had to do another slow reread.

What'd that mean, about his ex-wife? And I thought *my* baggage was heavy.

I had no clue what to say, and I highly doubted he was looking to talk about his ex any more than I'd be interested in talking about either of mine, so I swerved around that conversation and maneuvered back to the original comment.

Me: Can I come with you?

Alejandro: In the shower or to your house?

Alejandro: Kidding, kidding. No way are you coming with me to your house.

Alejandro: 😉

Yup, I'm in trouble.

Me: Funny, are you?

Alejandro: I try.

Me: Well, I haven't been to my house since last night. I'd like to look around. Get a few more things since Trevor packed for me.

He didn't respond, and no bouncing dots indicated he was typing.

I returned to the bed, wondering if he'd bailed on me.

Of course, I had just basically alluded to the fact Trevor had packed my underwear as casually as he'd shared that his ex-wife tried to kill him. *I think I need Hollis to walk me through how to flirt. Because that was not it.*

Alejandro: We'll have to take that up with Trevor. I doubt he'll want you leaving until we know for sure the break-in was random.

I flinched at the vibration, at the fact he was back with me again. Then I went into defense mode after reading his text.

Me: He's not the boss of me.

Alejandro: . . .

Me: Those dots mean?

Alejandro: You know exactly what they mean.

Me: He may think he's the boss. There's a difference.

Alejandro: Mmhm.

Me: Meet-and-greet with Trevor go that well, I take it?

Alejandro: Only slightly better than it did with you.

Alejandro: Just so we're clear, I'm relieved it was you I saw naked and not him. I'd be traumatized for life.

Alejandro: ⬆ That's another one of those kinds of texts I should have reread first and most definitely not sent.

Another? Like the ex-wife-wanting-to-kill-you text? I almost asked him that, and I applauded myself for refraining.

Me: Anyway, take that shower so we can go. Trevor can stay here with Chase to keep an eye on him. I'll ensure T understands I'm safe with you.

Alejandro: You are safe with me, that I can promise you both.

Alejandro: But before we go, I'd like to see Chase. I miss him 🙂

Of all the things he could possibly say to me . . .

I swallowed, working that lump back down my throat since it had no business being there in the first place.

Me: He's probably seconds away from finding you and "pulling an Alex" and walking in on you too. Be sure to keep your head on a swivel.

Alejandro: Yes, ma'am. Will do my best 😉

I let go of my phone, dropping it next to me on the bed as I stared up at the ceiling, releasing a heavy breath along with it.

I replayed our exchange, trying to make sense of it. I wasn't sure how long I'd been lost in my thoughts, but the knock a few minutes later had me bolting upright.

"It's me! Why's your door locked?"

My little dude. I hurried over, not about to tell Chase that my new friend had walked in on me naked, so that lock was very much needed.

I opened up, not expecting to see Alex standing alongside him.

Chase quietly pointed to Alex as if I couldn't see him.

It was easier to talk through text than have a conversation with him eye to eye and pretend the naked thing and borderline flirty banter over the phone hadn't happened.

I smiled at my son, then gave myself a quick second (or five) to appreciate Alex for what I told myself would be the last time.

Broad shoulders strained against his clothes. A white cotton long-sleeved shirt hugged his hard frame, and his long legs were covered by dark jeans. Bare feet were planted solidly on the hardwood.

Muscles I bet were carved more by his job than by morning dates with the gym couldn't be masked by cotton and denim.

But it was his eyes that truly stole my attention—dark and deep, wrecking me. There was a look in them, like he craved the sun breaking through the clouds but refused to trust anyone enough to be that anchor for him.

Those eyes were laser focused on me now as if trying to get a read on me. Sharp and unblinking beneath thick lashes a woman would kill for.

I'd probably been staring too long, because he subtly cleared his throat while dragging his fingers through his inky-black hair. I couldn't help but follow the movement of his big hand over every unruly strand that refused to obey.

The left side of his mouth dipped slightly, a half smirk, half warning for us both.

Yeah, yeah.

Protector. Protected.

Best friend. Best friend's sister.

Veteran. Widow to a decorated war hero.

We were on the opposite sides of a few too many coins, and I doubted even the most skilled magician could make both sides work together.

Okay, I'm done. No more strange feelings of desire for this man, boxed up and ready to be shipped off to Siberia and never be seen or found again. Well, outside my fantasies, which maybe I should even stop having, too.

But when Alex's hand found a new home, slipping across the faint five-o'clock shadow on his jaw before settling firmly on my son's shoulder, the tape on that box peeled open. Ripped. Right. Apart.

"Someone found me." The awkward quiet was finally broken with Alex's remark. Damn, the husky quality of his voice pulled at something deep inside me, tempting me to step closer to him.

"Earth to Mommy!"

Yeah, Mommy's staring, isn't she? "Just tell me you knocked on Mr. Rodriguez's door instead of bursting into his room?" One naked encounter for the day was plenty.

Chase held up a room key, closing one eye. "I may have borrowed the spare key from Dad when he told me what room Uncle Alex was in."

Uncle Alex? My heart did a weird little stumble at those two words strung together. Not because I thought of him like a brother, but . . .

"He didn't barge in." A quick throat-clear from Alex. "Not really. I was in the shower, so I didn't hear his knocking. He gave me time to dress." He was defending my son, and I kind of loved that.

"Chase." I tried to pull off serious, but my son's wide-mouth grin was far too infectious for that scolding to hold any weight.

"Sorry, I was just excited. I want another snowball fight. That okay? Dad said he's in, too."

Alex and Trevor in a snowball fight? Two men who'd both seen me naked, huh? Because today couldn't get any more awkward.

"Mommmmyyy." Chase waved his hand, trying to coax me out of my head, which was currently a messy place to be.

I forced my attention on my brother's friend, the sexy man assigned to watch over me, as I relaxed my arms and pushed my sleeves to my elbows.

The side of Alex's mouth lifted, revealing that one lone dimple I'd clocked the moment he first smiled back at me over Christmas.

"We were planning on heading to our place to grab some stuff, but I think we can squeeze in a quick snowball fight first if Alex is up for it." I met Chase's eager eyes. "Which team will I be on?"

"Daddy says you have to watch because of your head."

Of course he did. "I'm fine," I reassured him. "No way are you having a snowball fight without me."

I could feel Alex's glare land hard. He was about to side with Trevor on this, wasn't he?

"You and Daddy together, then! I'll have Uncle Alex's six."

Oy. I worried at how easily Chase paired my name with Trevor's, like there was a little hope for reconciliation clinging to the edges of his words.

This right here just became my new concern about the dangers of sharing a roof with Trevor. Chase would never want me to move out. He had his parents together again, and he didn't understand that didn't mean we were *together* together.

This was the definition of the "start over" I knew Chase was secretly hoping for when Trevor had first asked us both to move out here last year.

"How about boys against girls?" I asked. "I'll pull Aunt Eden onto my team. Two against three."

Chase laughed, already sprinting down the hall.

Alex watched him go, the smile slipping from his mouth as he turned back to me. His hand braced lightly on the doorframe, head tilted in question. "Are you okay?"

The warmth in his voice made my chest ache, same with that sincere expression crossing his face.

"And I'm not talking about what happened to you last night," he clarified, eyes shooting to my temple as if now noticing where I'd been whacked and regretting not playing doctor sooner to see if I was okay.

With his free hand, he reached out, brushing my hair away to inspect the damage without touching my skin.

I angled my head, allowing him to see the bruise and knot.

"A man that hits a woman deserves, well . . ." He briefly closed his eyes, mouth tightening.

Yeah, tell me about it.

"Trevor's right. You should watch only, not join." His throat bobbed with a deep, anguished swallow before he reset his attention on me, his hand falling to his side.

"I'll be fine, don't worry. Just don't go whacking me too hard."

"I wouldn't dream of whacking you hard." His eyes lit up, then he gave me a hesitant smile. "Anyway, I was asking you something, right?"

I forgot myself, too distracted by the gentle way he'd checked on my injury.

"Right, I, uh, was saying that this can't be easy for you to be here together. For any of you."

"We haven't been under one roof in a long time," I admitted, my body relaxing a little despite the fact I was doing something I hadn't done with a man in forever: opening up. Heck, I hadn't even done that with Ryder yet. "I need to be here with Chase, but it's going to be hard for him when it's time for me to leave."

I had a feeling Alex was about to share some words of wisdom, but Chase's "Hurry!" killed his chance.

"We should get a move on so we can head to my place afterward." I glanced at our bare feet. "You have boots?"

Alex smirked, that dimple flashing again. "What kind of operator would I be if I didn't?" He gestured toward his room. "Meet you downstairs. Might want to warm up that throwing arm. I have excellent aim."

"I would hope you do."

His answering look made my stomach flip.

And also, did I just flirt? Mildly successfully, too?

"Audrey?" he said quietly.

"Yeah?" I whispered right back.

But before he could say anything more, Chase returned, full of energy and exasperation.

"What's taking so long?" Without hesitation, he hooked his arm with Alex's and tugged him down the hall.

Alex shot a parting glance my way, and I couldn't help but smile, watching how easily Alex fit into our world. I also couldn't help but notice the way his mouth tilted into a helpless grin as he surrendered to Chase's commands.

I saluted my son, catching a subtle wink from Alex before he vanished into his room, Chase right on his heels.

It didn't take long to bundle up and make our way outside. The sun was low behind the mountains, painting the snow in a pale gold.

As expected, the second Trevor saw me, he started in on his lecture. Orders to stand down. Sit on the sidelines.

My response was to pack a snowball and let it fly right at him. He reluctantly agreed after that, but not before barking out "Go easy on her" commands to everyone.

Chase then pulled Trevor and Alex into a huddle, gesturing animatedly as he mapped out their battle plan as team leader. I loved how both men deferred to a nine-year-old without missing a beat.

Eden's boots crunched across the snow as she joined me. "Think we have a chance?"

"A pretty good one, since they're going to treat me with kid gloves."

She laughed, tugging her pink hat lower over her short blonde hair. "Your brother's friend is cute, by the way. Like sexy, manly hot—not boyish cute."

I knew she wasn't pointing out the obvious because she was interested. She was trying to let me know it was okay if I noticed a guy. A gentle nudge of support. We may not have been sisters-in-law anymore, but we'd stayed friends since the divorce.

"I have no plans to date again."

"So you keep saying, and I'll keep hoping you change your mind." She hip-checked me.

Before I could shut her down, Chase's excited shout cut through the air, along with a snowball. It smashed into Eden's jacket, dead center.

Eden and I took cover, pelting them back as fast as we could.

I landed a decent shot against Trevor before spinning around and getting hit in the butt by one. Not too hard, but enough to surprise me.

I faced forward, finding Alex smirking, another snowball already cocked in hand.

"Aren't you supposed to take it easy on me?" I reminded him.

"Believe me, I am," he returned, that handsome, lazy smile doing a number on me.

Like distract me from my snowball-making mission.

I knelt for more snow too abruptly and became dizzy. I lost my balance and fell.

Alex somehow not only caught me, but he also managed to pad my fall, using his body as a cushion. But now I was smack on top of the man. Sitting right on his crotch, because, you know, why not make things more awkward?

"You okay?" His breath clouded the air between us.

"I got a little dizzy. Thanks for the save," I whispered, hating that both men had been right about me not joining in on the fun.

Alex continued to stare into my eyes like he could read my thoughts and see my soul.

It took Trevor slicing through the tension to remind me we weren't alone. "You good?" he barked out, and I remained sitting on top of this man like it was the most natural thing in the world for me to be doing.

What is wrong with me? Oh, right. Bump to the head to blame. Phew.

"Are you okay?" Trevor asked again, but in a slightly more neutral tone than he'd used before as he offered his hand to help me up since I had another man trapped beneath me with nowhere to go.

"Mm-hmm," I murmured once on my feet as Alex stood.

"Time to sit out," Trevor ordered, and I decided to behave myself and listen.

Alex gave me a small smile before Chase hit him with a snowball. "Turning on me, are you? Well, then . . ." His husky laugh filled the air before he took off after Chase, and my son squealed and ran.

Trevor joined in on the pursuit as Eden came over.

"Sorry about my brother ruining that moment you two seemed to be having."

"Moment?" I shrugged. "What moment?"

She smiled. "You know what I mean." She nodded toward her brother. "Trevor can be such an overprotective pain in the ass sometimes with the people he loves. He may have looked jealous, but he's just like that. Heck, my boyfriend's the sheriff and he gives *him* a hard time."

Exactly what I'd hoped to hear. *Not jealous, just a pain. Good.* "Speaking of Beau, you think he could meet me at my house? Let us in?"

"Why do you need to go back?"

I peeked over her shoulder and lifted my chin toward the guys. "Alex wants to check out my place, and since he's going, I'd like to grab a few things. I'm sure the other overprotective man in my life told him to go over there. A.k.a. my brother's orders."

"Brother . . . ," she said on a sigh. "Still can't believe you have a big brother. Damn."

You and me both.

"Trevor will want to go with you."

"He needs to stay with you and Chase," I reminded her. "I can't go anywhere without knowing he's protected."

"Those guys were serious pros. I just don't think you should go home until—"

"What?" I cut her off, and she closed her eyes, her shoulders falling in disappointment, indicating she'd slipped and said too much. I knew Trevor had been holding back, dang it. "What is he keeping from me?" I reached for her arm.

After a hesitant pause, she lifted her head and frowned, eyes on me. "I heard him on the phone with our cousin this morning while you were asleep."

"Which cousin?"

"Tessa. Her dad's a general, remember? But that's not why he called her. Anyway, he wanted to talk to—"

"Her husband. Army Special Forces. Now co-runs a security company. Also, he's the son of the secretary of defense." I let those overwhelming facts sit heavy in the air, trying not to surrender to the worry that came with them. Kind of hard not to. "Chase loves Tessa and Gray, and their baby, Penny. And, of course, their cute dog, Lucky." The memory produced a smile, but it fell away fast. "Why in the world would Trevor think the break-in would require the help of someone like Gray?" *Unless my suspicions are right and it wasn't random.*

"Trev's just overprotective. No stone unturned, you know him. It's who he is. He won't rest until he knows without a shadow of a doubt it was random and you and Chase are safe at home."

"He said as much to me." I closed my eyes, the pain in my temple now making a comeback as I connected the dangerous dots I'd tried to ignore earlier. "Does he think someone is using me to get to him?"

"Maybe. Possibly. Or, well, more likely an enemy of—"

"Mitch," I breathed out, nerves twisting me up. "An enemy of the man Trevor never liked or trusted in the first place."

CHAPTER SIX

Alejandro

"It was bad enough you could've gotten hurt during that snowball fight, but like hell are you going back to your home after—"

"After what? What is it you're keeping from me?" Audrey asked Trevor, standing her ground. "Don't keep me in the dark."

Nope, not interested in third-wheeling an argument about to take place, either.

"Ryder and Reed will be here tomorrow. Let's wait and talk then, okay?" he requested, then looked over at me for an assist.

Shit, was he serious? "Er, uh, maybe he's right. Let's wait until we have more coverage before any of us go back to your place."

"Coverage for what?" She pointed her angry glare at me now.

"Tomorrow. Just wait until then." Trevor strode over and shockingly parked his ass right alongside me to face her.

Audrey groaned but thankfully didn't put up a fight. "Fine. Answers tomorrow, along with my things." She shook her head. "Things I want to pick out myself. So when my brother is here, and there's all this 'coverage' you need for some reason, I'm going over."

He scoffed and approached her. "What kind of things?"

I worked my way backward a few steps, trying to make a clean exfil without their notice.

"You packed my stuff, and I don't like some of what you packed."

"You're not moving in," he grunted back in the same tone. "So why does that matter right now, especially considering—"

"Considering *what*, exactly?"

The man had walked right into that one.

"Just tell me what you need. I'll get it tomorrow," Trevor deflected.

"I'd prefer not to say it in front of our guest." Her voice softened that time as her eyes darted to me.

"Just say it." Trevor gestured at her to continue.

Her shoulders dropped. "You packed my oversized *that time* underwear, ya know? There. You happy? As embarrassed as I am now?" She did this adorable wrist twirl, distracting me from what she'd said, but she also had me forgetting my mission to leave without drawing their eyes. "I know I'm moody, but it's for a different reason—just FYI—and I know that's why you grabbed those."

Trevor barked out a low laugh. "You're always moody, woman. And I have no damn clue what 'that time' underwear means. I just threw shit in a bag without thinking about it."

Yeah, I really don't belong here.

Trevor tossed a look over his shoulder at me as if remembering I was there and they were discussing his ex-wife's underwear.

"Doing a perimeter sweep," I mumbled on my way out, shutting the door behind me.

I barely made it three steps outside the lodge before Audrey called my name and tossed out a quick "I am so, so sorry about that."

"Nothing to apologize for." I kept on walking, hoping she wouldn't follow.

"I don't know what's worse: the secrets Trevor's keeping from me, you walking in on me naked, or hearing that conversation," she said in a small voice, and now I had no choice but to turn around and face her.

"No clue what you're talking about." I forced the side of my lip up into a semi-smile, hoping we were about done so I could check the property. If I was lucky, maybe I'd find someone or something to shoot.

She reached for my arm, doing her best to get a grip through my heavy jacket. "That was wildly inappropriate. Seriously, I'm so sorry."

I slanted my gaze to where she was touching me. "The naked thing, or discussing your underwear in front of me?" I casually tipped my head toward the woods, letting her know I had places to be. People to possibly kill and all.

"Can I walk with you? I need air."

I suppressed the groan of frustration trying to escape. She'd misread it as being jackass-like, when in reality, I just couldn't breathe around her for some reason, and it drove me nuts. "You sure you want that air? It's frigid."

"Will it numb my brain so I forget what happened today? Forget the fact there's clearly more to this break-in story no one wants to share with me?"

"Air won't help, no." I frowned. "But you can come anyway."

She nodded her thanks, then tucked her bare hands in her jacket pockets. We were seconds away from starting that walk we shouldn't take together when the door flung open.

Of course.

"Wait." Trevor cut straight over to me, avoiding eye contact with Audrey, and discreetly tried to hand me a 9mm, checking over his shoulder to ensure no guests were around in the process. "Can't sweep the property unarmed."

"I have a Glock at my back. I'm always armed, don't worry." There were ways to fly commercially with weapons. Though my 9mm was all I'd brought for this trip. Left my M4 with the guys back in Wyoming.

"Good." He hid the Glock before anyone could notice, then disappeared as fast as he'd come, probably not realizing Audrey planned to do that sweep with me.

"I really am sorry about him," she said, breaking the silence once we were alone again.

He regrets losing you and wants you back. "He cares about you," I said instead of speaking my thoughts as I started to walk, already forgetting I'd just changed my mind about her coming along with me.

"We're friends. That's all." Those words hit me harder than I'd expected, for some reason. "He just knows me well, and—"

"Still knows a lot about your underwear. Makes sense."

"Apparently he doesn't, based on what he packed and that conversation back there. And I still can't believe I said all that in front of you."

"Because I don't know you well?" Shit, that came out . . . well, not sounding all that great.

"Well, yeah. Or *no*?" She paused and let a *hmm* fall from her lips that I could hear even with my back to her. "Somewhere in between?"

I kept on moving, not able to dissect her words.

"You said you were married before. So you understand what it's like to have those conversations, right?"

I had no clue what she was talking about. What was I supposed to understand? I had no plans to talk to Beth ever again. Even if we were the last two people on the planet and the fate of humankind relied on us having a five-minute fireside chat, I wouldn't. The world had had a good run. Rest in peace.

"Sure, I'd absolutely be discussing her underwear with her. I totally get it," I grumbled under my breath, accidentally slipping into jackass mode.

"Ouch." One quick breath before she tacked on, with a touch of sass, "Well, that answers the question I had, though."

"Oh, does it?" I whirled around to face her, remembering now she shouldn't be out here if the break-in wasn't random.

She ate up the distance between us. "Now I know I'd rather you see me naked than to have heard that conversation with my ex."

And there she went, distracting me again with that comment. Fuck, I was in trouble.

"Well, I both saw you naked *and* heard your talk. Both happened. No takebacks." I winked, trying my hand at being funny, but dammit, it came out asshole-like again. What was wrong with me? "Sorry," I muttered, my gaze sweeping over her as she made the unwise decision to close that last bit of space between us.

We were at the edge of the woods.

Just us, nature, and God.

She worked her eyes up my body before making things slightly worse by removing her hands from her pockets like she might reach for me next.

Please don't.

"You're in an awkward situation." She tipped up one shoulder. "Babysitting your best friend's sister alongside her son's father."

I arched my brow, deciding to abandon ever using the word *underwear* again around this woman, given that I'd already seen her without any on. "So no more talk of your preferred drawers?"

"Drawers?" She smiled, and there went her eyes. Lighting up like lights on Christmas morning. "Um, yeah, let's not talk about those." She pursed her lips briefly. "Good idea. Best idea I've heard all day, in fact."

I couldn't believe we were talking about her underwear after her home had been broken into and she could've been raped or killed. Maybe she was looking for a distraction, though, so she wouldn't get lost in the what-could've-been's instead?

I could hear my mother's voice in my head, proud of that psych degree she made me get before joining the army. I had to admit, it did help me better understand people sometimes.

When Audrey reached out and set her hand on the front of my jacket, over my heart, I dropped my gaze there and gently took hold of her wrist with every intention of breaking free of this situation I'd somehow found myself in.

Only I couldn't let go. I just held her. Hand to my heart, with all those layers in between not mattering. We quietly stared at one another, locked in the moment the way we had been when I caught her from falling during the snowball fight.

You've been through hell, walked through fire and all the damn things, and so have I. I'm not doing it again.

No going back to ever using that heart of mine for anything other than an organ to keep me alive.

Take her back inside. Head on a swivel and focus up. None of the reminders landed like they needed to. What kind of operator was I? "Audrey."

She blinked and pulled her hand away, resting her palm on her cheek as if doing a quick temperature check. "I'm so sorry. I think it's . . ." She brought her hand to her temple, working her fingers beneath her white fleece beanie. "I was hit in the head. That has to explain why I'm acting so out of character today. Not locking my door while showering." She stepped back. "Talking about *drawers*." Another step away from me. "And this strange feeling in the pit of my stomach . . . Ummm."

That next step was about to send her falling over an exposed tree root.

I moved as fast as I could. Leaned in and swooped my arm behind her back, catching her.

"No falling for me." *Shit.*

She stared up at me, eyes going wide.

"No more knocks to the head, I mean." I did my best to backtrack out of that mess as fast as possible, knowing damn well I'd meant what I'd actually said.

There'd be no falling of any kind.

On the ground.

Or over any cliffs now nicknamed Where Old Souls Go to Die.

And sure as hell no falling in love.

CHAPTER SEVEN

Alejandro

I'd done my best to avoid Audrey the rest of the afternoon and stay mission focused, but I had no choice but to face her at the dinner table that night. I also couldn't turn down Eden's home cooking, even if the meal was served with a few too many questions from her boyfriend, Beau.

"How long have you two been dating?" I needed to turn the tables on the sheriff before he wound up knowing everything from my Social Security number to my dick measurements.

"When did we meet? Four months ago, when my car broke down. All that swagger rolling up to help me." Eden's laugh was contagious enough for Chase to pick it up too.

Only he ran in a different direction from what she'd probably intended, poking fun at her. Something about lovebirds and trees. Kissing, maybe?

I lost track of his teasing because Audrey was staring at me from across the table, and I couldn't *not* stare right back at her.

And now I was struggling not to think about her naked. Perfect time for that memory to hit me, with her ex-husband at my right and her son off to my left.

"So, um, my slightly rude boyfriend has asked you just about everything," Eden began while playfully elbowing the sheriff, clearly looking for a distraction from Chase's teasing, "except for where you grew up."

"I'm more of a show-than-tell kind of guy." I set down my fork so I'd stop stuffing myself with her good food, and went for the deck of cards I kept on hand like a security blanket, thanks to my father.

At the sight, Chase abandoned his silverware and the lonely green beans still on his plate.

"Nope, if you want to see a card trick, you have to finish your vegetables." Cards removed from the box, I began shuffling them, unable to miss the smile parked on Audrey's lips.

She pointed at Chase's plate. "You heard the man. Do what he says."

"Let me guess," Beau began while patting his mouth with his napkin before leaning back and hooking his arm over the back of Eden's chair, "your cards are a clue to where you grew up?"

"I have to say, I'm disappointed you didn't run a background check on me. You should already know that." I looked down at Chase. "Don't you think?"

Around a mouthful of green beans, he mumbled, "Mm-hmm."

I lifted my eyes to his beautiful mother, momentarily forgetting his father was on my other side.

"Vegas?" Eden guessed as I bridged the cards, shuffling them some more. "Magician?"

"Magician's son. I grew up backstage." I continued doing a few easy tricks that only involved shuffling while waiting for Chase to finish up. "My parents left Cuba in the early '80s so my dad could follow his dreams. He landed his own headline act while my mom was pregnant."

Audrey set her napkin on her plate. "How'd that never come up when we hung out before?"

"You didn't ask." I grinned, then side-eyed Trevor, feeling the full weight of his scrutiny now. *Fucking fantastic.*

"Didn't want to follow in your dad's footsteps?" Beau continued with his inquiry. Something told me he'd come from a long line of men in uniform himself. In his case, probably in the law enforcement field.

"I think I went the route I was supposed to," was all I could give him.

"Delta, right?" Beau gestured to Trevor. "He mentioned Ryder is, so I'm guessing you were, too?"

I nodded as Chase clapped and announced "Done!" while still chewing. "Show me your tricks now. Can you make yourself disappear, too?"

Unfortunately. In more ways than one. I kicked that shit thought to the side and did what I did best: cut through tension with both humor and magic, distracting everyone from their problems.

I wasn't sure how long I entertained Chase, along with everyone else at the table, but time flew by.

"How about we all watch a movie? I'm sure Alex is tired now," Eden proposed, and I was grateful for that suggestion because I was running out of magic tricks that involved cards. "Sound like a good idea?"

"All righttttt." Chase stood and picked up his plate. "Only if Uncle Alex comes."

The last thing I wanted to do was intrude on more of their family time. "We'll see."

I waited for him to leave with Eden for their living room, and after Beau pulled Trevor aside to talk about the case, I busied myself with helping Audrey clear the dishes.

Of course, that meant we were now alone, together, in the private kitchen.

"Thank you for helping get his mind off everything," she said as I joined her at the sink. "He'll sleep better tonight for that." She playfully hip-checked me. "You've got skills, though. Impressive."

"Yeah, well, I had no choice but to learn." I rested my side against the counter and grabbed a dish towel to dry the pots and pans after she rinsed them. "You should've seen me get sawed in half when I was a kid. Or break free from chains inside a tank of water."

"You can do all that, too?" She turned off the faucet and faced me.

"That I can." I smiled, setting the last of the dishes on the rack. "A man of many skills."

"Including how to dodge a sheriff's questions with a certain *je ne sais quoi,*" she teased, pulling out a French accent.

"Wrong language," I teased back, instead of acknowledging the fact she'd read me right in not wanting to talk about why I'd chosen the military over stepping into my father's shoes like he'd hoped. I barely talked about that with people I knew well, let alone a stranger.

"You want to hear me talk *en español*, do you?" Her entire face lit up as she stared at me. "Unfortunately, if you don't use it . . . you lose it. Forgot everything I learned in school." She wet her lips. "But I'd love to hear you talk to me *en español*."

"If you're lucky, maybe I will." That deep rasp in my voice should not have been present. I quickly cleared my throat and backed away, remembering I was supposed to be putting up walls to protect us both, and there I was building her a drawbridge she could use to drop on over anytime. "Anyway."

She smiled. "I like that word almost as much as using L-O-L at the end of texts. Great awkward-killer."

This woman and her blunt honesty were going to send me.

You know, over the edge.

Falling hard.

I may have had a soft spot for women who told the truth. Wonder why?

"*Anyway*, I should probably skip the movie."

"Why?"

I arched a brow, and I couldn't help but say the only thing that came to mind: *"Esto es peligroso. Tú y yo."*

"Translate, please." She parted her lips, their color a perfect match to her nipples, which I definitely remembered.

"Not on your life." I smirked, but then she pulled out her phone from her back pocket like her own personal deck of cards and gave it a voice command.

"Translate: *Esto es peligroso. Tú y yo.*"

Ah, fuck.

Whoever talked back to her didn't have a female British accent like my phone did. A computerized male voice came back, betraying me with *"This is dangerous. You and me."*

My cue to exfil. I patted the counter at my side twice, then turned, but she caught my arm with her free hand.

"Translate to Spanish, please: It doesn't have to be."

"No tiene por qué ser así," the AI voice responded.

She went and killed me by repeating the words to me in Spanish despite the fact I'd just heard them.

If I had to listen to her speak Spanish one more time, my control would snap. "I should say good night." There was no way I'd survive standing here another minute and keep up my walls.

"Hey, you two good?"

Trevor. Of course. I couldn't escape without another awkward confrontation, could I?

"I'm going to get some rack time. It's late." I checked my watch. 2100 hours. Yeah, well, I supposed white lies were okay.

"Negative. My son wants you in there and right next to him. So, too damn bad." Trevor shook his head, eyes on Audrey now. "He wants ice cream. Mind getting some for everyone?"

She pocketed her phone, then started for the fridge. "On it. Vegan for him. What do you want?" she called over her shoulder.

"The real stuff," Trevor grunted as if surprised she'd need to ask. "See you *both* in there," he said before bailing, leaving me alone again with his ex-wife and now no choice but to join their family tonight.

"Chase is lactose intolerant," she explained while setting two tubs of ice cream on the counter. "What about you? Which kind should I scoop for you since you're staying?"

"Vegan," I grumbled, knowing it was going to take more effort than I thought to keep my distance from her.

"Really? Are you intolerant, too? Because I know you're not vegan." She began scooping the chocolate into a bowl. "You pretty much inhaled Eden's pot roast."

"The last home-cooked meal I had was at Ryder's mom's place at Christmas. So do you blame me?" I grinned. "But no, no allergy." I tossed a look toward the hallway, thinking about Chase. "Just don't want him to feel alone."

CHAPTER EIGHT

Audrey

I stared down at Chase in my bed, the morning light peeking through the blinds, which made him groan and turn away to hide his head beneath the covers, falling back to sleep in a second.

After the movie, he'd asked to stay in my bedroom instead of his.

Trevor had offered to bunk with him, but we quickly realized Chase didn't want to sleep next to me because he was scared. He was offering me *his* protection from "*the bad guys,*" as he'd called them.

"Unless Daddy wants to sleep with you instead. Or Uncle Alex can!"

My son's offer had seemed to give both Trevor and Alex a coronary at the same time. Me, too, especially since I'd had a fantasy about sharing a bed with Alex two or *five* times since we first met at Christmas. It was never supposed to become a reality, though, and certainly not like *this.*

"Five more minutes, sleepyhead," I told him while checking the time. "Your uncle should be here soon." While Chase was normally up before any of us, he hadn't gone to bed until almost midnight since he'd begged for a few more tricks from Alex after the movie, and Alex had been unable to refuse his pleas.

"Okayyy," he murmured, half asleep already as I went to the bag Trevor had packed me to find something to change into.

Granny panties and a plain-Jane bra it is. Thanks, Trev.

I changed in the bathroom, then pushed my hair to the side to check on the knot at my temple. I'd like to continue blaming my weird behavior on the bump to the head, including my flirty-ish conversation with Alex after dinner, but that'd be a lie, and I was a horrible liar.

"Annnd I need makeup, or everyone will think I'm not just a hot mess, but sick." I rolled my eyes, then went in search of my purse. Trevor hadn't thought to pack any makeup, but thankfully I kept emergency mascara, a brow pencil, and eyeliner in my bag at all times.

Once I was done, I returned to my room to send Hollis a quick text before waking Chase.

Me: He's better in person than in my fantasies. How's that possible? No one is supposed to be better in real life.

Hollis: That's good. Right?

Me: Also, I flirted a little. Somehow, it came naturally after dinner, and I didn't even have wine. Maybe I was channeling you?

Hollis: Again, this is good. Why am I hearing "this is bad" energy in your texting tone?

Me: Because it IS bad. I don't want to like anyone.

At the sound of chatter coming from the lodge, I assumed that meant my brother had arrived.

Me: I gotta go. Stay safe wherever you are now.

Hollis: On a beach in Bali. Tomorrow? Who knows. But I should be there with you.

Me: No, no. I'm sure everything is fine.

That was a total lie. Trevor was keeping secrets from me, which meant that so-called "random break-in" hadn't been random at all.

But I had to admit, now I was a little grateful he'd kept me in the dark yesterday. Chase was able to have a relaxing and normal day because of it.

Me: No need to stress. Talk later. Love ya.

"Is that Uncle Ryder I hear?" Chase sat upright, tossing the covers aside as I shoved my phone in my back pocket.

"Why don't we go see?" I offered him my hand like he was still only six, and we made our way downstairs.

My brother was by the two front doors with his beautiful fiancée, Seraphina.

Reed and Alex were also with him. Trevor too.

Alex gave me a small nod hello, and yup, things were still awkward. *And why wouldn't they be, after the last twenty-plus hours of our interactions so far?* Kicking things off with him seeing me buck naked and ending with me wishing he'd give me a good-night kiss before bed last night?

He had on all black again today. From his boots to his jeans and long-sleeved shirt. A sexy combination with that scruff on his jaw, midnight-dark eyes, and matching black hair.

I forced myself to look away from the ridiculously handsome man and over to my brother, who was lifting my son up into the air.

I have a brother. I have a brother. Some days I really did have to repeat that mantra a few times. The shock and awe of it had yet to wear off.

Seraphina rubbed Chase's back as he remained glued to his uncle's large frame, hugging him. She peeked over at me as I joined them, an infectious smile lighting her face. "Hey, you." She strode over and wrapped me in her arms. And you know what? Yeah, I needed that hug more than I knew I did.

A handshake from Reed next, before my brother untangled Chase from his arms so he could pull me in for a hug.

"How are you?" he whispered as I kept hold of him, nearly crying into his shoulder at the comfort of having someone there who I knew wanted nothing from me. Just cared. Just loved me even though he didn't have to.

"I'm okay." Like Chase, I wasn't ready to let go.

I was also too afraid I'd face reality and break down if he untangled me from his arms. It was only now, in this moment, that I realized I never did cry after the break-in.

Because I'm okay, right? Minus being a head case yesterday, I really am—so that's what I have to focus on. Be strong.

"Sorry it took me so long to get here. Hope Alex took good care of you for me," Ryder said into my ear.

"Great care," I choked out, finally breaking free of him, accidentally catching Alex's eyes in the process. I looked back at my brother, who was sporting a small, nervous smile while patting his chest. "Hi."

"Hi." Ryder took hold of my cheeks and rested his forehead against mine. "Can't lose you, sis. Just got you."

Yeah, keep talking like that and I'm going to ugly-cry. A shiver rolled right on through me as he lifted his head and locked eyes with me.

I heard Eden introduce herself to someone, and when I twisted around, I realized it was Jason Reed.

He swallowed her petite hand with his big one, shaking it before Beau appeared to break up their introduction with one of his own.

I should have known he'd hang around for their arrival so they could talk.

"I have to head out soon. Don't want to rush the welcome party here." Beau tipped his cowboy hat. "But mind if we chat first?"

Trevor motioned toward the side hall. "In my office, away from the ears of the guests, would be preferable."

"I'll have your bags brought to your rooms for you," Eden offered. "And Chase and I will start whipping up eggs and bacon for everyone."

"Oh, I'd be happy to help." Seraphina took Chase's hand, and I nodded my thanks to her.

Trevor blocked my path to the office. "How about you join them?" He tipped his chin toward the kitchen as if I didn't know my way around.

I shook my head. "Nope, no boy talk. No excluding me." I kept my voice down so guests couldn't overhear. "You promised you'd tell me everything tomorrow, and that day has come."

Trevor raised his brows and glanced at Ryder hovering at the entrance of the hallway, the only one still present since everyone else had dispersed from the foyer.

"Audrey." Was my brother joining forces with my ex in an attempt to ask me not to argue?

I shook my head as my response.

"Fine. I take it you're as stubborn as I am?" The side of Ryder's mouth quirked, then he waved me over to join him.

But first, I had to get around the Trevor roadblock.

"You really don't want me to know the truth for some reason." And now I knew it had everything to do with that call Eden had overheard yesterday with his cousin. "Please, just get it over with. What is it you're keeping from me?"

Ryder strode over to us, forcing Trevor to shift to the side and make eye contact with him. "Well, hell, now you have me worried, too," my brother remarked.

"You're going to be pissed at me." Not the best thing to hear from my ex.

"Why will I be?" I swallowed, and my heart thwacked harder as memories from our marriage pushed to the front of my mind at how many secrets he'd kept from me. Some because he had no choice. Others for his own reasons.

Trevor closed his eyes, letting his arms drop. "I haven't been honest with you. I lied to you about why I didn't re-up. I lied about why I retired at twenty instead of thirty years like I'd originally planned."

I reached for his forearm to give him a squeeze, a request to look at me.

"I wanted to be more present in Chase's life, don't get me wrong." Trevor finally opened his eyes.

"But . . . ?" I whispered, thankful my brother was at my side, offering his quiet support to help me through whatever I was about to hear next.

Trevor stretched out his neck, eyes on the cedar beams. "I was hoping I was just paranoid and wrong about him."

What in the world are you talking about? "Wrong about who? What had you giving up being a SEAL, giving up the thing you loved more than anything?"

His gaze instantly hit mine. "I didn't love being a team guy more than being Chase's father."

I deserved that look and tone. "I'm sorry, I didn't mean that. I meant leaving the navy to run a lodge. You were already a great father while serving. Chase understood what you did. You were always his hero. Still are, uniform or not."

Trevor's shoulders collapsed. "No, I'm talking about Mitch. I left because of him."

"Because he died? You felt you needed to help out? I, um, don't understand." But then Eden's words from yesterday hit me, and the real *why* Trevor left struck me even harder.

"I didn't want to ruin his memory for you unless I had to," he shared in a low, haunted voice. "I'm so damn sorry, Audrey, but I believe Mitch was a traitor. A possible enemy of the state. And I highly doubt it was a mechanical issue that took down his plane, but the terrorists I think he was double-crossing our country with that killed him."

CHAPTER NINE

Audrey

After Trevor dropped that bomb on me, he turned and went to his office, leaving me alone with my brother to pick up the pieces. It officially made sense why he'd asked me to hold off on this conversation until today.

Ryder pulled me into his arms, resting his chin on top of my head. "This is . . ."

"A lot," I whispered, cheek against his chest, his jacket still on but open. I could hear his heart thrashing loud, pulsing in my ear.

"Maybe he's wrong."

"Trevor's never wrong. It's an annoying trait of his. Always being right." Well, when it came to these kinds of things, at least. "Is he suggesting, though, that someone came to my house in search of something of Mitch's? They broke in for that reason? Why now?" I had a million other questions, but from the sounds of it, only one man currently had the answers.

This was becoming as messy as it was complicated.

Ryder backed up and let me go, searching for my gaze. "You're not crying. Are you in shock?"

I frowned. "Shock? Um, I mean, of course. Mostly yes." *A little bit of no.*

His forehead tightened as if preparing for something he didn't want to hear. "What is it?"

"Hey," Reed called out, saving me from spilling my guts. "You two good? Ready?"

Ryder and I looked over at him, and I started his way without another word. I wasn't ready to open up yet—not right now. Not after what Trevor had shared. I needed time to process.

Once we were all gathered in the office, the first person to grab my attention was Alex. He had his back to the room, arms folded, eyes out the window and on the mountain view.

As if sensing I was there, he slowly turned, arms falling to his sides in the process. There was a pained look in his eyes, which had me believing Trevor had quickly shared the Mitch news in my absence. I wasn't clocking sympathy from him, though. Nor pity. More like understanding.

"Ready?" Beau, in classic Beau fashion, stepped into the middle of the room while removing his hat, signaling that it was time to get the show on the road.

The door softly clicked shut behind me as Ryder remained at my side.

"Start from the beginning, please." My voice came out like a strangled whisper as I went over to the armchair by the closest wall of books and took a seat, deciding that'd be the best course of action for Trevor's revelations.

Alex remained a quiet and now unreadable statue by the window, and Reed joined him, leaving only my brother and ex-husband in my direct view.

"Talk," Ryder prompted while taking off his jacket and tossing it on the second armchair next to me.

Trevor went over to his desk and picked up a folder. "After Mitch died, something didn't sit right with me. There were red flags. Whispers of shit on base. I poked around and wound up poking the wrong bear. Pissed off some people."

Typical of you. Not surprised there. I gripped the chair's armrests, bracing myself.

"What didn't sit well with you?" Ryder asked him.

Trevor glanced at my brother, then over at Beau as the sheriff put his hat back in place. "Two months before Mitch died, his close friend Arlo turned up dead deep in enemy territory."

"He was captured?" Reed asked in a terse voice.

Trevor shook his head. "No, if Arlo was over there, he went willingly. Well, at first, at least. Clearly something went wrong. The rumors . . . it was rough on his family. He was labeled a traitor. Not publicly, but in our circles he was seen as a disgrace to the uniform. To our flag."

He gave us all a second to digest that before continuing.

"I believe the same people who took out Arlo were responsible for killing Mitch, because I think Mitch may have been double-crossing our country, too." Trevor lowered the file to his side, resting it against his jeaned thigh. "For some reason, the government didn't want anyone to know about it. Maybe they were worried about the fallout if another decorated pilot went rogue like Arlo, so they covered it up."

"What evidence do you have to substantiate any of this, or is this all speculation?" Ryder was probably hoping to defend my deceased husband's honor on my behalf, thinking I'd want him to.

"It's a working theory, but I'm doing my best to confirm it as soon as possible. I'm still running leads." Trevor held up the file folder. "There was just no way I could stay in the navy and worry half a world away that one day something Mitch had been into might come back and hurt you or my son. So I hired someone to—"

"Wait." I bolted up and approached him, not letting him continue. "You were having us followed after he died, weren't you? I felt like I was being watched back in Virginia. I even told you about it. You made me think I was paranoid and losing my mind."

"Until I could officially get out, I needed someone keeping an eye on you and Chase. What'd you expect me to do? You think I could be downrange fighting while wondering if you two were in danger?"

"You were the reason I became so paranoid. *You.*" I pointed at his chest. "And I was right all that time."

"Shit, I know." He surrendered his free hand. "I should have just told you, but without evidence, I didn't want to hurt you for no reason."

Alex and Reed faced the window again, giving us privacy. But Ryder remained, hovering like my protective shadow.

"So, let me get this straight." I held out both hands, slamming a finger down onto my open palm with each new statement. "You thought my husband was a bad guy, but you had no proof. Just a gut feeling based on rumors. Then you had someone babysit us without our knowledge, *then* left your career to personally watch over us." I shook my head, shock continuing to tear through me. "Did Eden even really need your help, or was that a lie?"

Trevor tossed an uneasy look at the sheriff as if remembering the man was in love with his sister and may not like his answer.

"Was it a ploy to get us out of Virginia to somewhere new?" I asked, and when he looked up at the ceiling, that was an answer in itself. "All of that because of a hunch?"

I wanted to be mad at him for overstepping in his typical and secretive way, but his goal had been to keep us safe. So could I be? No, I didn't think so.

I knew he'd go to the ends of the earth to protect Chase—and even me, despite our marriage being over.

"I thought I was doing the right thing, and as more time passed, I hoped I'd just been crazy. Or at least, if Mitch was a shitty asshole, that his past would never come back to bite you or Chase."

"But you think Friday night, it did?" Ryder broke through our back-and-forth. "Why?"

Beau spoke up. "Because the men who hit the house were professionals." At least this wasn't news to me anymore since Eden had spilled the beans yesterday. "It was a targeted team. Precise movements."

"Bypassed every one of my security measures that only someone with the kind of background I have would be able to do, and that's stretching it," Trevor said, picking up for the sheriff. They'd clearly talked about all this behind my back before now. "No way was that random, and I don't have any enemies I'm aware of since my identity was hidden while serving, which leads me to Mitch. So I made a call."

"To?" Ryder asked him.

"My cousin's married to Admiral Chandler's son. Secretary of defense." Trevor handed Ryder the folder. "I asked Gray to speak to his dad for me. Try and pull some strings. Poke the right bear to get answers I couldn't get a year ago on my own. In hindsight, I should've done that when Mitch died, even if I barely knew Gray back then."

Ryder passed the folder off to Alex and folded his arms, rocking back in his boots. "We're familiar with the secretary. With Gray's team, Falcon Falls, too." I could read his uneasy expression as he spoke, as if he wasn't allowed to share much more than that.

"I take it the secretary confirmed your suspicions about Mitch?" Reed asked while looking over Alex's shoulder as Alex flipped through some documents.

"Not yet. Gray's father is with POTUS in the Middle East right now, wrapping up a meeting." Trevor's shoulders dropped. "Gray will reach out as soon as he talks to him." He pointed to the file in Alex's hands. "In the meantime, I asked Gray's team to do some digging since they have extensive resources. That file contains everything he found on Mitch. I haven't had time to really dive in and take a look yet, though."

"Were these files obtained by legal means? I see half the information has been redacted, so they're clearly still classified records." Reed half smiled, then held up his hands in apology to Beau, as if forgetting he'd been talking about hacking in front of law enforcement.

Beau waved him off with a flick of his wrist.

At that, Reed continued, "Was Gwen Montgomery behind getting the files?"

Gwen? It took me a minute to connect the name. *Right. Wyatt's twenty-something-year-old daughter.* We'd briefly met once.

"I know better than to ask Gray's team how they do what they do." Trevor lifted his chin, gesturing to the folder. "But I'm sure there's something in there that'll point us to the fact my gut's right about Mitch. Gotta be a breadcrumb or two."

Alex stopped flipping through pages, keying in on something in front of him, and his facial expression, and every line of his body, visibly hardened.

"What is it?" I asked, but instead of acknowledging my question, he remained in some kind of daze, quietly closed the folder, and passed it over to Reed.

"Let's say we believe your theory, that Mitch is a traitor and was killed by terrorists," Ryder began, pulling me back to the problem at hand. "Why come after Audrey now? Something doesn't add up."

More like a few somethings, right? "Because maybe Friday really was random." The words fell flat even as I said them. "Fine, fine—but why'd only a few men come to my house if I'm important for some reason?"

"To keep a low profile. Get in and out with whatever they were after before anyone found out," Trevor said in a gritty voice. "My hope is they were after something there, not you, and they didn't expect to find you home."

I rubbed my forehead, forgetting the skin was sensitive at my temple. "I have no idea what they'd want. Mitch certainly never opened up to me about anything op-y. Not ever."

"We'll figure out what they wanted. Don't worry." Beau removed his hat, using it to motion to everyone in the room. "We've got your six."'

"I appreciate that." I did my best to give them a hopeful look, when in reality, I was ready to crawl under a blanket and *I Dream of Jeannie* my way out of this mess with one wish: Make this nightmare vanish. Go back to yesterday, when ignorance was bliss.

"Let me know as soon as the secretary talks to Gray, will ya?" Alex hiked a thumb toward the door. "I think I'll head over to Audrey's and have a look around. I take it you have eyes on her place in case anyone tries to break in again?"

Beau nodded. "Deputy parked out front."

"Wait," I jumped in. "Shouldn't I go with you? I mean, I knew Mitch. None of you did. Maybe I—"

"Absolutely not," Trevor interrupted.

"Take Reed with you for backup," Ryder ordered before turning to face Beau. "Can you send an extra cruiser over to park out front while my men are gone as an extra deterrent?"

Beau began texting someone as Reed quietly joined Alex at the door, where he'd been hovering—and why did Alex look like his dog just died?

Also, why the heck didn't I feel that way? *Because I already know Mitch is a bad guy,* I reminded myself. I'd had a damn good reason to divorce him after all. I'd known he was bad, just not working-with-terrorists bad. Well, *allegedly*.

I closed my eyes and touched my cheek, remembering why I'd demanded the end to our marriage. And for the first time that weekend, I let the tears fall.

CHAPTER TEN

Alejandro

"See you two managed to get yourselves a real vehicle," I said, buckling in as Reed started the engine of the F-250.

"As opposed to . . . ?"

I waved him off, letting him know to ignore me and my shit mood.

After that, he gave me five minutes of silence to stew. I'd have preferred all twelve the GPS said we had for the drive.

"You, uh, okay after what you saw back there?" His hesitant tone was on point with the question.

I sat taller, caught off guard that Jason "Doesn't Do Feelings" Reed had even asked me that.

"No clue what you're talking about." My fingers dug into my palms where they rested on my legs. "Just tell me about the visit with POTUS's guy yesterday. No one's filled me in."

"First tell me if you're—"

"I'm not okay," I snapped. "You know that, dammit." I shut my eyes, cursed in English, then Spanish. "I can't escape that woman. Every time I think I'm done with her, she comes back from the dead."

"If only she *did* die." His flat tone had me parting my eyelids. "Sorry," he quickly added, "but you know how we all feel about her."

"I know, I know." I couldn't argue there. "Fate is cruel, though."

"Or the world's just small when it comes to who works with whom in the Tier One community."

I glanced at him. "Is that you, Mr. Doom and Gloom, being optimistic?"

"Just realistic." He shrugged. "Beth was CIA. And from what we saw in those case files, Mitch worked with the Agency more than once in the last two decades. Just a coincidence he piloted an op your ex was also on. A security company was attached to that mission, too. Doesn't mean anything."

I wanted to believe that. Because the idea that my ex—currently rotting in a black site halfway around the world—might've crossed paths with Audrey's dead husband? That had me ready to jump from the damn truck.

"Don't forget," he went on, "Beth was busy being a traitor and running that drug operation here the last few years. No reason for her—"

"To be in the Middle East on that plane," I said, cutting him off. "Exactly my concern."

So no, I wasn't ready to rule out that my ex was somehow up to no fucking good right alongside Audrey's ex. Because, as I'd stated moments ago, fate was cruel. Not the slap-in-the-face kind of cruel, but the knife-in-the-heart (and in-the-back) kind.

And now fate was doing a number on Audrey, too. She'd lost her husband twice. First to death, now to dishonor. Well, that was still an unsubstantiated claim made by Trevor, but something told me he wasn't wrong.

It'd been unbearable to not wrap Audrey in my arms when she broke down and started to cry. And to walk away from her with tears cutting down her face had gutted me even more. *But* she had Trevor and Ryder to hold her up, and who was I to do it?

"Talk to me about Wyoming now that we're away from civilian ears." I needed to shift gears before I unraveled. "Tell me you two convinced the president's new point man we're good as we are. No more recruits."

"Fine," he grunted, thankfully giving in. "Ryder reminded them our unit's purpose is to track enemies and create target packages for the government. We don't need more than three of us to do that." There was a note of irritation edging his tone. "But they insisted we need backup in case things go sideways like they did with Seraphina's case."

Also known as the op where we took down my ex-wife. "Everything worked out okay."

"Well, you did die on us. So, not totally okay."

"For five seconds. Doesn't count. Didn't even see the other side. I was joking about the whole near-death-experience thing." I shook my head. "Please tell me you hit them back with a good argument."

"We told them if we need backup, we'll call President Bennett's dark money SEAL teams again, like last time."

I couldn't believe we were now one of those off-the-books teams, too. I'd always heard rumors over the years that there were different clandestine units working for different presidents and a select few high-up cabinet members, but to now be one of them? It was wild.

The op that had brought Seraphina and Ryder together last fall was the one to change us back to active-duty status and have us report directly to President Bennett and the secretary of defense, Admiral Chandler.

"But apparently," Reed continued, "getting an assist from POTUS's SEALs 'might not always be an option,' yada-fucking-yada."

I reached back to rub the knots forming at the base of my neck.

"So I pitched the idea of standbys." He flipped on the blinker as we approached Audrey's neighborhood. "Vets who don't want to operate full-time but miss getting their hands dirty. They'd be ready to roll on short notice when needed. Decent payday, too. We'd get them classified status like we have, dot the i's and cross the t's and all that, then we'd be good to go." He jerked a thumb over his shoulder. "Hell, I could see Trevor doing that."

Trevor? "No, I'm not operating with him."

"There something we need to know about him? He another Mitch?" His tone edged into protective mode, like Audrey was suddenly his little sister, too.

Too bad I don't see her that way. "No, it's not that." I stared at the cab's ceiling, jaw tight. "I just . . ."

"You just what?" When I didn't answer, he filled the silence. "I thought you were done with all that. Thought Beth screwed you up for good. You seriously catching feelings for the boss's sister?"

"No, of course not," I said a little too fast, too defensively. "And yeah, I am done. With vows, marriage, and all that nonsense. Good for Ryder, he found the real deal. But me? Never again."

We pulled onto Audrey's street, and I silently thanked God this conversation was about to die.

"Standbys," I muttered, dragging us back on track. "POTUS bite?"

"Not sure yet. He's—"

"In the Middle East in a meeting, right." I shook my head.

"But I think he will. We'll have a two- or three-man team we can call in as needed."

"Not a bad idea." *As long as Trevor's name never comes up again.*

We passed the cruiser the sheriff had outside Audrey's house; the deputy inside gave us a nod as we rolled by. I tipped my head in return. Beau must've given him a heads-up that we were coming over to check the place out.

Reed parked in front of the one-car garage, and I was out before the engine ever cut off. I glanced up at the small two-story house with pale shutters. Something about it reminded me of my childhood home in Vegas.

"Let's just get this over with. I don't want to be away from her long." *Shit. Freudian slip.* "I mean, from everyone," I added quickly and ignored the what-the-hell look he shot me.

Reed unlocked the front door and disabled the alarm once we were inside. We cleared the house room by room, ensuring no one had slipped by the deputy.

Once we confirmed it was clean, we began looking around. For what? Hell if we knew. Just something. Something someone had broken in to get if it wasn't a random break-in. *Unless they were here for Audrey.* Not an idea I wanted to entertain.

By the time we reached the primary bedroom, we still hadn't stumbled upon anything helpful. So this was our last shot.

I paused in the doorway, feeling awkward about invading her personal space.

Reed didn't hesitate and strode right in.

Better you than me.

"Trevor said they didn't have a chance to go through her room before he showed up, right?" Reed asked. "Room looks untouched."

"Yeah," I murmured, still stuck near the threshold. "That's what he told Ryder."

"Well, are you just gonna stand there like a depressing shadow?" he muttered before disappearing into the closet.

Right. I forced myself to move farther into the room, though every step felt like I was trespassing.

I spotted a box tucked away in front of the window. Scissors had been discarded on the floor beside it. Half a glass of wine waited on her dresser with an open record player nearby.

What were you doing before they showed up? Unpacking?

I crossed to the dresser and picked up a framed photo, and I couldn't stop the grin from forming at the sight.

You have a photo of me in your bedroom. Okay, technically it was a picture of my team, with Ryder and Chase front and center. But there I was in the background, profile visible.

I'd spent maybe five days in total around Audrey since we met at Christmas, but never one-on-one. No deep talks. No personal confessions. Just casual hangouts, light and easy.

Nothing feels remotely light or easy now.

The second Reed stepped out of the closet, I returned the photo to its place, careful not to knock over the wine, then turned toward him.

He went straight for the box on the floor and lifted it onto the bed.

"I think she was going through that when they showed up." I nodded toward the wineglass, then the record player. "That box feels personal. Something she'd been putting off."

"How do you know?" Reed asked, peeling back the flaps as I joined him by her bed.

"Just a hunch." But in truth, as someone who had a box or *three* myself, I could relate. Mine were in a storage unit in DC, and unlike Audrey, I had no plans to ever take a look at what was inside.

"Mitch's stuff. Maybe it's in here," Reed said while picking up an envelope. "Shit."

"What is it?"

"Divorce papers," he shared, and the pressure in my chest built. "Only her signature. Dated shortly before his plane went down last year."

You were going to leave him? What'd the bastard do to you? And no, I didn't feel guilty calling him that. Not now. Not if he was a traitor like Beth. And especially not if Audrey had wanted out of her marriage. *This changes things.* I erected a mental wall before I let that thought take root and grow. *No, it* doesn't *change things, because I'm not allowed to feel anything for her.*

"Ryder never mentioned this." He slid the papers into the envelope and picked up a small ring-size box and opened it next, revealing a plain wedding band. "You think Mitch was the guy Trevor's made him out to be?"

"The divorce papers don't help his case. From the looks of it, she filed, not him. Still, the timing of this whole thing is off."

I removed the band from the box and turned the weight of it between my fingers.

A symbol of commitment. Of promises. Something I'd lost faith in and, clearly, Audrey had as well.

We really did have more in common than I could process right now.

I closed my eyes and let the wedding band drop fully into my palm, then curled my fingers around it.

"What are you doing?"

"Something's not right." I opened my eyes to take a closer look at it.

There was a subtle ridge along the inside. Muscle memory kicked in, and my fingers moved on instinct. A narrow groove slid open, revealing a laser-etched strip of numbers, thin and precise. A sliver of code was hidden within the band.

"What in the magic shit did you just do?"

"My dad had stuff like this. And I think we just found what they were after."

Reed and I locked eyes, the weight of that realization settling between us. It would be impossible to view the break-in as random now, which meant Trevor was right.

"It could be GPS coordinates or an alphanumeric cipher. A decryption key. I'll examine it under a microscope back at the lodge."

"Here." I handed him the band. "Take the whole box just in case." My gaze flicked to the envelope. "But having this stuff at the lodge does paint a target on it. Call Ryder. Tell him to have Trevor clear out the guests. Send them packing until we know more. We need to turn the place into a fortress to protect Audrey and Chase, and whatever the hell we just found."

"Guests'll be pissed, but better that than dead." He slid the ring box into his pocket and put the envelope back in its place.

"I'll be right out," I said, needing a second.

"I'll make the call. Meet you outside." He grabbed the box and headed for the door. "Don't be long. Pretty sure these assholes still have eyes on the place and the lodge. They tried to be discreet last time, but I doubt they'll bother next time."

"Why haven't they hit the house again while it's been empty?" I asked, that bad feeling clawing its way up my spine. "They had all day yesterday. They were pros—these guys don't strike me as the type who'd be deterred by a cruiser out front."

Reed's jaw tensed. "Because they're regrouping. Possibly bringing in more people now that Audrey's at Trevor's. And, uh . . ."

I nodded. "They want Audrey. Friday's break-in wasn't just a search; they were here to take her, too, which is why they'd need to bring in more people to hit Trevor's place."

"And I'm sure they know we're here now, too."

"Not just that. They knew if they hit her house again, it'd put us on alert at the lodge and we'd go into full lockdown mode before taking her somewhere else. They need us to think it was random so we keep our guard lowered. And then they'll hit the lodge and her place here again at once."

"I'm calling Ryder," he said on his way out the door.

I stayed behind, glancing around her room, acting as if I had all the time in the world for some reason.

My gaze landed on the dresser, and then came the stupidest idea of the day.

I told myself it was for her. To give her a sense of normality and familiarity in the chaos of all this. That was the only reason I went and found a duffel bag and opened her top drawer.

God help me, I packed this woman's lingerie.

Silk. Satin. And lace.

So much lace, too. Black. Red. Pink. Purple. She didn't discriminate. Lace in every damn color. How the hell would I stop myself from wondering what shade of lace she was wearing on any given day we spent together?

Shit, what was wrong with me to be thinking about that right now? Trevor's name flashed through my mind like an electric jolt, serving as another reminder to get my head on right.

Trevor is Chase's dad. He and Audrey will end up back together, the perfect family unit. I don't belong in that picture. I'm not screwing anything up for them.

I had to stay away. For Chase. For Audrey. And yeah, selfishly, for my own heart.

Because the only way to protect everyone was by not falling in love.

CHAPTER ELEVEN

Alejandro

The mostly quiet ride didn't do a damn thing to slow my racing thoughts, though I appreciated that Reed hadn't questioned the hot-pink duffel bag.

By the time we made it back, Beau and two of his deputies were guiding guests from the lodge to the parking lot. Ryder moved fast. *Looks like Trevor does, too.* I hated that I was no longer completely hating that man.

Clearing my throat, I shoved down the uncomfortable lump rising in my chest and got out of the truck with Reed. We weaved through the crowd of disgruntled guests.

"I'll go find Ryder and Trevor," Reed said before heading off.

I went searching for the woman who made my pulse fly for reasons I was determined to ignore.

I found Audrey in the living room with Chase and Seraphina. Chase was deep into building a LEGO *Star Wars* ship on the coffee table, a roaring fire behind him while the two women talked and watched him work.

My body stalled at the sight. Because of her. Him. Safe and smiling as a family. Something I'd convinced myself I didn't want after Beth and I blew apart.

Apparently, all that self-talk back at Audrey's house to convince myself I couldn't interfere in a family that may be being rebuilt was out the window. Because now I was standing here like I couldn't breathe unless I was part of the picture too.

"You're back." Her soft voice tugged me out of that dangerous spiral and back into a world where I had to live and die alone.

"Look what I'm building, Uncle Alex!" Chase's proud voice saved me from myself.

I tore my gaze from Audrey and took in his progress. "Very cool. Box says ten plus, huh? Crushing it." I winked, then gave Seraphina a nod before turning to Audrey. "Here." I handed her the bag. "Please don't smack me for going through your stuff, but it seemed important yesterday that you had, well . . . your stuff."

Her eyes widened slightly. "Drawers?" she mouthed, stepping closer while positioning her back to her son and Seraphina.

"Among other things." I couldn't stop the grin from landing hard.

Color rose up her neck and into her cheeks. Pink, to match the pair of lacy ones I'd packed.

I set down the bag and shrugged out of my jacket. The fire had me roasting while standing before her. The *heat*—not the thought of her in pink lace—had me burning up.

"Mind watching Chase for a second?" Audrey asked Seraphina, effectively back-seating my thoughts, cutting off that avalanche of a disaster on the verge of happening in my head imagining Audrey in only pink panties.

"Of course," Seraphina offered.

Audrey nodded, then gave me a subtle gesture. Time to get away from her son's ears for whatever conversation we were about to have.

"How much did Ryder already tell you?" I asked while following her down the hall, past the kitchen, to a small nook tucked off to the side, just big enough for a love seat and not much else.

"Ryder told me it's not safe for the guests to be here. Hence the herd of people flooding outside when you showed up." She dropped onto the love seat, elbows on her knees, face in her hands.

Not exactly an encouraging sign.

I considered sitting beside her but opted to keep some distance. I leaned against the wall, arms folded, trying for casual. It felt about as natural as Reed telling a joke.

She slowly lifted her head, hands falling to her lap. "Alejandro."

It wasn't just that she'd used my full first name—it was how she said it. Soft. Intentional. Like it meant something. And damn if it didn't knock the wind from me.

I held still, waiting for her to follow it up, trying not to breathe too hard. If she knew the effect she had on me, I was screwed.

Before she could continue with whatever she'd planned to say after my name, I rushed out, "How are you feeling? Still out of character, or are you back in the zone today?"

Her lips twitched like she assumed I was joking.

I wasn't.

"Well, I was starting to feel like myself again until the hammer was dropped about Mitch. Why?"

Right. Him. The reason we're in this mess. And as much as I wanted to ask her about those divorce papers, I figured Ryder should be the one to do that, especially since he'd told Reed over the phone before we arrived that he hadn't known about them.

"Just curious." I shrugged.

"And now I have a question for you: Why'd you put up a mini wall between us yesterday only to go and pack my stuff today?"

I still couldn't believe she had my words translated last night. I had to be more careful when I let the Spanish slide out loud. "It was only a mini wall, like you said. Doesn't mean I can't pack you a bag."

"Going through my underwear doesn't qualify as dangerous?"

Way to throw that back at me. It hit me just as hard in English, too. "Only dangerous if you want to slap me for doing that." I tried my hand at a smile, doing my best to be charming and hoping nothing I did was creepy. I mean I *had* gone through her dresser.

"Not mad at all. In fact, very grateful. Skipped right over the thank-you I owe you. *Gracias.*"

"De nada."

Her smile was contagious, and I gave her the best one I had in me right back. Well, my mom said it was. A little teeth. Let the dimple show. Something like that. Probably looked like a psycho instead.

"So, um, why'd you do it despite being all wall-y on me?" She made a little *hmmm* noise. "*Wall-E,* ha. One of Chase's favorite movies. We should've watched that last night."

"I've, uh, seen that a few times myself." I tipped my head toward the hall. "Don't tell the guys."

She laughed, and it was as innocent as the expression on her face.

How were we stealing a quiet, easy moment like this after what she'd gone through? I had no clue, but I didn't want her having to deal with any dark topics again. I wanted to keep her in the light forever.

"I was just trying to be nice. Friendly. *Brotherly.*" Partially true. Not the *brother* part.

"You see me as a sister?" Both brows shot up.

"Not even a little bit," I couldn't help but admit. "Don't have one to know how I'd act around a sister, though," I tacked on.

"Right." She flicked her tongue across the front of her teeth.

Yeah, don't do that.

"I'm not supposed to even be talking about this, am I? I promised to not talk about *them* yesterday, right?"

Them? Underwear. Drawers. Panties. Pretty in motherfucking pink. *Not that I'm gonna ever find out.* "You can talk about whatever you want." I waved the white flag, surrendering. How could I not? She was smiling, and when this woman smiled it made my chest feel too small to contain my heart.

"Because friends can talk about anything?" Was that a question or a statement? "But one thing I know for sure: Friends don't let friends wear granny panties."

I wasn't sure what I was doing, but instead of answering her, I dropped down on one knee in front of her. A totally normal thing to do. And to an outsider, it probably looked as though I were about to propose. Hell, thirty minutes ago I'd been holding her husband's wedding ring. So this absolutely made sense.

I rested my forearm across my leg, and she took me by surprise by reaching for my hand. Our fingers threaded together like it was the most natural thing in the world.

Dios mío.

She exhaled, shaky and soft, the sound brushing my skin.

"Friends don't see each other naked or talk about their underwear, now that I'm really thinking hard about it." She kept a tight grip on my hand. "Well, Hollis knows why I have so much lace, but she's never had the pleasure of seeing me in any of it," she added in a teasing tone. "That's my best friend, by the way."

"Ah, I see." I was tempted to ask to be the second person to know why she loved lace, but I managed to behave. "I hate to say I've seen your brother in his skivvies before, but happy to report our friendship somehow survived. You can just put that in the 'shit that happens during war' box, though."

Her smile reached her eyes, and I could barely breathe at the sight.

"Anyway."

At my use of the awkward-killer word, as she'd called it yesterday, that beautiful smile of hers stretched even more.

"I think we'll survive what happened and forget all about it soon enough." I'd try, at least.

And now, time to pull away and locate that wall I was supposed to have up. But before I had a chance to do that, Trevor walked in with his impeccable timing, like he'd done in the kitchen last night.

"Everything good? Why are you on your knees?"

Good question, Trevor. No damn clue.

Audrey didn't yank her hand away like I expected, so I had to do it.

"Something wrong?" Ryder joined the party, too.

Perfect. Just perfect. The hits kept coming. I finally got my ass up to stand and face two of the three reasons why I needed to keep my distance from her. Thank God Beth wasn't physically around to remind me of number three. *No, just her name in that file to haunt me. Close enough.*

"He was, um, trying to calm me down," Audrey said quickly. "You know how I get. Panic attack. I, uh, started spiraling, and he rushed over. I owe him one. He kept me from fainting."

I could've kissed her for that lie, but I was distracted by the envelope in Trevor's hand.

The divorce papers. His grip tightened on it as his jaw visibly tensed. *He didn't know, either?* That realization hit harder than I'd expected, and it felt worse, because I had to assume Audrey had been afraid to tell him.

"We have an update?" She stood and stepped alongside me.

Ryder and Trevor exchanged a quick look as Trevor discreetly hid the envelope behind his back.

"Reed took a closer look at the inscription inside Mitch's ring while you were, uh, calming down my sister . . ." Ryder cleared his throat, apparently now realizing how flimsy that excuse sounded. "He figured out the code was incomplete. Don't ask me how. Over my head."

"Wait, what about Mitch's wedding band?" She shook her head, clearly confused.

Right, we'd skipped over that explanation. I'd been too distracted by discussing her panties and the fact we should no longer talk about them to give her the heads-up about the ring.

"There was a laser-etched strip of numbers hidden within his wedding band," Ryder explained.

"Where does Reed think the other half of the code is?" I asked as Audrey processed the news.

"We think those men were looking for both their rings, not just Mitch's. Reed believes the rest of the code is in hers," Ryder answered.

Two halves make a whole. In marriage. In secrets. Heck, in life. Would I ever stop being haunted by the memory of my own vows?

"Where do you keep your band?" Trevor asked her.

Audrey pressed a hand to her chest. "It's in a different box, not the one you must've found. The only other unopened one I have. It's in the attic, just off to the left side of the folded-up ladder in the ceiling."

"Reed believes the rings themselves are keys. If they're scanned together and held up to the right reader, it should unlock something."

"So you need both," she murmured. "Takes two to work." She shut her eyes, her voice becoming smaller. "I grabbed that box Friday night while you were at the movies to go through it. But wait . . . does that mean you also know about—"

"Yeah, we know," Trevor cut in. "We know you planned to get a divorce and that you kept it from everyone." He waited until she looked at him before adding, "What I want to know is, why?"

Her eyes flicked to mine, and the look of raw pain and regret burned through me.

All I could think was one thing: *How do you bring a man back from the dead just so you can be the one to kill him?* Because whatever that look meant . . . I was going to need to do exactly that.

CHAPTER TWELVE

Audrey

"Not here. I need four walls to prevent Chase from overhearing this conversation." I started moving, circling my brother and Trevor, who were standing like a barricade to my escape. Jaws tight, fists clenched, and ready to fight battles they couldn't win. Not this one. Not when Mitch was already gone.

Trevor stepped around me, taking the lead. Presumably to his bedroom, since Reed was probably at work on something ring-related in the office.

Once inside, Trevor tossed the envelope onto his bed, and I went over to the only window, hoping to ground myself in the view of the mountains as the door clicked shut behind us.

"I shouldn't be here," Alex said quietly.

"No. Stay." My words came out sharper than I'd expected. "You'll find out soon enough anyway."

He didn't argue, and Trevor didn't protest.

"I need to know why you didn't tell me you were getting a divorce." Trevor's voice was gritty but not angry. Well, not with me, at least.

I crossed my arms, rubbing my hands up and down my sleeves. My mind flicked back to what my conductor used to tell me before a performance: *Picture yourself in your underwear. It'll calm your nerves.*

I'd always teased her back, *Aren't I supposed to be imagining the audience in theirs?*

She'd just grin and answer, *If you're picturing everyone looking at you, you stop worrying about hitting every note perfectly.*

It made no sense, and yet it had always worked. And that was why I'd developed a habit of buying pretty lingerie. Even after I'd stopped performing, I'd always wind up in the lingerie section of a store, thinking, *One day . . . one day I'll play again. One day I'll wear that pair onstage.*

At my brother murmuring my name, I remembered where I was and why I was there.

"The night before Mitch's last deployment, we had a fight," I finally shared. "Chase was with Trevor's parents that weekend." I continued massaging my arms as if that could hold me together. "Mitch had been acting different for two months. Going out at all hours. Drinking. Just acting strange. I tried to be understanding and patient since he'd lost his best friend not long before that, but then I started wondering if he was cheating on me."

I should've turned around to face them for this, but I couldn't handle the weight of their reactions or the reflection of my pain in their eyes.

So I kept my back to them, chin lifted and eyes on the jagged mountain peaks beyond the glass. A fortress out there—I needed that kind of strength right now.

"I wound up confronting him about it. I wanted the air clear before he deployed. To know if he was unfaithful." The words tasted bitter as they came out. "He was furious that I'd asked him that, and he snapped. Flipped it all on me. Told me how dare I accuse him of that with everything he was going through, and he'd only ever been trying to protect me. That he loved me more than I could possibly understand. He was so mad."

My stomach clenched so tight it felt like I might throw up. The memory slammed into me with the force of a closed fist. *Mitch's* fist.

"I'd never seen him like that before. One second, he was yelling, and the next—he was raising his hand, and he hit me. Hard enough that I fell."

I rested a hand on my cheek, like it was still bruised. Phantom pain bloomed alongside the real ache already there.

"He panicked right after and began apologizing. Blamed drinking that night, something he didn't often do. Then he punched the wall while yelling at himself for putting his hands on me. When I was too scared to talk or go near him, he picked up a bottle of Jack and took off."

I slowly turned around to see the three of them in a line, spaced apart but connected in one purpose: protecting me.

My son's father.

My brother.

And the man I wanted to let in, even if I didn't know what that meant yet.

"I decided to leave him. I was sorry for whatever he was going through, but the damage was already done. No amount of excuses or apologies would cut it." My heart thudded rapidly as my voice became smaller.

Trevor's arms visibly flexed, his hands curling into weapons. For a second, my gaze dropped to the shield of armor with the red cross on it, then shifted back up to his face. To the rage radiating from him like heat.

I didn't give them time to speak. I needed to rip the rest of the Band-Aid off and get this over with.

"That night, Mitch came home late and crawled into our bed drunk, pleading to make up. He begged, even cried. Pleaded for me to accept his apologies, saying he'd do anything in the world for me and it'd been an accident."

I could feel Alex's eyes on me, steady and burning, like he was trying to absorb my pain just by witnessing it. I'd told him I'd stop making things awkward between us. And there I was, dropping the ugliest pieces of my past at his feet. But he didn't flinch or look away.

"Then he forced himself on me. He said he needed me before he deployed in the morning and that he wouldn't survive without having me." My voice was raw and scratchy as I attempted to push through and share one of the worst nights of my life. "He said I was his wife and it was my duty. That he'd die if he didn't have me one more time before he left."

At Trevor's sharp inhale, I closed my eyes.

Until now, only my lawyer had known the truth. Not even my mom or Hollis knew.

"What happened?" Trevor asked, terror and fear seeping through his tone. "Please tell me he backed off."

Shame crashed over me like a wave, destroying the last of my composure.

My bottom lip quivered, and then I broke.

Tears streamed down my cheeks, hot and fast, as I sank to my knees.

"I gave up fighting and resisting. That's what I hate myself for the most. That I let my noes go ignored. I told myself it'd be quicker to just cry my way through it and let it happen. Then he'd fall asleep and ship out the next morning, and I'd be safe."

I covered my face with my palms, feeling so damn small. Crushed by the weight of that memory, forced to relive it anytime someone offered me their condolences for his death. Forced to keep my mouth shut about what had happened to me.

"The next morning, he didn't even acknowledge it. And that was the last time I saw him."

I'd been a statue, eyes burning, as he took hold of my arm, leaned in, and kissed my cheek to say goodbye. He'd stared long and hard at me as if he had something he wanted to say, and I doubted that something had been an apology. But nothing ever came.

"My God." Ryder wrapped his hand over my shoulder.

"I should've pressed charges, but I didn't. I couldn't. I didn't want anyone to know. And I was also afraid of what would happen if I did, of what he'd do."

Silence settled in the room, broken only by the sound of my breathing, still hitched and shallow.

"This is my fault." At the feel of Trevor holding my wrists, I heeded his request to lower my arms so he could look at me. He was crouched in front of me, and he let go of my wrists and cupped my cheeks. "I should've protected you. I'm so sorry, and I'm so fucking sorry you didn't feel you could tell me this."

"I couldn't tell you. You'd have killed him, and I didn't want Chase's father in prison for murder."

Trevor's eyes glinted with unshed tears. "There are visiting hours in prison."

I pressed a hand to his chest. "Is that supposed to be a joke?"

"I'm not being funny." He rose slowly, giving me a clearer view of Ryder still kneeling beside me like he had no plans to leave until I was steady again.

"I'm sorry I wasn't there for you." Ryder's voice broke, cracking under the weight of his guilt. The tear down his face sent more down mine.

"If you'd known me back then . . ." I forced a half shrug. "I wouldn't have told you. I wouldn't want my brother behind bars, either."

My gaze drifted to Alex next. He hadn't said a word. His hand was over his mouth, eyes on the floor. His chest rose and fell in a heavy, uneven rhythm, like he was trying to physically breathe through the pain I'd laid out.

"I worked quietly with my lawyer while Mitch was deployed," I continued, steadier now. "He rushed the paperwork, and I let Mitch know what was coming. His response was that we weren't getting a divorce; then he hung up on me. Two nights later, his plane went down."

The silence that followed was an almost mournful type of quiet.

Trevor went to the bed and picked up the envelope. "I, uh." He stared down at what was in his hands as if the contents inside had personally betrayed him. "I need a minute to just . . ." His words faded as he abruptly went for the door and walked out.

Ryder stood, then extended a hand. I took it, letting him help me to my feet. My legs were weak, like grief had rearranged my center of gravity.

I turned toward Alex, searching his face to get a read on him. "Do you regret staying?"

Alex's hand plummeted to his side as he glanced at Ryder before meeting my eyes. "I only regret that anything ever happened to you. *And* that he's already dead, so I can't kill him."

My shoulders rolled forward at his words. Chills spread across my back—not from fear, just from feeling too much at once.

"I guess Mitch wasn't cheating, huh?" I tried to force levity, even though my voice sounded as though it were caught in quicksand, going down fast. "Or maybe he was. Who knows, and I guess, who cares." I forced a shrug to better sell my words. "The secret phone calls and late nights must've had to do with whatever he was involved in, though."

"We'll figure this out and protect you. End the threat, I promise," Ryder said steadily.

"I promise I'll always love you and take care of you." Mitch's empty words from the day we exchanged vows came back to haunt me, and a forgotten memory slammed into me.

My ring. "A few weeks before Mitch's last deployment, my band went missing. I don't wear my rings to bed, and when I woke up, only the engagement ring was there. Mitch told me I must've misplaced it. He even accused me of losing my mind. Then he went out of town for a few days on some boys' trip to Vegas, and a day or two later, after he was home, he found it under the bed."

"He had to have taken it with him and had them modified with the inscription. Doubtful he really went to Vegas." Ryder turned to face Alex next. "We need to go through the files Gray provided Trevor. Timeline everything. If anything Mitch was involved in lines up with that window—"

"It could explain why he modified the rings," Alex said. "He knew something was coming, and he built a fail-safe."

A backup plan? "Sounds like he also knew he wouldn't be coming home to me, but what in the world was he involved in? Why would he betray his country? He wasn't always that man." At least, I didn't think he had been. I would've seen it, never let him near my son if that were the case.

"People change," Alex said flatly. "War can do it. Trauma. Money and power, too. Even to people we thought were unshakable. People who said they loved their country." His voice hitched slightly.

I tried to read the storm behind his expression but failed. "How, um, did you even know there was some hidden inscription in his band?"

Ryder tipped his chin toward Alex.

"It's a sleight of hand trick. Magician stuff," Alex explained. "There was a pressure point in the band, just like my dad used to do with fake coins." That hint of a smile was the first spark of light I'd seen in his eyes all day.

Maybe this man really could abracadabra my problems away. God, if only.

"Well," Alex started, clearing his throat, "we should get your band before someone beats us to it."

And just like that, he seemed to be shifting back into his role. Protector. Operator. My . . . *what,* exactly? *Bodyguard?*

"I'll ask Beau to send in his deputy parked outside Audrey's to grab her ring. None of us are leaving here alone." Ryder moved toward me, and I could tell he wanted to say something else. Maybe apologize again, which I didn't want. I needed us all to move forward.

"We need to find a secure location to get to while we wait on the secretary to reach out. We'll work the case from there. I'm sure we have eyes on us as we speak," Alex said in a grave tone. "They could hit anytime."

Hit anytime? My stomach wrenched. "What if we get rid of the rings? Would that remove the target from our backs? Can we hand them over to the government?"

"Maybe, but we have to find a way to get them to someone we trust. But we don't know for sure whether the people who broke in Friday are after you, too." Ryder grimaced, that detail clearly weighing heavily on his mind. "I need to talk to Beau and Trevor about tightening up security until we can put together an exfil plan and get you and Chase somewhere safe." Ryder reached for my arm and leaned in, preparing to kiss the top of my head. "Love you, sis."

I froze. The words *love you* landed like a punch to the chest. The good, restarting-your-heart kind.

Before I could answer, he turned to Alex. "Watch her. Don't let her out of your sight, got it?" He paused. "Maybe leave Trevor's bedroom, though."

He took off after that, and I gave a small nod to Alex and started for the living room. I peeked in to check on Chase. Satisfied he was laughing and absorbed in building LEGOs with Seraphina, I shifted back into the hall. That sound and sight were proof that some piece of normalcy could still exist amid the chaos.

I'd started to turn, unsure where I planned to go, when Alex blocked my path.

"I'd like to go outside, please."

He frowned. "And I'd prefer you stay inside. I never should have let you walk with me yesterday near the woods. I wasn't thinking clearly."

"Well, did you know the truth about Mitch yesterday?"

"No, but I know the truth now."

Fair enough. But I pressed my hands together in prayer position anyway. "Eden's probably in the kitchen. The office is booked for mission stuff. Just sixty seconds on the deck for fresh air? No venturing into the woods, I promise."

"You're asking me to not think clearly again, is that it?" He braced a hand against the wall, staring down at the hardwood.

"Just asking for air." And why'd I get the feeling this man would give me almost anything I asked for?

He slowly met my eyes as he retrieved a Glock he had hidden at his back. *"Peligroso,"* he warned under his breath.

"But . . . ?" I lifted my brows.

"But you win." He shook his head. "Now, get your jacket."

I patted his chest twice in thanks, grateful he'd listened, also feeling a little guilty about the power I seemed to have over him, which he clearly didn't like.

We bundled up and went out to the back deck before he could come to his senses.

The mountain air was crisp and clean, and I pulled it deep into my lungs like it might wash away everything.

"I think I'm still out of character. I may not feel like myself until this whole mess is over, not just because of the knock to my head." I shifted around to face him.

"So am I, because you shouldn't be out here." He quietly studied me.

"Can I ask you something?" I found myself whispering.

He scanned the yard. "Down to thirty seconds out here, but yeah."

I'll make the seconds count, then. "In the office earlier . . . the way you looked at me when Trevor told us about Mitch's alleged betrayal, it felt like you understood what I was going through. Why do I feel like you've been through this yourself?"

He didn't answer right away, but he didn't deflect, either. He just looked at me with the same quiet intensity that made me feel seen. "Because I have." His rough voice scraped across my skin.

That was all he said. No details, just the truth. But it was enough.

"Does it get any easier?" I asked. "Living with it? Trying to move on?"

He checked the property again, always vigilant, then met my eyes. "It doesn't." He paused. "Or maybe it does? I don't know. For me, it's been almost two years since we divorced, and I'm still trying to . . ."

"Move on?"

"No, I'm very much over her. It just seems that when I think the past is behind me, it comes back to bite me in the ass."

Well, that wasn't what I wanted to hear, but I did appreciate him being honest. "I hate that you can relate to what I'm going through."

"I hate that *you* can relate," he echoed in a somber voice. "And I really, really want to hug you right now."

"Do it," was all I could get out. Because his arms around me was all I wanted. "Inside, if you prefer, though. Think we exceeded my time limit."

He smiled and started to gesture for the house when something behind me caught his eyes, and his expression turned deadly.

"Get inside. Now," he ordered, using his body as a shield.

I bolted for the back door when I heard it. The *crack*. A single shot rang out.

Ryder yanked the door open before I could reach it, dragging me inside as Alex hissed what Ryder clearly already knew: "Breach! We're under attack!"

CHAPTER THIRTEEN

Alejandro

Gunfire cracked behind me, closer this time. The window didn't shatter. Reinforced glass.

I dropped low, scanning the tree line before bolting for the same back door Audrey had used a minute ago. My Glock was useless against trained snipers in broad daylight. No sense standing out there like a damn target.

"Where's Chase?" I asked the second I spotted Ryder moving solo down the hallway. He had an M4 slung around his body and my rifle in hand, along with a radio.

"Trevor's got Chase and the women moving to his safe room," he said.

Thank God for Trevor's paranoia.

I should have been more paranoid, never given in to her request for air. Should never have let Audrey step outside. She could've been clipped. Killed. *Fuck, fuck, fuck.*

"Sheriff and his deputies are holding the front with Reed on the first and second floors," he continued. "Audrey's house is also under fire. Beau said his guy parked out front never made it inside. Outnumbered and had to pull back."

"He make it out?"

"Yeah, he's safe." Ryder handed me a radio already tuned to our frequency, along with my M4.

"Multiple targets. North and east flanks," Reed reported over the radio, remaining calm. At least one of us was. I was a disaster, knowing Audrey and Chase were here.

Ryder started to issue orders but stopped when Trevor rounded the corner at a near run, shotgun gripped tight.

"I've got the safe room upstairs," Trevor said without hesitation. "I'll hold the hallway outside it myself."

Ryder gave him a short nod, then turned to face me. "You take the back. I'll cover the northeast."

"Room 11 upstairs has the clearest angle of the back," Trevor said, tossing me a set of keys.

I caught them midair and took off. "Any prisoners?" I called over my shoulder.

"We need one alive for questioning," Ryder replied. "Everyone else goes down."

I sprinted for the stairs.

Room 11 gave me exactly what I needed: an unobstructed line of sight across the trees.

I unlocked and opened the window. Cold mountain air hit my face as I spotted a figure repositioning behind the brush.

Muzzle out the window, I steadied, exhaled, and then fired.

"One down," I said over the radio. "Two more visible inside the fence line on approach. One's circling northeast."

"On it," Ryder answered.

I tracked the lead target as he sprinted toward the garage entry in tactical gear with a suppressed weapon.

One breath and one shot. He dropped fast. The moment the body hit the gravel, I saw another blur of movement through the trees.

Someone was cutting low around the ridge, slipping through the brush on the west side. Too close to the lodge for a clean shot—not with the way he was using cover.

"Contact on the west side. Impending breach," I said into the radio, getting nothing but static.

Shit. Comms were jammed. Hopefully only temporarily. Knowing Reed, he'd pull back to handle that and turn the tables on our marks. Kill their feed instead. Rescue ours. In the meantime, we were flying blind.

I yanked the rifle back inside, slung it over my shoulder, and drew my Glock.

I hit the stairs hard, boots pounding, and crossed the first floor in seconds. As I neared the back exit, I heard metal skimming gravel, followed by a hiss and smoke.

Gray tendrils curled across the yard, thick and rising fast. Classic conceal-and-breach tactic we usually used ourselves. I wasn't used to being on the other side of things like this. Always the attacker, rarely the attacked.

Multiple tangos would be advancing, and we'd be in the dark until it was too late. I had to do something.

"Ryder," I barked into the radio again. "They're pushing in."

Still nothing.

I burst out the back door and collided head-on with the bastard I'd seen circling from above.

We hit the deck, crashing onto the boards. The world turned into a swirl of smoke and fists. I lost my pistol in the chaos; then I scrambled into top position in time to block the blade he drove at me.

We grappled, and I ripped the knife from his grip, turned it fast, and buried it in his side with a hard twist. His body went limp, but I didn't stop there.

I retrieved my Glock from the deck, switched weapons, and put one final round through his head to be sure.

A shotgun blast echoed from inside the house. *Trevor?* The only reason he'd be shooting would be because there'd been a successful breach.

My radio crackled back to life. "Tango down," Trevor reported.

"We're back online," Reed said, stating the obvious. Thank God for that man's tech skills.

Ryder announced the good news: "Looks like they're falling back and using the smoke as cover for their retreat."

"Do we have anyone alive, though?" I asked, doubling back toward the rear door, my breath burning hot in my lungs.

One by one, voices came over the radio: "Negative."

So, all clear, but no survivors. And no survivors meant no answers or leverage. We needed both if we were going to keep Audrey safe.

My hand froze on the doorknob; then I turned toward the woods. The smoke was thinning out but not gone.

At the far edge of the clearing, just visible through the last veil of haze, there was movement. Two shadows. Two targets. Two *chances.*

"I'm going out. Cover me," I said, mind already made up, taking the steps off the deck at a run.

"Alex, dammit, stand down," Ryder snapped over the radio. "Do you hear me? Do not risk—"

"I have to." For her. For Chase. For the one thing I hadn't let myself admit that I wanted: something that looked a hell of a lot like a future. "I've got this." I dropped my voice to a hush, blending in with the breeze and dying smoke. "I'll vanish. They won't see me coming."

The Houdini in the field. That's what they used to call me downrange while in the army.

"Alex," Ryder hissed. "So help me, brother, you better make your ass reappear—and damn soon, or I'm coming out there to find you."

CHAPTER FOURTEEN

Audrey

"It's going to be okay." I tried to keep my teeth from chattering as I made the promise to my son. If I let him see how scared I was, then we'd both fall apart.

Chase trembled in my arms, his face pressed tightly to my chest, as I rocked him back and forth without pause, like maybe the rhythm could trick us both into believing we were safe. That this was normal. That this wasn't the second time in his young life that chaos had erupted and his father had to protect us.

The safe room's metal walls seemed to close in and collapse all around us, making the air feel thinner with every breath we took.

Eden and Seraphina were across from us in the cramped space. Seraphina was calm in a way that unnerved me, though the way she quietly rubbed Chase's back said she probably understood me more than she let on. I also knew she trusted Ryder with her life, along with ours, which made me feel a little better. Because of that, I tried to do the same. To trust. To pray. And to not let panic win.

I did my best not to let the sound of gunfire replay in my head like a sick lullaby. To ignore the shotgun blast that'd sounded far too close a few minutes ago. Trevor had more than likely cut someone down, keeping us safe.

This was all my fault. Every painful minute. They were all in danger because of me. Because I'd married a man who'd turned out to be a ghost wearing a mask. I thought I'd found safety and a new life with Mitch. Instead, I wound up inviting a monster into my life. Even worse, into my son's.

Had it all been a performance? Had I ever truly known him at all?

The fact we were in a safe room because of him served as a resounding *no*.

I flinched at the tap on the door a minute later, followed by the "It's me," from Trevor before the door creaked open. His hand was the first thing I saw. While our marriage had failed, it was never because he'd been a threat or danger to us. "It's over. For now."

Just four words from him, but they shattered something inside me. Air flooded my lungs. My grip on Chase loosened.

"Dad?" Chase twisted in my lap, searching for Trevor.

Trevor stepped into the doorway, arm extended. "I got you, buddy. You'll be okay."

Chase launched himself into his father's arms, clinging to him with the kind of trust only a child could so freely give.

Trevor held him tight, one hand splayed across the small of his back, before stepping aside so the rest of us could file out.

"Are you all right?" he whispered to me as Eden and Seraphina brushed past. His gaze flicked to mine, then over my shoulder, always assessing.

"I'm . . ." I swallowed hard, shoulders still tight with tension. "Is everyone okay?"

"Beau?" Eden asked before he could answer, a desperate plea in her tone.

"He's good. Held the front." That troubled and guarded expression wasn't what I wanted to see from him, though. "Alex went into the woods. He's trying to bring someone back for questioning since we, uh, had to put down everyone here."

Put down. Kill. Chase was smart enough to read between the lines. But as long as no one on Team Good Guy went down, then I was fine with any measures necessary to protect our family.

Trevor gently lowered Chase until his feet hit the floor. He clung to Trevor's hand but turned, looking up at him with wide, hopeful eyes. "Did Uncle Alex get the bad man and bring him back yet?"

The innocence in his voice broke something in me. How could he still sound so calm and trusting? I was grateful he was, but it was hard for me to believe. Probably because I was unraveling by the second while waiting for Trevor to tell me Alex was safe.

"I'm sure he'll be here soon." Trevor ruffled his hair with a half smile sitting on his lips. "Why don't you wait with Aunt Eden and Seraphina in your bedroom for now, yeah? I don't want you back in the safe room unless you have to be, but we need you close to it in case this flares up again."

This? Another attack? Was that in the realm of possibility?

I reached for Chase's hand, unable to help the tremor in mine. "There are windows in his bedroom." Fear had rewired everything inside me, and I'd be stuck in overprotective mode for as long as any threats loomed.

Trevor's jaw flexed. "Bullet-resistant glass throughout the place. Blast protection, too. Same stuff the DOD uses. They'll be safe in his bedroom."

"You really did overprepare for the just-in-case worst-case scenario, huh?" I murmured. "Thank you for that."

He lifted one shoulder in a modest shrug. "Eden, can you take them to his room? We'll catch up with you in a minute." His eyes cut to Seraphina next. "Ryder will be upstairs soon to check on you, I'm sure, but he's getting a little antsy."

"Waiting on Alex to come back?" I asked him.

Trevor's eyes darted to Chase, who was watching him closely. "Ryder will go after him if he, uh . . ." He didn't finish his sentence.

Not with Chase's blue eyes pointed at him in anticipation of his father delivering only good news.

Yeah, well, I'd like some good news myself, please.

"How about you show me your room?" Seraphina took hold of Chase's hand, coming in for the save. "I bet you have some LEGOs on display in there."

"Thank you." I forced my fingers to unclench as I let go of Chase's hand.

I waited until the three of them had slipped into Chase's room out of sight before I backed up against the wall and dropped my face into my hands.

The dam cracked. Every ounce of control I'd clung to bled out in a silent quake through my chest. I was nowhere near okay. Heck, I didn't even know what okay looked like anymore.

"Hey, now." Trevor took my wrists, gently prying my hands from my face. "You know I'm not going to let anything happen to you. That man hurt you before." His eyes became watery with the kind of emotion he'd never shed when we were married. "I will *not* let him do it again. Not even from the grave. You hear me?"

My shoulders jerked as I fought back the sob trying to break free. All I could do was nod. Because the second I talked, tears would flow, too.

I had to pull myself together, shake the fear still wrapped like vines around my lungs, stealing my breath. For everyone. Most of all, for Chase.

I had to have faith that everything would be okay. You know, whatever *okay* still meant. That word was being redefined by the second.

Trevor's jaw tensed as he dropped my wrists and walked back a step, running a hand through his hair.

"Hey!" Ryder's voice snapped down the hallway, slicing through the tension.

My heart stopped, then kicked back to life again.

"Alex made contact," he continued, his rifle slung across his body. "He's on his way to the lodge. He has someone with him for questioning."

I didn't think, just moved.

Relief surged through my chest so hard my knees buckled, forcing me to use the wall in the hall to guide me to my brother so I wouldn't collapse.

I walked straight into his arms and clung to him the way Chase had to me in the safe room. I ignored the cold metal of the rifle wedged between us.

Ryder exhaled sharply, holding me for a few long breaths as Trevor said, "Tell Alex to take the guy there."

"I'm going, too." I pulled back from Ryder, swiping at my tears with my sleeves.

"No, I don't want you running around this place when we have no clue if another team may strike," Ryder said firmly. "Stay with your son."

"I just have to see him." I sidestepped my brother in a hurry to confirm for myself that Alex was okay after risking his life.

"Wait, hold up!" Ryder called out. "Keep on the lookout up here," he added, probably to Trevor while in pursuit of me.

I made it to the bottom step before he caught up with me.

"The lodge is locked down and secure for now, but I don't like you being—"

"I'm going with you. You'll keep me safe." I had no plans to listen to orders or change my mind.

"Fine." He took hold of my arm and led the way, and we passed Beau standing guard near the front entrance.

Beau gave a grim nod but didn't stop us, and that was when I saw Alex. He was at the far end of the hall, forcibly dragging someone behind him.

Alex had blood smeared on his jacket and up the side of his neck.

Please don't be yours. I broke into a run, pulling away from Ryder. I reached Alex before I could talk myself down, and he quickly shoved the asshole over to Ryder to catch so he could then catch me.

With the prisoner secure in my brother's arms, I crashed against Alex's chest and threw my arms around him, eyes stinging with tears.

Alex carefully shifted me to the side, pinning me gently but firmly against the wall with his body like a shield as Ryder forced the man farther away from me. "Don't let her out of your sight," he yelled on his way down the hall with the prisoner.

Alex didn't answer; he simply stayed where he was, hand braced against the wall beside my head, dark eyes fixed on mine.

"I was worried. Are you okay?"

"I'm fine." His gravelly voice sent a shiver through my body.

I reached up for the side of his neck, needing to feel something solid. Something real. I dropped my forehead against his chest, barely understanding the connection tethering me to this man, but I couldn't deny it. Not when I could feel the hard thrumming of his heart against my forehead. "About that hug you were going to give me before all hell broke loose . . ."

"Yeah?" he murmured.

"I need it now, please." A half sob caught in my throat.

Alex didn't hesitate. He wrapped me in his arms, becoming my anchor. Holding me like I belonged there and he never wanted to let go.

He didn't say a word—just held me. And that was more than enough.

"I'm glad you're okay." I sniffled. "I mean, who else would I *not* talk about my underwear with, right?" I half laughed, half cried, the sound breaking as it came out.

"Relieved you're okay, too." He tangled his fingers in my hair and held the back of my head the way I'd held Chase earlier. "But, Audrey . . ."

"I know." I lifted my head to meet his eyes, blinking back fresh tears. "And I should never have asked you to let me go outside, and you—"

"Should never have said yes," he bit out.

"Maybe this is dangerous? Or at least complicated."

He quietly nodded, probably knowing exactly what I was talking about since he'd been the one to use that word last night. And he had to know I wasn't referring to the danger we were in now because of Mitch.

We were on the same page, but it felt dog-eared. Bookmarked for later. But something told me we'd wind up back on a shelf, simply collecting dust. Destined to never try to uncomplicate things. To just be, well, *friends*, like I'd said I wanted to be earlier.

"We need to focus on getting you and Chase to safety." He cupped my face, his thumbs skimming along the line of my jaw. Even covered in someone else's blood, he was gentle with me.

"Of course." I swallowed, never losing hold of his gaze.

He let go and stepped aside, then placed his arm protectively behind me as we walked.

When I heard the unmistakable low hiss of pain he was clearly trying to hide, I twisted free to confront him. "Did you lie about being okay? Is some of that blood yours?"

He closed one eye, pressing a hand to his side.

"Alex," I said in my mom voice, and I shifted his jacket and shirt up. "You're hurt."

"Not that bad. Relax," he grunted, shoving my hands away. "I'll deal with it later."

I opened my mouth to protest, but he shook his head and tipped his chin forward in the direction he wanted me to go.

"Fine," I relented, then hooked my arm around his back, careful of his bad side, in case he was the one who would need support but never ask for it.

We made it to the office a moment later, and the man Alex had gone after was now tied to a chair at the center of the room. Ryder was currently crouched in front of him, a knife in one hand, anger etched into every line of his face.

Reed stood off to the side, pistol drawn, jaw tight as he gave us a nod and the door closed behind me. "He says he's military."

Why'd that possibility feel so much worse?

"What do you want from me?" I asked him, freeing myself from Alex's hold to draw closer. "Who do you work for?"

The man's lips curled in a sneer as he spit out blood. "You won't kill me," he said instead of answering me.

Ryder pressed the blade against his neck. "You're a traitor. The second you turned on the uniform, you stopped being one of us."

The man laughed, a wet and broken sound. "You don't know who I am or why I'm here."

"Then enlighten us," Ryder barked out. "And don't lie and say you're here on government orders."

"You don't think he's been watching you?" His voice turned almost conversational, laced with something cruel. "He tried to be nice, you know. Planned to take you Friday when your son wasn't home. Keep things quiet and neat."

He? A rush of heat worked up into my face with feverish intensity.

"Then you ran straight into your ex's arms. Predictable. So, here we are." He tried to laugh again but wound up coughing up more blood.

Alex clearly had done a number on him outside, and Ryder must've finished the job in those few minutes I'd stolen with Alex in the hallway.

Ryder drew back slowly, his expression too hard for me to decipher as he glanced at Reed.

Alex stepped alongside me, keeping close.

"He said if we got caught . . . if plan B failed, then . . ." He groaned, doubling over slightly. "That we move to plan C."

"What's plan C?" Alex demanded.

The man lifted his head. His lips peeled into a grotesque smile.

I couldn't look at him any longer, so I forced my gaze away. It landed on the bookshelf and the spine of the book I'd held in my hands only yesterday. *Silence of the Lambs* vibes going strong here. It made my stomach turn.

"He said to give you a chance to surrender peacefully. If you want to keep your family safe, he'll text you with a location where he needs you to meet him with the key."

My heart lodged in my throat, and I blinked my way back to him.

"There's a phone in my pocket," he continued. "He'll make contact; then he'll tell you where to go."

"Who?" I repeated, louder this time. I stepped forward, fists trembling at my sides. *"Who?"*

Alex mirrored my movements, closing the distance in lockstep. His presence at my side gave me enough courage to stand tall.

The jerk shot me a smile again. Slow, deliberate, and full of satisfaction. "Your husband." His blood-smeared teeth flashed. "Mitch Langston. He's alive."

CHAPTER FIFTEEN

Alejandro

Be careful what you wish for; you just might get it.

My father's words growing up slipped through my mind as I stared at the traitor.

The news was a blessing and a curse. I could now kill Mitch with my own hands.

Unable to stop myself, I hooked my arm around Audrey, worried she might actually faint this time.

Ryder grabbed hold of the guy's chin, forcing his eyes on him. "Try again."

He attempted to resist Ryder's hold to look at Audrey, and I noticed she was gripping the front of my jacket, practically turning right into my arms.

I needed to get her out of there, but Ryder's clipped voice drew my attention back to our subject. He leaned over him, getting in his personal space, the knife resting at his side. "I don't believe in ghosts. Demons, maybe. Looking at a man possessed by one now—but no, not ghosts."

"The plane crash was a cover-up." The side of his mouth lifted into a partial smile. "Body too burned to allow for an open casket."

Audrey released my jacket and held up her hand, staring at my blood on her palm. "You should, um, clean that wound," she said in a daze, ignoring the asshole's remarks.

"Wait, you got hurt? That's *your* blood?" Reed redirected his focus on me, where it didn't belong. "Need the medic kit?"

"It's just a scratch. I'm fine." I took hold of her arm, worried she'd topple over without support. "One of his buddies out in the woods who won't be getting up again did it."

"We all knew what we were getting ourselves into," he spat out. "The risk was worth it. Despite what you think of us, we're patriots."

"Oh really?" Ryder circled his chair, probably about to apply more pressure to get him to talk.

"I don't think she should be in here." I tipped my head toward Audrey, a statue of shock at my side.

Her long lashes fluttered in some type of rhythm.

Blink. *Shock*. Blink.

She blinked her way over to Reed. "That medical kit you have, where is it?"

"Whatever bedroom Eden put my stuff in. In my duffel bag," Reed answered, eyes darting to my side and my torn jacket. "How bad is it, really?" He came over, forcing me to let go of her so he could have a look for himself.

"Not a big deal. Just . . ." I closed my eyes, memories of being shot by Beth last fall cutting through my mind. "He reopened an old wound, is all. That's why it's bleeding like this."

Theme of the weekend: reopening old wounds. Try not to bleed out, physically or emotionally.

"It's not that old of a wound." He tacked on in a low voice, "Damn that woman." He glanced at Audrey, jaw tight. "I have something in my bag that'll seal his wound better than a regular bandage."

"Great." Blink. *Shock*. Blink. "I'll take care of him. You just stay here and get the truth from him, because there's no way Mitch is alive." Her voice was raw and heartbreaking.

"Hold up," Ryder said, removing the radio clipped at his side. He quickly communicated with Beau, then Trevor, checking to make sure the property was still secure.

"The front is clear," Beau responded.

Trevor transmitted the all clear: "And I have the surveillance feeds up and nothing but wildlife in the woods for now. No thermal movement beyond the ridge. Back's tight."

"Stay put. Keep me posted," Ryder replied, then directed to me, "Go ahead. Get yourself patched up. Stay with her." He asked Trevor next, "What room did Eden put Reed's stuff in?"

"Three. First floor. Another set of keys are in my side desk drawer," Trevor answered, and Reed was already on the move to retrieve them.

My body relaxed. First floor. *Good.* I wasn't sure I'd be making it up the stairs with how much blood I was losing from that "scratch."

"If you two need my help, let me know." Reed handed the key to Audrey, as if I were a victim incapable of moving on my own. Damn him.

"Come on." I reached for Audrey's arm, needing to hold on to her as much as she probably needed me.

At the doorway, she stopped and faced the room. "Why does he want me? If he's really alive and it's him behind all of this, why? Can't you just take the wedding bands and be done with me?"

Ryder moved aside so she could see, but I doubted the jerk would respond. Not truthfully, at least.

"You're his wife. That should be reason enough." He coughed up blood, spitting it off to the side and away from Ryder.

"No, I'm not. Not anymore, and he knew I was—"

"Leaving him? But he didn't sign those papers, now did he? So guess what that makes you? Still. His. Wife. Under the eyes of the law and"—he looked up at the ceiling—"under God. You're *his*."

"Get her out of here," Ryder ordered. "I don't want her seeing what I'm about to do."

"Wait . . . you said being his wife 'should' be reason enough—but it isn't the actual reason, is it?" Her voice was so damn fragile it pained me to hear. I was worried she'd break. Yet she kept her chin up and remained boldly staring at the traitor.

Unable to handle her being in his presence any longer, I opened the door and urged her to step out so Ryder and Reed could talk to him.

I let her lead the way to Room 3 since she was familiar with the layout. "Are you all right?"

"Not sure I can be okay after learning my husband may be alive," she murmured as she let us into Reed's room.

I unhooked the radio from my side and tossed it onto the bed before dropping down next to it.

"Take off your jacket and shirt." She wiped her hands on the sides of her jeans as if it were no big deal she was wearing my blood, then removed her jacket and knelt in front of Reed's duffel bag.

"I see what you're doing," I said with a laugh, pretty sure I was losing more than blood now—losing my mind, too. "*Venganza*. Payback for seeing you naked."

Her hands went still in her pursuit of the cure that would hopefully fix my sanity as well. "Thought we were supposed to forget that happened?"

"*Imposible.*" Why'd I keep switching back and forth between the languages? I needed to get a grip. Clearly no grips to be had, because I went and shared, "Well, I did see you, so . . ." I unzipped my jacket, trying to stifle a groan at the pain the movement caused. "I'm trained to key in on every detail in a matter of seconds, and now I'll never forget."

Another round of blink, *shock*, blink from her.

I had to stop oversharing. Had to stop speaking in both English and Spanish altogether. At least, nothing about us or my feelings.

I pointed to the bag, forced myself to get with the program, and told her what she needed to get from the medkit and how to use it to stop the bleeding and seal the wound.

"If Mitch is alive," she said in a soft voice, changing the subject, "then I guess I really am still his wife?"

"If he's alive, he won't be staying that way."

She stood and faced me as I tossed my shirt. "Alejandro."

"Don't 'Alejandro' me," I grunted, looking down at my hand to find it covered in blood, like a metaphor for what I planned to do to Mitch if he still had a pulse.

"Shoot, I better move faster. I'm so sorry." She dumped the supplies on the bed, then ran into the connecting bathroom and returned with wet towels.

Sitting next to me, she began cleaning the wound, and now I was the one feeling lightheaded. Groggy. A little blink, *shock*, blinking myself as she doctored me.

"Mind if I ask how you got this original wound?"

I do. I swallowed, eyes nearly rolling to the ceiling. "Beth. It's from Beth." I reached for her forearm, hating myself for opening up as easily as this old wound had.

"Who's Beth?" she asked while using the syringe on me next, injecting the trauma gel into my wound.

"My ex-wife." My head rolled forward. "She tried to kill me last fall. She was CIA. Betrayed our . . . like Mitch . . . and apparently, they've been on an op together." I had no idea what words made it from my mouth to her ears, but clearly she understood enough, because she was staring at me with narrowed, sad eyes.

"Oh."

Yeah, that was about the only thing one could say.

A vowel sound of shock.

"There," she whispered after covering the wound with a bandage. "Bleeding has stopped. Really no stitches needed, huh?"

"Yeah, I'm all set, don't worry," I said under my breath, relieved she wasn't addressing the truth bomb I'd detonated and left to explode between us.

"How do you feel now?"

"No." I frowned. "How do *you* feel?" I dropped my eyes to her handiwork. Now I just needed an IV or something sugary to wake me back up.

"I'm more concerned about you." She used the towel to clean her hands, then did something I didn't expect: She set her hand on my cheek. "You risked your life to get answers. I wish you hadn't done that. The idea you may not have come back to us is too terrifying to think about."

"So don't think about it, then." I pushed through the fog and the discomfort and remembered something critical. Something important. Another reason why I had to keep my distance from her. "This is what I do. Mission first, my life second." I let her in on another bit of truth I doubted she knew. "We're not private security anymore. We work directly for President Bennett now." That was classified. *And* I didn't care. "My life could end at any moment. Country over self." I'd done it again. Taken a page from her book and continued to remain out of character. To overshare.

"Alejandro." She shifted closer, resting her forehead against mine, never losing hold of my face.

"Please don't say my name like that." I covered her hand, her warmth grounding me more than the bandage ever could. "Please don't say that name at all."

"Why not?" Her mouth pinched tight, etched into a sad line that hurt me to see.

"Because I like how it sounds too much," I confessed.

Her eyes narrowed, slanting toward my lips. "Oh." There it was again. That little sound that I wanted to catch with my tongue.

"Peligroso," I reminded her, my heart hurting more than my side. "Dangerous."

"Which part?" Her brows lifted.

"Talking about myself, because I just might tell you things I shouldn't."

"Like?" she whispered.

My stomach muscles tensed, but my throat didn't constrict, and out the truth came despite my efforts to stop it. "That I used to think

I could have it all. A career. Wife. Kids." I swallowed. "A dog, too, so Reed would visit, since he's better with animals than people."

"And she ruined the idea of that for you?" she asked in a tentative, nervous tone, like she was terrified to hear the truth. To hear the *yes* fall from my mouth.

So I gave it to her in Spanish, knowing damn well she'd still understand. "*Sí.*" I dropped my voice lower when promising, "But I won't let Mitch destroy your future the way Beth did mine. I won't let him take your peace. Got it?"

"Alejan—"

The door flung open, sending my name from her lips to the ether, and she immediately jerked back, hands falling to her lap.

Reed. *Not* Ryder or Trevor. That was something, at least.

His gaze volleyed between us, his eyes landing on the bandage at my side. "You good?" he asked me.

Not even close to being there, so of course I lied. "Yeah."

Audrey pointed at the phone he was clutching as he approached the bed. "What is it?"

"A text came through over the burner the guy had on him. Curious to see if you could confirm whether Mitch really sent it, based on what it said." He handed her the phone. "Although looks like these guys know a lot about him, so they could be faking it. Pretending to be him for some reason."

Unknown: Audrey, it's me. Yes, I'm alive. And I need you. All our lives, including Chase's, depend on you helping me. Be in touch in 72 hours with instructions. Do NOT lose the key. I'm trying my best not to hurt anyone you care about, but if you keep putting up a fight, you may give me no choice. Love you. Don't forget you love me too. —HELL

"Chase," she gasped. "Is he threatening him, too, if I don't do what he asks?"

"Are you sure that's Mitch?" Reed asked her before I could wrangle my angry thoughts and form a coherent sentence after reading his message.

"That's how he signed off on texts when he'd send me a message from an unknown number so I'd know it was him. He used to say HELL was his brand. He said, 'I sign off with *hell* because that's what I raise.' It started as a joke, but it stuck," she explained, her voice trembling.

"But his friends would know that," Reed said, "so that doesn't mean this is really him."

That ugly, dark part of me that wanted him alive so I could be the one to kill him just got uglier and darker.

Drain every drop of his blood for hitting her. Raping her. For endangering her and Chase.

All the things.

All. The. Fucking. Things.

I'd make him pay.

And only then, after he'd suffered, would I kill him.

CHAPTER SIXTEEN

Alejandro

"Here. Wear something of mine." Reed rummaged through his bag, pulling out a long-sleeved black shirt. He gestured for me to lift my arms.

"And what, exactly, do you think you're doing? I'm injured, not dead. I'll put my own shirt on, thanks."

He rolled his eyes and shoved the shirt at my chest.

"You could use the help." Audrey morphed into mom mode, not a woman *potentially* being hunted down by her psychotic ex-husband.

And yeah, I'd be referring to that prick in the past tense. He was *not* still her husband. Screw the law.

"You're not dressing me, either." I bit down on my back teeth and put on my shirt, refusing to let anyone help me.

It honestly wasn't that bad anymore. I was lightheaded and in some pain, but I'd dealt with worse.

"He's stubborn." Reed waved me off as I pulled the shirt over my head. "Let him be."

I brought the shirt to my nose and sniffed it. "Why does this smell like you?"

Reed leaned forward. "Probably not washed yet." He stood tall again, then jerked his thumb toward the door.

"Places to be, I know," I grunted in response to his quiet gesture to focus.

She gently patted my arm. "You smell good, by the way."

"I'll take that as a compliment. Pretty sure that's my cologne you're smelling," Reed said as we left his room. "Unless you're talking about blood," he added, stealing a look at her over his shoulder. "Then that's all him."

I huffed out a low breath of irritation. "Told you he's better with dogs than people."

"The humor stuff while on a mission . . . that the norm for you guys?" She smiled.

"I think it's a requirement in the military. They'll boot you if your humor isn't on point," Reed tossed out casually as we neared Trevor's office.

"Then you'd have been kicked out long ago," I shot back. "He's not remotely funny, trust me."

"He's kind of right." Reed went for the door handle, then asked her, "You ready?"

"No." She frowned. "But let's go in anyway."

He nodded and opened up, and I stayed close to her as we walked in together. I was able to breathe easier now that our subject wasn't in the room, just Ryder.

"Tied him up and relocated him for now," he let us know. "I didn't want him in earshot for our call with Secretary Chandler. Trevor reached out to Gray and told him we were hit. Gray put in an emergency text to his father. He's about to call now." His gaze cut down to my side. "You all good?"

Reed shut the door. "He could probably use antibiotics and a juice box, but he'll live."

"I can grab you one of Chase's apple juices. And I think I saw a pill bottle in your medkit." Audrey started to move, but I secured a gentle hold of her wrist, stopping her.

"You're not leaving my sight. I'll get something soon, don't worry." I gestured to the second chair, the one left empty during the interrogation. "Why don't you sit?"

"*You* sit." She stared me down, making it clear she wouldn't take no for an answer.

I probably caved faster than Chase would've. With a sigh, I dropped into the chair and glanced up at the ceiling. "How's the property looking?"

"Still locked down," Reed replied as Audrey leaned against the bookshelf, arms folded tight across her chest.

"What do you make of the text?" Ryder asked her.

"'Hell' was Mitch's signature. His brand." She shrugged, a motion that probably took more effort than she let on.

"Doesn't mean it's actually from him," Ryder said while checking his phone. "We've got incoming from the secretary."

My body tensed, bracing for the worst though I was desperate for something else.

"We're all here, sir." Ryder placed him on speaker. "Audrey, Mitch's ex-wife, is on the line, too."

"I also learned she's your sister," Chandler responded in a low voice. "What I'm curious about is, why I never knew she was family before now?"

"I, uh, only found out she existed at Christmas," Ryder faltered. There was a note of vulnerability in his voice I wasn't used to hearing. "I'm guessing Gray shared that with you before this call, but if you're bringing that up because you're about to tell me to stand down given our relationship, then—"

"Let's table that conversation for later," Chandler said, cutting him off. "First, walk me through what happened."

Ryder opened his eyes, exhaling. "How much do you already know?"

"Gray briefed me that Audrey's home was broken into Friday. Today, Trevor Sloane's place was attacked. Fortunately, you were all there. You held the fort and the attackers retreated."

My gaze drifted to the bloodstained chair next to me as Ryder shared, "We took one alive. He claims he's military. He could be lying to keep us from killing him. We'll upload his photo for ID, along with pictures of the bodies we dropped. But the guy told us who allegedly sent the team and why."

"Unless he's lying about that, too," Reed mumbled beneath the hand parked across his mouth.

"He said it was Mitch Langston; then we got a text from someone claiming to be Mitch as well," Ryder went on, his voice wavering.

"That's not possible." Static crackled over the line, followed by a long, strained breath from the secretary.

"Yeah, dead people don't text," I growled out in a low hiss.

"No, that's not it." Another pause from Chandler, followed by another deep breath.

My legs were weak, but I forced myself to stand, and Audrey immediately came over to me for an assist. "I'm fine," I mouthed, though my balance said otherwise. She didn't seem to buy it and stayed at my side, hovering like she could catch all two hundred and five pounds of me.

"What aren't you telling us?" Ryder asked as his gaze met mine, and I felt it coming. We both did. The storm. The tsunami on the horizon.

"He can't be alive," Chandler remarked in a steady tone. "No way he's behind this. I know that because I was part of the team that helped fake his death last year. But on his way to the safe house, he was killed." He gave us a what-the-hell moment of silence before continuing, "For real that time."

CHAPTER SEVENTEEN

Alejandro

Audrey's legs appeared to give out, but I caught her in time, easing her into my chair, dropping down with her to one knee. My hand remained locked with hers, and I had no plans to let go.

Ryder held up the phone after giving me a quick nod of thanks. "Explain," he demanded to Secretary Chandler, who was still on speaker.

"We can't talk about this now," Chandler replied, his voice tight. "But I saw the footage. Mitch is dead. The men guarding him lost their lives, too. DNA was a match. I don't know who the hell is out there pretending to be him. *But* if I'm wrong and Mitch is truly alive, then he's stayed off-grid for a year for a reason."

Audrey was trembling and pale. Fading. I tightened my grip on her hand, and she held mine back with equal force.

"We know what they're after," Ryder said, breaking through the quiet. "A key. Mitch said he'd text Audrey with a location within three days and she'd need to bring the key. We think it's split into two parts. Reed discovered a code inscribed in Mitch's wedding band, and we believe the second half is in Audrey's. Only we didn't have a chance to recover hers. Her house was hit when the lodge was, and we believe they have their hands on the second half of the key."

Chandler cursed—low, hard, and a little too civilian-like for the secretary of defense. Something told me he had a clue as to what those ring-keys unlocked, and he had no plans to tell us. At least, not now. "This changes things," he muttered. "I'm pulling in backup. Echo Team. This needs to stay off-book."

"Assign the op to Delta Shield." Ryder said what was storming through my mind as well. "Bring in Wyatt, Gray—the whole damn alphabet of operators, for all I care. Just don't sideline us."

"You told President Bennett's guy in Wyoming you don't need a full team," Chandler shot back. "That you just track people and assemble target packages, right?"

"This is different and you know it." *Way to throw that back in our faces.* "The guy we're tracking may have faked his death twice now. We're the only ones with a chance at finding him."

Ryder brought the phone closer to his mouth. "If it was your daughter in danger, would you stop your son or her husband from protecting her?"

After a beat of silence, he finally answered, "No, they'd hog-tie me if I tried."

"Sir?" Audrey's soft voice cracked through the tension in the room. "They don't just want the key; I think they want me, too." She rested her free hand on her chest. "That means my son needs to be far away from me."

I shot Ryder a quick look to get a read on how he'd respond to her, assuming we'd be on the same page of *Hell no.*

Ryder's jaw flexed. "You're not offering yourself as bait. Not happening."

"Sounds like we need her one way or another," Chandler said steadily. "I'll tell you everything once you're in a secure location."

"Does that mean you're tasking us to lead the mission?" Ryder asked, his spine going straight as he waited for the only acceptable answer.

"Just protect the assets. Retrieve the second band. Find what the rings unlock. And locate who's behind all this," Chandler ordered.

"She's not an asset." The words barreled out of me, tight and controlled. No room for interpretation. My message: Audrey was to be protected only, not to be used.

"Seems to me Audrey may be the only one who can draw this asshole out," Chandler responded in a heated tone. "So if you want this op, she's part of it."

Audrey's eyes met mine, red rimmed and resolved. Like she was about to beg us to follow the admiral's orders and not protest.

I'd keep quiet for now. Not rock the boat to ensure no suit in Washington or someone with a badge tried to take her away from us.

Audrey spoke up, loud enough for the secretary to hear her. "Trevor needs to take Chase somewhere safe. Somewhere no one can find him. I'll do what needs to be done *if* he's safe."

I had to give it to her—she was tough. Bold in standing up to the man and making her own demands. Not that I'd allow her to place herself in danger, but I could understand and respect a mother's mission to protect her child above all else.

Ryder closed in on the two of us, eyes fixed on her. "You should be with your son."

"I can't," she whispered. "You saw what happened here. I have a target on my back."

Ryder lowered the phone, shaking his head. "Then we have to find a place to take you that no one knows about."

"I have two locations in mind," Chandler offered. "My son-in-law's cabin in Boulder for your team. And for Chase . . . Michael Maddox has a secure property in the state. Not sure if you're familiar with him, but he can be trusted. I'll call his sister to confirm it's empty. Her husband is part of Echo Team."

"We'll draw the heat and be the decoy so Trevor can escape with Chase," Ryder said on an exhale, and I knew it was killing him that Audrey would be with us as part of that decoy. But what choice did we have if we were to keep her son safe?

Audrey focused on me, a glimmer of hope cutting through her panicked state. "Well, you're good at disappearing people. So you'll be our Houdini and make my son vanish, right?"

I was good at making myself disappear. The only time others went missing when I was around was because I'd killed them. I wasn't about to run with that thought, though, so I nodded instead.

"As long as my brother's team is in charge, then I'll do whatever you need, Mr. Secretary," she said after a quiet moment had passed.

She was giving another demand I could get behind, minus the "do whatever you need" part.

I closed my eyes, the weight of all this sinking in.

"Mitch—or whoever that was—said they'll be in touch." At Reed's words, I forced open my eyes. "They're watching us and waiting. They have to be. And anyone who hits a Tier One operator's property in broad daylight is aware of the risks and willing to do it anyway."

"Yeah, well, a hundred bucks says the men we laid out didn't know what they were walking into, but our guy tied up in the pantry did, which is why he's still alive and breathing," I muttered.

"None of this feels real," Audrey said under her breath.

"Let's just get you to safety; then we'll figure out who's pulling the strings and why." Ryder kept his eyes on his sister. "Once we're at the cabin, I expect full disclosure from you, sir. Every name. Mission. Anything tied to Mitch."

"Fine," Chandler agreed. "Your people are in charge. I'll authorize everything to be sent to you." He ended the call before we could ask more questions, and Ryder chucked the phone onto the desk.

"What does the key unlock that's so damn important?" Reed rested his hands on his hips, scanning the two of us.

"Secrets." Audrey's whisper sliced through the room, cutting right through me. "It's always about secrets."

CHAPTER EIGHTEEN

Audrey

Bags packed, everything and everyone ready to go except me. Because my little man was wrapped up in my arms as we sat on my bed, his face buried in the side of my neck as he squeezed me tight.

"I don't care about ice fishing or making new friends. Not even missing school. I just want to be with you. Why can't I stay with you?" Chase's scratchy, raw voice and the tears hitting my skin intensified the pressure already building behind my rib cage. "Mommy, please. Stay with us. We need you with us."

More pressure.

An unbearable ache.

It felt like something was pushing between my ribs and would pierce my flesh if I didn't wrangle a deep breath soon.

"You're going to have the bestest, bestest time," I whispered, doubling down on his favorite word.

Thank goodness his favorite "bestest" hockey player in the world hadn't been the grandfather who'd rejected him. Why was I thinking about that now?

Oh, I know . . . because I'm about to walk away from my son, and what if I never come back? What if I die and leave him without a—

"Your mom can't breathe, buddy." Trevor sat on the bed next to me, the mattress sinking under his two hundred pounds of solid muscle.

I shifted around to rest my chin on top of Chase's head so I could see Trevor. "I can't do this," I mouthed, hoping he could read my lips.

Trevor set his hand on Chase's back and gently stroked it. "I want you with us, too."

He knew why that wasn't possible. My very presence painted a target on the back Trevor had his hand on.

"I know what happened today." Chase shifted upright, forcing me to ease my head back so I wouldn't knock noses with him. "Daddy sneaks and lets me play *Fortnite* when I spend the night here, and so I know it was bad people out there today that wanted you."

Trevor cleared his throat. "Sorry, I know we didn't discuss him, uh, playing that kind of game yet . . ."

"Not what I'm worried about right now." My voice sounded as raw and drained as I felt on the inside. "I'm going to be fine, I swear to God. I just need to help your uncle with something while you get to play hooky and miss school."

"Daddy says I'm not supposed to swear to God, so why are you?"

I closed my eyes. He had me there. *Inhale. Exhale.* That was the right rhythm, right? So where was that deep breath I desperately needed?

"Your mommy is right. I want her with us, but she can't be." Trevor's solemn tone had my eyes opening in gratitude for the save. "And everything will be okay." He stood and walked around to help untangle Chase from his locked-in position and pulled him to his side to hold him like he was four, not nine. Only he could do that, with his towering height and frame, after Chase's recent growth spurt last summer.

I patted my cheeks with the backs of my hands to try to discard the evidence of my emotions and slowly stood, hoping my legs wouldn't give out. My gaze slanted over to the frosted window. "The snow's picking up."

"The snow will work to our advantage, cloaking us," he answered in a hoarse voice. His eyes were on his forearm, on the angel tattooed there that Chase was tracing with his index finger. "Consider the snow a gift from the Big Guy. He's going to protect us. Shield us from harm. Right, buddy?"

Well, shoot, now I was going to ugly-cry.

"Protect us from the bad people?" Chase's voice was so small that time, so full of innocence. "Like you do?"

"I can't do anything without God, but yeah." Trevor met my eyes next. "I won't let anything happen to you. And Ryder won't let anything happen to your mom."

I went over to the disposable iPhone Ryder had given me and opened it to the app he'd programmed in there. "I'll always be able to see where you are, and you'll be able to track me. The blinking dots represent us."

Chase took hold of it with his free hand, keeping the other curved around the back of his dad's neck. "The dots are together right now. Why can't they stay that way?"

My hand went to my heart on autopilot at the squeeze of pressure there. *Breathe, dang it.*

"Those blinking dots will be back together soon enough." Trevor let Chase slide down his side until the little black combat boots he'd laced up for him a few minutes ago hit the floor. Like father, like son. They were dressed alike. In camo, for the snowmobile ride they'd soon be taking while I served as the decoy to hide their escape in the other direction.

"Eden?" Trevor called out, tipping his head toward the hallway.

She appeared a moment later, so I had to assume he'd asked her to wait for us out there.

"Can you take Chase to Ryder for me?" he asked her. "We'll be right out."

"It's okay," I promised, and he hesitantly let go and went with his aunt while clutching the phone like a lifeline.

Once we were alone, Trevor tore both hands through his hair, eyes shooting to the ceiling. "This has to be one of the hardest things I've ever done. And this is coming from someone held captive by the Taliban for six weeks."

A story he'd never been able to fully tell me about. One he'd kept locked up deep, deep inside that had eventually destroyed our marriage.

"I know Chase is in good hands. You won't let anything happen to him. That's the only way I can do this." My hand raced across my lips, both my mouth and fingers trembling.

He pulled me into his big arms like a blanket of comfort, and like Chase had done to me, I nestled my face at the side of his neck and held on for dear life. "Love you, Trev. Like family, you know? And I just . . . I need to hear you say this will all work out. Because if you say it, I'll really believe it."

"Love you, too." Emotion squeezed around his words, and they came out raspy. "As family, of course," he emphasized, the way I had. "And you have to have faith. Believe. And then it will be." He added in a gruff voice, "And I trust your brother and his friends. They're good people. All of them. Even, uh, Alex."

There was something in the way he'd said Alex's name that gave me pause. Like he was telling me to trust Alex with more than my safety, and I wasn't sure what to make of that or why he felt compelled to tell me, but I didn't have time to psychoanalyze it because—

"Sorry, I didn't mean to interrupt."

I shifted away from Trevor to see Alex hanging in the doorway.

"We're ready to move out," he let us know. "The storm is giving us enough cover to go now instead of waiting for nightfall."

A true blessing that would literally disguise us.

Alex leaned his shoulder against the interior doorframe, keeping his arms at his sides, his gaze drifting between Trevor and me.

"Let's do this, then." Trevor glanced at me. "Meet you downstairs." He picked up my bag that he'd packed for me on Friday night, not knowing Alex also had one waiting downstairs. "I'll give you two a minute."

"That's not necessary," Alex said, brows drawing together.

Trevor patted his shoulder, and Alex moved out of his way. "Take that minute anyway."

When it was just the two of us, Alex went back to being a fixture of steel in the doorway.

"How's the wound? You take antibiotics yet?"

"Yes, ma'am, I did. And the wound is fine."

"Tell me that during all your escape planning, you managed to get fluids, too. At least that juice box." I crossed my arms, trying to chase away the chills that wouldn't relent.

This man always gave me butterflies despite the situation. Not the bad, anxious ones, though. More like the excited and eager fluttery ones.

"I did. Drank two, in fact." He gave me a hard, practiced nod, the kind I'd seen Trevor give his commanding officers in the past. "I'll be fine."

Satisfied by his response, I let my gaze wander down his body, taking in the fact he'd changed. Upgraded his civilian clothes to military-ish-looking ones. Since I knew I'd be sporting a bulletproof vest soon, I had a feeling he had a chest plate beneath his vest that was also packed with ammo.

I couldn't believe my son would soon be sporting armor while riding a snowmobile to escape.

Never in a million years would I have expected that when I let Mitch into my life, I'd wind up on the run because of him. That was the thing about life, though. You go left, not knowing you were meant to go right.

"Will you run the plan by me one more time?" I hated that my teeth were chattering again.

Alex straightened and stepped into the room to join me, a touch of hesitancy still lingering in the lines of his body.

"Trevor's emergency escape route wasn't compromised during the ambush. Thermal imaging and surveillance verify it's still secure."

"And still zero evidence anyone has gone near the snowmobile he has hidden, or the Jeep two miles away that's camouflaged, either?"

"Right." He nodded. "And we've got my rental, Ryder's truck, and your SUV parked in the three-car garage now. We'll exfil using all three. Once we roll out and get far enough away to be the decoy, then Trevor will move out with Chase. Once they're in that unregistered Jeep, he'll head to the next location, where we've planned for him to swap vehicles and make his way to Michael Maddox's cabin."

"And Michael is there now with his family for a ski trip, and he really doesn't mind Trevor and Chase crashing their vacation knowing what's going on?" I brought my hand to my stomach. Bye-bye, good flutters. Hello, pain and nerves.

"He's an excellent operator in his own right. You know, even for a marine." He gave me a lopsided smile. "And his security will be off the charts. He told the secretary he's happy to help, and Chase can play with his kids."

He closed the space between us and lifted his hand like he wanted to touch my shoulder and offer his support, but then he let his arm go back to his side.

"I needed to hear that one more time." At least no one had tried to lay siege to the property again. "And Eden's being escorted by Beau to the Jefferson County Sheriff's Office. She'll be protected by them at the precinct while we're gone." I couldn't handle anything happening to her, either. "Better for her to be with Beau, though, or us?"

"It's what she wanted." He lifted one shoulder as if not totally sold on Beau's protection abilities, which didn't sit well with me. "They want you, not anyone else."

"And if they try to use her to get to me?"

"What makes you think that just because Trevor's letting Eden make her own choices he's not still calling in extra reinforcements to keep her safe?"

Good point. Trevor was uber protective of those he loved. Case in point, what he'd done to keep us safe this last year because of a hunch about Mitch—a hunch that had turned out to be right. *Well, maybe right.* If Mitch had been en route to a government safe house, had he been helping them? Not a traitor? *Ugh, who knows.* It didn't matter right now. I still didn't even know if he was really alive.

"And no one aside from Trevor knows our plans and where we're going, or where Chase will be staying. Not even Eden."

Safer for everyone all around. I was on board with that.

"If anyone tries to come for us on the way to the airport, we'll lose them. And at the airport, we'll swap vehicles. Ryder has friends picking up Seraphina. They'll keep her safe, and then the four of us will go to Boulder and hopefully get answers from the secretary."

"And Wyatt and his wife will have eyes on us the whole way, yes?"

"Big Brother—or in this case, Gray Chandler's *sister*—is watching us." He smiled, attempting to pull off that casual, it's-all-good attitude I was lacking.

I knew he was just trying to make me feel better. Probably also hoped I'd forget he'd been cut right in the spot his ex-wife had shot him last year. Talk about a shocking admission we'd need to unpack at some point.

"You okay?" He tipped his head, eyes narrowing on me.

"I'm not remotely okay, but thank you for this plan. For everything. And for finding a way to Houdini my son to safety."

"None of that is thanks to me." He shook his head. "Your husband had it all covered. You didn't even need me."

Ouch. On so many levels. "*Not* my husband. And I do need you."

He frowned. "Sorry, you know what I meant."

Not sure I did—and why did I feel like there was some unspoken message sitting here between us that I wasn't quite picking up on?

He nodded, keeping quiet, but I could still feel the weight of everything he didn't say. "Ready to go?"

Not at all. "I'm not ready to leave my son."

"I don't think any parent is ever ready to do that," he said in a somber voice. "It's never easy to walk away from those you love."

CHAPTER NINETEEN

Audrey

The little blinking dots moved farther and farther apart, and it took all my restraint not to cry. The goodbye with my son remained on repeat like I kept hitting the same note on the piano over and over again.

"They're on the move," Seraphina told me, sitting in the front seat next to Ryder as the three of us drove down the icy, snowy roads in Ryder's rental truck.

Chase's little blinking light was no longer stationary. That meant he was now on the snowmobile with Trevor, making his escape.

There went my already-in-overdrive heartbeat, soaring at an even more dangerous speed. "I see," I whispered, finally ripping my gaze from the disposable phone.

"Don't leave me, Mommy!" Chase's cries before Trevor had to pull him off me so I could get into the truck haunted me all over again, and I shut my eyes and rested my head against the side window.

"We're coming up on that turn now," Ryder said a few minutes later, ushering in a new wave of panic.

"What'd Alex nickname this turn?" Seraphina's soft, easy voice was comforting. If she didn't seem terrified, maybe I didn't need to be?

Eyes open again, I focused on Chase's dot like it was a heart rate monitor. Every blink was a beat of my own, remaining alive as long as he was safe.

"Something like 'Where Old Souls Go to Die,'" Ryder said as he slowed down, and I twisted back to see Reed, driving my SUV behind us, do the same.

"So, he's going to send his rental off the cliff, and with it, the burner phone that text came from." I repeated what they'd told me earlier, needing to digest that idea all over again. "And you said you, um, mirrored that phone so if contact is made again, we'll still get the message?"

"Exactly. We're just trying to burn our trail and send whoever's keeping tabs on us in the wrong direction for now." Ryder briefly caught my eyes in the rearview mirror.

"Because they're not literally driving behind us, but they did tag that phone and . . ." I let my words drift just as the truck did a little side slide, too, sending my stomach along with the movement.

Ryder easily corrected the steering. "Presumably, yeah. They'll expect we'll try and ditch them, and that we might be successful, which is why you received that text as well. Scare you into thinking that, to protect Chase, you have to help whether you want to or not."

"Alex is done rigging everything now; then he'll set the car to coast over the cliff to buy us a little time to get to the airport," Seraphina said, still studying an iPad. "The snow helps, but this is just an extra decoy."

Alex had left ahead of us, bravely leading the way to create a diversion.

"And Beau's sending deputies for those bodies and the one you kept alive to keep questioning him, yes?" I asked despite knowing the answer. I had to stop doing that, but it made me feel better to hear their confirmations.

"Yeah, and hopefully we'll get a hit on their identities by the time you all make it to Wyatt Pierson's cabin in Boulder," Seraphina replied as the road narrowed into a winding bend flanked by snowbanks. I could see the drop-off looming ahead since the snow had stopped falling a few minutes ago.

Ryder slowed the rental truck to a crawl, then pulled off to the side and cut the engine.

I turned around to see Reed parking behind us.

"It's time?" I asked Ryder, and at his nod, I followed up with, "What if someone goes off that cliff because we took out the guardrail?"

"Natasha made a call to have two snowplows come block off access to this road from both sides to prevent civilians from getting into an accident." He twisted in his seat to study me, his 9mm resting on his lap as if it were an extended limb. "The plow drivers will clear out, so if the assholes show up to follow the trail, no one's here to get hurt."

Good. I couldn't live with anything happening to an innocent person because of me. "Will the bad guys really bite and believe we went over that cliff?"

"Probably not. But we'll have the only way on and off this mountain blocked, and it'll be obvious a car did go off the cliff, right along with their tracker," he replied. "All of this is to buy us time to get to the airport to switch vehicles."

Misdirection. An illusion. A decoy to get my son and us to safety. I needed to have faith, but gosh, I was still lacking in that department right now, and I hated myself for that.

Ryder faced forward as a call came over the dash. He placed it on speakerphone.

"Hey, Natasha here, patching in from CIA aerial. No thermal pings from your route yet. You're clear. All of you."

I let the comfort of those last three words sink in, and checked Chase's blinking dot again—still on the move, which was a good sign.

"We watched the vehicle go over the ridge. We're going to jam all external frequencies in a ten-mile radius after this call and induce a short power outage on the grid. We'll blame the snowstorm that rolled through your area. But that means you'll temporarily lose all signals as well," she went on.

I vaguely remembered meeting Gray's sister at some point in the past after he had married Trevor's cousin, but we hadn't had a chance to really speak too much. Thank God she worked for the CIA and her father was who he was, though.

Here I am, constantly thanking God, and yet I'm still lacking faith that all will be fine. What is wrong with me?

"Roger that," Ryder confirmed. "If they do have airborne support, they'll be blind, unlike you." He peeked at me in the mirror, adding, "And don't worry, our drone won't be impacted."

"The snowplows are almost to your location. Your ten-minute window starts in thirty seconds. Visibility is going to drop again for you in about two miles, where the storm is hitting now. Be safe."

"Thanks, Natasha." Ryder ended the call as someone was walking our way outside.

My heart squeezed at the realization that it was Alex. He waved at Ryder, then kept on walking.

The second he was in the passenger seat of the SUV with Reed, Ryder pulled back onto the road and the little blinking light on my phone went offline. My stomach muscles banded tight at the loss of the visual.

"We're ghosts now," Ryder said, and a few seconds later we passed the area where Alex had sent the rental car over the cliff.

"No one I'd rather be dead with than you," Seraphina said in a teasing tone, reaching for his hand on the steering wheel.

"Real funny." He shook his head. "She loves to give me an ulcer."

"We're going to be fine. I can make jokes because I trust you." She twisted around to look at me. "You're in good hands, and when they get you to Boulder, they'll figure this all out."

I nodded my thanks to her and closed my eyes.

The next ten minutes were going to be the longest of my life as I waited for that little blinking light to return.

The second it did, a breath of air whooshed free from my lungs, and a text quickly followed from Trevor's burner, which I'd preprogrammed into my phone.

Trevor: In the Jeep. All clear. Our son is safe. I have every intention of keeping him that way.

I texted back without hesitation, relief bubbling up inside as a shocking smile hit my lips.

Me: You shouldn't be texting while driving.

Trevor: Voice texting, relax.

Me: Talk about deja vu.

Trevor: No repeats of Friday night, please.

Trevor: And the fact you're responding means you're safe too. Good. Stay that way.

I let go of another deep breath and shifted around to ensure the only tail we had was the one we wanted. At the sight of Alex and Reed right behind us, I faced forward and texted Trevor back.

Me: I plan on it.

Me: Tell Chase I love him infinity times infinity.

Trevor: He says he loves you infinity cubed.

I clutched the phone to my chest while letting them know: "They're okay and now in the Jeep."

"I can see them on my screen," Seraphina confirmed. "Natasha patched us in so we can share the view."

Technology could be both a blessing and a curse, and right now I was grateful for it. "And Eden? She good?"

"She's at the sheriff's department with Beau. All good," Seraphina answered. "He has our hostage in a cell."

"Y'all really did Houdini us to safety. Thank you. I don't know what I'd have done without you. If my mom didn't tell me about you at Thanksgiving, then . . ." Tears gathered in my eyes as the memory grabbed hold of me, right along with the fact I'd barely spoken to my mother since that night, still so hurt that she'd kept a brother from me all my life.

"Speaking of your mom . . . who have you told about what's going on?" Ryder asked.

"Just my best friend." *And, oh shit.* "Is she in danger now? We need to give her a heads-up. And before you ask, yes, I trust her. We've been friends for almost nine years."

Ryder nodded, then requested I give Seraphina Hollis's phone number. "I'll handle it. No contact with anyone from here on outside of Trevor, though, got it?" he asked once I'd rattled off her number—one of the few I had memorized.

"Yeah, okay." I nodded.

"But you really didn't tell your mom about this?" He peeked at me in the rearview mirror, clearly surprised by that news.

"No. I'm still trying to forgive her for everything."

My mom knew our father had been married when they'd had an affair. Four months into her pregnancy, she met my dad, who raised me as his own.

"You know I don't hate her, right? I haven't met her, but I, uh, don't blame her for our dad walking out on my mom. He left them both," Ryder said. Seraphina reached over and rested her hand on his leg in quiet support. "He'd have left us no matter what."

I had no idea what to say to that. I hadn't even known I'd been abandoned until this Thanksgiving, but Ryder had spent thirty-plus years living with it.

"I'm still sorry," was all I could manage, my gaze falling to Chase's little blinking dot as we kept moving farther and farther apart.

"You owe me no apologies. And, Audrey?" He stopped at a red light and looked back at me. "Does it make me fucked up that I'm glad

Dad cheated? You wouldn't exist otherwise, and I wish I'd known you sooner—but at least I know you now."

And that.

Right there.

Sent me into the deep.

Into the thick of it.

Into an avalanche of hope, believing everything truly happened as it was meant to, which meant everything would work out now. It had to.

CHAPTER TWENTY

Audrey

From inside a private hangar at the Denver airport, my brother turned to face me, a worried expression crossing his face.

The secretary of defense must've pulled some strings to discreetly get us in here. No way would we have rolled through security with these guys armed to the teeth.

"Are you sure I can't convince you to get on this plane with Seraphina?" Ryder asked.

I peeked around him to look at said plane, with the name COSTA scrolled in billionaire black on its side, then found his eyes. "I've got a list of things I swore I'd never do. Want to guess what's on it?"

He smirked. And yeah, we could smile right now. Because my son had FaceTimed me from Michael Maddox's cabin ten minutes ago while we were waiting for this plane to pull into the hangar, and he was fine. We all were.

"I take it you're going to tell me it has something to do with planes?" Ryder lifted his brows.

"More like private jets. They're the real reason I never want to get rich. They feel like an obligatory purchase, along with a Birkin bag—two things I can live without." I smirked. "Jumbo jets are way more my speed. I need something that looks like it could survive an attack."

"So I shouldn't let my soon-to-be wife on board, is what you're saying?" He rested his hand on my shoulder and lightly squeezed. "What if I get you a bigger plane? One of those two-story ones. Will you leave then?"

I rolled my eyes.

"That's what I thought. You're not going anywhere until this mess is done. And I suppose size doesn't really matter. At least, not always."

"You sure you don't want to go with us?" Seraphina joined the party in trying to get me to leave, too. "Come to New York with me. Keep me company while they take out the bad guys." At her request, Ryder let go of me so she could take over, and he rejoined the rest of his team, along with the four men who'd been on the jet.

"What would you do if you were me?" I asked her once everyone was out of earshot.

"Truth?" she whispered.

"Yes, please." I fidgeted with the tactical vest weighing me down, anxious to get it off me.

"I'd jump straight into the fight myself. I mean, I did go undercover with a psychotic drug smuggler to seek revenge for my family, so I'm not the best at taking the advice I give." She looped her arm through mine as Ryder talked to Reed and the four mystery men set to whisk away my brother's bride-to-be.

Ryder must've really trusted these guys.

Also, how lucky were we that they'd just left Vegas for New York? And, thanks to Secretary Chandler, were able to make an emergency stop in Denver?

Not luck. Fate. Everything has to be okay. We're going to get out of this, and Chase will go back to having a normal and wonderful childhood free of bad guys and danger.

The only thing keeping my legs from giving out and my stomach from doing full-on somersaults right now was the fact he was safe now with Trevor, in some type of fortress-cabin off the grid.

Alex turned to the side, casting a quick look my way. We'd yet to speak since we departed the lodge.

"Who are they?" I asked her.

"Ryder's friends with the only guy over there who doesn't have *Costa* as a last name." Seraphina discreetly pointed toward the non-Costa. "That's Hudson Ashford. Maybe he even knows Trevor. He was a Navy SEAL, too. He's now married to Isabella Costa. Well, suppose she's an Ashford now."

Before I had a chance to ask a follow-up question, Ryder called us over.

The sooner we got this show on the road, the better, I thought. We still had to swap vehicles and get to Boulder.

Natasha, our goddess of a cyber helper today, was currently covering our tracks with the CCTV footage while here to ensure no possible hacker on Team Mitch (or Team Counterfeit Mitch) could track us.

If they figured out we came here after the lodge, they'd begin chasing their tails trying to find where we would go next. Those were Natasha's words, at least.

"Guess we better go over to him before Ryder comes and tosses the both of us over each shoulder. Knowing him, I bet the man would actually do that, too." Seraphina kept her voice light and teasing, probably hoping to calm my nerves.

Ryder began making introductions to Seraphina and me. It felt nice to hear "This is my sister," come from his mouth with such pride, too.

A chorus of *nice to meet you*'s followed as each of the men shook my hand.

"You just happened to be in Vegas heading home, huh?" I should've ditched the curious tone there, but it'd come out anyway.

The four men exchanged a look before one of them broke forward from the pack, his thumb grazing his jaw. "We had business there." There was a notable accent. Italian?

"The kind of business my brother's acquainted with?" My lips teased into a smile.

"Maybe." The guy smirked before turning toward Ryder. "Ready?"

Ryder reached for Seraphina and pulled her to the side. "Give me a moment and we will be." Holding her hand, he walked her out of view to the other side of the jet, where I had a feeling he'd be spending that moment kissing her.

"Congrats, man," Reed said to Hudson, not elaborating on why; then he turned toward one of the other men while picking up Seraphina's bag. "I heard your wife's pregnant with a girl and that, uh, you have a teenage son?"

"She is, and I do." A man of few words.

"Glad everything worked out in Italy. I heard things got a little intense and that you died?"

And then there was Reed. Apparently a man of *direct* words.

"Just for a couple of minutes." The mystery Costa nodded at Alex for some reason. "Heard you had a close call, too?"

Your ex-wife shot you. I still couldn't get over that. How much baggage did we have in common?

Alex brushed the spot I'd patched up like he could still feel the memory under the skin. "I'm fine."

"Well, you're in good hands, Audrey," Hudson commented as Reed handed him the bag.

I sighed. "I know. Thank you. And thank you for keeping Seraphina safe while we, um, figure out whether . . ."

"Your husband's really dead?" one of the other men said, his accent fainter.

"Enzo," Hudson snapped, giving him a death stare as Ryder and Seraphina returned. "Way to be blunt."

"It's fine—and you're right." I chewed on my lip, unsure what to say next. I was grateful I didn't have to speak, because Ryder did it for me.

"Natasha called; she says we're clear to roll out. We better go." Ryder let go of Seraphina's arm and offered his hand. "Constantine," he said with a tip of the head, then went down the row of men. "Alessandro.

Enzo." When he got to Hudson, he gave him a quick one-armed hug instead. "Thank you. I owe you."

Constantine stood tall in a crisp suit and gave off leader energy. And while Alessandro and Enzo carried themselves like businessmen, it was obvious all three were also the kind of guys who could kill you and still make it to a dinner reservation. Hudson was the only one who smiled like a human instead of a loaded weapon.

Constantine stepped forward. "Happy to help."

It was good to pair names with faces now.

"Seraphina can stay at my place. My wife will love having you around. My son . . . well, uh, he can be a lot, but—"

"I can handle him, don't worry," Seraphina reassured Constantine before Ryder pulled her back into his arms and kissed her.

My brother didn't give a damn who had eyes on him. And somehow I loved him even more for that.

After a few more goodbyes, Ryder ushered us out a side exit where a black Suburban waited, parked like it'd appeared by magic while we were inside.

Alex tossed both my bags into the trunk, and I whispered softly, "Thank you. For everything."

He gave a tight-mouthed nod and quietly reached out to adjust the plated vest I'd forgotten I was wearing. He gestured toward the SUV—my cue to get inside. Of course, he beat me to it, opening the door for me, and I let another thank-you brush from my lips to his ears in a whisper.

Reed was already behind the wheel with Ryder at his side, now holding the iPad Seraphina had been in charge of before.

"She's going to be fine." Reed elbowed my brother, then put the SUV in drive and pulled forward.

Ryder glanced out the window in the direction of the hangar. "I know," he returned after a deep exhalation. He peeked back at me. "So will you."

I nodded, unable to get any words out, then dug into my pocket where I'd stashed my new phone to keep an eye on Chase's location.

A text popped up a moment later. A photo of Chase watching a movie alongside Michael and Kate Maddox's kids.

Me: Thank you for this. We're leaving the airport now.

Trevor: Good. Be safe.

Me: Always.

I closed my eyes, only to have them startled open when my brother hit me with words I didn't want to hear: "We just received word from HELL."

HELL. Why did that signature feel like it had an all-new meaning? The man might have very well come back from there himself.

"What'd he say?" I sat taller, planting a hand on the back of Reed's seat while side-eyeing Alex, noticing him shift uncomfortably at the news.

"Here." Ryder handed me a phone, a different one from what Mitch had given us, but presumably the "mirrored" version of it—whatever that meant.

I held it out so Alex could look with me.

Unknown: I know you, Audi. I know how you think. You're not with Chase. You placed yourself in danger to protect him. Of course you did. It's what any good mom would do. —HELL

Unknown: Nice trick with the car and snowplows. You bought yourself some time. I expected you to get away. You're resourceful.

Unknown: But if you want to keep everyone you love safe, I expect you to do what I say.

Three images popped up at once.

I stared at the first one, which had to have been taken in Fargo at Christmas. Alex and Chase building a snowman.

The next was of my brother playing hockey with my son.

The third was me alongside Seraphina, watching Ryder, Reed, and Alex in a snowball fight with Chase.

Oh my God.

Another photo came through, this one of us at the edge of the woods with Alex at the lodge.

Unknown: Don't tell me you're falling for another man in uniform. Delta. Really?

Unknown: I'm still your husband, Audi. Till death do us part. You better remember that. You're mine. We're in this together. For better or worse.

Unable to stop myself, I pulled the phone back to my lap, about to fire off a reply, but Alex rested a hand over mine. I looked up at him, and he shook his head, mouthing, *Don't.*

I gave him the phone before I did something stupid.

That fragile feeling that maybe everything would be okay vanished in an instant. I started shaking, unable to stop my body from responding in such a way.

"That text came from Mitch, I'm sure of it," I whispered as I shifted my gaze to Ryder. "He's the only one who called me Audi, and I just feel it deep in my bones. He's alive." My voice cracked. "And that means he's right. I'm still that man's wife whether I like it or not."

CHAPTER TWENTY-ONE

Alejandro

"Leverage. Yeah, that's what I'm saying. I don't give a damn how many people you have to pull in to—" Ryder stopped talking over the phone, shoulders falling. Rage still simmering, same as me. "Everyone, yes. I don't care if they're second or fifth cousins. I mean every-damn-one."

I sat back in the seat, glancing at Audrey, who was quiet next to me. Hands wrung together. Eyes out the side window. Fragile, but not broken.

"He knows our names. He has photos of us—including my fiancée—he took at my mother's house at Christmas. Mentioned Alex is Delta. So, yeah, everyone close to us, too, not just Audrey and Trevor." Ryder paused, a low hiss leaving his lips. He wasn't hearing what he wanted to. "Well then, find the resources. I don't give a flying fuck if you have to shake a tree on the White House lawn and make it rain cash. Make it happen. Everyone gets protection." Ryder ended the call, not taking shit from anyone, and dropped his phone onto the center console between the front seats.

"Go that well, huh?" I muttered, doing my best not to reach over to Audrey again. Let her hold my hand instead of squeezing hers together like she was both praying and trying to break something between her palms.

"That was President Bennett's guy, the one he sent to Wyoming." Ryder twisted around to look at me. "He thinks asking for protection for all of our families is overkill, and all I'm trying to do is keep everyone from getting killed."

Audrey spoke up for the first time in thirty minutes. "Used as leverage to get to me."

Ryder's gaze dipped to her palms, and he shifted his seat belt aside, stretched out his arm, and placed a hand on top of both of hers. "We won't let that happen."

"But if Mitch is capable of having a drone that went unnoticed up over Trevor's lodge to take photos, and he can find out Alex is Delta, then does that mean he has someone on the inside?" she asked as I swapped a quick look with Ryder.

He sent me a concerned expression back that read *This isn't good.*

"We may need to call in a favor. Who do we know and trust who can protect our people?" Reed quickly added, "I might not like my parents, but I'd prefer for them to continue breathing." One of these days, maybe the man would tell us more about himself other than slipping in clues that didn't bode well for his upbringing.

"We already have Hudson and the Costas keeping an eye on Seraphina in New York. I don't want to ask them to do more." Ryder let go of Audrey and faced forward.

"Don't those SEALs that work for POTUS run a security company as a cover story?" I asked at the memory. "They take on legit jobs on the side as well, right? They have retired SEALs working for them in a couple locations."

"If POTUS won't pull protection in for everyone, then I'll make the call. I can see what Gray and his people can do for us, too. They might already be stretched thin, but it's worth a shot." Ryder grabbed his phone and wasted no time in sending texts.

I checked on Audrey, finding her hands no longer clenched together but now gripping her legs. "You okay?" I asked her, not sure what answer I expected to hear other than *no*.

"Trying to be," she said softly. "I'm so sorry I've pulled you all into this mess."

"We're family. Don't apologize," Ryder responded. "By the way, that friend of yours, Hollis . . . she's something else, huh? She demanded I send her updates three times a day about your safety, but she doesn't seem to be concerned about her own."

"Yeah, well, that's Hollis for ya." Something told me there was more to her best friend's story than that, but no one in the vehicle pressed since we'd made it to our destination.

Once Reed parked inside the garage, I opened the door to get out. For the first time in my life, I wanted to be cold. I needed to put out the fire burning beneath my skin and extinguish the fury flying through me that Mitch had created.

"I'll do a perimeter check," I offered.

Ryder shut his door, standing in front of me while shaking his head. "No, you need to get inside and change your bandage. Reed will do it." The man morphed into Delta One, going so far as to block my path. "Don't argue with me. I'm not in the mood."

I knew better than to fight fire with fire. So I soldiered forward, grabbed as many bags from the trunk as I could carry, then followed him and Audrey through the interior door after he'd unlocked it with the security code.

The cabin was quiet but prepared. Someone had been there ahead of time to set things up for us. The heat was even running. Kitchen probably stocked, too.

"Wyatt said there are three bedrooms upstairs. Primary downstairs," Ryder said as I dumped the bags in the kitchen.

Audrey wandered off, her phone in hand, probably texting Trevor that we'd arrived and anxious to talk to Chase again.

"You take the room down here. I'll stay upstairs next to her." Ryder picked up her bags, prepared to bring them to Audrey's new quarters. "Not that any of us will do much sleeping tonight." He lifted his chin since his hands were full. "Grab the medkit. Check your wound. Take more antibiotics if you have to. Need you in top shape."

I nodded my *roger that* at his orders.

"Natasha and Wyatt should be calling soon. I'll get the laptop set up in the living room in a minute," he said before taking off.

Once I was alone, I braced my hands on the counter.

But before I let myself go off the deep end, thinking up a bunch of negative shit that didn't belong in my head, my body went still.

Is that music? I followed the melodic and resonant notes as they became louder, more powerful.

If pain were ever to be described as a sound, that's what it was. But it was also oddly peaceful.

I rounded the corner, surprised to find a doorless open space with a Yamaha, and Audrey parked behind it—playing.

Her eyes were shut as her fingers gracefully moved.

I leaned against the wall, mesmerized by the music. Well, by her.

One tear trailed down the length of her cheek as she played, and my hand climbed up my chest as I followed her fingers over the keys.

When her fingers came to a stop, she lifted her head and opened her eyes. She startled at the sight of me and hurried to stand. "I couldn't help myself. I left my piano in storage in Virginia. I was worried it'd get damaged in the move. I'll get it one day."

"I, uh, had no idea you even played."

"You didn't ask," she said, repeating what I'd said to her the other night about my Vegas-childhood question.

"What was that piece called? It was sad."

She picked up her phone and headed my way. "It's by Jurrivh. Called 'Crying Alone.'"

"It was . . . well, you were incredible." I wanted to reach for her. Be the one to take away her pain so she wouldn't need to cry.

She stopped in front of me, tucking her hand into the collar of her protective vest as if uneasy wearing it.

"Let me get that off you," I offered, and quickly went to work removing it so I wasn't touching her too damn long. I tossed the vest off to the side. "Where'd you learn to play, and why'd you stop?"

I had a million more questions for her, and I knew now I'd need every single answer. I had to know everything about her.

"New England Conservatory of Music in Boston." She gave me a small smile, letting her free hand fall to her side. "I was part of an orchestra after college. We traveled. Performed." She lowered her head, losing my gaze when she added, "That's how I met Trevor. Military ball in DC. He approached me after the performance."

Trevor. The roadblock between us, not Mitch. Not the man she was still technically married to.

"I apparently met Mitch that night at the ball, too. And we bumped into each other at another ball a few years later that I was attending as a guest, not performer. I'd been pregnant with Chase then and kind of dismissed him." Her shoulders fell with a sigh. "Our paths wound up crossing again after Trevor and I were divorced, and he said it was fate that we kept bumping into each other, so we should date."

She visibly cringed, and I clocked every tremble of her body while taking a beat and a breath to recalibrate from the mere mention of that man's name.

"Anyway, um . . . being pregnant, though, that's why I stopped performing. That's why I started this story, right?"

I gave her a small smile, nodding, when in reality the mere idea Mitch had ever been near her in the past had me wanting to swallow cyanide. Or maybe forcing Mitch to take it. *No, shit, what am I thinking? Reed's right, that's too humane.* Mitch needed a much uglier and more painful death for his third and *final* time dying.

"I told myself it'd be temporary until Chase was two or three, but then life happened and I just never went back. But maybe one day I'll play again. That's why I have so many, um—"

"Everything okay?" Ryder cut her off, killing my chance at learning why she had so many of something.

My guess? Lace. But how that related to playing the piano, I had no clue.

"You haven't done what I told you," Ryder grunted before we could answer him, pointing to my side as if I didn't know my left from my right.

"You're starting to love this Delta One thing a little too much." I tried to pull off my typical joking tone, but to be honest, I was pissed.

Pissed at Ryder for coming in and interrupting us.

Pissed at Mitch for hurting her.

And pissed at myself, knowing that even if I kept letting my guard down around her, it'd never stay down for good.

CHAPTER TWENTY-TWO

Alejandro

By the time I'd removed the heavy weight of my vest, cleaned up the wound, and redressed it, Reed had returned, and Ryder had already synced his laptop to the TV screen in the den back by the primary bedroom.

Audrey was on the couch with a mug in hand, steam swirling out of it. More than likely tea, not coffee, unless she was like me and could have caffeine any hour of the day and still pass out five minutes later.

"You good?" Reed asked me, and all I could do was nod as Ryder connected the incoming call from an unknown number.

Wyatt and his wife, Natasha, appeared on the TV screen, sitting at a desk somewhere. Probably at the Pentagon or Langley.

"Welcome to my place." Wyatt leaned back in his desk chair. "Good to see you safely made it there."

"Thanks to your better half, we did." Ryder locked his arms over his chest, tipping his head in thanks to Natasha.

"I won't argue with you there. I'm bloody lucky to have her." Wyatt still had his British accent even though he'd moved to the States several decades ago.

Natasha nudged him in the side while turning her attention on Audrey. "You hear from Beau yet?"

"He sent his deputies to Audrey's to confirm whether or not her ring was taken." Ryder opened his palms, revealing that they were empty. "Looks like we both have one half of the key now."

"Shit." Natasha pivoted, eyes back to Audrey now. "Sorry, I should have opened with asking how you're doing. I can't imagine."

"My son's okay, and we're all okay, so I'm focusing on that. Trying to keep my eye on the positives so I don't drown in worry." Her voice was hoarse, and I wanted to go to her, but I kept my ass parked at a distance.

Ryder did what I wished I could do, sitting beside her. He didn't say anything, just rested his hand on her knee.

"You can sleep sound there, I promise you. We've got the entire state lit up with layered surveillance," Wyatt said. "And there are about five hundred ways someone would trip the security system around my cabin or Maddox's place," he went on, as if realizing she'd yet to buy the safety he was trying to sell, "and no one is getting through a single one of them without us knowing."

I had to assume that was a slight exaggeration on Wyatt's part, but I'd heard rumors about how overprotective he was of his cyber-genius daughter, Gwen, and his younger daughter, Emory, so maybe not.

Audrey brought the mug to her lips but didn't drink. Her fingers stayed wrapped around it, her gaze somewhere far off, as if she were trying to see through the layers of betrayal fogging up her life. "Okay, um, thank you." She set the mug on the table and sat back.

"We've got you." Natasha folded her arms on the desk like this was another briefing, not a nighttime drop-in at their vacation home. "Before you arrived, I sent someone over I trust with our daughters' lives to stock up the place with a week's worth of food. Clean sheets and all that."

"Thank you," Ryder responded as Reed circled the couch, his hand resting on his sidearm like it was his security blanket. Knowing that man, he slept with his piece. "What about our request to protect our families?"

"I lost patience in waiting on approval for you. I put in the protection orders myself," Natasha said.

Wyatt side-eyed his wife, smirking. "Daddy's girl. The admiral will do what she says. He'll sign off on it. Don't worry."

"Like you aren't also putty in Gwen and Emory's hands?" Natasha rolled her eyes, fighting a smile before facing us again as if remembering she had an audience.

"Thank you." Ryder nodded. "That's one less thing we need to stress about."

"Echo Team's on standby to support you when we have more intel to go on as well. And Falcon Falls has your backs if need be, too," Natasha let us know.

"That include Gwen?" Reed asked. "I assume she's the one who sent Trevor those files on Mitch. She still on the case?"

Wyatt tipped his head, gaze cutting to Reed as if he might be interested in more than just his daughter's computer skills. "She is, and she'll keep us posted if she finds anything of use before we talk to my father-in-law tomorrow."

"Tomorrow?" Tension beat up my spine, landing firmly at the base of my skull. "He's not going to brief us tonight?"

"We'll tell you what we can. But the admiral's yet to give us his side of the story, so we're still in the dark ourselves. He promised to brief us as soon as he lands in DC tomorrow. He's on Air Force One with POTUS right now," Wyatt shared. "I know that's not what you want to hear, but what's important right now is that you're all safe and no one knows where you are. No one outside our circle, at least."

"Circle of trust," Audrey murmured. "I once trusted Mitch and now . . ." She shook her head and looked up. "Sorry, I wasn't insinuating you can't be trusted."

"We get it, don't worry." Natasha waved her hand. "As for what we can share now, we don't have too much. Unfortunately, the pool of suspects who *might* be working from the inside is larger than I'd like it to be. We'll work on narrowing it down."

"But we did find something interesting when we ran facial recognition on the photos you sent over," Wyatt noted. "We got a strange hit on the guy you questioned."

Natasha clicked a remote, and the face of the man from the lodge—the same man I'd dragged from the woods—filled the screen, only he was in a tropical shirt and not tactical gear.

"He's a fisherman living in the Maldives," Natasha explained. "Address and information check out. I even have footage of him there as of a week ago. No red flags aside from bad interior decorating. I hacked his internal security cameras to view the live feed. Nothing is recorded, so I couldn't rewind and have a look back into the past. But everything looked normal."

"Please tell us how this innocent fisherman wound up working for Mitch and attacking us today?" Ryder pressed before I could.

"His cover was good. And when I say *good*, I mean too good for me to realize it wasn't real." Natasha visibly cringed as if mortified by that fact. "Thankfully, Gwen's better than me and better than whoever created his legend." She clicked a button, and a younger version of the so-called fisherman popped up. This time in a uniform. "Real name is Rhett Robeson. Was a naval pilot like Mitch. Joined around the same time he did."

"*Was* a pilot?" Ryder's chin jutted forward. "So he's no longer active duty and living under an alias in the Maldives, you mean?"

Natasha shook her head. "No, 'was' as in is dead. As of 2011."

"Clearly someone forgot to tell him," I hissed. "It appears we're having a real problem with dead men that keep on walking."

"What about Arlo, that friend of Mitch's that died two months before Mitch and was rumored to be a traitor? He happen to be one of the men we killed today?" Ryder asked.

"No, he wasn't," Wyatt answered, arms tight over his chest. "Whether he's also among the living and not really dead, though? No bloody idea."

"Rhett's our only confirmed former serviceman that hit the lodge." Natasha turned off the screen behind her. "The rest of the bodies were all guns for hire, from what we can tell. Easily identifiable, too. Long rap sheets. Looks like everyone else out there was disposable to Mitch. Not the brains behind anything. None of them would be able to bypass Trevor's security. My guess is someone else was hanging back in the woods opting to remain unseen when you went hunting."

Great. "So we're either trapped in a ghost story, or someone's pulling the strings on a whole damn graveyard." A chill flew up my spine and curved right around to my side. No longer phantom pain from being shot, but real pain from having my flesh peeled open.

Audrey eyed the screen. "Mitch was a pilot like Rhett, not some spymaster. He doesn't have the background to pull all this off."

My blood boiled again as the thorn of Beth in my side faded and a new one took hold by the name of Mitchell Fucking Langston.

"Someone's definitely helping Mitch. Probably whoever must've pulled your files is responsible for Rhett's fisherman persona." Natasha's eyes narrowed. "Either Mitch is aligned with someone, or he's just a pawn like Rhett probably is."

"Pawn?" Wyatt grimaced for some reason. "Not a word I want to think about after everything we went through with that asshole." That sidebar conversation was lost on me, and from the looks on my teammates' faces, them too.

"But why would Mitch send someone to the lodge that we could tie to him? Unless he believed Rhett's alias would hold up?" Audrey's soft voice and questions brought our focus back to her. "Also, why out himself as being alive with that text?"

"Mitch wants you to know he's alive. He doesn't want you doubting him. He needs you to help him," Natasha proposed. "He believes you'll do anything to protect your son, as most mothers would. And it's possible he really did try to start this quietly on Friday."

I couldn't help but speak up. "I think it's more than that. I think he's masterminded everything from the start, right down to the break-in." I swiped the back of my hand over my stubbled jawline as I continued to work through my thoughts.

"Maybe everything that's happened this weekend is how Mitch wanted it to play out, right down to us escaping today," Reed tacked on in agreement. "Maybe Mitch sent his people for the key, but his goal wasn't to have you taken on Friday. He *wanted* to send you into Trevor's arms." He squeezed one eye closed as if regretting his phrasing. "Well, you know what I mean."

"He knew Trevor would bring Audrey to his place after the break-in," Ryder said with a nod, sounding as though we were on the same sick page. "Rhett confirmed as much, right? And Mitch also knew exactly who Trevor would turn to for help, because he knows who Trevor's cousin married."

Gray Chandler, son of the secretary of defense.

"Not just that." Natasha gave us an uneasy look before stealing a glimpse at her husband, and he gave her a nod of what felt like permission to share something. "I take it Audrey's yet to sign an NDA?"

Ryder shook his head. "But she already knows plenty at this point, so you might as well spit it out."

"Yeah, okay." Natasha blew out her cheeks. You know, great sign to see from an experienced officer. "Your ex-husband knew my dad before my brother married Trevor's cousin, Tessa. Not just because Trevor was SEAL Team Six and my dad was an admiral."

Wyatt dropped the news on Audrey fast. "Secretary Chandler asked me to recruit Trevor to run Charlie Team. This was a few years back."

"Wait, what?" Audrey's words echoed my own shock.

What were the damn odds?

"Trevor said no." Wyatt gave Audrey a moment to continue wrapping her head around the news. "He said secrets destroyed his marriage and he wouldn't let secrets be the downfall of your friendship, too. And he knew if he were to run Charlie, he'd only be able to tell you if you were his wife."

Audrey covered her mouth, eyes falling to her lap, visibly shivering. It was becoming increasingly harder and harder to dislike Trevor. Hell, he sounded like someone I could hang out with on the regular. Even operate with.

"Any chance Mitch knew Trevor has been in tight with your dad for longer than we thought?" Ryder asked Natasha.

"No clue. It depends on how closely Mitch was paying attention to Trevor over the years. Did the two know each other before you started dating and married?"

"They weren't friends, no. But they were both in the navy and attended a few events at the same time," Audrey shared.

Wyatt stood, pushing his chair back. "Well, let's assume the worst here, and that's Mitch was aware Trevor had a friendship of sorts with my father-in-law long before Gray married his cousin, and he was banking on that close relationship for some reason."

"Which means *what*, exactly?" Audrey asked pointedly.

"It's clear Mitch wanted to make sure there was no doubt in anyone's mind that he's the one behind all this," Natasha said. "Which is why he sent Rhett today, so we'd discover Rhett is also supposed to be dead. Then Rhett could give us a direct line to Mitch with the phone."

"So Rhett more than likely planned on being caught, which is why he hung back on the edge of the property waiting for what he expected us to do," I said in agreement with Natasha. "He put up a decent fight for show, then surrendered on purpose. He told us what Mitch wanted him to say and gave us the phone, so then Trevor would go to—"

"My father," Natasha finished for me. "Mitch wanted this to get back to the secretary of defense, to the man who faked his death in the first place. He's either framing my father, or he's forcing him to step into the deep end right along with him."

With Audrey and all of us now, too.

"This is . . ." Audrey stood and turned toward her brother, and he pulled her into his arms, catching my eyes over her head as he held her.

"We'll put a stop to this," Natasha said firmly. "Mitch has no idea what he's done by dragging us into this mess with him."

"He's made this personal for all of us, and he'll realize his mistakes fast," Wyatt added, fire in his voice. He let his temperature cool off faster than I'd be able to, and switched gears from war to rest. "Just head to bed, get some sleep for now. We'll figure out the full picture when we talk to my father-in-law in the morning." He pushed away from the table and stood, signaling the conversation was coming to an end whether we wanted it to or not.

Silence passed between us as Audrey freed herself from her brother's hold to look around at everyone.

"Dead men walking. Secret ops and ghosts." Reed shook his head, eyes locked on me like I had all the answers for some reason. "What kind of mission is this turning into?"

My stomach squeezed as I gritted out, "One that I'm afraid is just getting started."

CHAPTER TWENTY-THREE

Audrey

The bedroom was warm and quiet, reminding me of the honeymoon suite back at the lodge but a little smaller. Same smell of fresh linen and pine.

The windows rattled from a strong breeze outside, like nature was cocooning us in the shadow of a snowstorm so we'd remain cloaked from danger.

I stared down at the pink duffel bag alongside the black one on the bed.

The one Alex had packed.

The other? Trevor's doing.

I knew what Trevor had packed, but what had Alex chosen? I wasn't sure if I should check with him still hovering protectively in the doorway. What if we wound up in underwear-talking territory again? Or, worse, while I held a pair in my hands?

I was so overtired and emotionally spent, I just might talk about my "drawers" again. I didn't trust myself.

"You didn't have to walk me to my room, though I appreciate the gesture." I slowly turned to face him. "Ryder and Reed are just doing a quick perimeter sweep because Ryder's overly cautious, right? They'll be back inside soon." It was too cold, snowy, and windy for them to be out in that mess. At least we'd made it here safely before the storm had picked up.

He set his shoulder against the interior doorframe and quietly stared at me. "Mm-hmm," he finally said.

"Not going to leave until someone is upstairs with me, huh?" I forced a smile, shocked I was still capable of such a thing.

Before he had a chance to answer, a text came through. I glanced at the lock screen to check who it was. Of course, there was only one person who had this number, so who else would it be? Ryder would get the messages from Mitch, not me. "It's Trevor."

Alex straightened at my use of his name, taking one step back, nearly into the hall. Was Trevor coming between us even when he wasn't here?

Also, had Trevor really turned down leading a special group at Secretary Chandler's request because he didn't want to lie to me?

I had no clue what to make of that. Heck, I didn't know what to make of anything I'd learned today.

I picked up the phone to open his text. He'd sent a photo of Chase curled under a blanket with a dog sprawled across the bottom of the bed.

Trevor: He's asleep. Hope you get some too.

I sent back a quick message and a thank-you before returning the phone to the nightstand. "Chase is good. Sleeping with their dog. Now he's going to want one, too." Probably not a bad idea after what he went through this weekend.

"Trevor will move mountains to keep his son safe," he said in a low voice. "And apparently do anything to protect his relationship with you—even turn down a job the majority of Tier One operators would kill for."

There was something in that statement, something that went beyond the surface. He was trying to tell me Trevor wanted me back, wasn't he?

But he doesn't. I mean, I don't think.

"I have a feeling you would move mountains, too," was all I could manage, not sure if I should unpack the second part of his statement right now.

"Of course." The tight nod he surrendered didn't do wonders in helping me believe he was understanding what I'd been saying.

My eyes drifted to his side where his wound was currently covered by his shirt. That scar had been torn open today, a brutal reminder of the betrayal we both carried.

"So, who's been in charge of texting my best friend?" I asked as I forced myself to look away from him, deciding to check the bag he'd packed even though he was still there.

I undid the zipper as slowly as I had cut the tape on Mitch's box last Friday.

Who knew I'd be starting a game of Jumanji by opening that box? And now we had to keep playing until someone won, or we'd be trapped forever in this hellish world Mitch had sucked us into. *Too bad I used to play that game with Chase. Never again now.*

"Ryder placed Reed in charge of talking to her."

I smiled—not that he'd see my reaction. "Chose the guy who doesn't like people to handle my best friend, huh?"

"To talk to the only person who knows why you have so much lace? *Sí*," he said in a husky voice. Was that a request for me to tell him why, too?

"Well, um, I can assure you that she won't talk his ear off about what's in my dresser. She'll just demand you protect me or else she'll send her father's security guards to do it." I peeked back at him. "Her father's rich. Old-money rich." I focused on my mission of exploring what was inside, smiling at the fact he'd tossed in my perfume, along with a candy bar.

I wasn't sure why the sight of both lifted my spirits so much with how high the stakes had been raised tonight, but sometimes the simple things in life were all you needed to push you back in the right direction of happiness.

"You found my secret candy stash I kept in my dresser." Thankfully, I didn't have a vibrator in there. If I had, and he'd packed it, I would have turned as red as a strawberry. "Thank you for packing my perfume and something sweet to eat, too."

"Figured if you were hiding candy in your room, you had a sweet tooth and might want it."

"More like keeping it from my son's sweet tooth." I held the bar between my palms and turned to face him. "I'd never get any chocolate if I didn't stash away a little for myself."

A handsome wolfish grin I hadn't expected chocolate to produce cut across his lips. He even walked a step forward, eliminating the distance he'd placed between us moments ago. "I have to hide my stash from Reed. I get it."

"You should do that more often." I lowered my arm to my side.

"What's that, exactly? Share my chocolate?"

"Smile." I sighed. "A girl could get used to chocolate and smug smiles."

He lifted his chin, making a *tsk* noise. "I don't do *smug*. I do *mysterious* and *charming*."

I couldn't believe it, but I laughed. Some of the tension even evaporated. I could feel the edges of everything else, all the worry and fear, slipping farther and farther away.

There was an earnest depth to his tone that matched his eyes. "You know," he began, his smile fading and a seriousness slipping back to his face, "you scared me today. Being out on that deck when we were shot at . . ."

"I can't imagine anything scaring you," I murmured honestly.

"That's just an act. *Una ilusión*. The man behind the curtain is a mess." The roughness in his voice shattered what was left of the wall between us that'd been fighting for its life.

"You're *not* a mess."

His eyes met mine as he came closer, and the room became smaller. Quieter. Only the howling winds outside.

He brought his fist beneath my chin. "All roads lead to disaster when it comes to me." His forehead tightened, and my breath hitched at his anguished tone. "You need to remember that. The last thing in the world I want to do is hurt you. And yet, knowing that, I can't seem to—"

"Keep away?" I gulped. "I don't want to hurt you, either, because I'm a mess, too." I leaned forward, our bodies nearly brushing up against each other. "I don't know what this is. But there's something between us, isn't there? And I don't think it's dangerous."

"It's there." He narrowed his eyes, like he was worried that if he blinked, I'd disappear on him. Become one of his father's magic tricks. Vanish before his eyes and never be seen again.

Thing was, I felt exactly the same.

Had the same fear.

Gosh, we were a pair.

"I should go." He pulled his fist away but didn't move his body. "Good night." Then he did something I hadn't anticipated. Slanted his head, drawing his lips to my cheek for a kiss.

When he straightened, I couldn't help but do the same. A whisper of *good night* from my lips, followed by a kiss to his cheek. Only when I started to pull away, I let my lips wander toward his mouth.

We remained there for a few seconds.

Just breathing.

Our lips close but not touching.

And then he brought his mouth to my other cheek and repeated his goodbye. Copied me as well after, drawing his lips toward mine.

His breath caught, and mine disappeared entirely.

Then he did it.

He kissed me.

Tilted his head and brought his hand to the back of my neck and lit me on fire.

"Dios mío." His words vibrated against my lips as the candy bar fell from my hand.

Close-mouthed kissing that somehow felt erotic and sensual. I went as far as living out my fantasies in real time by slipping my hand under his shirt.

Touching his hard, hot skin, feeling the tight band of muscles clench beneath my palm.

My problems evaporated with his lips on mine, him holding me there with my hand on his body.

I nearly cried at the sense of peace he was giving me in this moment. Peace I probably had no business having, given what was at stake, but I couldn't change the way I felt any more than I could turn night into day.

But like the final note in a performance, I could feel the end coming, about to close out. I even heard the lingering sway of sound dance between our bodies as his mouth went still.

Reality hit him, and he let go of me and stepped back.

Breathing hard, he continued to stare at my mouth as if in a state of shock.

"I have to go." He turned for the door and nearly collided with the frame. He muttered something in Spanish, and I was pretty sure it translated to the same chaos echoing in my mind.

The door clicked shut behind him, and I stood there with my heart thundering, my lips tingling, and my knees questioning their purpose. And my heart? That was a lost cause.

I bent down, picked up the candy bar, and opened the drawer of the nightstand, hiding it, chasing some sense of normalcy. To pretend Chase was down the hall asleep in his bedroom, and no one was in danger because I'd trusted the wrong man.

I thought back to Alex's orders about locking doors at the lodge, and obeyed that command now. Then I focused on the two bags.

To the one thrown together by the man I still trusted with my life, and to the colorful one packed by the man whom I was not only starting to trust . . . but also starting to fall for.

CHAPTER TWENTY-FOUR

Alejandro

I remained outside her door with my fists clenched, resting against the frame. I did my best to channel every ounce of self-control I had, to not go back into her room and slip my tongue inside that sweet mouth of hers this time and let her kiss destroy me.

Lock the door. Keep me from coming in.

I gritted down on my back teeth.

Fighting the urge. Fighting my basest instincts to take her in my arms.

I dropped my gaze to the slight rattle of the handle. She'd locked me out. *Good. That's what I want.*

I shoved away from the door and went for my phone to check Ryder and Reed's status. They were still outside checking the property, their signals blinking at a comfortable distance. Comfortable enough to give me time to do something dumb. To *not* walk away.

Don't do it. Turn around.

I shoved the phone in my pocket and did the damn opposite.

Two quick knocks as my heart tried to break free from its prison, a place it was supposed to remain. Never freed. Never let loose to feel anything ever again.

But Audrey had to go and open that door. She had to look at me with those beautiful eyes of hers while whispering, "Checking to make sure I was good and locked in?"

She had to go and be perfect. Sweet and kind. *So* incredibly kind.

Dammit, she had to go and be everything I never knew I wanted.

And when she *Alejandro*'d me again as I quietly stared at her like the human version of a wrecking ball trying to withhold the swing, I snapped. Momentum and gravity were forces that just couldn't be stopped, after all.

I lunged forward.

Crossed the line.

Reached for her face and anchored my palms on her cheeks, dropping my mouth near hers and waited. I waited for her to give me permission. To cross the line with me. To let me know I wasn't alone in this.

And when she parted her lips and pressed up on her toes in invitation, I took it. Fuck, did I ever.

My mouth crashed over hers. Tongue slipped between her lips while backing her against the wall.

She arched into me, grinding. Searching. Chasing something. Like how hard I was.

There was nothing hesitant or cautious about this moment. It was as intense as my heart was beating. And as dangerous as I knew it would be, and then some.

Soft, decadent moans left her full lips as she let her hands wander over my body.

I relished every touch.

Every bite of her fingernails into my flesh.

She rotated against me, stealing her lips from mine to drop her mouth to my neck and kiss me there.

I died.

For real this time.

The way she kissed me, clinging to my body for dear life as I nuzzled my face against the side of her neck.

When her eyes returned to mine, a soulful look in hers before she urged me down to capture her mouth again, I knew I was done. It was game over.

I felt it in my bones, in the very fabric of my entire being, that I belonged to her. It didn't have to make sense; it was true.

In this moment, at least. In this room and in the mountains of Colorado, I was hers. For now. She owned me. All of me.

I was ready to deliver my soul on a platinum platter for her. Let her etch her name into my heart, too.

This was different.

This was . . . *This is how it's supposed to be, isn't it?*

And *that* terrified me.

I had to stop before I did something crazy, like make love to her. Fill her. Hell, if she asked me to, I'd offer her something I never thought I'd give anyone because of Beth: a child.

You have a son. With Trevor. That reminder slammed into me. Had me feeling like I was cheating with another man's wife even if that made no damn sense.

I backed away. Let go of her. Searched for my sanity and my sense of control.

She was breathing hard. A hand over her heart and another between her legs, as if I'd left her in pain there. In both places.

"Audrey." Her name was a snarl from my lips. A demand to stop me. To tell me to walk away. To tell me to not fall to my knees and take her pants down along with me. I'd taste her, get her off; then I'd pick out one of the pairs of lace panties I'd packed for her and guide her legs into them, only to slide them out of the way to lick her senseless again.

"What was that?" She covered her mouth now, resetting my attention there.

It was me falling. Off the cliff. Into something more. Into the deep.

I held my hands up in surrender. In request to not let me do all the things the caged beast inside me craved to do.

"I have to go," I said in a hoarse voice, feeling the pull of my flesh and desires draw me closer to her, my arms falling to my sides. Barrier removed now. Time to extract myself from this room. "Lock the door. Don't open it."

"Not even for you?"

On my way out, I glanced back at her. "Especially for me," I hissed before leaving, shutting the door behind me.

Not trusting myself to stick around any longer and wait to ensure she locked up, I took off down the hall.

I descended two steps at a time, finding Reed coming back inside once downstairs.

"Yup," he said while removing the M4 slung across his chest and setting it aside. "You definitely kissed her."

I stopped in my tracks. What gave me away? The raging hard-on I was still sporting? My eyes, which were probably dark and soulless right now?

"Don't follow me," I warned, blowing past him while muttering a few choice words in Spanish on my way to my bedroom.

Naturally, Reed didn't heed my order.

"You not hear me?" I snapped, turning halfway around.

"Loud and clear." He was completely unfazed as he kept up behind me. "Ryder's not inside yet, and I don't owe Hollis an update for another ten minutes. That gives us time." A flicker of a smile cut across his face.

I ignored him, continuing on my mission to get to my bedroom. He remained right on my ass, dammit.

It wasn't lost on me that Ryder had placed me downstairs and away from his sister, and he was just fine with Reed being upstairs.

Smart man. I'd nearly had sex with his sister. *Un*protected, too. Never thought to pack that kind of protection. And maybe I was being a cocky asshole to believe she wanted to have sex tonight, but the way she was rubbing against me, my dick still painfully hard as a result, told me it'd be a yes.

"We need to talk."

I flicked on the light in my room just in time so I wouldn't trip over my bag. "There are two things you suck at," I bit out, turning my frustration on him when he didn't deserve it. "Humor and feelings."

"Agreed—but here I am, outside my comfort zone, and I'm trying anyway." He leaned inside the doorway with his arms folded, signaling that he had no plans to leave.

Damn you. I dropped onto the bed, leaning forward. Elbows to my legs, I slowly lifted my head, unsure if I should let him look me in the eye or not, worried he'd see that I'd left my soul upstairs, since eyes were supposed to be the windows to it and all that . . . or however the expression went.

"I can tell you're pissed. Or, well, confused. You look like you just found out your whole deck of cards is rigged."

"See. Right there. Humor and talking aren't your strengths, man."

He stepped inside, deciding to double down, not back down. "Just because you learned a thing or two from your father, living in his shadow most of your life, doesn't mean you're him."

My dad? Was he really trying to psychoanalyze me right now? I didn't have any childhood trauma. No shitty memories growing up. My parents had left the country they'd loved to escape communism so my dad could pursue his dreams here, and they'd given me an incredible life.

"Your dad's a good guy, don't get me wrong," he added as if reading my confusion as to where he was going with this. "Million times better than my old man. But I know somewhere in that head of yours growing up behind that curtain onstage with him had you thinking that everyone and everything eventually disappears at some point, and that has to be—"

"Don't do this." I dropped my head into my hands.

Because dammit, he was right. A little bit, at least.

"You joined the military because you needed something real, right? Something solid and not built on illusions?"

His words jolted my head upright again. *How the hell do you know that?*

"I get that. I really do. And I can tell you're feeling something real now, and with her. It's impossible not to see the way you two look at each other. From the second you shook her hand at Christmas, your eyes lit the fuck up, man. And it's been scaring the hell out of you ever since."

"Please." I lifted my hand. "We're working a mission. That's what we need to focus on." That was rich, coming from me after I'd made out with my team leader's sister. "I should be the least of your concerns."

"Don't bullshit a bullshitter," he grumbled. "You may always put the mission before your own life, but there's one thing you still put above everything else, and that's the people you care about. So don't you sit there and tell me I'm not allowed to give a damn about you right back."

This was a side of Reed I rarely saw. I wasn't sure how to handle Mr. Doom and Gloom being all . . . well, whatever this was.

"Let's just regroup in the morning and act like this heart-to-heart never happened, 'k?" I stood and lifted my shirt, checking the bandage there. A memory of Audrey's hands on my skin as we kissed dropped a veil over my sight, and all I could see was her and nothing else.

"Fine, whatever you want. It's your life."

Shit. I was being such a dick. "Reed?"

He paused in the doorway.

"For what it's worth," I said in a low voice, "thanks." I flicked my wrist, lightening my tone. "Now, go text Hollis so Audrey's best friend doesn't worry."

"That woman, I can't deal with her for much longer. Drives me nuts." He rolled his eyes. "Something tells me she would, and even *could*, find us. I better look into her background tonight, make sure she checks out." He shook his head, and silence continued to stretch between us before he muttered, "Just do me one favor, okay?"

No, dammit, I'd rather talk about why Audrey's friend is annoying you. Not that it was hard to annoy that man. I did it just by breathing. "What?"

"Just remember that you don't have to be the magician anymore. You never wanted to be anyway, right?" He nodded. "Be who you really are."

I let go of my shirt, eyes shooting to the floor after he left. *And who's that?* Because at this point . . . I was starting to think maybe I had no damn clue myself.

CHAPTER TWENTY-FIVE

Alejandro

I managed to avoid Ryder and Reed the rest of the night—because I hid like a coward. Like that inner magician I just couldn't seem to shake no matter how much I tried.

I'd volunteered to patrol during the storm to avoid talking to anyone. Wound up spending half the night walking in a frozen tundra (mildly exaggerating, but I grew up in Vegas, so sue me) when there was no need to. I'd been numb to the cold, too focused on what Reed had said to me and what had happened with Audrey.

Now I was about to come face-to-face with her, and I wasn't sure if she'd even open the door when I knocked after I'd told her not to last night.

I knocked on her door like I was a salesman hoping the door wouldn't open so I wouldn't actually have to do my job. Barely a tap, then I turned, planning to tell Ryder to come up himself when he was off the phone with his mother.

I was mid-escape when the door opened.

"Thought I told you what to do if there was a knock," I muttered, swiveling back around, not prepared for the sight in front of me.

Blonde hair in a messy bun with a few loose strands that begged for me to reach forward with my hand and brush them behind her ears. Her skin was pink, as if she'd been scrubbing away evidence of tears, matching her reddish eyes.

And then there was the white sweatshirt with piano notes on it that hung off her shoulder, paired with black leggings that hugged her long legs. Bare feet and pink-painted toenails.

Basically, she was a vision I'd give anything to come home to every day after work. Minus the possibly-just-cried part.

"You okay?" I rushed out before she could tell me why she'd opened her door for me.

"Chase misses me. He's worried. We were FaceTiming."

Yeah, that'd do it. And I had no way to help fix that problem. Not yet, at least. Not until Mitch and every potential enemy were dead and buried for good.

She moved out of the way like an offer to come in, one I probably ought to refuse after what had gone down last night.

I, of course, did the opposite. At this point, it'd be more shocking if I actually heeded my own commands to stay away from her for once.

She set her back to the wall by the door and bent her knee, propping up her foot.

I caught a whiff of the perfume I'd packed now that I was in the room with her. Lancôme Idôle. I'd memorized the label, telling myself it wasn't because I planned to buy a bottle after this op so my place would smell like her. I wasn't that obsessed. Or so I kept telling myself, at least.

"Breakfast." The word came out like a rough demand as I remembered why I was up there alone with her again. "Reed's cooking. One of the few things he does well, aside from killing people. Well, that and memorizing every detail involving human history."

She began tracing the piano notes on her sweatshirt, and I followed along with every swipe of her finger as she whispered, "I thought you were here to talk about last night."

Talk? Doubtful that was possible. But I kept doing the same shit over and over again while expecting a different outcome anyway.

"Though I have a feeling you're going to tell me we should lock that up in the Never Happened box, along with seeing me naked and talking about my underwear."

"Who saw you naked?" Ryder's question, and his sudden appearance, had her shoulders startling and me damn near jumping out of my skin.

If anyone were to get the drop on me, it'd be Delta One.

"Rodriguez?"

And you last-named me. Great. I met Audrey's eyes, unsure what to say and how to save my neck here before I faced him.

"I forgot to lock my door at the lodge," she said, taking the bold and brave route of honesty. I kept forgetting that was an option since I'd been lied to so often by Beth in the past. "He thought it was his room," she continued while sidestepping me, "and I'd just been getting out of the shower. It was an accident."

"I'm sorry, what?" The disbelief in his tone felt like a mercy kill was coming. He'd make it fast and painless, but the end result would be the same.

I was a dead man walking.

"Any news yet? And all good so far with our families? Protected, yes?" Her attempt to redirect Ryder was appreciated, though I wasn't sure how effective it'd be.

"All safe," he confirmed. "But you're not about to speed by what I overheard. Naked. Underwear talk. And what's the other thing that you're supposed to forget happened?"

Ah, you know, nothing. Just the fact I almost put my face between your sister's legs. I was certain that'd go over really well if I actually spoke my thoughts out loud.

"Alex." At least he'd reverted to my first name. "Why can't you look at me? What the hell happened?"

"Nothing, seriously," Audrey whispered, her tone giving away that *everything* had almost happened.

But it didn't. And I focused on that while finally manning up and facing my best friend.

Audrey set her hand on his forearm, imploring him to turn his attention on her instead. "There's nothing between us. You need to relax and let this go."

Nothing.

Between.

Us.

Those words cut that wound of mine open again, sending me backward and over the threshold of her door.

You're not mine. Can't be. And maybe Reed hadn't correctly Freuded me. What was going on between us wasn't real.

Just two people thrown together in extraordinary circumstances, mistaking this for something more. That was more plausible than anything else. It couldn't be that I was falling for my best friend's sister. It couldn't be that I . . . well, had already fallen.

CHAPTER TWENTY-SIX

Audrey

The lie burned as it left my tongue and I freed my hold on Ryder, no longer caring about calming down the bull. Because now all I could focus on was wanting to take back what I'd said, even in front of my big brother.

Ryder circled his hand around my wrist, stopping me from joining Alex. "I need to talk to you in private."

"Which one of us?" I asked, my stomach in knots.

"You." He pierced me with those eyes that were just like mine, the same color provided by the man who'd abandoned us both. "Secretary Chandler is due to call any minute." He let me go and focused on Alex. "We'll meet you downstairs."

He didn't push Alex to talk like I'd expected, but I wasn't sure if dismissing him like that was even worse.

"Excuse me." Alex cleared his throat and made his exit.

Then I watched yet another man walk away from me.

"Inside. Door shut. Privacy needed." My brother was as good at grunting out demands as Trevor.

I decided not to challenge him, given what he'd walked in on. After heeding his orders, I dropped down on my bed, waiting for the full impact of the lecture I felt coming. "Please don't be mad at Alex."

His shoulders slumped, the opposite reaction I'd been anticipating. "I'm not mad at him. I'm worried about him. And you." He slowly walked over and dropped down next to me, the bed shifting under his weight. "I've known you were my sister for a few months, but that man's been my brother for fifteen years, and he has the biggest heart of anyone I've ever met." He glanced at me, half smiling. "Well, now that I'm getting to know you more, probably tied with you in that department."

Was he waving the white flag here? Giving us the green light? Not that we had plans to actually go anywhere and explore this obvious thing between us. We both had quite the baggage at our feet. "What are you trying to say?"

He hung his head, resting his elbows on his legs. "That I feel stuck in the middle."

I set my hand on his back. "That's the last place I want you to be."

"I'm supposed to protect you from getting hurt, but I also have a duty to protect him." He kept his gaze shielded from me. "You've both been through a lot. I don't want either of you . . . You know?"

I filled in the dots. Not hard to do. "You don't want to see us hurt." I was on the same dog-eared (okay, *bookmarked*) page. "I've had two failed marriages. I was adamant I'd never let myself feel anything for anyone ever again. You should see the number of texts I said exactly that to Hollis in the last year." My mom, too, before I'd found out my life had been a lie.

"And now? Do you feel like it's possible again?" He glanced at me without lifting his head.

"I honestly don't know. I never expected fantasy to become reality." I cringed at the realization of what had just come out of my mouth. I let go of his back to cover my face in embarrassment. "Anyway." Doubted that awkward-killer word would work right now. "All I know is, we seem to understand each other. Maybe we have a connection because we know what it's like to survive betrayal."

"And how long have you two been in the same boat?"

At least he didn't press on my fantasy remark. But was that him asking if we'd hooked up? "My boat is sinking. There's a hole in it. Ship's going down." My hands returned to my lap, and I stared at my ring finger, which had been bare ever since the morning Mitch deployed, the last time I saw him. "As for his boat? I don't know. You'd have to ask him."

Talk about taking the long way to not actually answer his question. I hoped he wouldn't notice.

"I have no idea what you're talking about."

Neither. Do. I.

"I take it that means you two haven't actually . . ."

"You could just ask me instead of letting me roam into vague boat metaphors."

He lifted his head, cracking a small smile, and it was good to see. "I'd rather not ask my sister, who I've only known since Christmas, if she's sleeping with my best friend." He covered his eyes as if realizing he'd kind of just gone there anyway. "Guessing it's a no, though, based on the conversation I accidentally stepped into."

"It's a no," I confirmed. "Very innocent. Like, first-base territory." Though had the man asked me to get naked and on the bed for him last night, I would have *Yes, sir*'d the heck out of him, easily forgetting where we were and why, just to have one perfect night with him, one free of pain and both our pasts.

"I prefer hockey references," he said with a half smile.

"Okay, okay. No goals made. We only kissed." *And I nearly had an orgasm from rubbing myself against his erection while we kissed.* Points for keeping that to myself. "Please don't kill him. Or me."

He shook his head, sitting up taller, not yet giving me his eyes. "I'm pretty sure it's not my place to tell you what you can or can't do with your life. As much as I'd love to step in for our asshole father and protect you like that, I know I shouldn't."

I put my hand on his shoulder. "You're doing a great job at being an overprotective big brother, which is all I both want and need."

"And are brothers allowed to tell their younger sisters what to do?" His gaze slipped my way, and he smirked.

"Yes, and it's my duty to not listen and do the opposite."

He laughed, and some of the tension seemed to lift off into the ether along with the sound. "I love ya, Audrey. You know I do, right?"

"And I love you." It occurred to me that it was the first time I'd told him that, and based on the grin on his face, he'd enjoyed hearing it. With my hand off his shoulder, I nudged him in the side. "But if you could tell me what to do, and I'd actually listen, what would you say?"

He lifted his eyes to the ceiling. Cue change in the air and mood. *Shit.*

"Alex's ship isn't sinking—it's already at the bottom of the ocean. That's what I'd tell you. And I don't know if he can ever resurface." He peered at me again. "Sorry, I went back to the boat thing. Not sure I made sense, either."

"You did. And I think you should know that Alex came up for air last night. It felt that way, at least. And I'm pretty sure I did, too."

"Which means?"

"There's hope?" I shrugged. "I think?" Maybe. I had no clue. First, I had to repair whatever damage I felt I'd done with my "nothing between us" comment, which had come out of my mouth like a bad reflex.

"I can't handle your heart getting broken after what you've been through, and I can't watch him get hurt after what he's dealt with, either." He stood. "Just promise me you'll take things slow." He rested his hands on his hips. "Please don't do the opposite because I said that," he added with a small smile.

Before I had a chance to respond, even though I was unsure what I planned to say, Reed called out from somewhere, "The secretary's on the line."

"Coming." Ryder offered me a hand to stand. "You ready for this?"

"Talk to the secretary of defense about why my husband is back from the dead? Not to mention, he tried to recruit Trevor to work for him? Sure, no problem. An absolute walk in the park after this awkward conversation with you."

His expression turned glum. "I forgot to ask you how you're handling that news about Trevor."

How *was* I handling it? Clearly not well. "Not sure what to think about it, to be honest. I feel bad that he turned down what sounds like a dream job for an operator because of me." Maybe I'd lied to my brother and my ship wasn't sinking. It was already at the bottom of the ocean, alongside Alex's.

"Do you think Trevor wants to get back together?" He frowned. "Better question for me to ask is if *you* do."

"I'll always love him, but not in a romantic way. Maybe I was too young when we met. We rushed into things, and I don't know . . ." I forgot he didn't know my backstory yet. "I'm not a bad person for not wanting to get back together with him, even though Chase could have—"

"Chase needs his mom happy, that's what he needs." He pulled me in for a quick hug as Reed called out again.

"Yeah, yeah, we're coming," Ryder hollered, releasing me from his comforting bear hug. "Let's get this over with."

I followed him out of the bedroom and down the stairs, hating the fact I wouldn't have a chance to clear the air with Alex before the call.

I wasn't sure what I planned to say other than to apologize, but that felt like the best place to start. *I just need to get through a secure call with everyone first and pretend like there isn't a war going on inside me.*

When we entered the den at the backside of the cabin, Secretary Chandler's face was already being broadcast on the TV screen. I barely acknowledged him, my attention shooting straight to Alex.

Alex was standing off to the side of the room with his back to the wall, one hand loose at his side, the other resting over his heart.

Two wounds. I felt responsible for both.

"What can you tell us?" Ryder's voice cut through the fog in my head, snapping me back to why we were there, and I took a seat on the couch, folding my legs underneath me.

"Before I say anything, open your email and have Audrey electronically sign the NDA. What I'm about to share can't leave this room, and she doesn't have classified status." Secretary Chandler motioned to Ryder's laptop sitting on the coffee table with a sense of urgency. "My daughter told me she already shared a little too much in her presence as it is."

Yeah, like about Trevor.

Ryder quickly followed orders, handing me the computer. I didn't bother to even skim-read, but I did catch a word or two while scrolling to the place to sign. You know, like *prison* and *treason*, so that was great.

Ryder took the laptop from me once I'd basically signed my life away and returned it to the coffee table. "It's done. Now, please, explain everything."

Chandler put on his glasses and leaned forward as if verifying he now owned my life; then he removed them and sat back in his leather chair. "Mitch reached out to JSOC last year in January, demanding he speak to me. He said he had sensitive information provided by a credible source that'd do serious damage if it got out."

I was going to be sick.

"Mitch thought I'd help, given his connection to Audrey and Trevor's ties with my family. He may have also known I knew Trevor for even longer than that. Mitch wouldn't share anything until I had him protected. And by *protected*, I mean faked his death. He believed he'd be killed, along with anyone he loved, if word got out that he was handing over the intel he had to us."

My hand instinctively lifted to my cheek, haunted by the memory of that "love." My thumb slid across my lower lip, tracing where Mitch had once split it open.

"'Love,' my ass," Ryder hissed, resting a protective hand on top of mine as if remembering what I'd shared with him yesterday. "Only loves himself."

Chandler let the tension sit for a moment before continuing. "I told him the US government's not in the business of faking deaths." He worked at the knot of his tie next, then slipped it off and set it on top of his glasses.

"But he manipulated you into agreeing, right?" I took a guess, and from his nod, I was clearly right.

"Mitch threatened to upload everything he had online if we didn't cooperate. And to prove he wasn't bluffing, he showed me a video of something that'd be damning if it were ever to see the light of day. He also said good men had been wrongly branded as traitors."

"Like Arlo?" Alex asked, and now the dots were starting to connect. "Was he his source?"

Well, I thought they were starting to connect. I was still in a bit of a daze.

"I'm familiar with that name, but not because Mitch shared it. He never had a chance to give me any names, because he was killed on the way to the safe house."

"What the hell did Mitch drag my sister into?"

"Stratos," Chandler replied as if that was supposed to mean something. "When I said we're not in the business of faking deaths . . . I meant not anymore." He slowly looked around the room, landing lastly on my brother. "But the government used to be."

CHAPTER TWENTY-SEVEN

Audrey

After Chandler's revelation, Alex took an immediate step closer to the screen. "What are you saying?"

Chandler let a quiet moment pass. "Before you guys joined us—and before private SEAL teams existed—there was Stratos."

"Stratos?" Reed echoed. "Greek for *army* or *multitude*. Represents unity and power."

Chandler stood, the tan, aged skin on his forehead creasing even more. "There have been clandestine units operating without congressional approval or knowledge since as far back as the Cold War era. Different programs. Different motives. Always changing under different presidents. Rydell and Bennett are the only two to ever see eye to eye and pass the baton instead of burying it."

"We're clearly aware of that," Ryder acknowledged, "given what my team does now. But we didn't know these kinds of teams went back that far."

"Stratos was created in response to the attacks on September 11. A unit composed of what they called ghost operatives. Men willing to have their identities erased. Men without family that could put country over self." He stared down at the desk, shoulders hunched forward. "They handled the dirtiest and most sensitive missions. Ones no one wanted their fingerprints on. That's what I was told, at least. They had the perfect cover stories and airtight alibis, because as far as the world was concerned, they either didn't exist, or they were—"

"Dead," I whispered, my stomach no longer sick but free-falling.

Chandler slowly looked up without meeting anyone's eyes. "President Rydell wanted nothing to do with the unit. He had it shut down when he was inaugurated in 2013, then started up his own teams. Bravo, Echo, and now Charlie Team." Chandler lifted his chin, eyes on Ryder. "Now President Bennett has brought Delta Shield in as well. But you're the only groups, outside of the help we get from Falcon Falls Security here and there, that works these types of off-grid ops now."

"Are you saying Mitch found out somehow that Stratos used to exist, and he was looking to expose a unit that had already been terminated?" Ryder asked him.

"No." Chandler closed his eyes. "What I'm saying is, Mitch discovered Stratos was resurrected from the dead, and without President Bennett's knowledge." Eyes open, he continued, "Mitch said he had files about the original program, as well as intel on the reboot of Stratos and who's behind it. He promised he'd turn over the evidence once he was secure in the safe house. Only he never had a chance."

"Was it a drone strike that took out his vehicle? Bodies so burned you couldn't even identify his remains?" Ryder guessed.

"Yes, but there was DNA evidence," Chandler confirmed. "Though I suppose it could've been faked somehow."

"And the key Audrey unknowingly had in her possession unlocks some type of safe or vault that holds the evidence he has on Stratos?" Ryder continued.

Right in front of me all that time.

"Mitch knew when you faked his death in the crash, his wedding band would be returned to Audrey with his personal effects," Reed pointed out. "It was a calculated move, and from the sounds of it, he had no intention of turning anything over to you."

"That means Audrey's not just Mitch's target," my brother began while rising. "She's become a liability to whoever's currently running Stratos, since by now, if we know he's alive, they must know, too."

"Why wait until now, though?" I shook my hands out at my sides, joining Ryder on his feet. "Why not come for the key sooner? Why wait so long?"

Ryder turned to face me, a muscle in his jaw twitching as he shared, "Self-preservation. The second he came after you, he knew he'd signal to the world—to both Stratos and the government—that he wasn't dead. That makes *him* a target, not just you."

"If Mitch is truly alive and behind what's going on, he needed someone on the outside to help him escape the transport vehicle to the safe house," Alex said, his attention on Chandler for answers.

"We'd assumed there'd been a leak inside JSOC, someone with ties to whoever started up Stratos again, and they wanted Mitch and the evidence buried. But we couldn't find the source despite only a handful of people knowing the location. So we believed it was a cyber breach, not a human one." Chandler dropped back into his seat like the weight of this was too heavy. "We clearly never caught who was behind it."

"We need everything you've got on Stratos. Including files on anyone who knew your plans with Mitch to fake his death and take him to the safe house," Ryder began, voice deep and authoritative despite who he was speaking to. "If you want us to find a ghost, we can't be working with guesses. And the files Gwen gave to Gray to send us might as well have been pages from a coloring book. Too much was blacked out. We need the unredacted versions on everything and everyone."

"I can do some of that. But unfortunately, there's nothing on Stratos to give you. Everything was scrubbed from existence the second President Rydell declined continuing with the unit."

"Why?" I couldn't help but ask—probably the only one who wouldn't get it right away, since I'd never served.

"To protect the current president from what the former one did. He kept his hands clean of Stratos by not knowing anything about it." He drew his hands together, tapping his fingers against his lips. "All information, along with their missions, was destroyed. One former Stratos team leader who'd been in charge of ops, but not an operator himself, was tasked with shutting it all down and assigning the men new identities and relocation packages."

"The president back then . . . he died two years ago," Ryder said after exhaling a frustrated breath. "What about the guy who was responsible for ending it all? Can he help? Or is he possibly a problem for us, too? He had access to everything, so maybe he—"

"He's also dead. No help to us now." Chandler quickly shut down Ryder's hope with that answer.

"And when did this new unit start up, according to Mitch?" *That's assuming we actually trust what he said.*

"Four years ago." Chandler dropped his hands to his lap as he added, "I had my best people, including my daughter, dig into everything after he was killed, but all roads were dead ends."

"Because the only two people who knew what happened were literally dead," I said in understanding. "Or fake-dead, and you didn't have their names to track them down to question."

"Precisely," he confirmed.

Reed spoke up. "The man who helped shut down Stratos . . . President Rydell clearly knew who he was since you do, and he must've trusted him. But given the fact we have a problem with dead men not being dead lately, you sure he is? If anyone would know how to fake his death, it'd be him."

"No, he's dead. And unfortunately, he betrayed President Rydell's trust in 2018 and wound up in the same kind of CIA black site prison Beth's in now," he answered while shooting a quick glance Alex's way. He paused and took a breath, then continued: "That man helped Rydell launch Bravo and Echo Teams. He practically wrote the handbook on the units, promising him he'd apply what he knew from Stratos to prevent the same mistakes being made."

"I'm sorry, *what*?" Ryder circled the coffee table to stand closer to the screen like he might reach out and grab the man's tie, then use it to strangle someone.

I had a few ideas who'd make a great target. Mitch. Beth. Rhett. To name a few.

"Who was he?" my brother snapped when Chandler remained eerily quiet.

"Will Hobbs, alongside Bravo One's sister, helped recruit Bravo One; then Will became a liaison for Bravo and Echo for five years before Bravo found out Will was a traitor."

"You're telling me this former Stratos guy was one of the architects behind the president's teams, and he's a traitor, and he's also dead?" Ryder hissed, hands clenching at his sides. Ready for war.

"It gets worse," Alex rasped, and I looked over at him as that bad feeling in my gut intensified. "Will Hobbs was a good friend of Beth's."

CHAPTER TWENTY-EIGHT

Audrey

I replayed Alex's words, realizing this man was only at the bottom of the ocean, ship sunk, because his ex was anchoring him there the way Mitch was trying to drag me down, too.

"Beth knew Will Hobbs?" Reed cut through my thoughts, moving toward Alex as if he might physically remove the words from Alex's mouth, forcing him to take them back. "Please tell me you're joking."

"I wish I was." Alex stole a quick look around Reed at me before continuing, "Beth used to work with him. They were friends. He was almost fifteen years older than her, and she told me he was more of a mentor-type figure, but I started questioning if they were having an affair." Those words came across as painful and bitter to hear as they had to have been to say. "Then, in 2018, Will went off the grid, and Beth never mentioned him again. It was like he'd become—well, like a ghost." He peered at Chandler, probably waiting for him to shoot down that idea.

"Although Will went by the Ghost back in his SEAL days," Chandler finally said, "he never became one himself. Or a ghost operative for Stratos—just their liaison. He betrayed our country and was placed in a CIA black site prison in 2018, but now he's dead. I confirmed with my own eyes that fact in 2022. And when Echo Team puts a man down, he doesn't get back up."

"I'm guessing his death had nothing to do with Stratos and their revival, or you'd have led with that," Ryder remarked.

"No, and believe me, after Mitch's transport was hit on the way to the safe house, I dug deep into Hobbs's past to ensure it didn't, considering we found out in 2018 Hobbs was being blackmailed." Chandler reached for his tie on his desk and began wrapping it around his hands, staring at it, not us. "And if Hobbs had any secret files hidden about Stratos or our current teams, we never recovered them."

"What about Bravo One's sister? Could she be of help?" Alex asked. "If she worked with Will Hobbs, maybe she can shed some light on—"

"She didn't know anything about Stratos. She wasn't *allowed* to know details about the previous program, or that one even existed. Per President Rydell's orders. It was safer that way. I still talked to her after Mitch alerted me to the fact Stratos was active again. Hell, I spoke with everyone on the president's SEAL teams. Nothing useful. First they'd heard that name."

"Well, Mitch obviously knows something we don't, and he's still alive to share it. And we have half the key to unlocking whatever evidence he must have on Stratos," Reed pointed out.

"This whole thing reminds me of what happened nine years ago, when Bravo Team found out Hobbs was a traitor the first time." Chandler tossed his tie, shaking his head. "Hobbs's fingerprints feel all over this, but I don't know how that's possible. I thought we were done with him."

"Well, whoever's working with Mitch now must have known Hobbs back when Stratos was first operational. Could be Rhett. Arlo, if he's not really dead, too. Anyone in plain sight, even," Reed said. "All I know for certain is, we need to get to Mitch before whoever's running Stratos 2.0 does. We're both after him now."

"And you have one part of the key, and Mitch now has the other, which means Mitch needs you as much as you need him." Not the most encouraging words from the secretary of defense.

"If Rhett was part of the OG Stratos, then why work with Mitch now? Why come out of hiding as a fisherman in the Maldives?" Alex asked. "Money really the motivator?"

"We'll figure it out, and I'll have my granddaughter go over all the files. She was working something else pretty big last year when this was going down, so we didn't pull her in," Chandler said. "If we missed something, she'll find it." He focused on me next. "In the meantime, the priority is keeping Audrey and that second key from getting into the wrong hands." He didn't bother to say goodbye. The screen simply went black.

"Well, shit," Reed muttered.

You could say that again. "I think I aged ten years from that call," I muttered under my breath.

"Well, you look good for forty-three." Ryder gave me a hesitant smile, clearly trying to lighten the mood. "Are you, uh, okay, though?" He reached for my arm. "You actually look a little pale now that I'm—"

"I do feel lightheaded," I admitted.

"Why don't you get a bite to eat? You didn't have breakfast yet." Ryder gestured with his head toward Reed. "Will you take her to the kitchen and make sure she's taken care of?"

Reed stepped around Ryder and offered his arm, clearly worried I couldn't walk without help.

"It's going to be okay," Ryder reassured me as I remained frozen, stuck there in shock at everything I'd learned.

I wanted to believe him. To cling to his words as fact, not just hopeful sentiment. But from the sounds of it, Mitch had sucked us deep into hell. And last I checked, no one ever made it out of there alive.

CHAPTER TWENTY-NINE

Alejandro

Ryder rested his hands on the back of the couch, letting go of a steady breath, and I felt something coming. Something I didn't want to hear. "There's something we need to consider doing."

My blood went cold, and I clenched my back teeth as I waited for the wound at my side to be peeled open again. "I'm not talking to her. I can't."

"Doesn't have to be you, but right now, we have one close lead tied to Stratos. And while Will Hobbs may be dead, Beth's not." Ryder circled the couch to confront me head-on. "If she was close to him, maybe he told her something he shouldn't have?"

I tore my hands through my hair, doing my best not to spin out. "I'd rather talk about the conversation you overheard upstairs than discuss my ex." Totally normal morning. Nothing weird at all about any of this.

"You want to talk about *that*?"

My hands landed at my sides like two grenades, pins pulled. "Pick your poison. But one woman makes me want to jump from a cliff, and the other one makes me feel like I already fell." *Shit.*

Ryder lifted his hands, nostrils flaring. Anger or concern? I wasn't in the best state of mind to get a good read on my team leader. "Which woman is which?"

Forget grenades in hand—*I* was the ticking time bomb. Ready to go off. "Ignore me."

Ryder gripped the front of his neck and rotated his head. At least he wasn't wrapping a hand around my throat.

"What about Beth's stuff?" I forced out as a memory punched through me. "I have a few boxes in a storage unit in DC. Stuff the government gave me of hers after she was locked up since she has no living family. I said I didn't want it, that I was her ex, but they made me take it anyway."

"You think there could be something in there that might help? Notes? Calendar and shit like that?" Ryder adjusted course back to where I needed him to be. You know, out of my head and not talking about my feelings.

"Maybe?" I shrugged. "I don't know. It's stuff I should've just burned." Including our wedding album. Our life together had somehow fit into one box, and the things the government had forced me to take fit into the other two.

"I'll ask Natasha to send someone to your storage unit and go through everything. We may have more luck with those boxes than talking to her."

I rattled off the information for my storage unit and then demanded, "If it comes to talking to Beth, though, let me make myself crystal-fucking-clear: no immunity deal."

"Trust me when I tell you that I'd never let that woman go free. You have my word."

"Good. Glad to hear," I grunted.

Eyes on his phone, he shared, "Just got a text from the Secret Service, checking in to let me know all is still good on the home front. Our families are secure."

Thank God for that. "Audrey's mom know she has eyes on her?"

"No, Audrey doesn't want her to know anything. Guess she takes after Trevor there, thinking it's safer for her to be in the dark. But she also mentioned to me on the drive here yesterday that she's barely spoken to her mom since Thanksgiving, so her silence might be for other reasons."

He needed to wipe that guilty look from his face pronto.

"Thirty-three years growing up thinking one thing, only to find out another . . . Plus, she missed out on having you as her brother all that time. I can't say I blame her."

"I'm not her mom's greatest fan, since she knew my dad was married when she hooked up with my old man, but at least Audrey didn't have to feel abandoned her whole life the way I did most of mine." He blinked a few times as if shocked he'd made that confession to anyone other than the woman he loved. "Anyway," he said after an awkward throat clear.

I'd never be able to hear that word and not think of Audrey now.

"I should call Trevor soon and fill him in on what we learned," he continued. "I'm sure Chandler's already sent him an NDA to sign."

"You think Trevor knew Will Hobbs? They were both team guys."

"It's possible. But Trevor's, what, forty? So there's a fifteen-year-or-so age difference between them, so maybe not. Will would've already been deep in Stratos territory when Trevor was only just getting started twenty years ago."

"I think I'd rather him not know Will and risk losing a lead." From the sounds of it, that man had been through enough. Last thing he needed was to have that asshole caught up in his past, too.

"I feel the same." He rested his hand on his chest. "And speaking of my sister . . ."

"You mean speaking of your sister's ex?" I grumbled, not liking where he was planning to about-face this conversation. When he didn't say anything, I couldn't help but blurt out, "I know you'd like to kill me, but we've already got enough bodies on our hands." The hoarse laugh that followed was out of self-preservation. "I'll stay away from her. I hear you. Loud and clear."

He quietly eyed me, assessing me like he was about to negotiate with a terrorist who'd hijacked a plane. "I don't know how I missed this before, this thing between you two, but I think Seraphina picked up on it the second you met."

Not the direction I'd expected him to go.

"I don't want you getting hurt."

I scoffed. "You think *she'll* hurt *me*?" I waved him off with a quiet *never mind* embedded in that gesture, hating that I was actually afraid of that very thing. "And who knows, maybe she'll get back together with Trevor."

I was hoping he'd shut down that possibility, but instead, he started his sentence in a way that didn't bode well for me having a future with Audrey. "Just promise me something." That long pause after, nope, not good, either. "Maybe hold off on—" He let his words die when an incoming call popped up on the TV, which was still synced to his laptop.

I'd never been so grateful for an interruption.

"We'll finish this later." He turned his attention on the laptop and accepted the call. "Hey, what's up?" he asked Natasha as her face appeared on the TV.

"Gwen's joining the call, too. One second. She's currently in Switzerland, but we've got a few ideas on how to expedite the search through the files. Gwen also had a question about the ring. Where's Reed?"

"In the kitchen. I can go get him," I offered, hiking a thumb over my shoulder.

"Either bring Audrey in here to eat or keep an eye on her in there." Ryder turned toward me. "Will you?"

Shit. "Yeah," I huffed out. "Sure." I made my way down the hall and hung back outside the kitchen at the sound of Audrey's sultry voice.

"Oh my gosh, this has to be the best thing I've put in my mouth in a long time." The light moan coming from her was going to send my blood pressure through the roof.

And now I was remembering the sounds she'd made while we kissed last night.

Reed laughed, which was unusual for him.

"What's so funny?" She paused. "Ohhh. You boys and your dirty minds. Just say it, you know you want to."

She gave Reed a chance.

Not too shockingly, he didn't take it.

"That's what she said," she joked, probably using air quotes as well.

I took a breath and a beat, then let her words from earlier—*There's nothing between us*—haunt me before rounding the corner.

Reed was sitting alongside Audrey at the breakfast bar, and he stood the second he spotted me.

"Natasha and Gwen need you," I let him know, doing my best not to look at the most beautiful woman in the world sitting there. "They probably need that big brain of yours for something."

A sly smile slipped across his lips.

"Mind if I stay in here? My brain could use a break from all that op stuff." At Audrey's tentative tone, I finally gave in and looked at her.

"Sure, but your brother doesn't want you alone, so I guess I'll be staying with you." *Just my luck.*

Reed came over, then gestured toward the hall with his head. "I have to borrow him. One second," he told Audrey without glancing back.

"Don't start with me," I said under my breath while following him out of her line of sight.

"I'm not going to press you about *her*." Reed set his back to the hallway wall. "More like the other 'her.'"

"Not interested in discussing either. Did that with Ryder already; I'm good." I started for the kitchen, but Reed grabbed hold of my shoulder, stopping me.

"Do you have any of Beth's belongings? I was thinking—"

"Already on it," I cut him off.

Time to open the boxes I thought would remain untouched. At least I wasn't going to be the one to do it. Audrey had more courage in that department than I did.

"Just go help Natasha and Gwen. I could use a brain break myself."

"Maybe eat something, too." He freed my arm. "How's your wound, by the way?"

"It's still there. Now, go. Don't worry about me." I rolled my shoulders back, drew in a deep breath, then entered the kitchen to confront the greatest obstacle I'd ever faced when it came to my sense of control.

"Now that it's just us . . ." She sighed. "I think it's time we talk."

CHAPTER THIRTY

Alejandro

Audrey slid her half-empty plate aside and brought her hands to her lap. "Your ex. Mine." Her gaze slowly lifted to meet my eyes. "Your past. Mine."

I kept my distance. Stayed on the other side of the kitchen, arms over my chest, back to the wall. Doing my best to switch from fire to ice in my veins.

"It's all one big mess, isn't it? And our lives feel entangled, too."

When she worked her bottom lip to the side of her mouth, catching it with her teeth, I made a mistake. I pushed away from the wall and took a step closer. Just the one.

"Are you okay? That call was heavy." Was she really asking *me* that? "Especially after the Ryder thing upstairs. Then the mention of your ex."

Those words sent my ass back that one step I'd taken. "No clue what you're talking about."

She let go of a deep breath and did something I wished she hadn't. She stood, circled the breakfast bar, and approached me.

I locked my hands into fists at my sides so I wouldn't reach for her, but at the thought of that son of a bitch hitting her in the past, I quickly unfurled my fingers. I needed to let her know I wasn't him and would never lay a hand on her.

"Audrey . . ."

"If I'm not allowed to say your name like that, then you don't get to say mine." Her chin tipped defiantly, but her lashes fluttered as she looked up at me, her voice softer now. "Fair is fair."

"Nothing about these last few days has been fair."

"Can't argue with you there." Her fingers drifted to the hem of my shirt. "When did you last change this bandage?"

"Before your brother found out I've seen his sister naked." The truth spilled too easily around her. If I wasn't already backed against a wall, I might've stumbled from the weight of it. "I'm good." I caught her hand, guiding the fabric back down over my skin.

She frowned and dropped my shirt. Only she didn't step away.

She stood there—still too close, too beautiful. Her scent wrapped around me, and with it came every memory of where my mouth had been the night before. Where my hands had wandered.

"About what I said upstairs—" Her voice caught, a small sound of frustration escaping her lips. "You know I was only trying to protect you from Ryder, right?"

"No idea what you're talking about." That tired line had to be worn to the bone by now.

Her hand brushed up under my shirt again, gentle and deliberate. She didn't stop until she reached my chest, resting her palm over my heart. "The only thing keeping me grounded right now is you. Your calm. Your presence."

There was nothing calming about her to me. She lit every fuse I had. Made my skin feel too tight. Made me ache to touch, to hold, to lose myself in her.

"Audrey," I warned again.

"Alejandro." She breathed out my name, and damn if it didn't undo me. "Talk to me."

I couldn't. Not without giving too much away. Like the fact I'd been drawn to her since the moment we met at Christmas.

She closed her eyes and kept her hand over my chest, as if she could will my heart back to life. "Come back up. Be here with me. Don't stay buried down there."

I knew what she meant. Drowning wasn't always physical. Sometimes it was silence. Memory. Guilt. And I hated that she understood that kind of pain.

"I can't talk about it. Not yet. I just need . . . *time*." I waited for her eyes to return to mine. "Play something for me instead?"

Her hand slipped away, sliding down my stomach, before it hit her side. And I could breathe again. Just barely.

"You want me to play the piano for you?"

I nodded, and she stared at me a moment longer before nodding, too. Maybe we both understood this was the only way forward right now?

I followed her down the hall to the small area where the piano waited. She moved to the instrument like it was an extension of her, then ran her fingers over the sleek black surface before sitting.

I circled to the other side so I could see her face as she played.

She touched a single key, then another. A fractured chord echoed, then softened into something raw and beautiful. Her spine straightened, her breath slowing as she lost herself in the music. And I lost myself in her.

She played like she was bleeding emotion through her fingertips. Every note hit something inside me.

When she stopped, I stepped forward, bracing my hands on the edge of the piano, begging, "Again." The word came out hoarse, broken, and as desperate as I felt.

Her eyes lifted to mine.

Hers shimmered.

Mine burned.

I nearly said it—*What are you doing to me?*—but she seemed to already know.

She began again without a word, and I moved around the piano, needing to be closer.

I watched her fingers dance across the keys, felt something inside me shift. And then I set my hand over hers, stilling her movement.

She froze and slowly turned her head to look at me.

"Stand," I said, voice gravelly as I slid my hand to her wrist, gently tugging her up.

The bench scraped back as she rose. I guided her to the side of the piano and lifted her onto it. Her arms wrapped around my neck, and I stepped between her legs, hands planting firmly at her sides. Anchoring myself as she tightened her thighs around me.

And then I kissed her. It wasn't soft or questioning. It was everything I'd held back last night. Every pent-up feeling I hadn't voiced.

I groaned and pushed my hands beneath her sweatshirt, searching for skin.

"Please," she whispered, and that was all it took for me to devour her again.

One hand skimmed up her back. The other slipped beneath her bra, found her breast. Her nipple hardened under my palm.

Our mouths clashed, and her hips moved against me, chasing friction.

I broke the kiss just long enough to find her eyes. "*Now* . . . tell me again how there's nothing between us."

CHAPTER THIRTY-ONE

Audrey

"I lied," I whispered. "I don't just feel something. I feel *everything*." The most honest words I'd said in years. Raw and unfiltered.

Now I had to wait for him to react. To show me he heard me.

He didn't speak. Just stared at me like he was seeing through every wall I'd ever built—like he recognized the fear in my honesty because he carried the same fear.

The air was thick from what he didn't say, and then he swallowed.

And just like that, the tension shattered.

His mouth covered mine, taking hold of my bottom lip. No hesitation and no holding back.

"Panties," he growled. "What color lace?" He pulled back, eyes fierce and burning with lust.

I found the strength to be bold. To not back down and hide inside a shell of shyness. "Why don't you find out for yourself?"

His brows drew tight, chest rising sharply. He murmured something in Spanish that slid like velvet down my spine.

"There's no lock," he said with a wicked glint in his eyes.

"There's no door." And I didn't care. I hadn't felt this free since the last time I performed onstage.

"Problem is . . ." He leaned in, lips grazing my jaw. "I don't want to just look."

"So tell me. What do you want?" I needed him to say it, to let his words crawl over my skin and burrow deep.

He slid the back of his hand down my arm, slow and reverent. "I want to touch you. Taste you. Make you feel *everything*." His mouth brushed my ear. "I want you to know how much I . . ."

How much you what? I threaded my fingers through his hair and whispered, "Be reckless with me. Just for a minute." I lightened my tone, teasing, "No door. No lock. No problem."

His breathy laugh tickled the side of my neck. "That minute worth getting caught?"

"No." I swallowed. "Yes?"

He leaned back, studying me like he was strategizing the best way to make me come without losing his mind.

His gaze raked down my body, his thumb a gentle whisper across my bottom lip. "You need to get off."

"I know," I said with a laugh.

He grinned. "No, I mean off the piano."

"Ohhh." I slid down from the Yamaha and landed straight into his arms.

"This is risky. You sure?"

"I need you touching me more than I need anything right now," I admitted. "And there's no one I'd rather risk it with."

He nodded. "I'm going to lower your pants now. That okay?"

"Yes, please."

He peeled my leggings to my thighs, then stepped back like he needed space just to look.

I lifted my sweatshirt, blocking his view. *"Rosa."* A shy smile hit my lips. "I still remember my colors."

His jaw flexed, gaze burning through me. "There's one part of you I haven't had the pleasure of seeing yet." Then came the order: "Turn around. Arms on the piano. Bend over."

My sweet guy had left the cabin. And I was here for it.

I obeyed. Piano in front of me, my ass on display.

The moment his hands landed on my flesh, I flinched from sheer anticipation.

"Perfect." He squeezed my ass cheeks. "I'm going to put my hands between your legs now. Okay?"

"Alex?"

"No," he said, pressing his erection against my ass. "Alejandro from now on."

Well then. "Alejandro." I sighed. "You have my blanket permission. Anything. Everything."

He groaned, fingertips digging into my sides.

"And while I usually don't take orders . . ." I bit my lip. "I want you to boss me around."

His hand slid over the curve of my ass, down between my thighs.

"I think I can manage." His breath was hot against my ear as his fingers moved under the lace.

My knees buckled. My fists clenched against the piano.

"You're soaked." A mix of Spanish and English came from him next as heat flooded through me.

He pumped his fingers in and out with perfect control.

And everything else disappeared.

The mission. The betrayal and chaos. It was just him. Just me. Just *us*.

"Come for me." His voice, commanding and deep, dragged me over the edge.

I ground back on his hand, chasing every ounce of pleasure.

"That's my girl."

He withdrew his fingers and gently fixed my leggings, all before I could blink. He spun me around and lifted me back onto the piano.

His hand, smelling like sex, cupped my jaw as he kissed me like a man possessed.

Yeah. We'd just done *that.* On a piano. With no lock. No door. And my brother and Reed down the hall.

"We need you."

Speaking of . . .

At Ryder's bad timing, I went still. "Aw, shit."

Alejandro backed away from me, and I jumped off the piano, trying to shield him with my body as he worked to down-boy his hard-on.

"Hi, what's up?" I faked casual, crossing my arms once I'd turned toward my brother.

Ryder shook his head, cursing under his breath without making eye contact. "Thirty seconds. Then the den." He left as quickly as he'd interrupted.

"Think a casual 'anyway' would have worked on him?" I teased, trying to relieve some of the tension. "I know. Crappy joke. But at least he came in after you'd removed your hand from between my legs."

Alex squeezed his eyes closed while adjusting himself. He was probably internally swearing, blaming himself for losing control.

"Should we talk about what happened before we join them?" he asked once he'd fixed his attention back on me.

"Mm. I think that conversation involves more than thirty seconds." I pointed to his crotch. "So, um, does it always take you that long to . . ."

"You really are dangerous," he whispered, then hit me with a much-needed smile. "And no, this is an all-your-fault problem."

"I kind of like being the cause of that problem." I set my hand on his chest, finding his heart beating strong and steady.

"I bet you do." He murmured something in Spanish that sounded entirely too sexy when we needed to wrap this up. "Well," he said while leaning in, dropping his forehead against mine, "just so you know, when we do have time for that talk, I'll be ready for it. No disappearing on you. We're in this together."

"Together and now in the same boat, from where I'm standing." I worked my lip between my teeth, my emotions suddenly all over the place as the reality of what happened between us kicked in. "I don't know if we're still at the bottom . . . or making our way back to the top."

CHAPTER THIRTY-TWO

Alejandro

Eyes on my reflection, I stared into the mirror while washing the sweet smell of that woman from my hand.

How'd I let things go that far, risking Ryder walking in on us like he wound up doing?

I clearly couldn't think straight when it came to her, as already established a few times back at the lodge. And what happened today was also the first time in a long damn time where I'd put my feelings above a mission. Also something I rarely did.

The problem? She was my mission. The priority had to be keeping her safe. *Not* exploring this thing between us.

Dangerous, all right.

There were half a dozen reasons why I needed to behave and focus up.

And none of them had mattered the second she asked me to take a look at her panties and touch her.

I turned off the water and dried my hands before slamming them onto the counter, shaking my head, needing to get a grip before I faced everyone.

It took me five minutes beyond the allotted thirty seconds Ryder had given me to get my ass to the den.

The TV screen glowed with overlapping data streams when I joined everyone.

Audrey was situated on the couch, and Ryder was on a knee in front of the laptop by the coffee table, an unreadable expression crossing his face when our eyes locked.

Yeah, I deserved a lot more than that look. And now I couldn't remember if I'd had a chance to finish that promise I'd planned to make to him to stay away from Audrey. The morning had been a blur of lips, heat, pink lace, and now guilt.

Ryder stood when Gwen and Natasha appeared on the screen, and I was all for a distraction so I wouldn't have to deal with any tension with my team leader.

Audrey was right. We couldn't "anyway" our way through this when it came to what he'd walked in on. I was still reeling as it was.

"Hey, I think we've met." Gwen waved at Audrey. "I'd say it's good to see you, but clearly not under these circumstances." She offered a small shrug, then shifted straight into mission talk. "We figured it'd be faster to upload every relevant unredacted file we now have our hands on into a program I built instead of going through it all manually ourselves. It'll scan for patterns, red flags, recurring names—stuff like that. We'll let AI do the heavy lifting."

"So, we're being replaced by machines," I muttered.

"Would you prefer to go through Beth's stuff from your boxes yourself?" Natasha asked, but not in a condescending way.

I gripped the back of the couch, noticing Audrey was a little too close to my hands now, but I couldn't back away. I was already there. In deep. In over my head. All the damn things.

"I'll take the algorithm, thanks," I said, unable to erase the bitterness from my tone since we were discussing my ex. "No need to visit Betrayal Lane."

I could feel Ryder's eyes burn a hole through me at those words.

Did he feel betrayed by me now?

Shit.

"My husband went to get your boxes from storage." Natasha's announcement saved me from making eye contact with Delta One, and that was how I needed to think of the man right now. "When he's back, I'll scan everything into the program. No need for you to look at anything."

Never thought I'd be grateful for AI when I wasn't a fan of humans being replaced by technology, especially as rapidly as it seemed to be happening lately. But consider me a fan right now if I could avoid Beth.

I forced my hands to relax, keeping them on the couch without death-gripping it. "So while your program sifts through the haystack, what do we do? You start looking into Arlo's background? Trace Mitch's last steps between when Arlo died and Audrey's rings disappeared before the plane crash?"

"Looking into all that now, yes." Gwen smiled. "Well, my program is."

"Could've used her last year when Mitch's transport was hit," Natasha commented, pride, not jealousy, in her voice.

"Well, you have me now. You all have the dream team with us." Gwen winked, eyes on Audrey as she clutched the pillow to her chest like I'd seen her do a few times today. "So, while you two were, um, otherwise occupied, we did figure something out."

Oh, she knows. How the hell does she know?

Ryder's spine went straight.

And yup, he knows Gwen just read the tension in the room, too.

"Thanks to Reed," Gwen continued, "we knew the cipher in the ring was incomplete, which suggested the key requires two rings to work." Her fingers tapped across a sleek and colorful wireless keyboard. "We also got lucky. Mitch's ring appears to hold the second half of the code, not the first. The final four digits helped us pinpoint what kind of vault the keys unlock."

I stayed behind the couch, grounding my hands more firmly on the backrest. "Like a routing number? A digital signature tied to a specific vault?"

Gwen nodded, clearly in her element. I was glad we had her on our team, but I also had to keep in mind Mitch had a pretty damn good hacker on his side to pull everything off he had so far. We couldn't get too comfortable.

"We narrowed it down to three possible vault brands, based on the sequence," Gwen announced. "These types of vaults are designed to require not only physical keys but often a biometric verification."

"So even if someone had the rings, they couldn't open the vault without the original owner." Reed gave us the shit news, confirming our concern as to why Mitch needed Audrey.

"So that's why Mitch wants me." Audrey said what we'd guessed back at the lodge. "But how'd he pull this off without me being physically present when he locked the vault?"

"Good question." Natasha slipped on what looked like a pair of blue-light glasses as she studied a different screen off to her side. "And I don't have an answer for you that won't sound sci-fi."

Audrey held up her hand. "I'm okay, then. I've had enough over-my-head stuff for a lifetime." She folded forward a little as if the weight of those words had physically hit her. I stole a look over her shoulder to see her knuckles whitening around the pillow.

"These types of vaults come with expiration dates," Gwen continued, eyes on something else and not on us, so she probably didn't notice Audrey turning a little pale. "If the contents aren't claimed and fees paid by then—"

"Wait, what?" I interrupted. Now they were losing me, and I *was* a sci-fi guy.

"There's a date embedded in the cipher," Gwen explained. "I found the sequence: two, twenty-seven, twenty-seven. February twenty-seventh of this year."

I didn't try to pretend I fully understood how she'd found numbers inside numbers, but sure. *Let's go with that.* "So that's the expiration date for the safe that the two rings will open."

"We believe so," Gwen responded. "The timeline fits."

"Why would he take the risk to cut it so close to the expiration date, though?" I asked. "For that matter, why store evidence in a vault that expires? What happens if he misses the deadline? Does the vault explode?"

"Unfortunately not," Natasha replied dryly. "That would've worked in our favor, especially in my father's. Think of it like a layaway. These companies charge an exorbitant fee for every day they store someone's assets. If the contents aren't claimed and the fees aren't paid by the deadline—"

"They keep it." Audrey's voice was hollow as she slowly rose from the couch, tossing the pillow aside. "Which means they must've seen what's being stored is of value. They know it's worth keeping if the owner doesn't come back for it in time."

"Precisely." Not the news any of us were looking to hear from Natasha. "And I actually think the timing feels intentional, like Mitch really did plan all of this out down to the last detail and minute for a reason."

Yeah, putting him five steps too many ahead of us.

"But in order to pay the fee, since last I checked he wasn't rich, he'd have to sell whatever's in the vault first, right?" Audrey asked while undoing her hair, shaking it free.

She slipped the band on her wrist before combing her fingers through her hair, distracting me at a time when I really shouldn't lose focus again.

"But wait," Audrey continued, "that doesn't make sense. He can't access the vault without the rings or me. *Or* without paying the fee first."

What doesn't make sense? I ripped my gaze away from her and back to where it belonged.

"He doesn't need the vault open to sell what's inside it. He just has to prove he has what he's promising," Gwen explained. "He'll probably show something like he did to my grandfather last year about Stratos 2.0 to attract the right buyer. Then he'll bring the money, rings, and you, Audrey, to open the vault at the exchange."

"And guess what's happening this Friday night?" Reed folded his arms, and Audrey and I turned toward him, clearly the last of everyone to catch up.

"There's an auction," Natasha filled us in. "It's held annually. This year marks the twentieth anniversary. Same family, same location in New Zealand. They sell black market antiquities. Stolen IP. Government tech. Whatever Mitch has would fit in."

"And one of the three vault locations you identified as a possibility is near this event," I said in understanding.

Natasha nodded. "An hour's drive in Arrowtown, on private land that was retrofitted with modern security. It's smack in the middle of a historic gold rush town in the mountains, which makes it the perfect spot for a secret bunker or underground vault."

Mitch really did coordinate this down to the last damn detail. And now he was backing Audrey into an impossible corner. If she didn't help him open that vault, the intel would fall into someone else's hands. More than likely, dangerous hands. Either way, someone would end up with whatever Mitch had locked away.

"I programmed my software to search everywhere Mitch may have been in that timeline we pinpointed as important," Gwen said. "And now that we know about this vault location, I've placed special emphasis in New Zealand to see if Mitch was ever there before he died. Well, fake-died."

This was feeling more and more like a legit lead. Good.

"But why didn't Mitch just sell what he had a year ago? Why go to such lengths to do all this? He wouldn't even need me, right?" Audrey scanned the room; then her shoulders dropped as if it'd just clicked. "Oh. Because he'd be a dead man walking. For-real dead and unable to spend the money. He knew he'd be hunted down forever. So he had to make sure everyone believed he was truly dead until the right time. Meanwhile, it was hiding in plain sight with me."

"The only one he probably trusted, especially since you wouldn't even know what you had," I said, shaking my head, tense all over again.

"But if everyone now knows he's alive, doesn't that place Mitch back in the same predicament he'd have been in last year then?" Audrey asked.

"No." I closed my eyes, the blood rushing from my face. "This isn't just about him becoming rich, it's about him buying his safety, which he couldn't do before. He probably didn't know who he could trust with the evidence, either, worried one of his low-life friends would stab him in the back and sell it themselves. You know, something he'd do." *Which is why he picked you.*

"And how does he buy his safety now?" Audrey's soft voice had me opening my eyes.

"With our help," I gritted out. "He's playing us. Trying to use us as his own personal army in New Zealand." I brought my hands to my hips, anger flying through me. "He knows about Chandler's off-the-books teams. Maybe not about us since we're new, but Bravo and the others."

"You're saying Mitch knows that after Stratos was shut down, new units were created by President Rydell and Will Hobbs in its place?" Ryder asked, his gaze cutting to me. "He also somehow knows Stratos was relaunched at some point outside of government hands, and who better to take out a clandestine unit of Tier One operators who'd want him dead—"

"Than to pull in another group of the best operators in the world to handle his problem," I finished for him. "Money. Safety. And Audrey. Then he's off-grid forever." I swallowed. "Will Hobbs had to have told Mitch about the new replacement units in 2013, Bravo and Echo."

"But something clearly sent Mitch over the edge to start all this up when he did," Gwen pointed out. "Unless someone else is calling the shots, and he's just a puppet?"

"Like Arlo dying." *Well, if he's really dead.* "Or the puppet could also be looking to cut his strings and get control himself." I couldn't help but unleash that sick idea, too.

Audrey dragged both hands down her face. "Does that mean what I think it means?"

"No." Ryder reached for her arm, waiting for her to look at him. "This absolutely does not mean I'm putting you in the cross-hairs of Mitch's mess. Like hell are you going to New Zealand. End of damn story."

"We have to get what's in that vault, though. And shouldn't you help shut down this Stratos unit? Who knows what kind of missions they're going on and why. I married this man, drawing you all into this, so I'll be the one to help you get out of it." Ryder opened his mouth to protest, but Audrey was quicker. Possibly even more stubborn. "So read *my* lips, mister." She lifted her chin like a challenge, then echoed his words back to him in a slightly friendlier way: "I'm going . . . end of freaking story."

CHAPTER THIRTY-THREE

Audrey

"Don't you dare blame yourself for Mitch's choices," Ryder shot back while sitting next to me. "He's clearly a skilled manipulator. How could you possibly know the kind of man you were marrying?"

"He was fourteen years older, charming, and I guess he tricked me into . . ." I backed down as soon as I realized where I was going with my words. I was about to slam headfirst into Ryder being right.

Not my fault. Only Mitch's. That didn't make the truth hurt any less.

The side of Ryder's mouth lifted in regret. "Everything's going to be okay," he promised. "But why don't we table the whole you-going-to-New-Zealand conversation for later, yeah? We need more answers first."

"I suppose you're right," I agreed.

"Of course I am." Ryder's teasing tone and quick smile were somehow exactly what I needed right now.

"We should also get Trevor on the line, don't you think?" There went Reed, poking a hole through the calm I'd managed to grab hold of with that. "See if he knows Hobbs?"

I locked both arms around the pillow. "Charlie Team." *Trevor gave up a dream assignment because of me.* Guilt and blame triumphed again.

"Go make the call," Ryder ordered, and Reed shot me an apologetic look before taking off.

"You okay?" Natasha asked, drawing my eyes to the screen. "Anything we can do to help?"

"You're doing quite a lot already." I shook my head. "But thank you."

"You play piano, yeah?" Natasha's out-of-the-blue question had me sitting up taller. Freeing my hold on the pillow a smidge. "I remember Trevor telling me how talented you are." She gestured toward the hall. "Maybe playing would be a good distraction? Someone on Wyatt's rich side of the family gave us a piano for a wedding gift. It's never been touched."

"Yeah, well, it's been touched now." Such a brother thing to grumble into a closed fist, and I couldn't help but let go of the pillow to send a solid elbow into his side.

"Ah, you already played?" Natasha smirked.

Something like that.

Ryder twisted around on the couch to face me. "Wait, you play piano?"

Yeah, I do more than make out with your best friend up against them. I had to be blushing. At least I wasn't spiraling. Natasha had helped after all. Kind of, sort of.

"Reed and I heard music a few times since we've been here, but I thought it was a radio you were playing because it was so good," my brother continued. "That was you, wasn't it?"

"Guilty." *Among other things.* "I played a long time ago." *All I have left are memories and a drawer full of regrets and lace underwear.*

"I still can't believe you didn't tell me." Ryder looked genuinely hurt that I'd failed to mention this. Now the music notes on my sweatshirt were probably clicking into place for him.

"We've been busy dodging bullets and discussing how our exes are enemies of the state." My attempt at humor didn't land and probably came across as sarcastic. "No time to share."

He called me out, not letting it go. "Why didn't it come up in the last two months?"

I looked over at Alejandro as if he could somehow save me from these questions. He had his arms folded, back to the wall, eyes on the floor.

"I'm surprised you didn't run a background check on me when we met," I said under my breath, turning to Ryder again.

Ryder rolled his eyes.

Okay, I deserved that.

"I went to school for music," I relented. "Performing is how I met Trevor. I was young. We didn't plan to get pregnant so fast, but it happened."

"I'm going to check on Reed." Alejandro left the room before we could make eye contact, probably sensing this was a brother-sister moment even though I wanted him here.

Natasha's screen went dark without so much as a goodbye.

"Guess it's just the two of us now."

Ryder reached for my hand and set his on top of it. "Tell me." His eyes narrowed. "Tell me everything you can handle sharing."

"Now?" I lifted my brows, unsure. "With everything going on?"

He took the pillow from me and set it aside. "Please."

Walk down memory lane. Could I do that and keep it together? We'd soon find out.

I gathered my thoughts, then ripped open that box containing my past as quickly as possible.

"I was part of an orchestra and performing at a military ball in DC. He swept me off my feet; then everything went fast between us because he had to spin up. We got to know each other while he was half a world away. When he came back three months later, he proposed. Next thing I knew, we were married and I was pregnant, so I stopped performing."

I paused for a beat to breathe. Then continued. Telling him everything. From becoming close friends with Hollis during that time to how she'd helped keep me from falling apart when Trevor was held captive by the Taliban.

When I was done sharing, he asked the one thing I'd left out: "Why did you two get divorced?"

He probably thought I was horrible, thinking I'd left Trevor after the man survived being a prisoner of war. "He left me, not the other way around."

"Oh." His eyes shot to his hand on top of mine.

"I'd considered it a miracle Trevor made it home . . . only to lose him again, but in a different way," I whispered.

"I don't know the details of that op, only that it went sideways and he was taken."

I didn't know much myself, to be honest. Part of the problem, in a way. Trevor hadn't been able to talk to me.

"Him and his teammate were both taken. It was an ambush. Trevor was rescued, but only after he had to watch his friend lose his life."

Ryder dropped the f-bomb, dragging it out as he hauled me closer for a sideways hug.

"He blamed himself for his friend dying and for him surviving, and it broke him," I went on after steadying my heart rate. "He was benched from operating for over six months, which didn't help. I think he didn't know who he was if he wasn't part of a team."

"That kind of trauma doesn't fade easily," he gritted out.

"He pushed me away after that. Wouldn't let me in. Then one day, he asked to separate. Next thing I knew, we were getting a divorce. I tried to fight for us, to save our marriage, but he wouldn't let me."

"He had to be able to save himself first. And based on what I know about him now, he got better and eventually went back to operating."

I lifted my head to look over at him. "We talked about getting back together after that, but we decided it was best if we just stayed friends. Eventually, I met Mitch and only agreed to be his friend at first, but he wore me down."

Thinking back now, he'd probably manipulated me, but I'd never seen the big picture of what he'd been doing to me then.

"I actually met Mitch the same night I did Trevor at the first ball. Both men tried to win me over. Clearly Trevor won out."

"Damn."

Yeah, I could think of a few more curses than that, and I wasn't much of a swearer.

"That wasn't our only bump-in, either. There was another ball Mitch was at, and he approached me while I was pregnant. Then . . . well, when I was single, my mom was babysitting one night so I could go out for drinks with friends, and I ran into Mitch at the bar. He claimed it was fate. He said, 'Third time's the charm.'"

"That line worked?"

I choked out a half cry, half laugh. "Not at first. I resisted. Wasn't ready to date. But he got to me eventually." I shrugged. "He was older, charming, a little cocky, and had that whole Maverick from *Top Gun* energy. But taller and younger than Tom Cruise, of course. He went so far as to take me out on his motorcycle for a 'friend' date. Gave me his jacket, aviators, with the wind in my hair." I blew out my cheeks. "He was persistent. Never gave up until I said yes to dating and yes to marriage."

Ryder let go of me and stood, dragging both hands through his hair.

"After we were married, he didn't want me working, but at that time he'd convinced me he was being sweet, not controlling. And he'd promised I'd play again one day." I shut my eyes, trying to wrap my head around how I'd fallen for it. "Was any of it ever real, do you think? Or was he always wearing a mask?"

"Maybe?" A question and an answer all in one. "About the guy you have feelings for now, though . . ."

That pivot had me on my feet now, too, but before he could continue, Reed walked in and shared, "You're not going to believe this. Trevor said he met Hobbs once. It was at the military ball in 2017, when Audrey was pregnant."

And there went my stomach. Free-falling.

"And guess who introduced him to Hobbs?" Reed continued.

"Mitch?" I asked, remembering he'd been there that night, too.

"No," Alejandro said, joining us now, too. "Beth went with Hobbs while I was deployed. He was her plus-one since I was in Afghanistan."

No, no, no.

Ryder held up his hand as if he could physically push away the facts. "You're saying Beth, Mitch, and Will were all at the same military ball in 2017? *And* you and Trevor were also there."

Alejandro's eyes narrowed, gaze focused on my brother. "This means I have to talk to her, doesn't it? I have to talk to Beth."

CHAPTER THIRTY-FOUR

Alejandro

The screen blinked to life, splitting between Secretary Chandler at the Pentagon and Trevor with Chase in what looked to be a nearly as secure location.

"Got a new friend, do you?" Audrey leaned in toward the screen, reaching out instinctively as if she could actually touch her son as he petted a golden retriever wagging its tail beside him.

"He just wanted to say hi real quick." Trevor knelt beside Chase and the dog, wrapping his tattooed arm behind his son's back.

"I miss you." Audrey pressed her hand to the screen, ignoring the fact we had the secretary of defense watching. "We'll be together soon, I promise."

"I know. Daddy says we'll all be together again."

Together again. His small voice and those words hit me hard. The thought that I could possibly be a roadblock to that happening sent guilt splicing through me.

Chase glanced at his uncle, who was hovering at my side along with Reed, as if they were both worried I might go find a cliff to jump from after realizing Beth was in the mix more than we'd thought.

"Keep Mommy safe—okay, Uncle Ryder?"

"You got it," Ryder said with a firm nod. "And then we'll hit the ice. Play hockey together like we did at Christmas."

Chase smiled, but it felt a little forced, like the kid knew how bad shit really was, but he was trying to put on a brave face for his mom's sake.

Like father, like son. Like uncle, like nephew.

"Love you, baby." Audrey pulled her hand away from the screen and stepped aside.

"Okay, go back with Michael and the others. Give your mom and me a minute." Trevor ruffled Chase's blond hair, then gently guided him and the dog from the room.

He returned in front of the screen a moment later, his expression hardening, letting his own mask of bravery slip even though I knew he'd want to keep it up for Audrey, too.

"I had no clue Beth Rodriguez was your wife." Trevor laid his comment on me quickly.

"*Ex*-wife," I clarified, the word always bitter in my mouth. I hated that she'd never dropped my last name after the divorce, clinging to it more than she had to the sanctity of our marriage vows. Ten years together before we split. Ten years of lies.

"Tell us what you know," Chandler prompted, the monitors pulsing behind him with data, the Pentagon's hum of activity alive in the background.

Trevor looked to Audrey. "I take it you now know about the job offer with Charlie Team I turned down?" When she nodded, his shoulders slumped. "What you don't know is that it was the second time I was asked, and I said yes the first time."

"I beg your pardon?" Chandler leaned forward, hands braced on the table in front of him.

"I figured you didn't know. The first offer came under the previous secretary. That's why I didn't mention it when you tried to recruit me for Charlie. I assumed if you knew, you'd have said something." He exhaled and met Audrey's eyes. "Beth introduced me to Will Hobbs at the military ball in 2017."

Reed had already delivered that shocking blow to us before the call, but it still managed to hit me with just as much intensity a second time.

"I was at the bar getting a drink, and you were off talking with friends. Beth approached me with Hobbs and introduced us. He said he'd been watching my career and was impressed. He told me he had a proposition that was of the classified nature, and it was a once-in-a-lifetime opportunity. Asked if we could meet privately in the morning."

"I remember waking up at the hotel alone," Audrey cut in. "And when you came back you said you were jogging, which was weird, because you hate running, and you—"

"I'm sorry." Raw, emotional pain, that I could detect from the man even through the screen, simmered beneath the surface. "Will offered me a position as part of a select unit of SEALs that he said would answer directly to POTUS. But first, I had to complete a trial run. A test op. Me and a few others."

"That's not—*no*." Chandler straightened. "I didn't know about this. Not because the previous secretary kept it from me, but because it's not true." He rubbed his neck as if expecting to find a tie, though he'd tossed it earlier when talking to us.

"What happened next?" Ryder asked, glancing at Audrey, who was clutching the base of her throat like she couldn't breathe.

"Hobbs said he'd need to send me on an off-the-books assignment before I could officially meet everyone and join." He gestured toward Audrey. "But she was pregnant, and I wasn't about to spin up and miss our son's birth. So he agreed to wait until I was ready and another mission presented itself."

What the hell went wrong?

Trevor cleared his throat, then coughed into a closed fist. "When it was time, two of us deployed to Afghanistan as planned with our team; then we were pulled out for a secondary classified op. It was total mission failure. We were both captured. Taliban-held village, underground cell. My friend was killed in front of me." He looked up at the ceiling, stretching his neck. Trying to keep it together.

Holy shit. I wasn't one to get chills, but I sure as hell was getting them now.

"Six weeks later, we found you," Chandler said, breaking the silence. "Bravo and Echo pulled you out, the same teams Hobbs lied to you about joining." He curled his hands inward, resting his fists on the table, hanging his head. "The mission details had been corrupted in the system. The former secretary of defense said he couldn't trace who sent you two on that op or why. And you wouldn't talk to them after. They blamed the trauma and closed the case."

"Pulled me from operating for a while, too," Trevor added in a terse tone. "I was under strict orders by Hobbs not to open my mouth if we were ever caught. Not even to my own unit."

Chandler slowly lifted his head. "I can assure you, Hobbs lied. We don't put our men through test runs like that, and there weren't any slots open on the teams. That was before Charlie Team was formed."

Trevor rubbed his chest, and I had a feeling his heart was about to break free. To learn what happened to him had been a lie, and that he'd been played by someone he trusted . . . Well, shit, I could relate, I supposed, because of Beth. But what he went through was much worse than what I'd survived.

"My decision to say yes to Hobbs cost me everything. My best friend. My marriage. My sanity. Everything," Trevor said bitterly. "And you're telling me it was all bullshit?" His hands tensed at his sides as he walked back from the screen.

Something told me the trap of PTSD was about to try to suck him back into its ugly vortex, which sometimes felt impossible to escape.

"I assume that's the real reason you turned down my offer to lead Charlie," Chandler remarked after letting Trevor process the news for a minute.

Trevor dragged both hands along the sides of his head. "I couldn't destroy what I'd worked so hard to rebuild." His focus cut to Audrey, an apology in his eyes I knew she didn't want or need.

The woman only cared about others, and her heart had to be breaking for her son's father right about now.

She reached out for him the way she had Chase a few minutes ago.

And I felt like an intruder to what should've been a private moment, but we all had no choice but to stay. His story was now tied to our mission.

"I have no idea why Will lied to you, but he had to have had his own motives. We discovered he was a traitor in 2018. Found out he'd committed war crimes," Chandler went on, dropping more bad news on him. How much could one guy take?

"That explains why I could never reach him." Trevor's arms fell to his sides, jaw remaining locked tight.

"It was intentional, wasn't it?" Audrey covered her mouth. "This Will Hobbs guy meant for something to go wrong on that mission, didn't he?" She surveyed the room as if we had the answers. "But why? What'd he gain by sending Trevor into a trap?"

"We don't know yet," Reed said, stepping forward. "But Beth might."

Beth. Fuck that woman and my life right now.

But in comparison to what Trevor and Audrey were going through, I could man up and talk to my ex, dammit. What choice did I have?

"We can't forget Mitch was at that military ball, too," Ryder remarked. "You didn't see him near Beth or Hobbs that night, did you?" he asked Trevor.

"No, I only remember Mitch because he couldn't take his eyes off my pregnant wife. He had the balls to ask her to dance."

Audrey spoke up. "I said no, of course."

"But something told me he had a thing for her, so when he reappeared after our divorce, I wasn't surprised." Trevor kept his eyes on Audrey, a world of hurt there. Anger. And probably a dozen other emotions. "I hated him from the start. Now I know I had every reason not to trust him."

"And I should've listened to you," she said, stepping even closer to the screen. "I'm so sorry. Your gut is never wrong."

"Who wants to listen to their ex about who to date?" Trevor grumbled. "I get it."

Fair point.

Audrey turned to the side, eyes on her brother. "What does this mean? What happens now?"

"It means I need to talk to Beth. I have to see if she knows why Will Hobbs targeted Trevor," I said. The words felt like acid, but they were the truth. "She might be our only hope in figuring out what the hell is going on."

CHAPTER THIRTY-FIVE

Alejandro

"Are you okay in there?" Audrey's voice floated through the closed bathroom door.

I opened up and stepped out into my bedroom, shirtless, jeans riding low on my hips. "I thought I locked that."

"You forgot," she said, already halfway into my room like she owned the place. "And I opted not to knock." She stopped a foot away from me. "How's the wound?"

"Which one? The one on my back where that woman stabbed me multiple times?" I tapped a finger above my bandage. "Or this new one?"

She didn't answer right away. Instead, she erased the space between us, resting her hand flat against my chest, right over my heart.

My pec muscle involuntarily twitched beneath her touch. "My wounds don't seem nearly as bad as yours must be."

"My heart feels ripped out. Like it's not even in there anymore. I feel numb. Is that normal?"

"You should never feel that way." And now I was angry all over again at Mitch, and now at a real dead man—Will Hobbs—for making her feel this way.

She trailed her fingers down the center of my chest, soft and slow, like she wasn't even aware she was doing it.

When she reached the ridges of my abs, she followed the line to the waistband of my jeans, teasing just above the edge of my boxers.

"Underwear." Her voice was glass, fractured and on the verge of totally breaking. "We keep circling back to that topic."

"Oh, we do, do we?" I rasped as she skated her finger along the band of my boxers, my abdominal muscles tensing at her touch.

I caught her wrist, halting her before things went somewhere they couldn't go again.

"You're in shock. That's why you're reaching for something else. But this isn't what you want or need. Not now, at least."

That call with Trevor changed things for them, didn't it? It had to.

"Mitch would've never ended up marrying you had my ex not introduced Trevor to Will Hobbs."

Her expression cracked, and I saw it hit her—the sting of hindsight.

"And then you and Trevor would still be married," I added, voice rough. "Chase wouldn't have been caught in all this. His family wouldn't have been torn apart."

"How do you know what happened in Afghanistan is why we ended up getting divorced? I told Ryder that, not you."

I released her wrist and stepped around her, grabbing my shirt. "I saw it in your eyes on that call. His too." I yanked the shirt over my head, the movement pulling at the wound in my side. "It's not hard to figure out that kind of trauma screws with a person, especially when it was his decision to go in the first place."

"Oh." Her small voice had me turning around. "I know what you're doing."

I frowned. "And what's that?"

"Pushing me away. Putting up walls." Her voice trembled. "After that call, you regret what happened between us, don't you?"

Yes. No. I wasn't sure what I was doing. Right now, I only knew I needed to soldier forward and lock down my emotions for everyone's benefit.

"He's jealous of you, you know. Mitch." She fidgeted with the hem of her shirt, reminding me of when she'd lifted it to help me better see the pink lace between her legs. "He was fine with me going to Trevor's after the break-in, because he knew nothing would happen between us. It was what he wanted, clearly. But those photos he sent of us were personal. They were a warning not to fall for you. A reminder I was his wife. Until death do us part."

"Audrey," was all I managed, unsure what to say after that.

"Mitch sees you as a threat," she continued anyway. "And if he's had people watching me, he probably figured out Ryder's my brother after I visited our dad and was rejected. That's why he didn't accuse me of anything with him. But you? He saw something. Maybe at Christmas. The way I was looking at you, perhaps."

I stared at her in shock. Did she realize what she just admitted? And did I hear her right? "Are you saying you felt something for me when we first met?"

She let go of her sweatshirt, nodding. "I didn't want to. I told myself no more falling for anyone, but being around you . . ."

I removed what was left of the space between us and gently held her chin, needing to look her in the eyes.

"Who knows, Mitch may have even tapped my phone. He'd have learned a lot about my feelings for you if he read the texts with my best friend."

I'm really going to kill that man.

"But I'm starting to think this isn't just about revenge or a payday. I think he wants more than just for me to open that vault."

Yeah, me too. And it was destroying me to think about.

"Mitch wants to take me away. From Chase. From everyone. So he can keep me for himself. In his mind, I still belong to him like a piece of property he owns."

"I'll never let him near you." I brushed my thumb along the line of her lips. "You hear me?"

She didn't acknowledge me, only let go of a strangled breath. "He's obsessed with me, isn't he? I think he has been since the moment we met." She hesitated, then added, "Something tells me he's the reason Hobbs sent Trevor on that mission. He wanted Trevor out of the picture." She paused before whispering what I felt in my bones to be true: "He did it so he could make me his wife instead."

CHAPTER THIRTY-SIX

Alejandro

I didn't respond. I couldn't. My jaw was locked so tight that it ached as I kept hold of her chin. The woman in front of me had survived a quiet war.

If Mitch had been pulling the strings in her life for that long, then we weren't just up against a rogue pilot with a bruised ego. We were up against something much darker and more sinister. More calculated.

I swallowed down the burn-like pain in my throat, forcing my emotions into a box to deal with later. I didn't let go of her chin until I noticed Reed hovering in the doorway.

"Trevor would like a word alone with you." He gave a nod of apology for interrupting, and she turned away from us, probably trying to hide the evidence of her tears with her sleeves.

"Okay, um, thanks," she said, sniffling while turning back to face us.

"I should talk to Ryder and see where we're at on getting Beth on the phone." I started for the door, sidestepping Reed to make my exit, knowing he'd keep an eye on Audrey while she talked to Trevor, to a man who . . .

Well, to a man who might wind up back together with the woman I'd fallen for.

I did my best to shove my personal thoughts and feelings to the side when I joined Ryder in the living room. He was on one knee, leaning forward to start up the fireplace.

Great, setting the mood for my own personal hell with Beth. Flames and all. Makes sense.

"Chandler's working on getting Beth on the line," he said while standing. "And without any get-out-of-jail-free card, don't worry." He cleaned his hands off on his jeans. "How are you? How's my sister? I, uh, saw her go to your room."

"We're about as good as can be expected, given who we married and what they did," I admitted, then quickly laid the theory on him about Mitch being obsessed with her, possibly since they'd first met.

Ryder blinked a few times, dragging his hand over his mouth, processing.

"Talk to me as Delta One, not as her brother. You think that's the case?" I asked before giving him time to digest everything I'd shared. "Has Mitch been sabotaging their relationship since day one?"

Ryder's gaze slowly cut to my face. Ready to kill. I'd seen that look before, and I was right there with him.

"A man obsessed with someone is never an enemy I want to have."

I was with him on that, but there we were, more than likely dealing with that problem now. "The man's patient and dangerous. He could've made up his mind about Audrey and stalked her all that time while Trevor was still in the picture."

"He had to be shocked to learn about me at Christmas when she visited. And considering you were there, too, and Beth may be a link between the shit he pulled in the past—then to see you, Beth's ex, near Audrey . . ."

"But why not eliminate me as a possible threat after that? Wouldn't he be worried we'd do exactly what we're doing now, tying everything together? Why take the chance?"

Ryder gave me a sharp look. "You think you're that easy to take down?"

True. "I guess he doesn't care if we know the truth. He pretty much pointed us to it."

"And while he may have wanted POTUS's teams to handle his enemies for him originally, he probably decided who better to keep the woman he's in love with safe than her family? But once we outlive our usefulness—and he has his revenge, payday, and Audrey—he'll kill us." He lifted his hand, patting the air for emphasis. "Not that we'll let that happen." He dropped his arm, grimacing. "I hate that you're going to need to talk to Beth and convince her to help us. Putting you in this situation kills me."

"Not sure how much she'll reveal unless it works to her benefit." And that terrified me. "But I'll get her to tell us what we need."

"There's not a day that goes by that I don't feel guilty for not talking you out of dating that woman to begin with." Ryder turned toward the fire, resting his hand on the mantel.

"Remember me in my twenties?" I faked a laugh. "I didn't exactly respond well to being told what to do. I'd have doubled down on dating Beth if you told me to steer clear from her."

"You haven't changed all that much now."

I could feel where this conversation was going, and I wasn't sure if I could stomach it. "Go ahead. Spit it out. I know you want to say what you didn't get a chance to finish earlier." At least he didn't know I'd gotten his sister off against that piano.

He kept his back to me, head hanging forward. The fireplace crackled low, casting shadows over the worn-stone hearth as I waited for him to speak.

"You're thinking about your nephew. About Trevor." I finally said what I assumed was on his mind. "I know that because I'm right there with you."

He pushed off the mantel and slowly faced me. "If Mitch ruined their marriage on purpose, and God knows how many times and ways he actually tried, then what if—"

"What if they're supposed to be together and should never have split?" I went over to the armchair and collapsed into it. "I can't come between them. If they're meant to have a second shot, I refuse to be another Mitch and block that from happening." I nodded, my stomach twisting. "So you have my word: Nothing will happen with Audrey until they have time to figure things out. And if they get back together, then I'll say *sayonara.*" I saluted him with that goodbye, even though the casualness was utter bullshit.

"I just want you all to be happy, and it sucks if you finally found someone that makes you . . . ya know, feel something again, and you can't—"

"Can't be with her, I know." I took the illusion of being fine one step forward and shrugged before standing. "Some people just aren't meant to be happy." I gestured toward the hall, signaling to Delta Three. "I'll always have Reed to keep me company."

He lifted his chin, giving me a quiet *Shut up* embedded there. Neither of us were all that great at navigating feelings conversations. Like most operators, we sucked at it. And while I may have had the psych degree and often gave advice, I never took any myself.

"Listen, I'm not telling you to back off, but I agree with holding off until after Mitch is six feet under and my sister can see things a bit more clearly and figure out what—or, uh, who—she wants."

I'd expected a more direct order to stay away, and Delta One was leaving me with a maybe. I didn't know how to do *maybes.*

Hope and maybes were too dangerous. Because there was that inevitable coin toss of things not landing the way you prayed they would. And then what?

"Well, you have my word," I finished saying as Reed and Audrey joined us.

"Gwen's program got a hit," Reed let us know. "She was able to confirm Arlo made contact with Mitch before he spun up on the op that he died on."

I switched gears the best I could to focus up. Mission first.

"CCTV footage with a time stamp verifies it. The evidence of their meeting was scrubbed from surveillance footage, but Gwen found it. That had to be why it was missed before," he shared. "Don't ask me how she even knew where to look in the empty black hole space of the internet, or whatever she said. It's even over my head."

Which is saying a lot.

"But it looks like Arlo passed something off to Mitch," Reed continued. "Something small enough to fit inside his hand. Probably a flash drive."

"So, Arlo was murdered for whatever he knew, and since he gave the evidence to Mitch for safekeeping, Mitch must've figured it was only a matter of time before they'd come after him next. He hid the evidence somewhere safe and had a hacker cover his tracks." *Hopefully, Gwen can recover that footage from the internet black hole, too.*

"So, Mitch mapped out an escape plan. He wasn't sure who to trust since Arlo was killed and branded as a traitor. And maybe he ran out of people he could blackmail, or maybe they're tied to this as well," Audrey said, her tone sounding as unsure as I felt about all this. "But we know that man can play the long game. He's capable of waiting a year to reap the reward of his patience."

"Looks that way." But I also knew firsthand looks could be deceiving. I wasn't ready to commit to a theory yet. If my father had taught me anything, it was to always view everything as one of the three Ds: diversion, deflection, and deception. *Between that and Beth, it's no wonder I have trust issues.*

"Did Gwen find anything else?" Ryder asked him. "Any idea who could be operating Stratos now?"

"She's still working on retracing his last steps and confirming he was in New Zealand, but her and Natasha do have some working theories about Stratos 2.0 and who's running it." He rested his forearm on the mantel. "They believe it's one of the major security companies that are awarded contracts on the regular, who have high-level security clearance and access to a lot of military ops. They're narrowing down the list by cross-referencing flights Arlo and Mitch piloted where those companies hitched a ride or joined the op as well."

"And one of those flights Beth was also on," I said at the memory of what I'd read back at the lodge that felt like a decade ago. "There was a PMC attached to that op. I think their name was redacted in the file I saw."

"Well, we have the unredacted copies now, so Gwen should be able to find it fast," Reed said as he looked down at his phone. "A text from the secretary. One hour. Then it's time."

"Time for what?" Audrey asked, voice as fragile sounding as my current mental state.

"To face my demons," I said under my breath. "To talk to Beth."

CHAPTER THIRTY-SEVEN

Audrey

"I'm alone now, unlike earlier when you called." I sat upright against the headboard for support, balancing the phone in front of me as I FaceTimed Trevor. "So talk to me. Please. You called before, then said nothing."

Trevor was sitting on the floor of Michael's office, his back against the wall. He held the phone in one hand, the other resting at the side of his neck where three crosses were inked into his skin.

The same silence from earlier blanketed the call. And like before, it brought a cold wave of chills over my skin.

"This is my fault." His jaw tightened as he bowed his head, fingers pressing over the tattoos like he could draw strength from them. "Mitch was probably watching you. Studying you. Obsessing over you while I was deployed. Before we were married and after. What kind of sick piece of shit does that?"

"I agree with every word. Except the part where you blame yourself." I grabbed one of the throw pillows and set it on my lap, propping my elbow against it as I held the phone. "The only one at fault is that man." Something Ryder had helped me understand earlier when I'd tried to blame myself.

He finally met my gaze. "When you two started dating, something in my gut told me he'd always wanted you. But I told myself it was just jealousy. And I had no right to be jealous when I was the one who asked for the divorce."

Ohh. My stomach was already pretzeled beyond reason, but that? That somehow managed to twist it tighter.

"I convinced myself not to dig into his background when you two dated because I didn't want to violate your privacy, but I should've. I should've done it when he was still alive, not just after he died." He scoffed. "Well, faked his death."

"Would you have found anything?"

He grimaced, knowing I was right. There'd have been nothing. Mitch clearly knew how to cover his tracks and keep a low profile.

"Still," was his best defense. Like that one word would convince me to convict him, so he could freely shoulder the guilt.

"Trevor." His name came out as a warning and a plea as I tried to pack everything into those two syllables. All the grief, the truth, and the desperate need for him to stop blaming himself. "Not. Your. Fault."

"You won't ever convince me otherwise, sorry. I trusted Beth. Trusted Will. Trusted Mitch to be in your life and our son's. I only did a basic background check of the fucker instead of stalking his ass like we now know he was doing to you. I trusted all the wrong people."

"I repeat, and say it with me . . . *you didn't know.*"

"Exactly. I should have."

"Noooo, that's not what I meant and you know it."

"If I'd never come into your life, then maybe—"

"Chase wouldn't exist, and Mitch may have been in my life even longer." I tossed the pillow, needing to be on my feet. "You're the one always saying everything happens for a reason. God's plans, not ours. To just trust. You're the one who has to remind me of those things, not the other way around. Don't let evil win. Don't let this man get in your head. Don't doubt yourself and your beliefs."

"Well, I hate to break it to you, but I may have to be the man I was before again soon." I lost his eyes to his lap. "I have to do something I promised I wouldn't do again."

"Do what? Promised who?"

He slowly looked up at me. "Kill in cold blood."

I blinked, confused. "When did you do that the first time?"

"You don't want to know all my secrets, trust me. I have every intention of killing Mitch. I don't care if he waves a white flag; I'm taking the son of a bitch down."

He'd protected us at the lodge yesterday without a second thought, but this was different. He knew that. I knew that. And I couldn't let him do it. I brought the phone to my forehead as if I was resting against him instead. "I won't—"

"I'm sorry," he cut me off, refusing to hear it. "But that man hit you, raped you, and endangered you and our son." His rough, strangled voice deepened as he added, "And if I have to spend eternity in hell for taking his life, then so be it."

CHAPTER THIRTY-EIGHT

Audrey

I checked the time. T-minus ten minutes until Alejandro would be on a call with his evil ex, and he wanted to do it alone, so I'd have to sit here and wait. Wonder. Continue wallowing in sadness, replaying that call with Trevor. He'd ended the call before I could protest and beg him not to intervene and seek retribution. But when that man's mind was made up, it was up. Alllll the way up.

"Do me a favor and distract me." I gave Reed my best prayer hands, sitting on the couch in the living room in front of the fire.

"Me?" Reed looked up from his phone. "You want *me* to distract you?" He frowned. "I'll go find Alex, how about that?"

No, I needed a distraction from him, too. "Ryder asked you to watch over me while the two of them prep for the call, so please, help me get my mind off all the heaviness."

He sat upright, his spine going stiff, eyes lifting to the ceiling as if I'd just asked him to solve world hunger in sixty seconds.

"You could let me talk to Hollis." I held open my hand, hoping he'd hand over the phone he'd been using to contact her.

He grimaced. "She's become a pain in my ass."

"I feel like that's not hard to do." I chewed on my lip, resisting a small smile at the little tease there. And look at that, he was already distracting me from the weight of the world pressing down on us.

"Fair enough." He typed in his passcode, then handed me his phone. "Please tell her it's you texting and not me."

"Worried she'll think you're being nice?" I smirked, opening up his messages.

"Doubt she'd believe it anyway. She's . . ."

I lifted my brows, focusing on him, thankful he was temporarily lifting the stress about the call with Trevor and Alex's soon-to-be call with Beth off my chest. "She's what?"

"Nothing," he grumbled, picking up his laptop from the coffee table.

"Fine." I opened his messages, tempted to scroll through and invade their privacy and read their exchanges. Before I had a chance to do that, a new text popped up from her.

Hollis: I'm helping whether you want me to or not. She needs me. My mind is made up. I'll pick you up in Colorado. We'll take my plane and fly to NZ together.

"Wait, what?" *And aren't you in Bali, then heading somewhere new?* I held the phone up, waiting for Reed to give me his attention. "What is she talking about?" I knew Hollis's parents had money and a jet, and I'd always declined her offer to ride in it, given my disdain for the things, but . . .

His forehead tightened. "How much do you know about your best friend?"

"How much do *you* know about my best friend?"

He set down his laptop and twisted around on the couch, swiping the back of his hand over his cheek twice as if lost in thought. "I had to look into her to ensure she wasn't working behind your back with Mitch as some type of plant."

"What secrets is she keeping from me?" I rushed out, my body tensing up in preparation for the hit of betrayal.

"I had no choice but to confront her, given some weird patterns and inconsistencies Gwen and I picked up on when we both checked into her."

He took the phone from me and set it on the table, letting me know I wouldn't be texting her. At least not yet.

"Ryder told me not to say anything yet, that you had enough on your plate." He lifted his hand, patting the air. "And before you ask, Alex doesn't know about this. Figured his plate's full, too."

I rewound everything he said and unscrambled it. "You're not saying my friend has been working with Mitch, are you?"

"No. In fact, she seems to be beating herself up that she didn't know Mitch was such a bastard." He stood and faced me, locking his arms over his chest.

"Just tell me what you know; I can only handle so much."

"I thought I was supposed to be distracting you?"

"You are." Only I was now hanging by a thread and on the verge of spinning out thanks to this new distraction. "Please."

His arms dropped, and he studied the phone on the table. "This relentless woman is going to find a way to involve herself in our mission no matter what, so when you see her—*if* you go to New Zealand with us—then she can tell you herself like she demanded we let her do."

Sounds like a Hollis thing to say and do. Then again, maybe everything I thought I knew about her is a lie, so what do I know? "And how in the world would Hollis help on a mission? She doesn't even work—and while I adore that woman, her biggest problems are which city to choose to visit and what designer handbag to buy."

A hollow laugh left his mouth. "That's a front. Not real."

"Who the heck in my life is real?" I spat out, fighting tears. "And does Trevor know the truth?"

"I asked Trevor if he knew the truth about her. He said when he went fishing into the background of all your friends, he accidentally kicked a hornet's nest when it came to her family, forcing Hollis to tell him the truth."

"And that means?"

"That yeah, he knows she's been keeping secrets from you."

Seriously? "Does no one trust me with the truth? Everyone just thinks I'm some fragile woman that can't handle it." I wanted to scream, but I somehow managed to keep it together.

"I don't know what to tell you. Hollis convinced Trevor it was safer for you not to know."

"I'm really getting tired of everyone deciding what is and is not safe for me without my input." I sank onto the couch, prepared to throw a few walls up again and be mad at the whole world. *At least Alejandro didn't hide this from me.* "You let me look at your phone," I murmured a beat later when it hit me. "That was your way of letting me know without telling me. A loophole."

He lifted one shoulder. "I fuckin' hate being left in the dark, so . . ."

"For a non-people-y person, you're not so bad at it." I gave him a lopsided smile. "Thank you for being honest. Well, as honest-*ish* as you're allowed to be."

He sat next to me. "She's not a threat. More like an asset. But don't tell her I said that." He tore a hand through his hair. "I guess the second she learned about the attack at the lodge, she began working the case herself."

Working the case. How was any of this real?

"She'll tell you, I promise. I'll make sure she does."

Something told me he would. Happily hold her down and force the truth from her. "Yeah, now that she has no choice."

Before I could ask him another fifty questions, my brother joined us. "Alex is about to get on the call with Beth. He's in the den." He hung back by the fireplace, and as if picking up on the tension, cut right to it and asked, "Everything okay in here?"

"Hmm." I pushed up to standing. "Where do I start? How my ex-husband wants to risk his soul to kill Mitch? Or the fact my best friend has been lying to me, and you and Trev chose to keep this from me?"

"Oh," was all I got from my brother. More like, *Oh, shit.* I could hear it in his tone despite the lack of a curse.

"And Hollis is going to be a pain and demand she join the op. Just an FYI," Reed added. "Not sure if there is anything we can do about it. She did offer us a ride, though. And we may have to meet Echo Team in Queenstown, so we can't borrow their plane to get there."

"You want to work with her?" Ryder asked, eyes narrowing on him. "I thought she drove you nuts."

"She does," Reed grunted. "And when Gwen floated the idea that Hollis be my plus-one at the auction ten minutes ago, I told her absolutely fucking not. But—"

"Y'all are talking like I know who the heck my best friend really is," I said, cutting off their back-and-forth and about to lose it.

I couldn't believe my innocent distraction request had turned into *this.* I really could use my mom right now. Someone who wouldn't betray me.

Shit. She did, didn't she? She lied to me my entire life. Thinking she was protecting me. Everyone keeps trying to protect me, and now it's starting to feel like they're only trying to protect me from the truth. I'm a magnet for liars. This is just . . . I'm spinning out. I need to calm down.

"Let's just say your best friend is not who she says she is." Did my brother really just throw those words at me so casually and add a shrug as well?

"Don't do that." My eyes burned, and my body was now wound so tight I thought I'd snap. "Don't act like having *another* someone close to me lie is—"

"You're right," Ryder cut in without hesitation, stepping forward. "I'm sorry. I tend to see things through one lens and forget the other side."

Reed went over to the armchair and picked up an M4 that'd been sitting there like it now belonged more in my world than a piano. "That'll be my cue to leave."

Ryder gave him a quick nod and redirected his focus to me. "Whatever you want to know, I'll tell you."

"She asked you not to tell me, yes? So she could be the one?"

"She did." Ryder cleared his throat. "Repeatedly."

I huffed out a deep breath. "Fine, then I'll wait for her to explain face-to-face and decide then how angry I am. For now, I have enough to deal with." Time to shift gears and my energy elsewhere. "How's Alejandro?"

"Alejandro?" he repeated like a question.

Oh, right. I used his full name. But he told me to. I didn't need to tell my brother that right now, and no, that wasn't me being dishonest. I hoped it didn't count, at least. "Is he okay?" I deflected. "It can't be easy what he's about to do."

"No easier than these last few days have been for you. Dealing with people who've hurt you."

"We have to put an end to this. All of it." I closed my eyes as I let my past play through my mind in dizzyingly slow motion.

From opening that box on Friday to the inscription in the wedding band to Alejandro comforting me on his knees back at the lodge before I confessed Mitch's sins, to the hotness that happened by the piano. Everything. All of it. Landing lastly on something Reed had said before he took off. And the *aha* moment hit me like a bolt of lightning. "I think I may have an idea," I blurted out.

"Please tell me that your idea doesn't include you demanding to come to New Zealand with us, come hell or high water, like your best friend has?"

"You're the ones who told her about New Zealand, I take it. Should've left her in the dark like you did me."

He winced, and so did I at that jab.

"Sorry, still a little upset about the lie," I whispered.

"As you should be." His brows pinched as he explained, "But no, it was her brother who found out about New Zealand, we didn't tell her."

"Her brother? What do you mean?"

"He's apparently good with cyber stuff like Gwen. He was able to unfuck the destroyed footage tying Mitch to that vault in New Zealand before Gwen could." He held out his hand. "Gwen's a little upset that someone beat her to that, so maybe don't bring it up to her. Sensitive subject." He gave me an innocent smile.

"I'm still reeling over the fact Hollis has a brother she never mentioned." I took a moment to recalibrate before moving forward. "But if they haven't found Mitch on any other CCTV footage aside from that one time, he must really be holed up somewhere and waiting until the auction, right?"

He nodded.

"But, um." Shit, what idea did I have I never presented? When it slammed back to mind, I shared, "I think we should use Mitch's obsession with me to our advantage."

"What do you mean?"

"He doesn't just want to buy his freedom and safety. He wants me in his own sick and twisted way. Forever, right?"

"And you're saying that we give him *you*?"

"Yes." I shook my head. "No." I closed the space between us, my mind racing. "We give him the illusion of something he can't handle." *Here goes.* "Gwen suggested Hollis be Reed's plus-one. What if I go not only as Alejandro's plus-one, but as his wife?"

Ryder took an immediate step back, a hand shooting over his mouth.

That was a deep-in-thought, considering-it look, right?

"No aliases. But the cover story is the ring on my finger," I continued while he processed. "And Alejandro wears *Mitch*'s band. We don't hide from him. We remain in plain sight. And we make him come right for us, because what choice will he have?"

"And he'll snap seeing you, the woman he desperately wants, with Alex and his ring on Alex's finger." He slowly looked up at me, hand returning to his side. "We turn his sick jealousy and obsession into our advantage for the op."

"Your team can grab Mitch at the auction, and you guys keep him alive so we can get to the vault and open it. Then Secretary Chandler can ensure the evidence never gets in the wrong hands. After, track down the rest of Stratos 2.0 and shut it down for good."

Ryder's brows tightened. "And what about Mitch?"

"Once the vault is open . . ." I swallowed. "We kill him."

CHAPTER THIRTY-NINE

Alejandro

"Nicole Kidman."

That out-of-nowhere name from Reed's mouth had me shooting him a funny look. "What about her?" I ran a quick memory lap trying to recall what I knew about the actress and why Reed was bringing her up now while we waited on my evil ex to appear on screen.

We were currently in the den, staring at a small room with a single chair, a spotlight overhead, and nothing else.

"That's who Beth reminds me of. I don't know why I never thought of that before." Reed adjusted the sling holding his rifle across his body as he stood guard next to me.

He'd refused to let me lone-wolf this conversation despite my request to do exactly that. Something told me he had concerns Beth might turn into the girl from *The Ring* movie and crawl through the screen so he could finally kill her. Maybe that was why he was packing heat for a phone call?

When I continued silently staring at him like he was a few cards shy of a full deck, he scoffed. "You don't think Beth looks like a younger Nicole?"

"Just when I think I have you figured out, you go and say something to throw me off."

He kept his hands on his M4, casually shrugging.

It took two seconds too long for it to click. For me to understand what the man was actually doing. "You're distracting me. Lowering my pulse rate before the call." I waved him off.

Reed rolled his eyes and faced the screen. *That* was more like the guy I knew.

I dragged my hand across my chest, realizing my heart rate had noticeably slowed down, only to pick back up again the second I saw two bodies on-screen.

A guard was walking Beth toward the chair. A nightmare in orange.

Her blue eyes found mine as the guard cuffed her to a chair in front of a table that was bolted to the concrete floor.

My spine straightened at the mere sight of her, remembering I'd flatlined and died for a few seconds because of her.

The guard walked around and stood behind her chair. "You have ten minutes."

"I'll only need two," I remarked, eyes back on the woman who'd ruined my life.

She angled her head while staring at me, and I held my breath, anticipating her to use her CIA mindfuck tricks on me. "Alejandro."

"Don't say my name." There was only one woman outside my mother allowed to call me that, and she was in this cabin. "I know you've already been briefed by Secretary Chandler about what I want, and he's agreed to meet your demands."

"While I can make even a potato sack look couture, I'd prefer a new color and something a bit more pleasant to wear." She dropped her eyes down to her orange jumpsuit as if feeling the need to explain the first demand she'd made. "And the typewriter . . . since they won't give me a laptop . . ." She met my eyes. "I'm going to tell my story."

"I'm sure the CIA would love to publish it," I said dryly as she pivoted her attention to Reed. "As for your last demand," I hissed at the memory of what Secretary Chandler had said he'd agreed for me to do, "you want an in-person visit with me after this mission ends?" No Reed or anyone there to have my six per this demon-woman's request. "Why?"

"I'm helping you without asking for my release, aren't I? I know they wouldn't say yes to that, but I do need to see you. They've turned down every request I've made in the last few weeks to talk to you in person."

This was news to me. I'd had zero clue she wanted a one-on-one. I'd have denied her as well, but what was her endgame? *No, don't take the bait, don't ask. Just focus up. Mission first.*

"I'll tell you when you're here. And just so you know, I'd have told you what you wanted regardless."

I didn't buy that for a second, but I wound up asking anyway: "Why?"

"Because I'd do anything to help take down Mitchell Langston."

From the corner of my eye, I spotted Reed stepping forward, his interest as piqued as my own. I had no clue if this was a mind game from her, or if Mitch was an enemy of hers now making this an enemy-of-my-enemy-is-my-friend situation.

"Talk," I demanded, checking my watch, hating that we'd already used up one more minute than I'd wanted. When she didn't do as I said, I quickly figured out why. "Yes, I'll come visit you after this is over." A chill beat down my back as I bit out what she was waiting to hear. "You have my word."

She quietly nodded. "Mitch's specialty is not only flying, it's also blackmailing people. I was relieved when I heard he died. So trust me when I say I wasn't happy when I learned from Chandler he was back in the land of the living."

Trust you? Sure, I'd sooner trust eating gas station sushi or a cat with a laser pointer locating my target than I would her.

"I'm more than eager to help return him to the graveyard."

"Why?" Reed with that question this time, as he stood next to me, hand still resting on his rifle.

She lifted one blonde brow. "Why do you think?"

"He was blackmailing you?" I huffed out a hollow laugh. *Why am I surprised?*

"The man collected dirt on people and kept it stored for a rainy day whenever he found use for it."

"What do you know about him? What's his connection to Will Hobbs?" I asked, folding my arms, waiting for her to confirm if Audrey's theory was right.

"You know about Stratos, don't you?" Her tone dropped low, almost soft and hesitant. Out of character for her. "It was shut down in January of 2013. Will Hobbs was part of it. And yes," she said with a nod, "I know about the new SEAL Teams formed afterward thanks to a late-night pillow talk with Will."

She was outright letting me know she'd cheated with Will like I'd once suspected back in the day, and I had zero fucks to give about her faithfulness or lack thereof. All I cared about was taking down Mitch and Stratos so Audrey would be safe and could get back to her life. And here I was, doing the thing I promised I never would even if the fate of the world relied on it.

"Did Mitch force you to introduce Will to Trevor Sloane at the military ball in 2017?" I cut to it.

"No, I didn't know Mitch at the time, but Will did. And Mitch presented evidence of our affair to Will, along with some other dirty laundry of his that Will didn't want aired." She angled her head. "It was just sex. I loved you, you know. I'm sure you don't believe that, given everything."

"You shot me. So no, I don't believe you." I looked up at the ceiling, my muscles tensing, angry at myself for letting her get under my skin. "Just keep talking."

"Fine." She waited for my eyes before continuing. "I knew Trevor Sloane, so Will asked me if he could be my guest at the event and make the introduction."

"Because Mitch wanted Will to send Trevor on a mission that'd get him killed," Reed said before I could.

"Mitch didn't say why he needed Will to do that, but given the fact he married Trevor's then-wife a few years later had me putting two and two together. Guy was obsessed and pulled a David and Bathsheba."

"A David and what?" I blinked. Did she just refer to the story in the Bible about the king who sent a woman's husband into battle to die so he could marry her himself?

Beth ignored my question and carried on, "I didn't have to deal with Mitch for years after that, and I assumed it was because of what happened to Will . . . but then he called in a blackmail-favor, and I had to—"

"That's why you were on that op with him?" I asked.

"Mitch was piloting a flight for a private security company that was running an op on behalf of the government two years ago, and he needed someone to cover up the fact there'd be a secondary mission taking place the military didn't know about," she explained, and I couldn't believe she was playing ball so easily.

Then again, the one thing this woman hated more than anything was being betrayed.

"The son of a bitch blackmailed me into doing it by saying he'd tie me to that botched mission Will secretly sent Trevor Sloane and that other team guy on in 2018. I had no choice but to help."

"And this security company," I began, hoping we were finally getting somewhere, "are they a front for Stratos?"

"Stratos is operational again?" She looked genuinely surprised, and while she was a good actress—maybe even better than Nicole Kidman—something told me her shock wasn't fake.

I swapped a quick look with Reed before focusing back on the screen. "The name of the company?"

"I'm assuming you already knew I was on that mission, which means you know the name."

"How'd Mitch know Will?" I pressed forward. "You were dragged into Mitch's games because of Will, so how'd they know each other? The navy?"

"Stratos. Will and Mitch were both part of the unit. They were the only two operators who didn't have their deaths faked after it was shut down, so they didn't have to go off-grid after. That was the government's mistake: letting a man like Mitch walk away with all that knowledge, not expecting it to come back and haunt them one day." She was quiet before changing directions. "The government gave you my things after they locked me up, yes?"

I nodded.

"You destroy it all?"

"Unfortunately not." Wyatt had already collected the boxes from the storage unit, but I wasn't sure if they'd done anything with them yet.

"Good. The teddy bear you won for me on our third date at Six Flags . . . inside is a flash drive. When Will was sleeping, I downloaded a copy of his hard drive. You just never know who you can trust, and in case he ever turned his back on me, I needed something to hold over his head. He never betrayed me, so I never had the need to try and decipher what I'd downloaded. Everything is heavily encrypted. You'll need the best cyber expert out there to make sense of the files."

I called her out on that. "Bullshit. A woman like you doesn't sit on leverage like that. The file may be encrypted, but like hell would you not have taken a look yourself."

She lifted one shoulder, trying to act innocent.

"Check on the story," I asked Reed, but he didn't budge. Hesitancy crossed his face. The man was afraid to leave me alone with her. "It's fine, go."

"Time's about up," the guard said once Reed had finally left. He circled her chair and unhooked her cuffs from the table before forcing her to stand.

I was waiting for the moment when she'd try to escape. That moment didn't come, and that made me more uneasy.

"Alex," she said, thankfully not using my full name that time. "I do hope you take that bastard down, but don't die doing it. I still want that meeting."

"Why?" I couldn't help but ask. "Why do you need to see me in person?"

Now that she was closer to the screen, I could see something there I couldn't before. Something that didn't make any sense. Either my eyes were playing tricks on me, or the ice queen was—

"To apologize to the only man in my life who ever actually gave a damn about me." There was a touch of humanity in her tone I wasn't sure I could believe. "It took me being thrown in here to remember the woman I was before I became jaded by work. And now I remember the girl I was on that date when you won that bear. And while I don't think I deserve your forgiveness, I'm hoping that maybe because of that big, trusting heart of yours, you just might do it anyway."

"You're sure?" Ryder paced the living room by the fireplace in front of the couch where Audrey was sitting, raking a hand through his hair.

"It looks like Mitch was part of the Stratos reboot. In fact, he could have provided this security company everything they needed to kick it off, since he was part of the original group. It may have been all his idea." I thought back to what Beth had shared. "That's, of course, assuming what Beth said checks out."

Ryder stopped walking and faced me, but he remained quiet. Not ready to believe my ex—and who could blame him? I couldn't believe I was standing there doing exactly that myself.

"Helix International is on the list of PMC's Gwen and Natasha drew up as possibilities, and Beth was on that mission with Mitch along with Helix," I pointed out. "Mitch is clearly good at collecting dirt on people and using it to apply pressure to get what he wants. If Beth didn't lie, it looks like Mitch was manipulating people into helping Helix when they couldn't buy them off. And since this wasn't funded or run by the government, they couldn't erase identities of operatives and send them on their own missions."

"Mitch would've had the list of ghost operatives from the OG Stratos and could've dragged some out of retirement as well. Like Rhett," Reed pointed out, shockingly sounding as though he was on the same believing-Beth page as me.

Had the woman Jedi mind–tricked us? "But whatever Arlo told Mitch before he died changed things and made Mitch paranoid. Had Mitch wanting out before he wound up dead, too, even if he did hand Stratos over to Helix on a silver platter." I dropped down into the armchair by the couch.

Reed propped a hand on the mantel, eyes on me. "That's what happens when you create a monster—eventually it turns on you."

"We need to have Natasha and Gwen confirm if Helix is truly our mark. My guess is, Mitch is baiting them down to New Zealand like he is with us," Ryder said.

"If Beth was telling the truth, then there's a good chance Mitch not only has intel on Stratos, both old and new, but he might have—"

"The identities of everyone on Bravo and Echo teams since he'd been blackmailing Will back in the day," Ryder said, cutting me off as that horrible news sunk in. "This mission is now about protecting them, too." He removed his phone from his pocket. "If their identities get released, then they'll be forced to go off-grid."

"We have to do the plan we talked about, then," Audrey murmured as I got my ass back to standing. "We have no choice."

"And what plan might that be?" *What conversation did I miss while I was dealing with my own past?*

Ryder looked at me, ordering, "You'll need to sit for this." He closed his eyes. "The plan includes Audrey going with us to New Zealand, and you going as my sister's husband."

CHAPTER FORTY

Audrey

Ryder dumped my plan on Alejandro in one breath, casually tossing in the Hollis revelation like it was an afterthought. He barely paused between bullet-point beats. Then came the rapid-fire back-and-forth between the three of them. Everything from theories to power plays and the logistics of going from A to B to C were discussed while I sat there silently, as if I weren't at the center of it all.

I was on the verge of losing it as their words blurred in my mind. I also knew if I started rocking like I was having a nervous breakdown, there'd be no way Ryder would agree to let me go to New Zealand, so I needed to pull myself together.

A few words from Alejandro pushed through the noise in my head: *auction* and *absolutely no fake wedding.*

"No wedding, just the honeymoon," I corrected, though it was doubtful anyone had heard me.

Alejandro dropped whatever he'd been saying, speaking with his hands like my Italian father who'd raised me. He turned his gaze sharp on me as if I had two heads.

At this point, maybe I did?

"Mitch will never believe we got married." He hit the side of his hand into his open palm like a blade dicing an onion.

I was already peeling apart, so you know . . .

Makes sense.

"It's too risky—how can you not see that?" Alejandro asked, eyes on my brother.

"The plan falls apart without her and you know it," Ryder responded in a steady tone. "Bravo and Echo may be at risk, given what we now know. It's no longer just about protecting government secrets or former operatives."

"And we will protect them." Alejandro pointed at me. "Just not with your sister in the middle."

"How about a tiebreaker decision?" I was going to keep riding this train of crazy all the way to New Zealand if I had to. I found my backbone again, chucked aside both the pillow and my anxiety, and stood. "Reed. What do you think? You've been as quiet as I have."

Reed glared at me as if unhappy I'd dragged him between two men ready to go to war over how to best protect me.

"If Audrey stays in Colorado, you don't think Mitch will find a way to get to her here? And how are we supposed to open the vault without her?" Reed slowly pivoted toward Alejandro. "A magic trick?"

"Not funny," Alejandro hissed.

"I wasn't trying to be," Reed shot back.

Alejandro's dark eyes slanted over to me before drifting back to my brother like a target he'd dialed in on but didn't want to take the kill shot.

"For the record, I hate this plan—you do know that, yeah?" My brother spoke before Alejandro could present his next argument. "But this is our only plan for now." He pointed at him. "Don't like the plan? Come up with a new one. Until then, I'm calling Chandler and getting approval." He left no room for arguing, because he took off.

"I'm going to check in with Natasha and Gwen," Reed muttered, bailing on us as well.

Maybe that was my cue to leave. To let Alejandro calm down so he'd realize Ryder was right. There was no other way forward that didn't involve us being together.

It was a slow journey to my face before his dark eyes challenged my lighter ones in a duel. Who'd blink or turn away first?

"I should probably give you some space to think," I said, surrendering first.

"To calm down, you mean?" His eyes burned through me, peeling back more of my layers in a much different way right now.

I fidgeted with the sleeve of my shirt, tugging it down to cover part of my hand. *"Peligroso,"* I whispered. "This is dangerous, I know."

"Muy peligroso," he said, emphasizing each word slowly. *"¿Lo entiendes?"* He closed the space between us. *"Me estás volviendo loco."*

Loco. Crazy. I knew that one. "I make you crazy?" My breathy question redirected his focus to my mouth.

"Muy loco." He hit me back with a gritty answer, only to close his eyes. "Go before *I* do something crazy."

"And if I want you to do it?" Because I felt just as *loco*, if not more, than he did.

"Please," he begged, desperation in his voice. *"Por favor."*

I relented and backed up. "Just so you know, the danger out there might be real," I said while turning, preparing to leave, "but this thing between us is, too." I took off after that and went to my bedroom.

Once the door was both shut and locked, I checked my phone, ensuring Chase's little blinking dot was where it was supposed to be. Then Eden's. I didn't have a chance to toss my phone and hide under the covers, because a message popped up.

Unknown: I'm sorry.

Unknown: This is Alejandro btw. I don't think you have my number in that new phone.

Unknown: And I think you misunderstood me down there.

Unknown: I hope you know the ONLY reason I don't want to pretend to be your husband is because I care about your safety.

Unknown: I'd never survive anything happening to you.

I wasn't used to a man being so open with me like this. It was as refreshing as it was terrifying. Because the more honest he was, the more I had no choice but to be as well. To face the truth sitting in front of me.

I'd been so afraid of risking my heart getting broken again, I'd forgotten that risk can also come with reward. And hearts could be healed if the right person held it in their hands.

Unknown: I'm also sorry about your best friend. Can't be easy to find out she lied to you like that. That was news to me. I would've told you had I known. I knew Reed looked into her, but he didn't tell me anything.

Unknown: Beth asked me to forgive her. I'm sure it's a trick. A Trojan horse thing. It has to be. But IDK. It threw me off. But maybe prison changed her.

Unknown: I should probably stop talking to myself.

Unknown: Anyway . . .

I pulled back the covers and slipped beneath them, needing to sit before I responded.

Me: Hi.

I programmed his name into the phone.

Alejandro: Hi.

Alejandro: So, I'm not talking to myself?

Me: Not anymore, no.

Me: You don't need to apologize.

Me: As for Beth? I suppose miracles do happen. I do know hanging on to hate will hurt you more than it does her, though.

Me: And yeah, the Hollis news sucked. Still processing. Starting to feel like almost everyone in my life has lied to me. Has anything in my life been real?

Bubbles bounced.

Disappeared.

Came back again.

After a few minutes passed and no text came through, I messaged him.

Me: Are you okay?

Alejandro: No. Are you?

Me: No.

Me: We're a pair.

Alejandro: Well, since we're about to go undercover as ourselves but married . . . I guess it's a good thing we're on the same dangerous page?

Me: Does that mean what I think it means?

Alejandro: No one else I'd rather be dangerous with . . .

Alejandro: So, what do you say? Marry me?

I laughed, my glossy eyes fighting back shockingly happy tears in spite of everything.

Me: Talk about the proposal of all proposals.

Alejandro: I could come up there and get on my knees for you if you'd like?

Me: Something tells me that if you did, we might wind up getting in trouble.

Alejandro: Affirmative.

Alejandro: So, is that a yes? Feel like being Mrs. Rodriguez for a few days?

Alejandro: Just a warning, the last one tried to kill me . . . You don't plan on doing that, right?

Me: You're hilarious, you know that, right?

Alejandro: I'm the team's comic relief. It's in my job description.

Me: To use humor to try and hide your feelings?

Alejandro: Is it working?

Me: Not even a little bit. Because it's too late. You've already been too honest with me and shown me the real you. Can't hide from me. I won't let you.

Me: So, what is it that you really want to say? You know, if you could say anything without worrying about being considered loco?

Those bubbles began dancing again.

Alejandro: A few days being married to you doesn't sound so great. That's what I'd say. Not nearly long enough. Eternity sounds better.

Eternity? What a beautiful word.

Alejandro: And Audrey?

"Yeah?" I said out loud as if he could hear me.

Alejandro: This really is dangerous. This thing between us. For me, at least.

Me: I don't get it. Help me out? Why?

Alejandro: Trevor.

Alejandro: It looks like Mitch sabotaged your marriage. Maybe you two belong together. Deserve a second chance to at least see. And I would never want to stand in the way of you two trying again.

"Ryder was right about you," I whispered to myself. "You do have the biggest heart."

Alejandro: Don't respond to that now.

Alejandro: I want to hang on to the illusion for a little longer that one day you could be mine. And that this isn't crazy or dangerous. That it's meant to be.

My back hit the headboard, and I tugged the covers up tight to my chest.

I started to type, prepared to tell him I was not getting back with Trevor. To let him know I felt the exact same way as he did. Crazy or not, I didn't care.

Alejandro: Don't. Please.
Alejandro: After, okay?

After the mission. After this is over. Yeah, I can do after, I suppose. After's a fair request.

Alejandro: But just so you know, if there's a chance at a future with you . . . I'll wait on that chance forever.

CHAPTER FORTY-ONE

Alejandro

"You doing okay?" Ryder joined me in the bathroom as I redressed my wound, clearly taking my closed bedroom door as an invitation to come in. "I should have asked you that already. The call with Beth couldn't have been easy."

"None of this has been easy, man." I washed my hands and put my shirt back on. "But I'll be fine." I didn't feel like getting into the thick of anything right now. That text-talk with Audrey had also done a number on me. I was still trying to wrap my head around how I'd be calling her Mrs. Rodriguez, calling her my wife when I'd never planned to call anyone that ever again.

Now, there I was, terrified about the days after when I'd have to stop.

Stop calling her my wife.

Stop calling her mine.

Stop wanting the woman I was quickly (crazy or not) learning I wasn't so sure I'd be able to live without.

"You do realize the word *fine* is just as bad when a dude says it as a woman, right?" He'd given me a few seconds to spin out in my head before calling me on my shit.

"At least let me out of the bathroom before you Freud me." I gestured for him to make room to leave. "Hate when you try to hijack my job like that."

He smirked but followed my orders and went into the bedroom.

"Just tell me you have new information." I sat on the bed, resting my forearms on my legs, doing a bang-up job on selling the idea of *fine*.

"The flash drive was in the bear. Heavily encrypted. Gwen's working on it. So, yeah, Beth told the truth. Well, that she performed surgery on a stuffed animal and stitched it back." He observed me like I was both his patient and his friend, not a Tier One operator.

Didn't feel like I was myself right now, so I didn't blame him.

"Chandler wants us on a flight to New Zealand as of yesterday. If there's even a remote chance Hobbs told Mitch about Bravo and Echo—"

"I know. I'm on board with the plan." I sat up taller, eyes on my best friend, trying to figure out how I'd wound up falling for his sister, a sister he'd only just found out about. Not on my 2027 bingo card, that was for damn sure.

"Good, because Natasha also confirmed the two co-owners of Helix are in Queenstown, not even twenty minutes away from where the auction is being held on Friday. Highly doubt that's a coincidence."

"So, Mitch is drawing us all there so we can kill each other, and he can walk away with the cash and Audrey." I got my ass back up to standing at that news. "He wants us focused on Helix. Look one way while the real magic happens somewhere else. Oldest trick in the playbook."

"And he's had a year to plan this out, and we're running on borrowed time."

"How the hell does he think he's going to get Audrey away from us?" I grunted, the idea of that happening un-fucking-acceptable.

"I don't know what to think about anything anymore to be honest. The fact your psychotic ex is the one helping us now?" he hissed, pushing off the dresser. "None of this makes sense."

Yeah, same messed-up page. Still a dangerous one, too.

At the sound of Reed's voice gaining ground, clearly on the phone with someone as he walked and talked, that reminded me . . . "Hollis," I said under my breath.

"Who Reed is talking to now, actually. And we didn't tell you about her because I didn't want you to have to lie as well."

I lifted my chin toward the door. "What's her story?"

"A thing of make believe," he said with a smirk.

"And that means?"

He removed his phone from his pocket, then swiped it open before tossing it to me. "Have a look for yourself. You'll see exactly what I'm talking about."

I swiped through the screenshots of intel he had on Audrey's best friend, shaking my head in disbelief. "This is real?"

"Yup." He accepted his phone back. "Chandler's the one that gave me that information," he added as the door opened and Reed entered. The man looked pissed.

"Hollis has arranged for us to fly out of Denver on her Boeing 747 that she apparently owns. One of three, actually," Reed let us know.

"At least it's a jumbo jet, since my sister can't handle small planes."

"Chandler okayed this?" I asked in surprise. "He's allowing her to hijack the mission?"

"Join. Support. Follow *our* lead." Reed brought the phone back to his ear. *"Right?"* He huffed out a low, anguished noise while grimacing. "She's also secured our invitations to the auction. I don't even want to know how. Don't care."

The man really couldn't stand this woman, which was saying a lot.

"Yeah, I hear you. Got it," he said into the phone before taking a deep breath. "She has another team that'll be meeting us in New Zealand for backup, too. Approved by Chandler."

"Yeah, well, this just took an interesting turn," I said as he ended the call just as Audrey came up behind him to join us in my bedroom.

It was getting a little crowded in here. Perhaps the guys needed to leave. She could stay. Problem solved. *Fuck. No.* What happened to *after*? To waiting. To giving her time and space to think, breathe, and ensure she and Trevor didn't belong together?

"What'd I miss?" Her blue-green gaze journeyed around the room, landing on me last as she pulled the side of her lip between her teeth.

Mrs. Rodriguez. Wife. Mother of my future child. Yeah, that's where my head was currently. In that dangerous, dangerous place of hope. *I am so screwed.*

I cleared my throat, trying to remember I'd negotiated with terrorists before. Taken back a hijacked ship from literal pirates. And survived walking in on my parents "doing the tango in bed," as they'd called it when I was ten.

So, you know, I could survive another few days with this woman without wanting to pull that lip between *my* teeth instead.

I blinked my way over to Delta One, realizing words were being spoken and I'd been so busy staring at his sister's mouth that I hadn't heard a single one. "Who's going where?"

Ryder shot me a funny look, reading me loud and clear, I was mentally hedging on FUBAR status right now. He jerked his chin like a command. An order to focus up.

Roger that.

"Chase and Trevor are going to be transported by way of a military escort to Buckley. They'll stay on base there while we're in New Zealand." Ryder clued me in on the exchange. "Echo Team's on their way to Colorado. Echo Four and his wife won't be joining; they're stuck in New York. But the other four will be picking up Rhett and Eden when they land and taking them to the base, too. Chandler wants to have his own people question Rhett. I don't think Chandler wants Beau knowing much about this."

"Classified. True," I remarked in a low voice, doing my best to refrain from looking at Audrey so I could stay on mission.

"At least I know Chase will be on a military base while we're gone. Can't get much safer than that, I suppose," she whispered.

"Something tells me Trevor will agree with that and want to join Echo Team as their fifth when they fly to New Zealand to meet up with us," Ryder said steadily, eyeing his sister to get a read on how she'd handle that.

"Will Hobbs tricked Trevor into thinking he was joining Bravo before, and he risked his life for that. Then he turned down Charlie Team because of it. Now? He might actually work with Echo . . ." Her voice trailed off, leaving us with a nonanswer on her opinion about him rolling with us down there.

"Musical SEAL chairs," Reed joked, earning himself a death stare from Ryder and me. "Told you I wasn't funny," he said to Audrey. "Sorry."

She patted his arm. "You're funny to me, don't worry."

I had no choice but to look at her again. *I basically told you I want to marry you over text, didn't I?*

"I should pack, then." She tipped her head toward the door, letting us know she was about to leave. "Just need one bag, I guess. We're not going too long."

I stepped forward, and the words fell from my mouth before I could make sense of what I was saying: "Which bag?"

She slowly turned to the side, glancing at me, and my heart slammed against my rib cage as I waited for her to respond. Like her bag choice—the one I packed or his—might be a clue as to where her heart was. Getting back with Trevor. Or trying out a future with me.

Crazy. It was crazy to think this way. To hope.

But then she met my eyes and, in a steady voice, answered, "*Rosa.*" Her eyes narrowed, almost appearing glossy as she whispered, "I choose pink."

CHAPTER FORTY-TWO

Audrey

In the air

From inside my private suite on Hollis's plane, I stared at the little dot on my phone as it blinked steadily, tracking Chase and Trevor's movement. They were en route to Buckley, the military base in Aurora. ETA thirty minutes.

Echo Team had already landed in Colorado and were now on their way to pick up Eden and Rhett as well.

So far, all good. Everyone was safe. I just needed to convince my nervous stomach of that.

As if reading my mind, a text popped up from Trevor.

Trevor: We're getting closer. Stop watching the tracker. I can feel your anxiety from here, and you're up in the air.

Trevor: Talked to Hollis yet? You should . . . But I know you're still pissed at me for not telling you the truth after I learned who she was last year, so you probably won't take my advice.

Me: I was a chicken and told Ryder not to let her near me yet, which is probably a jerk move since we're on her plane, and she's helping us. But am I a magnet for liars?

I palmed my forehead as if he could see me.

Me: Do I have "Gullible" stamped somewhere?

My hand plopped back into my lap.

Trevor: 😟 You're trusting. Not gullible.
Me: Not trusting anymore 😟
Trevor: Don't blame you after the last few days. Also, I'm sorry for not telling you about her. She said it'd be safer if you didn't know.

I was in the middle of responding when someone knocked on the door of my closed-off suite, which was three times the size of one of those business pods on a commercial plane.

"I know you don't want to talk to me, but I'm not above begging."

At hearing Hollis's voice, I deleted what I'd planned to say and let Trevor know I was going to confront Hollis.

He wished me luck; then I set aside my phone and gave her the all clear to come in.

Hollis's look today was nothing like I was used to. Black combat boots, dark skinny jeans tucked into them. A leather jacket open to a white tee. Her dark-brown hair was in one long ponytail-like braid.

Badass vibes, not Barbie on a Beach like she'd tried to get me to believe.

"Hi." She sat in the seat next to me. "On a scale of one to ten, how much do you hate me?"

I frowned. "I don't hate anyone. Well, I take that back." I twirled a finger in the air. "There are a few people on that list." *Like Mitch.*

"Present company not included," I added in a small voice. "I'm hurt, not mad."

"Rather you be mad than sad."

I lifted one shoulder as my response. "Is Hollis even your real name?"

She shifted her braid around to her back, sitting up taller. "Lady Celeste Hollis Avery Wyndham d'Aragon, daughter of the Duke of Rothvale."

I only caught half that. Was she kidding?

"D'Aragon is tied to my old Iberian and Vatican bloodlines. Last time anyone called me by my full name, they were either trying to knight me, arrest me, or marry me." She gave a nervous laugh, suggesting she was kidding—but heck, maybe not? "I picked Hollis Avery to go by on an assignment in DC, and she became what felt like the real me. Maybe that's because you were the first real friend I felt I had outside my family?"

"I'm sorry, but *what*?" Something told me we'd barely scratched the surface, and I was already in over my head. "This is a lot." I blinked and pointed up. "Normal people don't just own planes like this. Governments do. Whole-ass countries, sure." I pulled the covers up tighter like a shield. "And they aren't knighted or have names that sound like they belong in a fantasy movie."

"I know." She nodded. "I'm not remotely normal." She faked another laugh, this one more nervous sounding than before.

"That's the only thing I believe right now." I blinked back tears, the feeling of betrayal hitting as hard as it had with Mitch. "How can you be a real friend when I don't know the real you?"

One reason I'd gravitated toward Hollis, despite being worlds apart lifestyle-wise, was because she'd seemed so authentically genuine. So real. Painfully blunt sometimes, but I liked that about her. Now to find out everything had been a lie. Ugh, yeah, *hurt* was an understatement.

"I don't know what you want me to say," she finally said.

"Start with the truth. Always a good place."

"Whether you believe it or not, you probably know me better than anyone outside my family, at least." She shrugged. "I'm myself with you. I get to be Hollis, the girl next door, when we hang out and talk. Not Lady Celeste, who has one of the highest kill counts of my siblings."

"Highest kill . . ." I couldn't even finish echoing that. "And since when do you have siblings?" I deflected, since I couldn't handle the whole murder thing.

"I have a twin brother, and he's a hacker-cyber-guru who's a little reclusive. Then there's my slightly younger sister, who drives me nuts, but I love her." She gave me a half smile. "And my other brother is . . . oh gosh, how to describe him?" She shook her head. "Let's just say he puts the *gray* in *morally gray*."

Understood. How was I going to get through more of this?

Hollis leaned toward a cabinet beneath the TV and popped it open.

Ah, not a cabinet. A mini fridge.

"Looks like you need a drink. We have a long flight, don't worry. You'll be sober before we arrive." She unscrewed the mini bottle of champagne. "No glasses in here," she said while nudging it my way. "Take a sip. Digest what I've said; then we'll continue."

Yeah, those were orders I could follow. I took a few more fizzy sips than planned, then wiped my hand across the back of my mouth as I waited for her to go on.

"I was only ever trying to protect you. I gave you the version of me that was safe to know. But if I'm being honest, maybe I didn't want you to know the other me. Not because it's risky, but because you're the only person who didn't expect anything from me. And it was nice not to have to wonder if our friendship was genuine or if you were afraid of me."

"Right, because you have a higher kill count than your *morally gray* gray brother," I said with as much sarcasm as I could pack into that comment.

She opened her own bottle and downed even more than I had of mine before responding. "I said 'one of.' Big brother has me beat by two."

"And do you have a chalkboard with a tally of these numbers at home or something?" More sarcasm, followed by another few sips of champagne. And maybe I really was mad, not just hurt. "I trusted you. You babysat my son." I slammed my free hand against my chest. "What if some guy attacked you while you were rocking him to sleep?"

"I'm sorry, but please know I'd have died protecting your son if need be."

"There shouldn't even be a *need be*," I shot out, feeling unhinged.

"I failed you. In more ways than one." She drank more of the champagne. "I have no clue how I missed the whole Mitch thing. I looked into him, and I didn't find anything. Of course, Chandler himself vouched he was really dead when I asked him last year."

I waited for her to continue. To rip the Band-Aid off and get through this.

"I've memorized this speech a hundred times since we met, just in case." She finished her bottle and tossed it in the trash. "My family . . . we're legacy operatives with titles across multiple empires going back over six hundred years. They've advised the Medicis. Funded exploratory work for da Vinci. Even smuggled artifacts out of Constantinople before it fell to the Turks and became Istanbul. My lineage was granted special diplomatic status by the Vatican in the 1600s, a status that was never revoked."

Another pause. Another sip that I took. Another chance for my head to explode over what she was saying.

"We're part of the first intelligence networks that existed centuries before agencies and their acronyms. We even helped design MI6's cipher system." She took a quick breath. "Heck, you should meet my mom. She helped dismantle three foreign governments without firing a shot." She smiled. "But we don't serve just one country. We serve *order*. And we also store secrets. Our vaults make the Smithsonian look like a gift shop." Her casual shrug would be my undoing. "I grew up in the US, that wasn't a lie, but it's because someone tried to put a bullet through my brother's skull when he was seven during a cello recital."

"A *cello* recital? You're kidding."

"The bullet missed." The casualness of all this was going to send me over the edge I was already teetering on. "The hit was linked to an Eastern European intelligence feud," she explained as if that'd make perfect sense to me. "So my parents relocated us here when I was three, but they kept all their other estates around the world active."

My God.

"I didn't stumble into spycraft; I was raised in it. My family has amassed priceless and sometimes questionable relics, one of which is coming in handy for this auction. The invitations were secured because of it."

Another casual lift of her shoulder as if this was all just a regular Monday and she wasn't shattering my perception of reality by the second.

"My family has been accused of hiding everything from the maps of Atlantis to the Ark of the Covenant."

I gulped back more champagne. "And do you have those?"

A faint smile crossed her lips. "Maybe? I've never seen the east wing's subbasement at our estate in Romania. If it glows and hums, I stay away."

That had to be a joke that time.

Right?

"So, what you're saying is you're a little Indiana Jones, James Bond, and Lara Croft all mixed up into one?" No wonder Reed said it'd be better to have her explain this herself.

"Well, they're fictional characters, unlike me. Rumors and legends of our family may have inspired their stories, though." She stood and rested her back against the partition wall, crossing one combat boot over the other. Shoes I'd never have pictured my alleged Birkin-bag-buying friend wearing.

"How'd Reed even figure this out?"

"I've helped out the government before. I actually helped gather intel to locate Trevor back when he was taken."

What?

She continued as if she hadn't just rocked my world with that comment. "So that's why it was easy to get Secretary Chandler to green-light my coming with you all."

"Hollis . . ." My chest constricted. "Thank you for helping him."

"Of course." She lifted one shoulder, then moved on. "My twin brother's also helped out Falcon Falls Security, whether they realized it was him helping or not."

"Why'd you tell me you were an only child?"

"Because I didn't want to lie about who they were and make it even more complex, I guess?"

I suppose that actually makes sense. I tossed the bottle in the trash, the champagne heating my veins and emboldening me a bit more.

"I was used to being offered weapons of war, not banana bread. Then you came along, being all nice and kind. Chatty. Annoying, at first, with the whole innocent thing." She laughed. "You grew on me; then I didn't want to give you up."

"It's the banana bread, right? It's damn good." I couldn't believe I'd just tossed in a joke after all *that.* "What were you doing living in my building in the first place? Looks like you could have bought the whole street instead."

"I was renting the penthouse to run surveillance on a double-agent politician with ties to a rogue intelligence cabal." She shrugged. "Anyway."

Yeah, if that word was ever needed, now would be the time.

"So, this other you I'm just now meeting, tell me more about her. Not about your family, but about you." I slid my legs around, sneakers to the floor. "Give me a few details so I can merge the two *you*'s I know in my head."

She lifted her eyes to the ceiling, thinking. "Well, I actually can't stand that bagged-tea garbage you always offer me, but I drink it anyway. My favorite car that I own is a 1967 Jag I keep in London." She dropped her chin, finding my eyes. "I was trained by Gurkhas while in Nepal, and that was a life-changing experience. I've never been a shouter, and yet people still seem to listen. And, let's see, I don't actually give a shit about designer handbags or sipping cocktails on beaches. I bet you guessed that by now."

"And relationships?"

"I really do have a thing for bad boys and have commitment issues. Now you might have a better idea of the reason behind that."

"Still processing, but yeah." The ping from my phone served like an intermission for her big reveal. "It's Trevor," I shared, relieved. "They're safe at the base." I clutched the phone to my chest.

Before Hollis could respond, my brother joined us. "Gwen decrypted the flash drive."

Hollis checked her watch. "In record time. Knew she could do it. She find anything that might help us?"

"Yeah," Ryder said with a nod. "There were files on the identities of every operative from Stratos, and she also confirmed Mitch and Rhett were definitely part of the unit. Mitch was a pilot. Just not a 'dead' one like Rhett. She's sending us photos of the rest of the operatives now to see if we recognize any of them."

There went my stomach again, free-falling at that confirmation.

"Meet us out in the cabin," he said while taking off.

I gently squeezed Hollis's arm. "I'm still upset, but you're also still not on my hate list."

"I'll take that," she said with a tentative smile before we went out to find the others.

The champagne was starting to kick in now. I should have come up with the drinking idea sooner.

The second we returned to the cabin, Alejandro caught my eye. We hadn't had a private moment alone since I basically told him I returned his feelings in a very big way with my "pink bag" proclamation. Well, I hoped he'd read between the lines there, at least.

"You okay?" he mouthed.

"Trying to be," I mouthed back, giving him the best reassuring smile I could manage.

"Jason," I overheard Hollis say, and she flicked her wrist for him to scooch over.

He moved over three seats. "I go by Reed," he grunted.

Something told me she knew that and enjoyed pushing his buttons.

"Here's what Gwen sent us," Reed said while syncing his laptop to the large screen at the front of the cabin closest to the cockpit. "Every operative is on here with their aliases provided when they were forced into retirement." He began flipping through images.

"Wait, go back. No beard and younger." I cupped my hands around my mouth. "Is that who I think it is?"

Ryder stood, phone to his ear. "Gwen, we've ID'd one of the men. Alert Echo Team they're about to walk into an ambush."

"Beau." I couldn't believe this. He'd been right in front of us this whole time—and oh God, Eden. "He's a ghost operative from Stratos . . . and Mitch is going to use Eden as leverage to get to me."

CHAPTER FORTY-THREE

Alejandro

We'd been ten minutes short of finding out the truth, that Beau had been a plant in Audrey's life.

Ten. Fucking. Minutes.

Echo Team would have arrived and stopped Beau and Rhett, taking them down. Kept Eden safe.

As Audrey talked to Trevor over the phone, I stared out the oval window at the clouds beneath us, searching for answers. Trying to find the *reason* written in the sky as to why we were ten minutes too late to protect Trevor's sister. It didn't make sense. I tried to rationalize it, to find a path forward, but I was coming up empty.

I lifted my eyes to the ceiling of the plane, keeping my hand on the wall by the window.

Silence. Why'd I expect to easily hear God answer me just because we were over thirty thousand feet in the sky?

I continued listening to Audrey talking, her soft voice competing with the hum of the engines and the broken chaos in my mind.

"We'll get her back, you have my word." Audrey's promise had me slipping my gaze over to locate her in the cabin.

At least Trevor and Chase had made it to the base safely. And the friends Trevor had asked to watch over the sheriff station hadn't been hurt.

Now I was really damn glad Ryder had made the decision not to give Eden any of our locations, even though we had hers.

Audrey ended the call a minute later and turned toward her brother as he asked her, "How's he holding up?"

"He's keeping it together for Chase." She clutched the phone beneath her chin. Her skin was pale but her eyes dry.

I'd caught a faint whiff of alcohol on her when I'd hugged her a few minutes ago, so I had to guess that was steeling her nerves to get her through this.

"Why didn't Beau attack us when the lodge was hit?" Audrey looked around the cabin, searching for answers the way I'd checked the sky. "He had two deputies with him. They could've used the element of surprise. We'd never have seen it coming."

Ryder stood and braced his hand on one of the seats, his gaze drifting to Reed and Hollis, who were working on laptops nearby with three seats of distance between them, which was probably still not enough for Reed. "He might have dropped one of us, but he'd have been a dead man after that. Dead for real, I mean."

"And the deputies were more than likely unaware of who he really was," Reed said, looking up at her from over his laptop.

"You think it was him and Rhett who broke into my place Friday? Beau was the first to arrive on scene. I bet they'd planned to ask me where the rings were, so they got ahold of them then."

"Thankfully, Trevor showed up before they anticipated." Now that I knew it was probably Beau or Rhett who'd hit her with the butt of their gun, I'd be returning that blow with a lot more force when I ran into them next.

"We told Beau where to find your ring." Ryder hung his head in frustration. "We handed it right over to the fucker."

"Not your fault." Audrey tossed her phone aside and went over to him. "And I told Trevor the same thing when he started blaming himself for missing the truth about Beau when he ran a background check on him after he started dating his sister."

"I take it Natasha checked him out this weekend and didn't find any red flags?" Reed asked Gwen over the web call.

"Yeah, my stepmom is also on the same guilt train as everyone else. Beau's cover was as bloody good as Rhett's, and she missed it. After we learned about Rhett, I should have checked myself."

"How about we cut the blame all around? Mitch had over a year to plan everything out, and we're working from behind." I lifted my brows, eyes sharp on Audrey with a silent directive I needed her to get on board with.

"As for Beau, he's more than likely just following Mitch's orders. Him. Rhett. They were both Trojan horses. Beau played the long game for him, and Rhett was brought in for the final play." Hollis joined in on the conversation while closing her laptop. "What I'm still trying to understand is, why Mitch did all of this in the way he did. Why not just give the evidence to Rhett or Beau to hang on to, come for Audrey when he was ready, then send word to Chandler that he's actually alive and bait everyone to New Zealand? No need for the vault. For Beau dating Eden. The attack at the lodge. Clean. Easy. And boring, sure, but . . ."

Ryder urged Audrey to sit, and once she was safe and buckled, he answered, "Our assumption is that Mitch is a paranoid asshole who didn't trust anyone with what he had. We also know he *thinks* he loves Audrey, so he wouldn't want to outright put a target on her head by storing the evidence in her possession. Safer for her to have the key without knowing about it. Or for anyone to know what the key even was—probably not until the last minute, when he needed Beau to grab it over the weekend."

"For that matter, something tells me Mitch would rather Audrey remain in our custody until the final showdown than Beau's or Rhett's.

Maybe he was worried if they had both her and the key, they'd cut him out. Or, well, worse." *Is Mitch keeping Audrey safe from two men who might want more than just money from her?* Was his twisted obsession, in some weird way, protecting her?

"I guess that makes sense." Hollis's hesitant tone wasn't all that inspiring as to whether she believed our theory. "Trust is important." She looked away from Audrey as if pained at the memory of breaking her best friend's trust by lying to her. "I can see Mitch doing what he did for those reasons."

"But you're still having doubts?" I asked her.

"Just trying to wrap my head around Beau, or whatever his real name is . . . moving to Colorado to embed himself in Audrey's life in preparation for this moment," she replied. "There had to have been an easier way to be a Trojan horse."

"Trevor," I reminded her. "They knew the kind of man they were up against. The security he'd have. Probably caught wind he was suspicious of Mitch and had poked around about it. They had to be careful. Play their cards right to earn his trust so they could walk right into his own house without Trevor realizing he'd invited the enemy to the dinner table."

Hollis nodded, but there was something in her eyes that still told me she wasn't convinced.

"Where are you in determining who's been helping Mitch out? Hacker or insider?" Ryder turned his focus on Gwen. "Someone had to have given Beau a heads-up that Echo Team was en route."

"It was Trevor," Audrey whispered. "Another reason why he blames himself. He told Eden they were being relocated to the base and SEALs were on their way to get them."

"Trevor also let Beau know we were Delta," I said at the memory, thinking back to dinner on Saturday night.

Audrey shot me an apologetic look as if that were her fault. No, not even close. Not Trevor's, either.

"So that's how they knew. No one had to look into our files. We told them everything ourselves." I cursed, tearing a hand through my hair.

"Well, this all makes a lot more sense," Gwen said a quiet moment later. "My grandfather personally vouched for everyone who knew Echo was on their way, so I'd assumed it'd been a cybersecurity breach. But this is a best-worst-case scenario. Otherwise, if someone had hacked my grandfather's servers, then we'd be dealing with a much bigger problem."

"Mitch still has to have someone highly skilled helping him with everything, right?" I asked Gwen. "Anyone capable of creating Beau and Rhett's new identities while also scrubbing CCTV evidence from existence the way they did are pros. But at least we have the original Stratos files and all the operatives' names." Beth saving our asses with that was another curveball I'd yet to wrap my head around. "Were the new identities provided to Beau and Rhett when they were placed into retirement different—"

"Different from now, yes," Gwen confirmed. "Which makes things a little tricky in trying to find if any other ghost operatives in these files are assisting Mitch. A simple search of the covers the government provided them in 2013 won't turn up anything useful if their names were changed again by this hacker."

"Need some help from my brother on that?" Hollis offered. "Two of the best cyber minds coming together should be able to easily handle one hacker, right?"

"Any chance I can get a name and face to go with this brother of yours who seems to be my rival?" Gwen smirked.

"Maybe one day." Hollis winked. "For now, you can get his help, though. Nothing breeds success more than healthy competition."

Before Gwen could respond, Audrey raised her hand. "I have a question unrelated to cyber stuff. But I'm confused. If Mitch prepared everything down to the last detail, including trading me for Eden once we arrive, then doesn't that mean he has a contingency plan if that doesn't work out?"

I hung my head, not wanting to be the one to answer that.

Because yeah, he would.

The man had gone to major lengths to set these domino pieces up as he did, ensuring that when he knocked the first one over, they'd all fall how he wanted them to and we'd end up in the mousetrap, while he'd walk away with Helix destroyed, rich, and worst of all . . . with Audrey.

"*He's* the backup plan," Ryder said, when clearly no one else wanted to be the one.

"I don't get it," Audrey whispered.

"If his plan with Eden fails, he has one more trick up his sleeve," I remarked in a low voice. "And that's to leverage himself if he has to."

"Because Chandler still needs what's in that vault," Audrey said in understanding. "And it takes both of us—and both rings—to open the safe before it expires and someone gets their hands on it either way."

Ryder nodded. "Mitch knows we need him alive, and the US government will do just about anything to contain this."

"They'll even cut Mitch a deal to make it happen?" Audrey unbuckled her seat belt and stood. "Would your grandfather really pay him off and then just *let* Mitch walk away scot-free?"

"He wouldn't pay him nearly as much as Mitch could get at the auction, but up to 10 million? Probably." From the sounds of it, Gwen had already discussed this with the secretary. "But Mitch would have to sacrifice taking you with him as part of the deal."

"Mitch wants you and a higher payout, though," Ryder reminded her. "So he'll do everything in his power not to rely on his backup plan."

"I . . . need a minute." Audrey walked around her brother and went down the aisle, not making eye contact with any of us as she started for one of the five suites in the middle of the plane.

Hollis stood as if preparing to go after her, but Ryder called out, "No, you lost the best-friend privileges for the moment, remember?"

Hollis's shoulders fell, but she pivoted to the side and nodded her okay to stand down.

"Keep working. Get me more intel to go on so we can get ahead of these bastards once and for all," Ryder ordered, sweeping his gaze around the room. "And I'll go, um . . . be who she needs right now. Her brother."

CHAPTER FORTY-FOUR

Audrey

Queenstown, New Zealand

Now I understood what time travel must be like. It was Wednesday night here, but still Tuesday in Colorado. After nearly twenty hours on a jumbo jet and skipping eighteen ahead, I felt like I had two left hands. Not ideal for playing piano—not that I planned to. Or sleep. The other thing my brother kept insisting I do.

The last "day" had blurred together. Mission prep, theories, cyber-something-or-other stuff that flew over my head, and betrayal. Complex layers of it.

Eden was out there because of me. And Mitch had done exactly what we'd feared: offered her as a trade, demanding we fly to New Zealand. He'd texted proof of life of her on a plane, along with a threat and his HELL signature. Then the usual: *Wait for next steps.*

And because Hollis apparently had a Rolodex that rivaled some legend named Carter Dominick, she had four SUVs waiting at a private hangar for us when we touched down.

Three were decoys, and we packed into just one to play a game of Follow the Wrong Suburban.

The team didn't want to risk going to the hotel where the auction was being held until Friday, so we were currently holed up in the penthouse suite of a resort and spa on Hollis's dime, and I couldn't seem to breathe despite the size and luxuriousness of it.

"I need a minute." I rushed from the living room, where everyone had gathered to talk mission stuff, and into my bedroom.

Out on the balcony, I went to the railing and braced my forearms over it, trying to slow my breathing, to calm down before Trevor arrived.

After Echo Team had confirmed Eden and Rhett were truly gone and went to Buckley, Trevor had worked on convincing them to catch a ride with them here. He'd even had their team dog, Bear, offer a paw as the tiebreaker vote in letting him join.

Based on my conversations with Chase while I'd been on the plane, he was excited for his dad to suit up again. And he was also excited Bear would be hanging back with him at base instead of joining Echo here.

Chase had proclaimed he now wanted to be a SEAL, not a hockey player. *"Just like Daddy,"* he'd told me. *"But only if I get my own Bear."*

Chase is safe; everything is okay. I needed to keep beating that mantra into my brain. Right along with *Eden will be soon, too*.

A chill slid up my arms as I stared out over Lake Wakatipu, the moonlight shimmering on the water. I needed the scenery to quiet the noise in my head.

If it doesn't work soon . . . champagne again it is.

"What are you doing out there?" Alejandro came up behind me, gently reaching for my arm. "I'm sorry, getting fresh air is not worth the risk." He guided me back inside, then shut and locked the door.

"I wasn't thinking clearly. Just couldn't breathe." I hung back by the door, keeping my eye on the scenery outside. "No one knows we're here, though, right?"

"They're not supposed to, no." He shifted to the side, blocking me from the view as if also offering himself as a just-in-case shield.

"Not taking chances with you after what happened last time you were outside."

We were shot at. How could I forget? "Sorry." I peeked around him at the view. The outside reminded me of one of those thousand-piece puzzles. Too beautiful for the chaos surrounding us.

"Sounds like you guys are making progress in there." I stepped away from the glass doors. "Almost like this is your job."

"I'm feeling more and more out of my element by the second, to be honest." He pulled the floor-to-ceiling curtains closed and turned to face me.

"Jet lag can do that." My hands fell to my sides as I resisted setting them where they ached to be. On him. His face. Pretty much anywhere, as long as we were connected.

"I might feel off for another reason." His husky words settled between us.

"Have anything to do with something or someone I know?" I lifted one innocent shoulder, a much better pianist than actress.

He sent me a lopsided smile, his dimple on display. "Maybe." He reached for my waist and took me by surprise by hauling me against him. "It was taking everything inside me not to do this before. Not to hold you on that plane aside from one quick hug."

I set my hands on his chest. His heart was beating as fast as my own.

"Are we erasing the word *after* from our minds for the time being?" I slid my hands up to the sides of his neck, brushing the pads of my thumbs along his stubbled jawline. "Hanging out in the moment?"

"May not be a good idea. Not sure I can go back to waiting until after if we do." His fingertips tightened where he held my waist. Desperation to draw me even closer burned from his skin to mine, right through our clothes.

"The world is on fire," I whispered, breathing him in. Absorbing every second of every moment with him while we had it. "All around us. And we're standing in the middle of it." And as it turned out, I didn't need air outside—just air with him.

His gaze flicked from my lips back to my eyes. "I won't let it touch you. You know that, right? I'll put out every fire to keep you safe." His voice hitched.

"Just not the fire burning between us, okay?" I swallowed. "I like that one."

He brought his mouth to my ear. "And I like that one, too," he whispered just as a voice called out from the living room, letting us know Trevor had arrived.

CHAPTER FORTY-FIVE

Audrey

Alejandro untangled our bodies before anyone spotted us, then offered his apologies to Trevor about Eden when he joined us in my bedroom, then left the two of us alone.

My stomach and heart hurt watching him go, and I now knew I couldn't wait until after to tell him how I really felt. My choice of the pink bag wasn't good enough. He needed to hear it from me now, not later.

"Audrey." Trevor's use of my name drew my attention back to him as he pulled me into his arms.

"I'm so sorry about Eden," I whispered as he held my head to his chest with one hand, keeping his other arm at my back. A broken sound I heard in his lungs came out as a gruff breath a beat later. "Everything will be okay," I reassured him, trying not to break down. The last thing I wanted was him trying to comfort me. "We *will* get your sister back, I promise."

"Mitch needs her, which makes her safe from danger right now," he said in a strangled voice. "So, yeah, I know she's going to be all right. And no trades happening, either."

I stepped back, looking up at him. "I feel a *but* coming."

"More like a *maybe*." He dragged his fingers through his hair. "Riding here with Echo has me worried I won't want to stop operating again after."

That was quite a different *after* from the one I'd been discussing with Alejandro.

"I don't want to upset you or Chase, though. I'm not even sure if it's possible to pick up again and operate, but—"

"But maybe it is," I said in understanding. "And you can be both a dad and a hero, you know. You were before." I squeezed his arm. "I don't get a say in what you do, but if you're asking for my thoughts on it, I want you to be happy. If that's operating, that's operating."

His shoulders fell. "Why are you so great?"

"I thought I was a pain in the ass?" I teased. "Always moody."

"I was kidding about that." He briefly closed one eye. "Mostly." He rested his hand over mine. "Does he know we're just friends? That we're only going to be friends even in light of what we found out Mitch probably did to us?" His gaze moved to the open doors.

Not the transition I expected.

His blue eyes landed back on me. "I'd have totally fucked it up all on my own had Mitch not gotten involved," he said before I could respond. "Unfortunately."

"Don't say that." I rested my free hand on his chest. "And who knows, it could've been me messing things up."

"You?" he scoffed. "Never. You're perfect." He smirked, only a mild flash of sarcasm there. "We're just, uh, not perfect for each other."

And he was right about that.

"Back to what I was asking: Does Alex know the news changes nothing for us?"

"Why are you asking about him?"

"I think you know." He angled his head. "He's the first guy that's come into your life I don't want to kill. Actually like. And I want to see you happy—so call me optimistic, but I was hoping maybe there's something between you two."

I closed my eyes. "I can't believe we're having this conversation after everything."

"Maybe it takes losing those you love to figure out what's right in front of you."

"And what's right in front of you?" I whispered, eyes opening.

"That just because I don't think marriage will ever be in the cards for me again doesn't mean I don't want the mother of my child to be happy. And you have me worried with your comment back in my office. Just making sure if anything happens to me this week that you—"

"Oh no. No, no, nooooo." I pulled away from him. "Don't you dare start with me on that." I made a zero with my hand. "No chance of anything happening to you. Zilch. You *will* be fine. You *will* raise your son." I folded my arms, standing my ground. "And I don't want to hear this BS about you not ever finding love again."

"How do you think it made me feel when you said as much to me?"

He had me there.

I puffed out my cheeks, then let the breath go. "I better hear you say you'll be fine, or you lose my okay on operating."

"So damn bossy." He winked, then flicked his wrist. "Come here. You win. I'll make the promise."

I lifted my arms and held his cheeks like old times. His hands found my waist, and he slowly leaned in, meeting me halfway to rest his forehead against mine. Then he said what I needed to hear, promising he'd return safely.

"Happy?" he grumbled.

"Hardly. We still have hell to get through. Literally." Mitch's brand name had me shivering. Talk about giving new meaning to that word. "But we *will* get through it. All of us."

"Yes, ma'am," he responded, voice thicker with emotion that time.

"Hey, am I interrupting?" Hollis asked, and Trevor cleared his throat and backed away.

I sniffled, swiping at a stray tear while turning around to face her. "No, we're good. What's up?"

"My brother found our hacker. Something to do with reading the numbers inside the numbers inside the digital footprint of her signature?" she said as if this was Greek to her.

She wasn't alone on that.

"No clue what he actually meant, but he knows who's been helping Mitch. Her hacker name is Cipheria. She's been active for over two decades. She's also someone who could hack the Joint Special Operations Command. I mean, she *has* breached JSOC's servers before. She did it five years ago as a game just to let them know she could."

Trevor stroked his jaw, shaking his head. "That means she could have found the transport vehicle bringing Mitch to the safe house, assuming Mitch didn't even know where Chandler was taking him. And she could've sent an unmanned drone to take out the vehicles to help fake his death. Probably had another team on standby in a nearby vehicle for his new ride out."

"Which means JSOC didn't do a great job at fixing their systems to protect her from getting back in again," Hollis said. "I have even better news, though. Gwen got a fix on the location for another former ghost operative from that Will Hobbs file. New alias for the guy, courtesy of Cipheria, and we caught him on CCTV footage here in New Zealand. We think this guy will lead us to your sister. Echo Team's already gearing up now to roll out."

"You're serious?" Trevor rested his hands on his hips, relief filling up his chest as he inhaled.

"Yup. Once we locate him, if we can confirm he's with Mitch and the others, then Secretary Chandler wants us to go ahead and end this now. Converge on their location, and we'll be done before sunrise. No need for the auction." She revealed what sounded like a possible end to this nightmare.

Wait, is this really happening? Was Beth literally going to be our saving grace on this? That was hard to wrap my head around. Liars being honest and bad people being good. Felt like an oxymoron. Or another illusion.

"And if we locate Eden but not Mitch?" he asked. "What are the orders?"

"If they can confirm Eden's safe, then the team sits tight. They'll wait and see if Mitch shows up. If he doesn't, then Echo Team will stay on Eden, then move in for the save on the night of the auction as planned."

"This feels a little too good to be true." I hated to be the one to say it, but something didn't sit right with me, like we were still missing the big picture. Too focused on putting together the thousand pieces first.

"It does feel a little too perfect," Hollis admitted. "Which is why we prepare for the worst and hope for the best." She gestured to the living room. "Your brother's team will stay with you, and I have no plans to leave your side after failing you the first time." She pinned Trevor with a curious look. "You still up for operating with Echo, or is Bear's vote going to waste?" She shot him a quick smile.

Trevor exhaled and looked back at me. "What am I doing?"

"You're asking me?" *Ah, right. You won't be able to stop helping people once you start again.* Not the worst problem to have.

He lifted his brows. "So?"

"That's a simple decision." I rested my hand on his chest. "Go be the man your son looks up to as a role model. And while you're doing that," I said with a smile, "I'll have your back here, waiting for your return."

CHAPTER FORTY-SIX

Alejandro

I tugged at the brim of my cap, using it to try to shield my eyes as I reemerged from the room I'd be bunking in and made my way to where everyone was gathered. Well, everyone except Audrey and Trevor, of course.

Hollis had come back without them after she went to share the news, since I'd walked my ass out of there upon accidentally witnessing what sure as hell looked like a reconciliation between Audrey and Trevor.

Hands on his cheeks. His head tilted forward as she leaned up. They'd been about to kiss.

I'd bailed, feeling like someone had cut my heart out. Since dead men kept walking these days, it made perfect sense that I'd still be functioning without that organ.

Audrey was allowed to change her mind. Just because we had a connection didn't mean there couldn't be another one between her and Trevor.

I'd only known her for two months, and she'd known Trevor for over ten years. What'd I expect?

I needed to find a way to be happy for them because that was the right thing to do.

But tonight, seeing them together, had me feeling like I'd fallen into the deep end of the ocean, in shark-infested waters, having forgotten how to swim.

Consider me down.

At the motherfucking bottom.

Never getting back up again.

Hopefully, one day, I'd actually be able to say, *Congratulations, glad your family is back together,* and mean it. I *needed* to mean it, dammit.

Right now, though, I was choosing the asshole route. Being a grade-A certified selfish piece of shit for wishing she'd chosen me. Wishing we were meant to be, since I'd never felt this way about anyone before.

I shoved my dark thoughts aside when Ryder joined me. "You okay?"

It took him coming over for me to realize I'd only taken one step out of my bedroom before I'd landed in overthinking, quicksand purgatory. I must've looked like I was off my rocker. No wonder he was doing a quick mental health check on me.

I *had* lost it. *Loco*, all right.

I'd fallen for an off-limits woman after promising myself never to fall again. Period.

"I'm great." I swallowed. "But Reed? Not so much. The man was hoping their team dog would be joining us. He's depressed."

Ryder squared up next to me, letting me know he wasn't going anywhere. The man always had my back, even when I didn't want it.

But when Audrey came out of the bedroom with Trevor, the mere sight of the two of them together had me walking back one step, preferring to be anywhere but here. Even visiting Beth in prison sounded like a better idea.

"You need air?" Ryder asked from the side of his mouth.

"I could use it, yeah," I muttered.

"Go. Do a perimeter sweep. Keep out of view of the cameras. We don't want anyone knowing we're here. Mitch's hacker might be monitoring all the hotels in the area for him."

"Roger that." I pulled at the brim of my hat as I started for the door, no need to say goodbye to anyone before they left. I'd already said my hellos and offered my thanks for their help. I wouldn't survive opening my mouth again with Audrey's eyes on me.

"Alejandro?" Audrey called out, and the name I'd told her to use now stung to hear. "Where are you going?"

I opened the door, and Ryder saved me from having to lie, telling her, "He's doing a property check for me."

I didn't turn back. Didn't acknowledge her. I couldn't. I had to find a way to focus on the mission, one that included having her share my last name come Friday. *God help me.*

In the hallway, I made sure to avoid the wide lens of the ceiling camera above the elevator. While Hollis's brother, a cyber magician, had apparently placed the cameras on a loop out here to protect us, my paranoia still lingered like smoke in my chest.

I spent forty-five minutes Houdini'ing my way through the place like a seasoned professional, both inside and outside, before finding myself standing in the jewelry shop on the mezzanine level, which was open for twenty more minutes.

Why I walked into that store? I couldn't tell you.

And why I stared at the mirror in there, my reflection blinking back at me like *I* was the ghost, not Mitch? No damn idea.

And when someone offered to help me, why I asked to see their women's wedding bands even though Hollis had already given one to Audrey? Well, that was easy.

I wanted to buy into the illusion for two more nights. The pretend reality where I was capable of falling for a woman who actually loved me back.

◆ ◆ ◆

I sent another text to Ryder for a status update about Echo Team and their op, then focused back on the view ahead of me.

It was barely fifty out and I was in short sleeves, but the breeze suited me just fine. Not to mention I wasn't ready to return to our suite yet.

I'd parked myself by the lake after buying the ring and stayed rooted to the view, the weight of my Glock at my back and the ring box still in my pocket.

Ryder: They're converging on the location now. A property twenty miles away from the vault in Arrowtown. Why aren't you back yet?

Me: I'm pretending I'm on vacation.

Ryder: Pretend from the room.

Me: Yeah, yeah, I'm on my way up.

I was about to put my phone away and remind myself I was Delta Two with a mission to complete when Audrey's name popped up on the screen.

Audrey: Where are you? You okay? Wish you were up here with us.

I couldn't respond.

I could barely think. Couldn't move. Couldn't do a damn thing.

How'd I let this happen?

This feeling inside me . . . God, it sucked. It was ten times worse than being shot by Beth. So much for waiting until *after* the mission to get to the truth about her feelings, which I'd clearly been wrong about.

Audrey: I miss you. Is that weird to say?

She'd stuck a knife in my chest with that message, then twisted it. That wasn't like her to hurt people. Was she back to being out of character? Was her concern about Eden or being away from Chase the cause? The jet lag?

Ryder: Echo Team has made contact. Eyes on Eden. She's alive and safe. Uninjured and with the operative Gwen ID'd.

I stood up at the news and started for the hotel.

Me: Mitch? Rhett? Beau?

Ryder: Negative. Only two heat signatures are inside the property. No one else was in there when they arrived.

Ryder: Rhett and Beau must've passed her off when they landed and joined Mitch somewhere else.

Since no one on our team had found Mitch on any CCTV footage after Chandler faked his death, the man was clearly doing a bang-up job of actually appearing to be dead. Keeping away from all cameras and laying low.

Ryder: Hold on, Echo's reporting a second SUV just rolled up.

Audrey: Eden's alive and looks okay, thank God. 🙏

I stopped walking, unable to handle being a dick and ignoring her.

I sent her a quick reply, letting her know Ryder already told me and that I was glad Eden was safe.

Another message came from Ryder as I started walking again, unsure if we'd be suiting up and joining them on an op to end this tonight.

Ryder: Four heavily armed military-aged males just exited the vehicle. None of our HVTs.

Me: Can they get clear images of them so we can ID who these other bastards are?

Ryder: They tried, but they're hunkered down far away and lighting is shit. They're using scopes and thermal imaging, and the men are currently all inside. If any come back out, they'll try again.

I went into the hotel, careful of the cameras, then took the service stairwell.

Me: What are Echo's orders?

Ryder: Sit tight for now. Wait and watch. Only move in if they feel Eden's at risk.

That's what I'd figured.

Ryder: I've requested additional reinforcements. They'll be cutting it tight, but I don't think we have a choice.

Ryder: Feels like we're going up against ourselves here, and I don't like it.

Me: Even worse. They're us but with ten to fifteen years more experience under their belts.

Ryder: Don't remind me. Now get your ass up here already.

I hurried to the eighth floor, returning to our suite. The door swung open before I could use my key. Hollis must've had eyes on the hallway and knew I was coming. She let me in and stepped aside.

Audrey was across the room by the windows. She slowly looked up at me. "Hi." The word sounded so damn small, while also somehow full of emotion.

I remained a statue as she started for me.

All I could think about, all I could remember, was that she'd kissed Trevor in her bedroom. Well, not that I'd witnessed that myself. God didn't hate me that much to force me to see it, I supposed.

"Are you okay?" She lingered in front of me, fingers drumming at her sides as if fighting the urge to reach for me.

"I need to be alone, I'm sorry." I moved around her, hating myself for being cold, but I was too upset to talk to her right now. "I'll be in my room. If something changes, let me know."

I took off my hat and tossed it on one of the two queen beds. I was about to shut the door when Audrey blocked my ability to do so.

"You can't just walk away like that and expect me not to worry." She opened her palms, staring at me with narrowed eyes. "Talk to me. What's going on? What happened?"

My jaw clenched, body locking tight. I was in an irrational state of mind. Hurt one too many times. "I can't do this, I'm sorry. I'm mad at you. I have no right to be, but I am." I looked away from her, unable to handle the sight of her being sad. "Please, just leave."

"Alejandro." She tried to come in farther. To challenge my current shit mindset.

I lifted my hands in a request to back up. "I *need* you to leave."

Beth had cheated. Shot me. Fucked me over. None of that hurt as much as losing a woman who was never mine to begin with. Not even close. And I didn't know how to wrap my head around what that meant. It made no damn sense.

"O-okay," she sputtered, and my heart fractured in half at the fact I was hurting her right back and she didn't deserve it.

I waited for the door to click shut; then I went over and locked it before removing the ring box from my pocket.

I'd planned to give it to her tomorrow and savor the time we had together, even if it was pretend. But how could I pretend when her heart belonged to someone else?

It felt like cheating, and there was one thing I'd never be, and it was a cheat. I wasn't like my ex-wife, or anything like Mitch.

But hell . . . I *was* like Trevor, wasn't I?

And we were both in love with the same woman.

CHAPTER FORTY-SEVEN

Audrey

"How's Seraphina?" I asked after Ryder ended his call with her. I didn't even know what time it was in New York. Heck, I barely knew what day it was here. Were we in Thursday territory now?

Ryder slid his phone into his pocket. "She really likes Constantine's wife and son, so she's enjoying herself. Probably getting baby fever, too, since Juliette's pregnant. I'm looking forward to one day being a dad myself."

Well, that was sweet. I couldn't wait to be an aunt.

"But how are you holding up?" He rubbed a hand down his face, appearing as exhausted as I felt.

I dropped onto the edge of the bed and let my head fall forward. "You mean, how am I handling Alex being mad at me for some reason?" I'd gone back to calling him by his nickname. It was somehow a smidge easier that way. "Any idea why?"

Ryder sat beside me. "No clue. Something set him off, but he shut down on us, too. We tried talking to him."

Yeah, I'd noticed. Both he and Reed had attempted to get into the second bedroom and had failed. He was ghosting us all.

"Maybe try and sleep? Trevor's keeping watch on Eden. Chase is safe at the base. Gwen, Natasha, and Hollis's twin brother are digging for more leads. There's nothing you can do right now."

"Why aren't you digging, too?" I gave him a little nudge.

"Bah. I'm more of the rescue-or-kill guy. Give me a target package and send me on my way to execute the mission. A little intelligence gathering here and there is fine, but we're outside my realm of expertise right now, and I'm fine with admitting that." He peeked at me over his shoulder. "Find numbers inside numbers or ask me to be a Ghostbuster?" he joked. "Not my thing."

"Good at making me smile when I should be pouting, so points there." I rested my head on his shoulder. "Also, you're selling yourself short. You'd make an excellent Ghostbuster."

A husky laugh fell from his lips before we both sighed. "Anyway."

"Ah, you use that awkward-killer the way I do. We must be related." I lifted my head, stealing another look at him. "And also, since you're not doing the heavy intelligence lifting with the others, then why don't you rest, too?"

"I'd love to, but Alex locked us out of the other bedroom, and I can't sleep in here. Hollis is taking the queen next to you later. My future wife wouldn't appreciate me rooming with another woman." His laugh that time was light but tired, cutting through some of the tension. "Reed's passed out on the couch, somehow tuning out Gwen's web call with Hollis."

"You could kick him out and have him take the second bed in here," I suggested.

"Let a guy sleep in the same room as my sister? Not a chance." He gave me a funny look. "Don't think Alex or Trevor would be thrilled with that, either."

"I don't think Alex cares anymore." Even saying that tore me up on the inside. "Trevor wouldn't mind. We're just friends." I closed my eyes, resting a hand on my shaky stomach. "Trevor kind of gave us his blessing, actually."

Ryder was the one elbowing me now. "Elaborate."

"Not that I needed him to, but he wants me to be happy, and he thinks Alex makes me that way."

And he had, until he'd pretty much closed a door in my face, in what felt like him also shutting me out of his life. Shutting the door on any *after*-anything happening.

"Hey, sorry to always be intruding." I looked over to see Hollis standing in the doorway, waiting for an invite in, so I waved her over. "I came to tell you Echo Three managed to snap an image of one of the men at the house. We were able to ID him pretty easily since he's a veteran employed by none other than Helix."

"Helix?" Ryder stood, his tone sharpening. "I thought they were Mitch's enemy. And now ours, too."

"Didn't Mitch want us to clean up his mess so he could ride off into the sunset with me and his millions?" A shiver ran through me at that thought.

"Mitch must've turned him. Some of those other guys might be Helix, too." She jerked a thumb toward the hallway. "Gwen's updating Reed and running an idea by him as well. Maybe grab Alex, too, while I have a quick word with Audrey?"

"Sure." Ryder nodded and quietly left, closing the door behind him.

"I feel like we might need to have a heart-to-heart, but give me a minute to transition back from 007 to Hollis Avery." She smirked. "See, still the same me. I can joke and have fun."

"I'm starting to believe you are really *you* you. You know, beneath the badassery and all."

"Good, and you should know I'll always be on your side no matter what. Need a body buried? I'm your girl. Finish a bottle or two of wine and watch sappy movies I secretly can't stand but you love? Anything for you, babe." She smiled. "Team Trevor? Got your back."

Well, that was quite the jarring transition.

"Team Alex? Count me in. Team Kill Mitch?" She leaned in. "Already on that mission." Her expression softened. "You're my best friend. My ride-or-die. It just so happens I'm good at the second part a little more than you realized."

Seeing as though I really did miss my best friend and needed her, I went ahead and bulldozed my way through the hurt her lies had caused me and blurted out, "Alex and I kissed. In Colorado. Actually, we did a little more than that."

Her eyes widened. "You had sex?"

"No, but he, uh, got me off. Against a piano." My cheeks heated. "And I think he gave me more than an orgasm—he gave me hope. Made me feel alive and myself for the first time in so long, even with everything going on." I swallowed. "Like I could play the piano again in front of an audience. And I wouldn't even need lace to combat my nerves if he was there to watch me."

"I'm happy for you but also confused, based on what I thought I walked in on happening between you and Trevor."

"What are you talking about?"

"You two, in each other's arms, heads together. Looked like a post-kiss moment."

"No. We weren't kissing. It was a friendly, heartwarming kind of thing."

She frowned. "Well, shit." Her gaze dropped to the floor. "I thought that's what I saw. Alex must've thought so, too. Ryder sent him to get you two; then he returned looking like he'd seen a ghost and asked me to grab you instead."

"He thought I was kissing Trevor?" I bent forward, hands on my thighs, everything clicking into place. *No wonder he shut me out.* "After everything Beth put him through, he must hate me."

"It's going to be okay. An easy explanation." She gently rubbed my back. "He obviously has genuine feelings for you, or he wouldn't be so broken up about it."

"So hurt he can't even look at me," I whispered. "I need to go out there. Clear the air." I took off, hating myself for not having been on my feet and moving five seconds earlier. "Where is he?"

"Alex?" Ryder looked up from his laptop. "He's gone."

"Wait, what? Why?"

"Gwen identified more Helix agents in Queenstown. Alex offered to go have a look. See what they're up to, since they're not far from the hotel where the auction's being held." He set aside his computer and stood.

I started for the door, hoping to catch up with him.

"Where do you think you're going?" he asked, stopping me in my tracks.

"He needs to know how I feel." I pulled the burner phone from my pocket, fingers trembling as I tried to figure out how to tell him that what he thought he saw was wrong.

"You really want to text that?" Hollis asked, coming up behind me.

"No." My shoulders collapsed. "But maybe I could ask him to come back to the suite? Tell him I have something important to say." I opened our last text thread, prepared to type.

"Wait until he gets back," Ryder requested in a low, almost regretful-sounding voice. "As much as I hate asking that of you, the mission is about keeping everyone safe, so it has—"

"To come first," I finished for him, lowering the phone to my side.

CHAPTER FORTY-EIGHT

Alejandro

The morning sun crawled over the alpine peaks from where I sat in my elevated overwatch position. I was lying prone on the edge of the ridgeline overlooking the Helix-owned safe house in Queenstown. The place was nestled in a cul-de-sac of glass and stone. A sleek modern fortress perched with purpose.

Multiple-car garage. Shuttered windows. Strategic sight lines. A perfect place for a traitorous security company to hide out.

I took a moment to stretch my neck, and wiggled my fingers since they were cramping up. My suppressed MK 13 Mod 7 sniper rifle was steady on its bipod, the precision scope trained on the front entrance. Ten hours here in my stakeout, and aside from taking a piss twice, I'd barely budged or blinked all night.

Now that there was more light, I was able to snap a few photos and text them to the team to get names. I assumed they'd all be employed by Helix, which meant they were more than likely veterans.

That made my stomach turn thinking about possibly having to go up against them. The last thing in the world I wanted to do was pull the trigger and take out one of our own.

At the vibration of a text, I checked to see Reed warning me not to shoot, that he was coming up behind me.

"Thanks, I would have."

He offered a thermos of coffee, and I was almost in just enough of a shit mood to turn him down, but I grumbled and took it.

"I'm your replacement. You get to go." He settled in next to me.

"I'm good right where I'm at. You should have stayed at the hotel. Now that I have my coffee, go back."

"I can't deal with Hollis. I needed a break."

"What do you have against her, anyway? I mean, besides your usual hate for people."

"She gets under my skin. I don't want to talk about it." He flicked my arm with the back of his hand. "Now, stop hiding and go."

"Give you a turn to hide, you mean?"

"Exactly." He reached for the bipod and moved the rifle since I wouldn't physically reposition my body like he wanted. "Audrey needs to talk to you. She barely slept last night, and Hollis is worried about her. And Hollis on edge puts me on edge."

I acted ignorant, shaking my head. "What does she want to talk about?"

"How would I know? But you upset her, and that upsets—"

"Hollis, got it. Which means you're here to be a pain in my ass, now," I grumbled. "And I can't talk to her, because then I'll have to tell her I caught her making out with Trevor and openly admit it's over with her before it ever started." Shit. I was so tired I'd accidentally told him the truth.

"You saw her make out with him? When?"

"In the bedroom, right after he arrived last night and before he took off with Echo." I set aside the coffee, stealing back my rifle.

"I don't believe that."

"Well, I saw it with my own eyes." *Didn't I? Shit.* Jet lag and devastation were both doing a number on my head.

"You sure about that?"

"Yes." I exhaled a deep breath and admitted, "Well, no. They were about to. I tucked tail and walked away."

"So you didn't *actually* see anything." He stole back the rifle. Probably in safer hands right now than my unstable ones. "We have someone rolling up now," he said, voice tight, switching gears. "Black Mercedes." He read off the plate, and I pulled out my phone and texted the details to Gwen. "Female. Brunette. Looks to be in her mid-forties, and the two co-owners of Helix are personally greeting her. We need to send her image to Gwen."

"Something feels really fucked up about all this, and I don't mean what's currently happening here. You get that feeling, too?"

He said what I'd hoped he wouldn't: "Unfortunately, yeah."

I wanted to be wrong about that. "Like we're missing the bigger picture and falling for a trick? Probably just my dad's training drilled in my head that has me always questioning everything I see—but I don't know, man."

"In this case, I'm with you. Just get back to the hotel for now, will ya? Get some sleep; then maybe you can see the truth for what it really is."

He lifted his head, eye off the scope to park his focus on me, ensuring I'd heard him loud and clear and read his secondary message.

"Go make up with Audrey. And kindly remove your head from your ass so I can go back to being the grump on the team. Not a fan of sharing the spot with you."

CHAPTER FORTY-NINE

Alejandro

By the time I returned to the hotel, feeling like shit, I was met by my opposite. A woman who appeared to have sunshine radiating out of her despite her supposed bad night of sleep.

She slowly turned away from the window, her arms over her chest like a shield, and her eyes softened as they landed on me, but she didn't smile.

I didn't deserve it anyway.

I let the door click shut behind me as Hollis announced, "The brunette doesn't exist."

"What do you mean?" I blinked my way from Audrey to Hollis.

Ryder came into the room from our shared bedroom, spinning his ball cap backward as he joined us, a toothbrush hanging from his mouth, which he removed to share: "She's an unknown variable. No one has anything on her. Not us. Interpol. MI6. No one."

"Which means she's good. Really, really good," Hollis said, standing alongside Audrey, who'd yet to budge from her fixed position.

She had to hate me by now for my attitude, and she had every right to. I hadn't handled what happened all that well.

"Are you saying this woman is our hacker? Is she Cipheria?" I kept my back to the door. "And if she is Cipheria, why's she working with Helix? I thought she was helping Mitch. Aren't they enemies? Or is she an insider plant helping Mitch out?"

I was losing track at this point. Whose side was who on? Who was really dead?

"I don't know. This is all so fucked." Ryder shoved his toothbrush back in his mouth.

"Maybe she's not our hacker, then," Audrey proposed.

"Give me a second," Ryder said around his toothbrush before returning to the bedroom.

Audrey let her arms fall to her sides, and I slowly worked my eyes up to her face, then regretted doing so immediately.

I couldn't look at her and stay angry. It was impossible, like asking someone to hate the sun when it gave us light and life. It just, you know, also burned you if you weren't careful.

And here I was, standing here, deciding *fuck it.* Fuck the burn. I could take it. Maybe even stand in the way of Chase's family being reunited to fight that fire now.

I hung my head, thinking of that cute kid. *Nope, can't do it to him.* If Audrey made her choice, then I had to respect it and their family.

"I'm glad you came back," she finally said.

Ryder returned before I could respond, toothbrush gone now.

"I'm going to check in with my brother to see if he can help out. Maybe he'll have better luck in finding her," Hollis suggested. "The brunette clearly exists; you saw her this morning. We'll find her." She brought her phone to her ear and nodded at Audrey, then took off for her bedroom.

"When you learn anything, let me know. I'm going to change my bandage and get some rack time." Maybe work on getting my head back on straight, too.

"And my sister will be helping you change it." That sure as hell came out sounding like an order, not from my best friend, but from Delta One.

I opened my mouth to object, but he lifted his hand, jaw tight, letting me know not to argue.

I shook my head but didn't protest, then went into my bedroom, where Audrey caught up with me a few seconds later.

"Medkit in your bag or Reed's this time?" Her voice was so fragile it killed me.

"Mine." I peeled my shirt over my head and tossed it onto the bed, keeping my back to her as I removed the current bandage taped to my side while walking into the bathroom.

I turned on the water and rinsed my hands and face before cleaning up the wound. I had no idea how I'd survive these next few minutes with this woman doctoring me up without feeling like my heart would explode from my chest.

"What's this?" she asked.

I caught her eyes in the mirror before dropping my attention to the wedding band I bought after I'd lost my mind.

"It's for tomorrow. You know, when we have to play pretend." I set my hands on the counter and hung my head, not able to be this close to her. To look her in the eyes and not ache every-fucking-where.

How was it possible to feel this deeply for someone after such a short period of time? At first, I'd struggled to believe how fast Ryder had fallen for Seraphina, worried he was in rebound territory. He'd proved me wrong, but now there I was, in the same boat of falling almost as fast.

"A diamond eternity band in platinum for a prop?"

"*Loco*, I know," I gritted out, and at the feel of her hand on my arm, my palms were about to meld with the marble.

"I didn't kiss Trevor."

Those four words sent my heart into my throat.

"I know you think I did, but you're mistaken."

The thousand-pound weight on my chest eased up, but only by a fraction. I wasn't ready to believe my ears. Not when I still trusted my sight. But then again, Reed was right. I hadn't actually seen them kiss; I'd just assumed they were going to.

"Beth hurt you," she began in a soft voice, keeping her hand on me, "but I'm not her. I would never do that."

My stomach muscles clenched, anticipating the impact of a hit instead of the relief she was trying to give my mind and body.

"Back before Trevor used to deploy, he'd rest his head against mine and promise me that no matter what, he'd always return. A tradition we kept even in friendship. Since he was going to operate again . . ."

She let the words marinate, let them find a way through the logical part of my brain. And the weight on my chest began to levitate higher above it.

"There's nothing between him and me. But there is something between *you* and me."

I met her eyes in the mirror, waiting for her to continue. I needed to hear more so I could understand.

"I didn't think I'd ever be able to trust anyone again. To even want a future with anyone after what Mitch did to me before he deployed," she said in a shaky voice. "And not only did I want you on Monday, I *needed* you. You didn't just touch me, Alejandro. You undid everything he broke."

I remained staring at her. Trying to absorb the fact *after* was happening now when I'd already thought I'd said goodbye to that possibility. I swallowed, knowing there was only one thing left to do: apologize.

I guided her around to face me and gently cupped her chin.

"Lo lamento." A deeper form of regret than *lo siento,* but she wouldn't know that, so what was I doing? "I'm so damn sorry for how I acted. I went to the worst-case scenario instead of asking you. Jumped to conclusions," I said in a strained voice. "I was an idiot."

She shook her head, freeing tears from her eyes. "I'd have done the same thing. We're used to people breaking our trust and our hearts. I'm not mad at you, only sorry I couldn't clear the air last night."

It was taking all my restraint not to kiss her trembling lower lip, to take it between my own. To apologize a hundred times over.

"When this is over . . ." It was the best I could get out right now, because she was too damn close, her hands gliding up over my heated, bare skin.

I was coming up on three days without solid sleep, and if I wasn't careful, I might snap and ask her to marry me for real.

Mitch being alive—technically making her still married—didn't mean shit to me.

"Okay," she agreed in a soft voice of understanding.

I leaned in and kissed her temple where she'd been hit last Friday.

The bruise was nearly gone, but it still served as a reminder as to why we were in New Zealand.

Why I shouldn't carry her into the bedroom and make love to her.

Why I had to wait until *after* this mission like I'd promised her brother I'd do.

"We shouldn't be alone in here much longer."

She proved me right by rolling her hips forward, pressing against my ever-growing erection while skimming her fingers along my sides, careful to avoid my wound.

Unable to stop myself, I hooked an arm around her waist and slid my hand to the back of her neck, gently taking hold of her.

"Peligroso," I reminded her, letting her know I was hanging on to a very dangerous edge here.

"We shouldn't, I know." And yet she kept arching into me, keeping her breasts flush to my chest, her hands still exploring, tracing my scars like they were constellations in the night sky.

The one at my side was healing quickly. Something told me a few more days with her and every wound, both inside and out, would vanish.

Her eyes remained bold, locked on mine. Lashes fluttering. Lips damp and parted.

I didn't stand a chance with her here like this.

I brushed my mouth over hers and demanded, "What color lace today?"

Her tongue peeked out like a tease. "Black."

I caught the word with my mouth.

Had her up against the wall by the open door a moment later. I pinned her leg to my side so she could draw closer and grind against me. Feel the full weight of my erection pressing into her.

Moans. Cries. Pleas.

And then—

A voice.

Not hers.

Not mine.

I waved blindly toward the sound. "Not now."

"I'm really sorry, but it's important."

Hollis, dammit. Trying to steal my moment with this incredible woman, and we were both going to be left tense and unsatisfied.

"Go. Away," I growled between open-mouthed kisses, all heat and tongue and desperation. I didn't give a shit that we had an audience. Not even the pope himself could pull me away from Audrey.

Screw *after*.

This was happening now.

"I found something Gwen's AI program missed on that flash drive from the bear. Guess we still need humans after all," Hollis kept going like she didn't understand English.

Did I need to switch to Spanish?

I wasn't leaving until I made Audrey come.

"Do you want Ryder to be the one to interrupt? He will if you two don't . . ."

She was still talking.

Maybe?

I stopped listening.

She was now the bane of my existence, because my girl was still kissing me like she needed me to survive. Maybe we were both jet-lagged and delirious. But so be it.

"Beth lied," Hollis declared, revealing an ugly truth I should have seen coming five miles and one gunshot wound away.

My mouth went still and Audrey froze against me, her foot finding the floor as I let go of her thigh.

Then, slowly, as one, we turned to the woman who'd intruded.

Hollis's eyes narrowed as she looked directly at Audrey. Her voice dropped to a whisper. "It wasn't Mitch who forced Beth to set up the meeting between Trevor and Will Hobbs at the ball. And it wasn't Mitch who sent Trevor off to die."

CHAPTER FIFTY

Audrey

"Everything we thought we knew is wrong," Hollis dropped on us before leaving us alone.

"This doesn't make sense." I followed Alejandro into the bedroom as he grabbed a clean shirt from his bag, leaving his wound undressed for now.

Once his shirt was on, he gently took my arm, guiding me to face him. "Whatever we learn out there, whatever goes down . . . I got you. Right here, right now. We'll get through this together." He palmed my cheek with his free hand. "Even if it's all been smoke and mirrors," he continued, voice tight with emotion, "this—what's between us—like you said, *is* real."

He leaned forward and kissed my temple like he'd done in the bathroom not too long ago.

"No one, dead or alive, can take that away. So regardless of what we hear out there, focus on that if the floor feels like it's falling out from under us."

Chills coasted over my arms, and he gently smoothed the pad of his thumb over my skin as if he could chase the shivers away. Maybe he could. He wasn't just offering to be my anchor in the storm; he was saying *we* were the anchor. Together we could get through anything, and I had no clue how he'd said exactly what I didn't know I needed to hear, but he was spot on.

I wasn't in this alone.

We were in this together.

He brought his hand from my cheek to beneath my chin, tipping my head up so my eyes locked with his. "I've got you. Whatever the truth is . . . I'm not going to let anyone hurt you or your family, and that includes Trevor."

He was telling me he accepted Trevor as part of the family, which may not have been that easy to say. But it meant the world to me that he had.

He slanted his mouth over mine for a soft kiss, then stepped away. "Ready?"

"Are *you* ready?" My forehead creased, unease slicing through me.

He exhaled and went for the door, then stole a look over his shoulder at me. "I was so blinded by my hate for Mitch I lost sight of the truth right in front of me."

"And that is?"

"That Beth only cares about Beth, and my entire life with her was a lie. She manipulated me." He shook his head as if disappointed with himself. "And I actually thought maybe she was changing. Searching for redemption." He faced forward again and opened the door.

"It's not your fault." I came up behind him. "And we're all on the Mitch-hating train, and it's still possible we're not *wrong* wrong. Mitch is probably tied to all this somehow." But then Hollis's parting words came back to haunt me. "Guess we're about to find out the truth, though."

Alejandro stepped aside to allow me out first, then he followed me over to where Ryder and Hollis were standing by the desk, laptop open with Gwen on the screen.

Ryder looked up at me. "You're going to want to sit for this. The both of you." He gestured to two nearby chairs.

"I'd rather stand," Alejandro commented.

I was torn about what to do. Would my legs hold up the weight of what was to come?

Hollis seemed to think not, because she tipped her head toward the chair in a quiet request for me to sit.

"Fast without all the details?" Gwen offered once I took a seat. "Or slow and—"

"And painful?" I interrupted, because wasn't there a reason everyone wanted the Band-Aid removed quickly? It hurt a little less.

Hollis sat next to me and suggested, "How about somewhere in between." And since she knew the truth already, she'd know what was best. "While my brother and Gwen were trying to get a hit on Cipheria's real name and last possible location before here, I asked Gwen to send me a copy of Beth's flash drive so I could have a look."

Gwen's voice stayed steady through the laptop's speakers as she switched to screen share. "My program decrypted the flash drive Beth gave us, which had all Will's files on it. Then it flagged the files by keywords, dates, and name clusters. A few were marked low priority, and Hollis wanted to take a look at those to see if the software may have missed something."

"Because you doubted Beth was telling us the truth?" Alejandro asked her, and she shook her head.

"Actually, no." Hollis turned in her seat to face him. "Something told me there was more Beth wanted us to find that'd either convince us she was telling the truth *or* do the opposite. I didn't believe for one minute she never took a look at the contents of the flash drive herself."

"But why tell us one thing, then give us something that would contradict what she said so we'd think she was a . . ." I let my words drop as it clicked. "Ohh."

Hollis nodded, letting me know I was on the same page now. Beth had lied, and she discreetly helped us figure that out for some reason.

"When I opened one of the folders from the flash drive marked *Music*, I clicked through all the mp4s to ensure they were really songs and not voice memos or recordings. You know, blackmail. One of the files didn't work when I clicked it. Instead, an access box popped up, warning that it needed to be converted to a read-only note file instead," Hollis continued. "It was a string of code that made no sense to me. So I had my brother take a look at it."

"And her brother realized there was buried metadata inside the file. And within that, there was a weird file path," Gwen picked up for her while sharing the path on the screen.

C:\Users\Will\Photos\September2017\BlackBox\Stratos\Notes\TSloaneInquiry

"When we unlocked that file to see what was in it . . ." Hollis let her voice trail off, closing her eyes. "It appeared that Trevor stumbled onto something he shouldn't have, and he started poking around. And had he kept on the trail, he'd eventually have found out there were dead men running ops for Will Hobbs."

I blinked, shaking my head like that might help me process it.

"Former Stratos ghost operatives were being sent on side missions by Will Hobbs and led by Rhett," Hollis continued. "Looks like after President Rydell decommissioned Stratos, Will chose a few of the retired operatives he believed he could turn at the right price. Two of the men he asked said no. He killed them using a slight loophole. You know, since they were already dead."

"Wait, you're saying Trevor was close to uncovering this, and that would have led him to Will Hobbs and Stratos, so Will and Rhett came up with a way to have him silenced?" I covered my mouth, my hand trembling.

Alejandro came behind my chair and rested his hands on my shoulders, reminding me that he had my back and we were in this together.

I let my hand fall to my lap at the feel of his comforting touch.

I spied my brother stealing a quick look at us as Hollis continued, "Hobbs kept tabs on every former Stratos operative—including Mitch—up until he wound up in prison in 2018. Probably to ensure no one ever stepped out of line, not just the ones he pulled in for other jobs."

"According to these files, it looks like Beau and Mitch remained friends even after Beau went off-grid after he was forced into retirement in 2013," Gwen shared. "My guess is, after Hobbs was in prison, Rhett picked up the baton and continued without him. And he left Trevor alone even though he didn't die, because his time in captivity resulted in the same outcome Rhett needed. Trevor was now off the trail."

"And Rhett was probably the one who pitched Stratos 2.0 to Helix—not Mitch, like we thought—after Hobbs died," Hollis said, speaking plainly about all this. But it still wasn't sinking in.

I should have asked for the Band-Aid version of this. "So you're saying Mitch didn't blackmail anyone? He really didn't have Trevor sent on that mission so he could marry me?"

Gwen returned to the screen, then focused on my brother as if requesting him to handle this.

Yeah. This was one hell of a *this*, all right.

Ryder walked over and took a knee in front of me and offered me his hand.

I had a big brother in front of me and the man I was falling in love with behind me. So I was safe. Secure. And nothing could hurt me, but . . .

"So Mitch is innocent?" I needed clarification here. For this to be made very black and white. "And *Beth* handed us over evidence no one knew she had to help out and reveal she lied."

"We built our entire theory around Mitch being obsessed with you. Obsessed enough to try and destroy your marriage so he could be with you," Ryder said in a steady voice, squeezing my hand. "What Rhett said to you when we captured him. The texts with Mitch's alleged signature. The photos. Appearing jealous. Then Beth's testimony was the nail in Mitch's coffin. We believed her, because we wanted to. Because we hated Mitch." He lifted his shoulder. "I mean I still do, but . . ."

"We don't know why Beth told us it was Mitch pulling the strings, and Mitch blackmailing her, even on that Helix op, but it's safe to say—"

"Actually, Beth never mentioned Helix to me," Alejandro said, cutting off Hollis. "I asked for the security company name, and she told me she didn't have to share because I already knew. But maybe she didn't know. And if it wasn't Mitch blackmailing her and Hobbs in 2017, then it was more than likely also not him on that other mission two years ago, which means it had to have been Rhett."

"Because Rhett didn't want us to know about Helix. He was hoping we wouldn't find out about Helix," I said in understanding. "But how in the world would Rhett know you'd go to Beth and talk to her?"

Ryder let go of my hand and stood. "Because you were being followed. The second they spotted Alex with you, they found a way to turn what would've been a problem into a solution. They knew Trevor would lead us to Chandler and to the fact Mitch came to him last year, and that'd eventually connect Trevor to Will Hobbs, and Will to—"

"To my ex-wife and to the truth," Alejandro finished for him. "Someone got to Beth somehow in that prison, and they forced her to lie. Had her pointing us the wrong way so we'd be distracted and chasing ghosts. It was all an illusion, and we bought the lie. That way, we wouldn't know the real threats were right in front of us the whole time."

"One tied to a chair in Trevor's office," Ryder bit out in a firm voice. "The other? Sleeping with his sister."

A chill blanketed my body in head-to-toe shivers. "Everything we thought we knew really is backward." I looked back at Alejandro, my heart cracking open for him all over again. So many lies. So much deception. What was real and what wasn't? "We're not here to take out Mitch's enemies for him like we thought so he can get away with me and cash. So then why are we here?"

"Containment," my brother said under his breath. "Rhett needed the evidence from the vault before it could be made public to the world and out him."

"What exactly are you saying?" I asked.

Alejandro hung his head, hands going to his hips. "We've been chasing a dead man. That Mitch really did die that day on the way to the safe house." He slowly lifted his eyes to meet mine as he rasped, "They silenced him the way they did his best friend."

Silenced.

Killed.

Dead.

Never coming back, for real dead.

Is that what we're saying?

In a somber tone, my brother revealed, "They probably didn't know until it was too late that Mitch had evidence that could bring their entire operation down, whether he was dead or alive."

CHAPTER FIFTY-ONE

Audrey

While Gwen and Hollis's brother worked in the background to figure out how Rhett had gotten to Beth in that prison, Ryder shared over speakerphone what we'd learned with Trevor and Echo Team.

"Clearly Rhett and Beau had been working on their crazy plan to get hold of the evidence even before Christmas, because Beau was planted into our lives prior to that," I added when Ryder finished talking, taking a seat next to him. I wrapped myself up in a blanket before continuing, "The *why*'s and the *how*'s don't matter right now, though. Or the timeline. All I know is, we were manipulated from every side."

"But are we really believing Beth is good here?" Trevor asked in a steady voice, though he had to be shocked. "Did she truly give you the file so that you'd eventually figure out the truth?"

"*Good* is a stretch of the imagination," Alejandro said bitterly, standing by the couch on Ryder's end. He rubbed his stubbled jawline, gaze lowered. A world of hurt and blame clung to him for believing Beth.

We'd trusted the wrong people.

And Trevor's own actions in trying to do the right thing had unknowingly placed a target on his head in 2017, not because Mitch was some psycho obsessed with me.

"Maybe Beth didn't have a choice. Or maybe he promised something I couldn't give her—a way out of prison. Or, more than likely, Beth was playing both sides," Alejandro explained, grit in his voice as he closed his eyes. "She did what she agreed to do, but she didn't tell them she had evidence on them. That was her securing our favor in case we won at the end of this."

"Maybe," Hollis began in a hesitant tone. "*Or* maybe she had no choice but to do what Rhett said."

"No way Rhett overheard the secure call I had with Beth that Chandler set up. Plus, she told me about the flash drive. She wouldn't take that risk if she thought someone was eavesdropping," Alejandro remarked, now sounding a little like he believed Beth again. The poor guy had to be feeling so many emotions right now.

"Then why not just tell us the truth to begin with? Why the games?" I asked, speaking my thoughts out loud.

"This is still Beth we're talking about." Alejandro opened his eyes. "She did what she was told to do, knowing if we didn't follow the leads Rhett wanted us to, he'd know she didn't hold up her end of the deal and it'd come back to bite her somehow."

"By not outright telling us the truth, knowing we'd have to go get the flash drive and decrypt it, she bought herself a cushion," Hollis answered. "Beth earned herself a window of time so it looked to Rhett like she did what he wanted her to. And by the time we figured out the truth, thanks to the flash drive, Rhett wouldn't connect the trail back to her."

"And she'd know we wouldn't tell Rhett how we figured it out anyway. This is a lead we wouldn't want him to know about," Alejandro said. "But I still think we're giving this woman a lot of credit in choosing to do the right thing." He shook his head, dragging his thumb along the underside of his lip. "I'm biased, though, so I don't know."

The room went quiet as everyone processed the unprocessable. Our two enemy number ones might not be what they'd seemed. Not when it came to all this, at least.

And that reminded me: Trevor had to confront what had happened to him in Afghanistan, and why, all over again. "Are you doing okay, Trevor?" I broke the quiet and asked, eyes on the phone as I waited for him to respond.

"I'll be fine. Past is past, right?" Trevor said over the line, then redirected before I could shut down that lie. "If Mitch was really alive, I'd still kill him for what he did to you, though."

"And what did he do?" Hollis pierced me with her concerned gaze.

I'd forgotten she didn't know what had happened before Mitch's last deployment or that I'd been planning to get divorced. I wasn't looking to relive that night right now—not with Gwen on the call trying to save the day.

"Something I kept from you to protect you," I admitted, staying vague for now. "I was worried you'd want to do what Trevor still does and kill him. Now that I know the real you, it's probably good I didn't say anything."

Hollis's green eyes narrowed on me, hands flexing at her sides. Ready to do battle with a dead man. I'd been right.

"Anything yet, Gwen?" I needed to deflect, and fast.

"I'm almost there. Give me another minute. I'm close to solving this," Gwen responded, and hopefully she'd save me from opening up about Mitch to Hollis.

I didn't even know what to think about that man anymore.

What he did to me was still horrible and deserving of divorce, but did he deserve death? I didn't think so.

Plus, hadn't he died trying to do the right thing? Though, from the sounds of it, he wound up putting a target on my head whether he meant to or not by hiding the key with me, also requiring me to be there to unlock the—

"Wait," I blurted, forgetting no one was in on my thoughts. "If the vault requires both Mitch and I to unlock it, then how do we get in? And Rhett must know that by now, right?" The blanket became a distant memory as I tossed it to stand. "Beau and Rhett didn't know where to look for the key because they didn't even know what the key was, right?"

"Rhett and Beau would've realized you didn't know, either. So questioning you would've been pointless. They probably even discreetly searched your house back in Virginia while I was still in the navy. Maybe even before I started poking—" Trevor dropped his words and cursed. "I did it again, didn't I?"

"Did what?" I spun around, staring at the phone as if Trevor was physically with us instead.

"I woke a sleeping giant. Rhett found out I was digging into Arlo's death and Mitch's crash. That prompted Rhett to dig deeper. He thought he shut everything down when he killed Mitch on the way to the safehouse after Chandler faked the crash, but then he discovered Mitch hid something in New Zealand prior to that."

"And that's when Rhett realized his mistake. He killed the only person who could tell him where and how to get the damning evidence," Gwen chimed in.

"Which brings us back to how will any of us unlock the vault without Mitch?" Ryder asked, standing up.

"There has to be a loophole clause," Hollis said. "Doubt the company wants anyone to know about that fine print to prevent people from taking advantage of it. But I bet if one party dies, legal death certification will trigger a fail-safe, allowing the surviving partner conditional access."

"And that'd be me."

"They knew they had a time limit in locating the key for the vault. They played the long game by placing Beau into your life," my brother said as if all the *how*'s and *why*'s were now clicking. "Get on the inside and try to find the key that way. But they ran out of time and had to accelerate the process."

"Beau was the best choice. He knew Mitch the most. Stayed in contact over the years." Hollis reminded us of what Hobbs's files had revealed. "He'd know about his HELL signature. Nickname for you. They twisted this all around to blame a dead man who couldn't defend himself. And set the trap."

"And we walked right in it," Alejandro noted bitterly.

"Mitch went to my grandfather because of Trevor's connection to him. He didn't know who to trust until after he was in a safe location." Gwen softened her tone when adding, "And maybe in Mitch's own weird way, he was also trying to keep Audrey safe. You have to be alive to open the vault for whoever had the key, which made you off-limits from harm. For the year, at least."

"Mitch had counted on Trevor to keep Audrey safe if the worst happened," Alejandro commented. "He was relying on you two working together to finish what he started."

"And now I know how Rhett convinced Beth to help," Gwen shared, cutting through the tension in the room here. "He didn't blackmail her; he threatened her."

"You're serious?" Alejandro scoffed, and I went over to stand next to him.

"Cipheria hacked a government-sanctioned mental health app embedded in a prison-simulation game that the Agency allows their inmates access to for an hour a week to help reduce behavioral issues. Text chat is supposed to be disabled."

Gwen zoomed in on lines of code as they flashed across the screen. All gibberish to me.

"Cipheria reverse-engineered the platform. Built a hidden back door into the app's code, then used a cached server log to find Beth's ID." She paused to let us absorb what I never would. I knew piano notes, not cyber code. "Reconstructing the deleted conversations now. One second."

What had looked like Greek to me suddenly converted to English in the blink of an eye. Now there was only a message, which I read out loud: *"If I can breach this system, imagine what else I can access. You think you're safe? If you don't do what we say and offer Mitchell Langston's name, then I will make it look like you had a psychotic break and jumped from a walkway. Or perhaps slipped in the shower and fried yourself. Who knows. Accidents happen, right?"*

"The good news is, Cipheria made a mistake, and she left a breadcrumb in her code that I'm going to follow now with the help of Hollis's brother," Gwen continued after we let the shock roll through the room like a tidal wave. "We'll find out who she is—and my money is, she's the brunette you flagged this morning with Helix."

"What does this all mean? Now that we know who's behind this and what they want, what do we do now?" I asked, scanning the room while taking Alejandro's offered hand.

"We still don't have eyes on Rhett or Beau yet where you're at, right?" Ryder asked Trevor and Echo Team.

"Negative," Trevor responded, his tone low and bitter. Still pissed off and blaming himself. I'd need to talk to him later. Remind him of the hero he was and forever would be, and how his son wanted to grow up to be just like him.

"Then we Charlie Mike," Ryder said with a nod. "Mitch won't be at the auction tomorrow night like we thought, but we will be." He shot a quick look at Hollis to check if we were all set in regard to the event.

"Item to auction and invites secure," she confirmed.

Ryder nodded his thanks. "Echo, where are we on the other team for backup?"

"They'll be here in time," someone answered.

My brother scrubbed a hand over his face. "We'll keep eyes on both properties we know about. If Rhett or Beau don't show up before the auction, then we'll stick to the plan we put together last night and not deviate from it."

"There's one problem with that plan," Trevor remarked in a low voice. "Some of those men who work for Helix might not know the truth. They might think we're the enemies and that they're following the president's orders. I can't take the lives of innocent veterans. Some of these guys are our brothers out there."

"He's right," Alejandro said, tightening his grip on my hand.

"Hollis, what if we ask your brother to get hold of every cell number tied to Helix's operatives, and the second we're ready to pull the trigger and move forward with the plan at the auction, he'll text them the truth?" Gwen suggested.

"It'll be up to them to pick a side." Ryder nodded in agreement. "Good or evil. That's what it always comes down to."

CHAPTER FIFTY-TWO

Alejandro

The night of the auction

My hand was damn near trembling as I held the last thing I had to put on as part of my cover story: Mitch's wedding band. The fact it was a perfect fit was about to send me over the edge. Not sure why it bothered me so much. It worked in our favor, but still—it did.

I finally forced myself to get it over with and slid the symbol of forever that didn't belong to me onto my ring finger.

Maybe Mitch was no longer a traitor to the country, but that didn't change the fact he betrayed the oath he made to Audrey. No excuses for what he did. Irredeemable, in my eyes. *But* judgment and forgiveness weren't up to me. That was between God and Audrey.

I could hear music coming from the bedroom Audrey and I would never actually share as she changed into the dress Hollis had picked out for her before we swapped hotels earlier.

Jazz, of course. Maybe it helped ease her nerves, with everything about to go down. She was one brave woman. A hero for what she was willing to do for her country tonight, protect names and missions on a file that maybe should never have existed in the first place.

At the feeling of being watched when I was supposed to be alone, I turned around, not too shocked to discover Hollis had gotten the drop on me.

She was hanging by the front door, already dressed in a red silk gown. Reed was her plus-one tonight, not yet with her. He'd swapped places with two of Hollis's teammates so we'd maintain a visual on Helix's stronghold to track their movements when it was time.

No signs of Beau or Rhett yet. Only another fake Mitch text with instructions for the trade: Audrey and the ring for Eden. Location TBD. Time: 2200 hrs. —HELL.

The "trade" to get Eden back was a trap. They were looking to divert some of our team, knowing we'd rescue Eden while they went after their real marks: Audrey and the ring.

I tossed Mitch's empty ring box onto the couch and strode over to her.

She lifted her chin toward the closed bedroom door. "How is she?"

I turned to the side. "She's nervous but trying to pretend she's fine. She FaceTimed Chase an hour ago. Trevor too."

"And her mom?"

"Not her, no. Maybe they'll talk when this is over. And I'll make sure she gets through this so she can."

She nodded, then went for the door. "Audrey finally shared with me what Mitch did to her that night. She was right—I'd have killed him. Zero second thoughts. And not two in the head." Her gaze slipped south to my crotch for a second. Message received. "I'm really glad she has someone like you in her life to wipe the slate clean and start over with. And that you're so cool with Trevor being in her life. Maybe you two can even work together again?"

I'd once been against that idea; now I had every intention of being the one to ask him myself.

She took off, and I focused on the bedroom door again, wondering what was taking my date so long.

I went over and rapped my knuckles against it.

"Come in," she called out over the music, which had clearly drowned out my conversation with Hollis.

I opened the door and froze at the sight before me. "You're not dressed."

Not only was she *not* dressed, but she was standing there in a wedding-white lacy bra and matching panties. One foot on the bed, rolling up a black thigh-high stocking.

"I'm in *something*." Her smile reached her smoky, done-up eyes.

This was one of those times when I needed to walk away like I'd done at the lodge.

We couldn't make love now. Not tonight. Not in the fifteen minutes we had (I could stretch that to twenty, maybe), but still . . .

So I behaved. *And* also became immediately stiff. The woman was in see-through white lace, after all. Looking as much like a goddess as she did my wife.

Her black dress was laid out on the bed we'd never get to use.

The jazz music competed with the sounds of my heart beating wildly up into my ears.

"Mind closing my door so no one else sees me?"

Good point. I closed and locked it, then slowly and very stupidly punished myself by turning to face her. *Look but don't touch*—but this woman was just begging for me to do exactly that.

No padding for her bra, so her pink nipple poked through, calling to me like a Siren.

My chest rose and fell as I worked to keep it together.

"Does driving me out of my mind help ease yours?"

"Well, you are my husband tonight, aren't you? We have a few more minutes until our reality is shattered." That touch of sadness at the end slayed me.

We were hedging on mission-starting territory. One wrong move and I could die.

But I was right there with her in not wanting to rejoin reality yet. The way she was sliding her hand gently along the hem of her panties ignited something inside me and destroyed my resolve.

She was playing dirty.

Officially corrupting my chances to behave.

Then she turned, and I pressed a closed fist against my mouth, nearly biting my hand.

Her ass was *right there.* She had me wanting to press my cock against it, let her feel how hard she made me.

Unable to stop myself, I walked up behind the little tease and reached around between her legs.

She moaned and lifted her hand, hooking her arm around my neck. "Why can't this be real? Just you, me, here in this beautiful place, with the sole purpose of making love as husband and wife."

I closed my eyes, going still at her words. "Is that something you could ever see being again?"

"A wife?" she asked softly.

"Well, to be specific, *my* wife." I retrieved the eternity band from my pocket, sitting lonely without its box. "Tonight, at least. Will you?" I held up the ring.

She turned toward me. "And what would you say to me?"

I kept the ring between us, her beautiful eyes on me. Her blonde hair pinned up, showing off her neckline, the perfect sweep of her shoulders. "If I were proposing?"

"No, if this was the moment we said our vows. What would you say before you slid that ring on my finger?"

No longer was she standing before me tempting my flesh; she was connecting with my spirit. "Audrey." I inhaled.

"Just amuse me, please. Let me buy into the illusion for a little longer before you risk . . . risk yourself for me. For our country."

"Are you worried I won't make it out of this?" I didn't blame her if she did, given everything that'd happened to the men she'd married.

First with Trevor. Then with Mitch.

And had she processed yet that Mitch was gone for good? Where was her head about that? I didn't want to ask now, but something told me that if he was an obstacle for us, she wouldn't be standing here before me with her heart on her sleeve.

"Of course you'll make it out." Her hand covered mine as her gaze lifted to my eyes. "And while I know this ring is a lie, what it symbolizes for us isn't."

I swallowed, my emotions catching in my throat.

"Which is how we feel about each other."

I shifted her hand to the side so I could take hold of her other one. I brought the eternity band to her finger, but didn't slip it on yet.

In a shaky voice, I confessed, "I've spent my whole life second-guessing what I see, never trusting my own eyes. But then you walked in with that incredible laugh and adorable son, and you somehow made everything feel real. And because of you, I now know it's possible to have everything I ever wanted that I stopped believing in."

"I, um," she said with a sniffle, "feel the same." She blotted her tears with the back of her hand, trying not to ruin her makeup.

I gently snatched her wrists and kissed her before murmuring something in Spanish.

"Translate, please."

"Mmm. How about after?" *After* was becoming my least favorite word.

"After, okay." Her brows furrowed as her hands went to my shirt. "We shouldn't, I know," she whispered, undoing two buttons anyway.

And I should have stopped her.

Should have done a lot of things.

I didn't do a damn one.

She bypassed my open suit jacket, her hand settling on the buttons of my dress shirt as she pressed up onto her toes to kiss me.

I reached around to unhook her strapless bra, letting it fall between us.

Two more buttons undone as she continued talking about why we should wait.

Then she freed my shirt from the dress pants as I echoed her words back.

Wait. And *after.* All the things.

We ignored every last word as she undid my buckle as *now* happened.

My lips found the curve of her neck, one hand teasing her nipple while the other gripped her ass cheek.

With my white dress shirt open, belt free, and pants officially shoved down by the ravenous woman, I had to slam down on my back teeth as she reached through the hole of my boxers to wrap her hand around my hard-as-a-rock dick.

Her name broke in half in my mouth as I tried to say it while she fisted my cock.

We're doing this now, aren't we?

"I don't have a condom," I said before kissing her again as the blood rushed in one direction with her hand on me like that.

"I'm not on the pill."

Fuccccck.

"Just finished ovulating, so we should be fine if you pull out—but you know, if not . . ."

If not? She didn't say it, but I saw it in her eyes. A future. A maybe. A family.

I needed to take a moment. To regain my control and my senses. I stepped away, forcing her to let go of me.

Staring at this woman—in only her white panties and thigh highs, her full, luscious tits rising and falling on deep breaths and her lips swollen from kissing me—was going to be my undoing.

"*Loco.* Crazy, I know. We've known each other for only two months, and only intimately recently, but when you know, you know." She chewed her lip, her nerves catching as she stared at me, clearly nervous about how I'd react. "I believe everything happens for a reason."

"Kids?" I blurted out. "With *me*?" I covered my mouth, shock ripping through me. "You're willing to risk winding up pregnant with my child?"

"Doesn't sound risky or *peligroso* to me at all. Making a baby with a man as honorable, kind, and incredible as you sounds kind of perfect, in fact."

She'd just told me everything I never knew I needed to hear, but there was a small problem with this perfect plan. "You know your brother would murder me if I were to get you pregnant outside of marriage." My gaze slipped down to her pink, perky nipples. "Then again, there are worse ways to die."

"Loophole." She lifted her hand, showing me the ring. "We're married tonight, so . . ."

I stepped out of my pants so I wouldn't trip, then picked her up to carry her over to the bed.

"Is that a yes, then?" she whispered, hopeful eyes meeting mine as she stretched out sexily, waiting for me to join her.

I swallowed. "Are you sure? This is one of those no-take-back kind of things, you know. Like once I'm inside you, even if I pull out, there's still a chance I get you pregnant," I said steadily somehow, despite my heart rate flying.

"More than anything," she promised as I quickly removed and set aside Mitch's wedding band, not wanting to think about him while we made love. "So are we in the same boat?"

"I'm wherever you are." I leaned forward to kiss her before I stripped down to nothing.

Her gaze flicked to my side and the bandage.

"Eyes up. On me," I begged.

"But what about your wound?" she whispered.

"I'm healed," I promised. "*You* healed me," I choked out, and for a second, I wasn't a soldier or a protector. I was simply a man who was falling in love. Maybe already in the thick of it now. *Loco* or not.

Her dark lashes fluttered, eyes riveted to mine.

"Now," I added with a devious smile, "part your legs for me."

She obeyed, sliding her panties to the side to show me that bare pink flesh I'd move literal mountains for if it meant filling her.

I groaned and stroked my cock, forgetting all about what would soon be going down tonight. All of it ceased to exist outside the four walls of this room.

"I need to taste you first." I bent forward and hooked her legs at the backs of her knees and shifted her around, scooting her to the edge before dropping onto the floor before her.

With her legs over my shoulders, the silkiness of her thigh-highs sliding across my skin, I wasted no time in setting my mouth between her legs.

She let go and I moved the lace aside, her hands flying through my hair while I dragged my tongue along her sex.

"Alejandro," she gasped, hips arching.

My name on her tongue. I could die a happy man. *Almost.* I wasn't ready to go anywhere until I felt her walls tighten around me while our bodies connected in the way we were made to do.

"Take me. Now, please," she begged a few minutes later, panting hard as the jazz music thrummed louder and more intensely, like a soundtrack for this moment. "I need to come with you, not alone. Together, remember?"

Together.

That word from her freed something inside me. I'd said it yesterday, but hearing it from her . . .

Illusion or not, as far as I was concerned, this woman and I were bound to one another in this lifetime and our next.

I climbed onto the bed, freed her of her panties, then did what she asked of me.

Our eyes stayed locked, our fingers entwined above our heads, anchoring us together as I buried myself inside her, giving us both exactly what we needed. And when she whispered my name again—not from fear or sadness, but in love—I knew I'd carry this moment with me into whatever came next.

CHAPTER FIFTY-THREE

Audrey

After walking through metal detectors to confirm we weren't armed, I stepped through the arched double doors alongside the man who had just made love to me like he was, in fact, my husband. My body was still pulsing, overheated, and on fire.

It'd been far more than sex. A deep connection. A promise of something real in a world full of lies.

Maybe I should have felt guilty, given what was at stake. But it was hard to regret what had happened between us when it felt like it was meant to.

"You okay?" Alejandro whispered in my ear as we began weaving through the guests in the ballroom.

I peeked up at him. "I need to do what I heard you mumble to yourself upstairs while buckling your belt."

He gently squeezed my hand. "Did I say that out loud?"

I nodded. "'Focus up.'"

We both had to switch gears, from our stolen moment to what was to come. Saving Eden. Taking down the men who'd turned our lives inside out. I was ready to hit fast-forward and for it to be over now.

"So," I began as he turned me toward him, "are you focused up now?"

The full orchestra played nearby, and I didn't miss the painful irony of being so close to a woman at the piano.

He brushed his free hand over my cheek. "I'm focused on you at the moment."

Those dark eyes held me captive, turning the music into background noise.

We were in a room full of high-rolling criminals dressed in couture, sipping champagne and preparing to bid on stolen, smuggled, or traded artifacts—according to Hollis. And here we were . . . pretending we belonged. Pretending we weren't bait, the most valuable "item" there. To Rhett and Helix, at least.

Alejandro threaded his fingers through mine and lifted our hands, brushing a kiss across my knuckles.

Good thing our cover was as newlyweds. No acting required for us.

"There you two are." Hollis popped our moment. She had a habit of doing that. "Nice night, yeah?"

That was his cue. Alejandro hesitated, then subtly brought his hand near his head, activating the motion-sensitive comm in his ear.

"Why don't you get a drink?" Hollis tipped her head toward the bar, eyes on Alejandro.

Also planned. Reed was there waiting for him.

Alejandro leaned in and kissed my cheek. When he stepped back, my heart stuttered at the sight of him in the dark-navy suit. A crisp white shirt, collar open, two buttons undone. Tan skin I wanted to touch again.

Then my gaze caught the reason why we were there on his finger. Mitch's ring.

"You better go," I reminded him when he lingered, clearly reluctant to leave me.

If he was struggling now, how would he handle what we were anticipating would come next?

Hollis gave him a look that said *Move*, and while I doubted he liked taking orders from my best friend, he did it anyway.

The second he was out of earshot, she asked me, blunt as always, "You had sex, didn't you?"

Her words jolted me.

I lifted my chin. Unlike me, she had a comm in her ear.

"Not on yet." She fixed the skirt of her glamorous gown, then snatched a champagne flute from a passing server.

"Not one for me?"

"It's not to drink." She winked. No clue what that meant. "Now, tell me all about what happened upstairs. You look properly . . . you know."

I scanned the room for my brother and confirmed he wasn't nearby to overhear. "I look what?"

She sipped the champagne anyway. "You rarely swear, so I'm trying to be polite."

Ohhh. My cheeks flushed. *Properly effed?* Yeah, well, Alejandro had *properly effed* me, all right. I exhaled and smiled, feeling too many eyes on us. "Why's everyone looking at us?" I asked instead.

"Two beautiful women in a room full of men," she said casually, then glanced at the bar. "One of them, though, is glaring at me like he wants to murder me."

I followed her gaze to Reed. Yeah, if looks could kill.

They remained engaged in a silent standoff. One that could burn the room down.

"So," she said, finishing the champagne she wasn't supposed to drink, "how was it? Exceed expectations? Ten out of ten?"

I almost laughed. We were chatting about sex in a ballroom full of black market bidders, and I wasn't panicking or puking.

Maybe Alejandro had quieted my overthinking brain when he made love to me.

I rested my hand lightly on my stomach, remembering what I'd said about getting pregnant.

"It was . . ." I let my voice float, mingling with the sound of the saxophone.

"Wow," Hollis whispered, bumping her shoulder against mine. "That good?"

"That good," I confirmed as the orchestra transitioned to another haunting piece.

We'd been chasing ghosts—it only made sense to play that kind of music, I supposed.

"I'm glad you didn't let Mitch being dead for real get in your head and not be with the man who clearly makes you happy." Only Hollis could be so upfront like that. No-holds-barred. She really was the woman I'd gotten to know over all this time. "You deserve to be happy. I just still can't believe you didn't tell me you were getting a divorce. Guess we're even now, since I lied to you?"

I gave her a pointed look. "Not quite even." I lifted the skirt of my dress so I wouldn't trip, anxious to get closer to the stage for a better look.

"I have to turn on my comm. The auction is about to start. Stay in sight." She patted my forearm, then left.

I drifted toward the stage, the satin of my dress whispering against the marble. The jazz pulled me in. My fingers moved at my side like they were playing the keys again.

I lost track of time, lost in the music, to the memories of when I used to perform.

A shiver trailed up my spine.

I turned, and there he was. Alejandro. Watching me from across the room.

Our eyes locked. And just like that, I was back upstairs.

Our skin flushed.

Our breaths tangled.

The rhythm of our bodies.

After a few quiet moments, I forced myself to look away, nerves rising like smoke.

The music ended soon after, which meant the auction would begin.

I moved back into position, slipping into place beside my husband as he discarded his bourbon. His arm came around me, firm and protective.

A tall woman in silver stepped onto the stage, speaking in a sultry French accent. "The first item tonight," she said while gesturing to a holographic display beside her, "is a rare disputed manuscript linked to a fifteenth-century Italian monastery. Opening bid: 1.5 million."

"That's probably code for buying Vatican secrets for blackmail purposes," Alejandro translated in my ear.

Well, *that* sounded horrible for so many reasons.

Slender remotes lifted around the room. Glasses clinked. A mix of laughter and seriousness filled the air.

"Tangos on-site," were the next whispered words from my husband. I really could get used to associating that word with this man. Not a fan of the words he'd just said, though, because that meant it was almost time for shit to hit the fan.

I followed his gaze to see Reed slipping out of the ballroom through the service entrance to move into his position.

Hollis was now alone, watching the auction, her expression bored, her body language suggesting she didn't care.

The next item: an ancient knife rumored to have belonged to a pharaoh.

"Lot 113. Opening bid: 13 million," the woman said.

Right.

Definitely a front for something else.

Before any remotes were raised, the hologram began to glitch. It flickered once, then again.

I brought my hand to my chest.

Something was coming.

The auctioneer frowned. "Apologies. Technical diff—" Her mic cut out. A burst of static snapped through the sound system, and then darkness.

The ballroom was plunged into black. Screams erupted.

Then a single spotlight snapped on. It hit us. Alejandro and me.

A voice filtered through the room's speakers—cold, calm, and cruel.

Also, distinct.

A voice I remembered.

"Next item up for bid," Rhett said as Alejandro stiffened beside me. "Instead of ancient artifacts, how about something a little more contemporary?"

Gasps. Confusion. Movement.

"Tonight's prize: survival."

My pulse thundered.

"Who'd like to purchase everyone's freedom here?" Rhett asked, his voice low and steady. Not villain-like. Just cold and dead.

"The price? Step one: All you have to do is let that woman walk out with the ring on that man's finger without following her," Rhett continued as the spotlight burned above us. "You do that, and remain in the ballroom until you have my go-ahead to leave, and the charges beneath the room won't detonate and bring this whole hotel down."

"And—and what's step two?" a shaky male voice called out.

Two more lights flickered overhead, now spotlighting Ryder and Hollis, too. "You stop these three people from following that woman out. And then after . . . you kill them."

CHAPTER FIFTY-FOUR

Alejandro

"If anyone walks out of here without my permission, a sniper will cut you down." Rhett's voice was a low hiss rattling over the speakers. Eerily calm, like a man who'd sold his soul long before he faked his death. "Would anyone like to test me?"

No one moved. Not even the woman at the podium. Or the couple hosting this fake charity event.

These weren't average civilians. Criminals, yeah, but unarmed, like us. All of us motivated by different stakes. Rhett was banking on fear to turn them into human weapons.

"Didn't think so. Now, you have thirty seconds to leave with the ring, Audrey. If you want to give your brother and friends a fighting chance, you'll do as instructed."

I saw the flicker of fear in her eyes despite having known this moment would come. I squeezed both her hands, probably more terrified than she was that she'd be leaving without me.

"Exit out the balcony doors," Rhett continued. "A helo will be hovering. One of my men is waiting for you." He clearly wasn't the one piloting the bird. No rotor wash bleeding through the speaker.

"Once she's outside, the next timer begins. You'll have three minutes to kill them." The command was meant for the guests.

A timer blinked to life on the ballroom's far wall. Red digits. Thirty seconds on the clock.

"They're highly trained," Rhett warned. "Most of you in there aren't used to getting your hands dirty yourselves. Well, here's your chance."

A beat of silence before Reed transmitted, "This is Delta Three. Two tangos are guarding the service stairwell leading to the basement. That's our target location."

We'd planned for this. Knew Rhett would trigger something loud and fast. But this kind of psychological warfare? He'd taken it to a new level. Fortunately, we'd prepared, and sent Reed from the room before Rhett had hijacked the auction.

I looked at Audrey again, who was still holding steady even if I wasn't.

My grip on her tightened. We'd chosen to ignore this part of the evening back in our hotel suite, pretending as though it would never happen.

Now here it was.

About to become stained in blood.

And her walking out that door without me wouldn't be an illusion.

When the lights came back on, Rhett announced, "First thirty seconds starts . . . *now*."

The wall timer started its descent.

I pulled Mitch's ring from my finger and pressed it into her palm.

She stared at me, fearless despite the tremble in her frame as she kicked off her heels. "Tell me what you said in Spanish upstairs. Before I go, please," she whispered.

"After." I needed to believe an after would exist for us both before I could tell her. Until that time came, all I could do was beg, "Go," even though that very idea felt like the walls were closing in on me.

Her lips parted. Words on her tongue she'd have to wait to tell me after, too. Then she hiked up her skirt and sprinted barefoot toward the balcony.

"Neutralized the tangos. C4 confirmed," Reed said over comms. "Enough to level the structure. Countdown active. Three minutes. I'll handle it. Be safe up there."

"Roger that," Ryder replied.

Audrey cast one final look back. Locked on me. Then vanished into the night air.

The screen reset.

Three minutes. The timer ticking again. And that was the guest's cue: Kill or be killed.

Two shots cracked in succession. One from outside the ballroom but inside the hotel. Sharp enough to stop everyone cold.

Someone had tried to sneak out and had been dropped. Screams from outside the doors leading to the interior part of the hotel followed. Then another shot from the same location as before. One more down. Red light, green light. With blood.

Reality snapped into the place. Survival instinct. And just like that, they surged.

The three of us collapsed together like a triangle. Muscle memory took over, each of us guarding a different axis.

"You don't have to do this," I warned, arms slightly raised, body at an angle to minimize target profile. "We're going to get you out alive if you just stay calm. We don't want to kill anyone."

The hosts immediately advanced toward the bar with the French auctioneer and hid, letting us know they weren't up for fighting. The few other women at the event also peeled back, wisely not engaging.

Most of the men nearby remained hesitant, staring at us, frozen, until two broke forward, charging me at once.

One swung a cane at me, which I parried upward, redirecting its arc, then stepped inside his guard and hip-tossed him onto the other guy. Nonlethal takedown. Efficient. Fast. Doing my best not to get blood on my hands unnecessarily.

I kicked the cane toward Ryder, who snatched it and cracked it across someone's knee.

To my left, Hollis shattered her champagne flute on a table's edge, weaponizing it. She buried the jagged stem in a man's thigh and yanked it free, backing him off.

Mimicking her idea, I grabbed an empty, uncorked champagne bottle from the closest table, shattered it on the pillar to my left, and drove the broken glass into another attacker's deltoid. Not deep enough to kill, but enough to drop him.

The three of us continued like this, moving out of triangle formation.

Strike. Disengage. Repeat.

Someone switched it up by flinging a folding chair at me. I ducked under it, popped up inside his guard, and landed an elbow to his throat. He went down, choking.

Comms lit up again. "Alpha Two here. Sorry we're late to the party. What's the status? Package on the move?"

Gray Chandler. That was a relief, even as someone clipped me across the jaw.

I shook it off. Countered with a knee to the gut, then shoved the bastard into a column.

"This is Delta One, glad to have you. Now, I need you to track down a helo that took off seventy-five seconds ago with the package."

"Roger that," Gray answered. "Expected target location?"

"No, last-minute change of plans," Ryder grunted between dodging blows to the face while taking one in the side. He relayed the coordinates after dropping the asshole trying to shadowbox with him. "Expect obstacles on your way."

"Alpha One. That's a good copy. En route now. Alpha Team out."

Another man lunged from my left. I sidestepped, grabbed his jacket, and redirected his momentum, using him as a shield. The guy behind him plunged a pen into his gut instead of mine.

"Delta Team, this is Foxtrot Three," Hollis's team transmitted, crashing the party now, too, as planned. "There are ten armed men nearing the hotel entrance. Do you want us to push or hold?"

Thankfully, Hollis's people had the Helix operatives under surveillance after Reed had rejoined us at the hotel last night. Any second now, every Helix team member would be getting a message from Hollis's twin brother: Pick a side or die on the wrong one.

Ryder answered mid-fight, panting, "Hold until the text has been sent. Continue on mission after that. We've got this room covered."

Just barely.

"Roger, Foxtrot Three out."

After clearing the wave of aggressors, the next group hesitated, staring at us with panicked eyes. Scanning the room, uncertain what to do.

"Foxtrot is preparing to engage with the snipers out here. After that, we're moving in on Helix. Message sent," someone from Hollis's team shared as another man worked up the courage to attack.

Wrong move.

I twisted his wrist and broke it clean, dropping him.

I checked the ballroom timer, then my watch.

21:59.

Echo Team and Trevor would be breaching at 2200 hours. Visual contact made on Beau an hour ago. A lamb sent to the slaughter by Rhett.

The second I returned my gaze to the room, a new round of men looking to get beat up engaged.

They were sloppier. Desperate.

And then the crowd turned on itself. No cohesion. All fear and confusion.

Cracks of bone. Gasps. Screams.

Tables flipped. Bodies crashed into the decor. Furniture became shields and weapons.

Suppressed shots from outside the ballroom sounded. Closer this time.

"This is Foxtrot Three. Snipers down."

Ryder was back to being behind me again, covering my six as I tackled a wiry guy with a jagged fork.

I swept his leg, then knocked the guy unconscious as he attempted to fork me to death.

"Lobby's chaos," someone on Hollis's team reported as I hammered a guy's jaw with my elbow. "Civilians are clear. Staff too. Helix is cannibalizing itself. Plan worked."

"Good. Status on police?" Hollis asked her team.

"Five minutes out," someone answered. "So we need to be gone in four."

Before we could answer, Reed's voice came over the line. "There's a problem. I'm in the primary interface, but he split the encryption. Every thread loops back."

"Meaning?" I ducked behind a flipped-over table as a woman joined the fight, launching her damn stiletto at me.

"It's a logic trap," Reed answered.

Hollis this time: "A logic-based kill switch? Was he expecting us to find it? Giving us a way to beat this?"

"Down to fifteen seconds," Reed warned.

The red digits kept ticking. Everyone stopped moving.

They all realized the same thing: The bomb was still alive and so were we.

No one was safe.

"Wait!" I shouted when I uncrossed the wires in my head and realized what was going on. I jumped up from behind the table. "It's a bluff. Another damn decoy."

All eyes snapped to me.

"He's a greedy, smart bastard. Not a mass-murdering psycho who will take down a hotel with innocent women and children inside it. It's just—"

The timer hit zero.

I braced for impact in case I was wrong, as if that'd do any good to fight a blast and fiery inferno.

Nothing.

Just silence.

No explosion. No fireball or death.

"—a distraction," I finished, exhaling the truth with every breath I had left.

CHAPTER FIFTY-FIVE

Audrey

The wind from the helicopter's blades hadn't even settled before I was yanked out of the harness by two men in black tactical gear. Faces hidden, movements unforgiving. Either they hadn't received Hollis's brother's mass text—or they had and picked the wrong side.

My bare feet hit the concrete. I stumbled forward, barely catching myself as they dragged me ahead. My dress clung to my legs, sticky with sweat and dust from the airlift.

We were maybe fifteen minutes from the hotel, somewhere remote.

One truth kept me going, kept me strong: The teams would get to me in time.

"Keep walking," one guy at my left snapped.

My wrists were bound, but only loosely. Enough for some movement. They guided me toward a row of eight armed men standing like statues in front of a large garage-like building. More men were more than likely on the perimeter or hiding in the woods.

From the shadows, the mastermind himself stepped into the light. Rhett. Lit from behind, his features were unmistakable.

"Where's Mitch?" I called out, playing the part I'd been rehearsing since yesterday. This moment was inevitable, ever since we'd learned the truth behind the lie.

The explosives had been a twist, though. But this part? Expected.

The guy off to my right handed Rhett the ring he'd taken from me. It had burned my palm like iron before he pried it away.

Rhett ignored my question and studied the ring under a flashlight. "Mitch is dead," he muttered, then looked up. Calm and composed. Like he hadn't threatened to blow up a hotel.

A hand clamped down on the back of my neck, forcing me closer. Close enough to smell Rhett's breath. Close enough to want to puke.

The smug curl of Rhett's mouth said it all: He thought he was two steps ahead of the universe.

I wanted to do more than spit in his face. I wanted to end him. For endangering my son. For trying to send Trevor off to die in Afghanistan. For impersonating a dead man. Forcing Alex into a position to have to face his ex. And so on.

"Time to unlock the vault and end all of this," he said a little anticlimactically. "I'm sure you're just as anxious."

The building's huge doors groaned open. Floodlights bathed the aircraft inside in a sterile, surgical glow. Not a commercial-size one like Hollis's. Not nearly as big as the Costas' jet, either.

This was a matte-gray death sentence with no visible tail number. Probably no transponder, either.

The concrete under my feet wasn't a path; it was a taxiway lined with faint-blue lights and a retractable barricade. The hangar sat directly off a private strip, probably owned by some unsuspecting millionaire.

Standing near the jet was Cipheria—also known in real life as Lisa. Gwen had identified her this morning. From what we could tell, she was also Rhett's girlfriend.

Rhett pocketed the ring. Bruises still lingered on his face from when Alejandro had dragged him into the lodge on Sunday.

He brushed a loose strand of hair away from my cheek. "Looks like that spot where I hit you is clearing up."

I tried to knee him in the balls. Close to success, but one of his jerk friends held me back.

"Are you finally figuring out New Zealand was never the final stop?" He smirked. "You only *thought* Mitch came here because of footage you recovered. But my girlfriend sent you chasing after not only the wrong enemy, but the wrong location." He winked, the bastard. "I have a lot more experience than your friends in putting together target packages and executing missions. My playbook was handed down to them, after all. Don't feel bad."

Condescending piece of shit.

He touched his chest, his voice lower and more serious now. "We sacrificed everything for our country. And they erased us afterward. Sent us off like disposable assets." A gruff sound slipped through his barely parted lips. "Stratos didn't really die, though. It evolved." His voice cracked slightly. "It's still breathing. Always has been. Quiet. Effective. Right under POTUS's nose, even after Hobbs died."

"Do your men at Helix know who's really calling the shots and why? That it's no longer about country anymore, but money?" My job was to stall, to buy the teams time. So I'd keep poking the bear for as long as needed until they arrived.

He pulled out a phone from his pocket. "You have no evidence to corroborate that text sent to my men. Nice try."

"But it *did* work, didn't it?" I pressed. "I bet some of your men flipped tonight."

He flinched. Just barely.

"We'll deal with traitors later." To his men, he ordered, "Get her on board."

"And Beau, or whatever his real name is?" I asked as we began to move. "You sent him to Eden's location knowing he'd die tonight."

"Casualty of war."

"Who needs enemies with that mentality," I muttered.

One of the masked men at my side pulled a Glock from his waistband, gesturing for me to walk faster.

"And them?" I asked, nodding to the other guy at my side holding my arm a bit more gently. "Are they expendable, too? Already 'dead' in the system so no one notices when they go missing?"

The one not waving a weapon at me slowed just a little. Just enough for me to know there was a chance of winning him over.

Rhett must've seen the look in his eyes, the hesitation there. "She's baiting you," he snapped. "Focus."

"We don't fake deaths anymore," the guy with the Glock said. "We learned from the government's mistakes."

"Tell that to Arlo," I reminded them all. "His death is what started this. And Mitch? You killed him, too. Should've asked questions first."

Once we were inside the hangar, Rhett glanced at me before getting into the jet's cockpit with his girlfriend.

"You're really the one running Helix, aren't you?" I asked once I was strapped into the cabin, which was open to the cockpit. "Not whoever's listed on the website. Pretty sure the bylaws say dead men can't own security firms."

He turned, shifting his headset down. "You know what my biggest mistake was?" He met my eyes. "Letting Mitch walk in 2013. Should've either recruited him to stay on or put two in his skull back then. Saved us all the trouble."

"Everything happens for a reason," I murmured, picturing my loved ones waiting for me. Mission success meant I'd see my family, so I kept on pushing through the nerves and fear to hold strong.

"To be clear, you did silence Arlo—and then realized Mitch's plane crash wasn't real, which had you putting two and two together that Arlo talked to him. So you had to shut him up, too." I paused, trying to buy us time. Distract him. "You had your girlfriend hack JSOC and found his location before he arrived at the safe house and killed him."

I gave him another chance to stir. To get irritated as I pushed his buttons.

"How long before you realized your mistake and that he hid evidence first?" I kept my cool, not even sure who this me was right now. "Five or six months? Clearly before you created Beau, the sheriff. Tried using him to smoke out the truth. Figure out what the key even was and then find it."

The *if looks could kill* glare from Rhett wasn't aimed at me that time.

"Ah, I see. Your girlfriend messed up, not you."

"Shut up," Lisa bit out as Rhett faced forward and began hitting switches and tapping buttons, preparing to pull out of the hangar.

"You stumbled upon a new problem, though. My brother and his best friend. Alejandro's ex-wife and her ties to Will Hobbs." *Nope, not backing down.* "You ended up down to the wire with days to spare before the evidence would wind up in the wrong hands or out in the public."

"No, everything was calculated. You don't think I knew exactly what I was doing?" she sneered, twisting around to look at me. "I planned this perfectly, down to hacking your emails six months ago. Saw the communications with your lawyer. Hacked him, too. Found out what Mitch did and why you were divorcing him. I used your pain to blind you all to the truth."

Now Rhett's comments to me back in Trevor's office at the lodge made sense. I'd assumed the only way he could've known about the divorce was because Mitch had told him.

I drew every last bit of strength I had, thinking about my son and my future with Alejandro. "That's the thing about traps and illusions," I said softly as gunfire sounded outside the hangar, which meant help had arrived. "Eventually, you find out you weren't really behind the curtain. You were just part of the show."

CHAPTER FIFTY-SIX

Alejandro

"Alpha, come in. This is Delta One. Status update?" Ryder asked as we geared up inside the bird, preparing for infil.

"Alpha Two," Gray replied, his voice tight over comms. "We're in position. We had resistance en route here. Hostiles neutralized. We're moving in now on the final target. We've got eyes on a jet on the tarmac. Engines hot."

"Do not let them leave the ground," Ryder ordered. "We're two mikes out, approaching from the north."

Delta Shield, along with Hollis, were packed into a modified Black Hawk—one Hollis had arranged personally. Apparently, she could pull helos from thin air like one of the owners of Falcon Falls could.

We'd lifted from the hotel landing zone just before local law enforcement swarmed the site.

"We've got a plan to prevent them from flying out," Alpha Two shared. "We've got it covered."

"We'll get to her," Hollis reassured us as she strapped a Glock to her side. She'd changed from her dress into pants and a tee on board when our backs were turned.

The rest of us remained in our suits but lost the jackets and swapped our loafers for boots. We now had chest plates and helmets on, same as Hollis.

"Echo pulled Eden. Now it's our turn to get Audrey," she continued, talking over the mic attached to the helmet.

Something told me she was reassuring herself of that as much as she was us.

But she was right.

Two miracles had already happened tonight: The charges didn't detonate, and Eden was safe. We needed one more now. A fourth tomorrow to get to the real vault in time before that evidence fell into the wrong hands.

"We will, you're right," I said, locking a mag into my HK416. "But she's still out there alone, which kills me."

"This is Audrey we're talking about." Hollis gripped my arm. "She's stage-trained, remember? Performers adapt. Even pianists. She's got this." She let go of me and lowered her night vision in place.

Rhett didn't know we'd figured out the rest of his plan, and Audrey was going to do her best to act surprised when he didn't take her to the vault in Arrowtown like he wanted us to believe he'd be doing. Thanks to Gwen and Hollis's brother earlier this evening, we'd learned the truth.

We now knew Mitch had never set foot in New Zealand. It was all deepfake AI. The vault he'd planted the evidence in wasn't here. Tasmania, one of the three locations Gwen had originally ID'd from the inscription in the ring, was the real target.

"Alpha One to all units," Carter Dominick's voice cut in, punctuated by gunfire. "Boots on the ground. Engaged with perimeter tangos."

"Status on the plane?" Ryder demanded.

Gunfire crackled. Then Gray answered, "Alpha Two. Runway's compromised. We blew the asphalt. Aircraft is immobile. HVTs and hostage are still on board."

Ryder gave me a look. *Let's finish this.* He keyed his mic. "Delta advancing northwest. Four friendlies dropping down in thirty seconds."

"Copy that," Carter returned. "Perimeter's still hot. Watch your flanks."

"Delta Shield on-site," Ryder confirmed, nodding to us as the helo dipped low. "Fast-roping now."

We were lowered to the ground under cover of rotor wash. Gunfire erupted to our left as we advanced in diamond formation, Hollis protected at center.

"Three tangos, northwest fence line," Carter warned. "They heard your bird. Coming fast."

"Copy. Engaging," Ryder transmitted back, then went to one knee, sighting in.

I covered his six, squeezing two rounds into a hostile who'd broken from cover.

"Threats neutralized," Ryder announced once we'd taken out the three tangos.

We pushed forward. Every shot we took calculated. Every second a countdown.

We weren't dealing with amateurs, but with men who'd received similar training as us, which made my stomach turn.

Operators. Former military. Now turncoats.

"Alpha One." Carter's voice popped back onto the line. "We've secured the perimeter. All enemies outside the plane are now down. You're green to move on the plane."

Then came the gut punch.

"Be advised: Rhett's still inside with the hostage. He's requesting a face-to-face. Refuses to come out unless he talks to Delta."

"This is Delta One," Ryder said, his voice steel. "Roger. Moving now."

The hangar lights flickered in front of us, painting long shadows across the field.

We knocked our night vision up when closing in on Alpha Team holding the ground, armed and waiting for us. Our backup had saved the day, thank God.

Now to get Audrey out uninjured. Thankfully, this was what we'd been trained to do in Delta Force: hostage-rescue even from a hijacked plane. We would defeat this asshole. I had to believe that. No suicide missions taking Audrey with him.

"Alpha One," Carter said. "He's ready to talk to you." He gave us the frequency to switch over to as we closed in on Alpha Team.

I turned the knob, catching a new voice as I did. "This is Zero Tango. I know you're there." Rhett, the asshole I'd clocked in the woods in Colorado.

Ryder keyed his mic. "We're listening."

"I know how this plays. You breach, people die. Probably her. So let's make a deal," Rhett continued.

"You're out of deals and out of chances. Nowhere for you to run—not even for a dead man," Ryder hissed back.

"Maybe not, but I've still got the hostage. I also have both rings. I kill her, you lose her and the evidence in the vault falls into the wrong hands. You won't be able to access it without her, even if you have the rings. You. Need. Me."

"The fuck we do," I ground out, unable to stop myself.

"Ah, the boyfriend." Rhett's voice remained steady, as if he actually still believed he held all the cards. "Is that you, Rodriguez? Your ex-wife's a real piece of work. Though you already know that, don't you?"

I kept quiet that time, not looking to play into his hands.

"Don't do what he wants!" Audrey yelled in the background, giving me a heart attack. Both her words and her voice.

"I don't know how you found our location or figured out—"

"Your hacker girlfriend isn't as good as she thinks she is. If she was, she'd have figured out how to hack that secure call you knew I'd take with Beth. You'd have found out you'd been played."

"Bullshit." Was that Rhett's girlfriend? "She told you what we wanted her to. You fell for it all, or you'd never have come to New Zealand."

Ryder advanced toward the jet, methodical and calm, rifle angled low but ready.

Alpha Team flanked wide, their muzzles still trained on the plane, but they gradually peeled off to give us the lead.

Once the cockpit came into view, my stomach sank.

Rhett was in the pilot's seat, his arm locked tight around Audrey, who was crouched next to him, gun pressed to her temple.

His girlfriend was in the seat off to Rhett's right, armed as well.

Before I had a chance to process, Hollis nudged me. An elbow in the ribs, and I turned.

She held up a phone. A text response to the one her brother had sent out to everyone back at the hotel, and he'd forwarded it to her.

555-934-3438: Friendly inside.

I immediately killed my mic and tipped my head toward Hollis and whispered, "Who is he? Can we trust him?"

She pulled the screen back and flipped to a profile: *Army Special Forces. Joined Helix six months ago.*

New. Not yet corrupted. And probably realized he'd been sold a lie.

She showed me the next message forwarded.

555-934-3438: I served with Gray back in the day. I can see him outside the plane. What are my orders?

None of us had masked up. No reason to. That may have been our saving grace now.

"Show this to Alpha Two. Confirm," I told Hollis.

She went over to Gray and quickly returned a moment later. "He's the real deal. Not another trap," she let me know.

I leaned toward Ryder, murmuring, "We've got a man on the inside."

His eyes narrowed slightly; then he faced the plane and resumed speaking into his mic. "Best I can do is offer you a cell at a CIA black site instead of death. Maybe even let you bunk with your girlfriend. But this ends now."

As Ryder bought us time, I shifted out of view of the cockpit and told Hollis, "Tell me you have something on you to kill the power inside that plane."

Hollis smiled. "Of course." She reached into her pocket and produced what looked like a hockey puck. "EMP device."

"Tell our insider the power will go out in thirty seconds; he should make his move then. Get Audrey away from Rhett, and we'll take the kill shots through the glass."

She nodded. "Once I hit this button, three seconds later, it'll fry everything in a twenty-meter radius. We'll have five minutes before everything starts rebooting."

"Good." I let my sling catch my rifle, then waited for her to send the text before setting the timer on my watch. Another damn countdown. "Go."

I turned my mic back on and switched to our secure channel to include Alpha Team in on the plan since Reed and Ryder were still on the other line with Rhett.

We moved into position, preparing to knock our NODs in place. I discreetly signaled to Ryder and Reed the time to give them the heads-up, then readied my rifle. Time for one of our own distractions. *Us*, so Alpha could move in for the kill.

"Alpha Two," Gray said. "POTUS wants the HVT alive for questioning, if possible."

Fuck. "If it's him or Audrey . . ."

"Of course," he responded as Reed and I flanked Ryder.

Through the side cockpit window, I put eyes back on her again. On the woman I'd made love to tonight. The woman who could even be pregnant with my child right now.

I swallowed. Breathed. And readied myself for only one allowable outcome: her surviving this unscathed.

And then in three, two, one . . . it was go time.

A sharp click.

A dull *whump* of released energy.

Then total blackout.

"Snipers up," I ordered, and Alpha Team moved on target as the interior of the jet went dark. Lights, controls, and cockpit screens were dead.

Night vision in place, we didn't hesitate.

Gunfire from inside.

Audrey out of view.

Two targets acquired: Rhett and his girlfriend.

And one voice shouting the only word I wanted to hear from inside the plane after Alpha Team took their shots: "Clear!"

CHAPTER FIFTY-SEVEN

Audrey

I was disoriented, unsure what the heck had just happened. One minute, Rhett was burying his fingernails into my side, holding a gun to my head; then the lights went out and I'd taken the chance to wriggle free of his hold and drop down.

All I knew now was that I was free of him and there weren't any holes in my body.

"Audrey, you okay?" a voice called from behind me. Male, unfamiliar.

Still on my knees, head cradled between my arms as if I could stop a bullet to the head that way, I blinked into the darkness, seeing nothing.

I searched around, locating a motionless body to my right. The girlfriend.

But the groaning man to my left, the one now reaching for me—

"I got you," the voice said again, this time closer, more urgent.

Strong arms hooked under mine and dragged me from the cockpit into the cabin. I bumped into another unmoving figure and felt metal beneath my fingers.

"You helped me," I whispered as the realization hit. Had to be the guy I'd hoped to turn.

He didn't answer, just shouted, "Clear!" as the cabin door creaked open. "Sounds like Rhett's still alive in the cockpit," he muttered to someone outside.

"Audrey?" Alejandro's voice.

"Audrey!" Ryder that time.

"Audrey . . ." And my best friend.

My name echoed from all sides. Music to my ears. They were here. We were alive.

The man guided me through the darkness toward a figure waiting at the base of the ramp. He had to be using night vision to see me. I couldn't make out anything.

But the moment I reached him, he pulled me into his arms without hesitation. *Not* a friendly, brotherly hug. No, this was—

"Alejandro," I cried as he held me, squeezing me tight.

"I got you," he rasped in confirmation, voice thick with emotion. "Never letting go."

At the feel of a hand at my side, I knew who it belonged to. "Glad you're okay," my brother said. "Well, more than just glad . . ."

"Everyone okay? Eden? Trevor? Echo?" I asked them, still clinging to Alejandro for dear life.

"Safe and secure," Ryder answered, and relief filled me. "Get her into the hangar. Be right over."

Behind us, Rhett moaned. Somewhere nearby, someone reported, "Shoulder wound. Ear clipped. But he's alive. We keeping him that way?"

I didn't hear Ryder's answer because Alejandro picked me up, clearly remembering I was barefoot, and carried me to the hangar, which was still lit up, glowing ahead like salvation.

That feeling of peace left the moment he set me down and I spotted a man dragging a dead masked operator inside to lay him next to two others.

Helix employees who'd chosen the wrong side. The side of greed and evil.

"Never leave a man behind—not even these guys," someone I didn't recognize said in a remorseful tone. He knocked his night vision into place once he was back outside the hangar, probably to help search for more bodies.

I shifted back into Alejandro's welcoming arms, catching his eyes since his night vision goggles were at the top of his helmet.

I didn't want to see the blood and death, knowing they'd died, in part, because of me.

He cupped my chin. "Not your fault."

"But this still isn't over," I said, remembering. "The evidence is in Tasmania, not here. We were right."

"Thanks to you, we can get there in time. What you did tonight . . ." His voice was tight. "No body armor. Just armed with courage."

I sniffled and rested my hands on him, feeling the plate beneath his dress shirt. So, so grateful he'd never had to take a round to test the plate's effectiveness. "The explosives. You're clearly in one piece, thank God. What happened?"

"He never planned to detonate. It was a decoy," Hollis said, coming up alongside us. She pulled me away from Alejandro for a hug. "Hi."

"Hi," I choked out as more operators began flooding the room.

One of them had the mastermind asshole behind all this: Rhett. He was bleeding. Bound and gagged. The guy shoved him on the ground. "Celeste," the guy said in a low voice, nodding at her.

"I just go by Hollis now." She went over and patted his arm. "Thanks for the help tonight. I was worried for a minute you'd miss all the fun."

"Of course you two know each other. Why am I not surprised?" Reed grumbled while striding in, letting his sling catch his rifle.

The guy ignored Reed and turned to face me. "Carter Dominick." He smiled. "Happy to see you alive and breathing. You were brave." He focused on Reed and tipped his head toward my best friend. "And in my *former* line of work," he continued—whatever that was supposed to mean—"it paid to know someone like *Hollis*. Only person who has more money and gadgets than I do," he added with a light laugh as my brother joined us again.

"What are next steps? Orders from your dad?" Ryder asked Gray, one of the few people here who I already knew, thanks to Trevor's relation to his wife, Tessa.

Gray looked around at the crowded hangar. "Echo Team will take Rhett on their plane to the States. Delta Shield catches a ride with Hollis to Tasmania and gets the evidence."

Alejandro stepped off to my side, resting his hand at the small of my back. Part of me wanted to borrow that sidearm strapped to his outer leg and go whack Rhett in the temple the way he had me just a week ago.

"Who, um, killed Cipheria?" I asked in a tentative voice, worried about the men here having to take a woman's life. Something told me that wasn't the norm for them.

"I did." An operator walked in to join us while removing her helmet, shaking out her blonde hair. "The rings," she said, passing them off to Ryder before looking at me. "Sydney Hawkins." She stood alongside a few other guys from the Falcon Falls team who'd been acting as Alpha Team tonight. "It was you or her. Easy choice."

"Thank you," I breathed, relieved Cipheria was no longer a threat. Not so sure how I felt about Rhett living to see another day, though, and I knew Alejandro and Ryder weren't happy about that, either.

"Come on. Let's get you to the airport. Trevor and Eden are on their way there now, and they're eager to see you," my brother said.

"Did Beau make it out alive, too?" I asked.

Alejandro stopped short, then shot an uneasy look at my brother.

I swallowed. "What is it?" I whispered.

"Well, um," Ryder started, "Beau had been disarmed, when Eden reached for a fallen weapon. She went to shoot him, and Trevor saw what she was about to do."

Stomach wrenching, I squeezed my eyes closed at what I knew was coming next.

"Trevor went ahead and took the shot before she could," he continued, "not wanting her to get blood on her hands."

◆ ◆ ◆

"Will do, man. You ever need anything, I'm just a call away," Carter Dominick said to my brother from inside the private hangar at Queenstown Airport. He pivoted to Hollis next and grinned. "Stay out of trouble, will ya?"

"Me? Trouble?" she teased.

Reed coughed into his fist, clearly calling her on it, which earned an eye roll from Hollis.

Carter slung his knapsack over his shoulder and spun his finger in the air as a directive to his team to move out. Everyone would be parting ways now except Gray. He'd be coming with us to the vault in Tasmania to hopefully retrieve the evidence Mitch had planted there.

We were still waiting on Echo Team's arrival with Eden and Trevor before we could fly out.

I couldn't begin to imagine how Eden was feeling right now. Trevor too.

"Sooo." Hollis turned toward me. "You ready for tomorrow?"

"If it means putting this all behind us once that vault is open? You could say that." I nervously brushed my thumb along my lips.

"You'll figure it out; I have faith in you." Her gaze seemed to snag on something on my hand before she pointed out, "You're still wearing the ring."

"Forgot it was there." I held my hand out in front of me, but before I could decide if I'd be taking it off now or later, two Suburbans rolled up in place of the Falcon's vehicles that'd just departed.

You're here.

Trevor stepped out first, catching my gaze. He circled the vehicle as Wyatt emerged beside him, and they both helped Eden out of the back seat. She looked pale, dazed, her eyes flicking around like she didn't quite believe this was real. Beau—or whatever his real name was—had twisted her entire reality into something unrecognizable.

I stepped away from Hollis to get to them.

On the way, I met Alejandro's eyes. He was standing just inside the open hangar, arms crossed, quiet but watchful, alongside my brother. He gave me a small nod, and I knew exactly what that nod meant.

No jealousy. No questions. Just his trust wrapped around me like armor.

Tears blurred my vision as I nodded back.

And then Trevor caught me in his arms for a hug.

"Thank fuck you're okay," he said into my ear, his voice rough.

"You too," I whispered, eyes falling on Eden as she melted into Gray's embrace.

"You know what I had to do, don't you?" Trevor pulled away, eyes red. "He was unarmed. But I didn't have a choice. If I didn't take the shot, she would have. She froze up when I did; then Wyatt disarmed her before she could finish him off."

"And you did exactly what you needed to do," I said, trembling. "You saved her. Saved her from a life of regret and guilt." I blinked back an ugly-cry and stared up at the ceiling, needing to steady myself. Then I looked him in the eyes. "But, Trevor?"

"Yeah?" His shoulders dropped, the weight of everything he'd carried etched deep into his face.

"You didn't kill him. And you could've." *Easily.*

He squeezed his eyes shut, forehead dipping to rest against mine.

"You found a way to protect your sister from a mistake . . . while also protecting your own peace. And I'm so damn proud of you."

CHAPTER FIFTY-EIGHT

Alejandro

Tasmania
Remote private bunker site; vault 212

Thick concrete walls surrounded us, embedded with steel and reinforced glass. The room stretched wide and high, its design more military grade than financial—a fallout shelter crossed with a weapons depot.

There were multiple guards in paramilitary gear flanking the single reinforced entrance, and security cameras buzzed softly overhead. Even without seeing their weapons, I could tell these weren't the rent-a-cop type.

"Cutting it close," the woman in charge said. "Almost disappointed you made it, to be honest. Something tells me what's inside this vault is worth more than the fee you're paying to pick it up."

Thanks to Hollis, who'd fronted us the cash on behalf of Uncle Sam, so we had the emergency funds on hand for this moment.

"So, you've got Mitch's death certificate, the key, and me . . ." Audrey nervously wrung her hands together. "Do you need my handprint or eye scan or something now?"

The woman flicked her wrist, gesturing to a guard to hand her an iPad. "You weren't here with Mitchell Langston, so we had to improvise on our typical procedures. He was rather convincing and had an interesting pitch." She began typing on the iPad. "One second. Let me get it ready so you can activate your vault to unlock it."

I reached for Audrey's left hand, reminding her she wasn't alone. She had Ryder and me with her. We'd get through this together.

At the feel of her ring still on her finger, my chest constricted. We may not have really been married, but something told me that the wedding band no longer felt like a prop to her. Crazy or not, it hadn't felt like one when I'd picked it out.

Rhett might've been the reason behind the purchase, but that didn't change what it meant to me. I'd still put my heart into it when I slipped it on her finger.

"Here you go. Sixty seconds to unlock the vault, or the contents remain with us. Time starts now," the woman announced, handing Audrey the iPad and forcing me to let go.

Another countdown. *Great.*

"Why am I looking at piano keys on this thing?" Audrey asked, shooting the woman a nervous look.

"I assumed you'd know." The woman checked her slim silver watch.

I hated not being able to help her. Hated watching her hands shake and knowing I couldn't do a damn thing except stand there.

Audrey closed her eyes. "What song would you think I'd pick?" she murmured under her breath as if talking to a ghost. In this case, maybe she was.

"Forty-five seconds." This play-by-play from the woman was not helping.

"It's okay. You've got this," Ryder reassured Audrey, giving the other woman a death stare at the same time.

Audrey opened her eyes and exhaled a deep breath. "How many chances do I get?"

"Just the one." She checked her watch again. "Thirty-three seconds."

Audrey nodded, then clenched and unclenched her right hand as her left one shook while holding the iPad.

I slipped my hand under it to offer support; then she caught my eyes and her brows slanted.

"Lace," I whispered, reminding her of the story she'd told me over coffee this morning at the hotel—because talking about her panties had somehow become our thing. And I was good with that.

Now that I knew she used to buy lace underwear to help her nerves while performing, I was hoping she'd visualize herself in a pair to steel her nerves.

"Lace," she said back, nodding in understanding, her confidence returning.

"Ten seconds," the woman warned.

Audrey's fingers hit the fake keys on the screen, and then, on the fifth note, the sealed door hissed before opening with a hydraulic groan.

"Just in time." The woman took the iPad from her. "Too bad."

"Oh thank God." Audrey covered her face with both palms as Ryder looked inside the vault.

I pulled her into my arms, resting my chin on top of her head. "I knew you could do it," I said as Ryder held up a flash drive and an envelope.

"Who'd have thought our conversations about underwear would save the world," she said, pulling away with a half cry, half laugh.

"I predicted it," I joked. "I called it a week ago when I walked in on you and—" I abandoned that thought, remembering Ryder was still present. I'd been caught up in the moment with her.

"Still her brother. Still here," he reminded us, though a smile tugged at the corner of his mouth.

"*Still* owe you an apology for breaking my promise," I said once we were completely paid up and out of the maze, back up top in the land of the living. Breathing fresh air and no longer feeling like we were inside a crematorium.

"I don't even want to know what you're sorry for," Ryder said as Reed, Gray, and Hollis met us outside by our two parked SUVs. "And for the record, you only owe me an apology if you ever break her heart." He slipped on his Ray-Bans, only to pull them down to steal a look at me. "That better never happen."

He handed the flash drive off to Gray, who had a laptop open, ready to confirm the contents.

"So, what song was it?" I deflected.

"'River Flows in You' by Yiruma. Only song I figured Mitch might be able to play the first few notes of. He used to whistle along, but only stayed in sync for the first few seconds. It was his favorite, though."

"Music?" Hollis swooped in and pulled Audrey off for a sidebar conversation, asking her, "What happened in there?"

I joined the guys as Ryder removed a letter from the envelope.

He quietly read it over, his chest rising and falling in a steady rhythm, unease settling on his face. "An 'if anything happens to me' letter from Mitch." He removed his sunglasses and shook his head, then motioned for Audrey to rejoin us. "There's a note for you at the end." He handed her the letter.

I folded my arms and closed my eyes, not sure I wanted to know what his parting words to her were. Not after everything he'd put her through.

Audrey's voice was shaky as she read out loud: *"If you're reading this without me, that means I didn't make it. I'm sorry. I didn't want to pull you into this, but I knew I could only protect you by keeping you in the dark while also requiring Rhett to need you if he were to ever find out what I knew. I didn't know who to trust, but I hope you finished what I tried to start."*

At her pause to take a breath, I opened my eyes, needing to take a deep one myself.

"I know I've been acting weird lately. Drinking too much. Stressed. I hope it all makes sense now. I'm still sorry, though. But in truth? I haven't been the best husband anyway, have I? Not sure if a dead man's sorry is

worth anything, but if it is? I am. Hope you find someone who actually deserves you. I know I never did. Take care, Audi." She looked up from the letter at me. "Signed it with his usual em dash and HELL." She handed the letter back to Ryder.

"He was right about one thing: He didn't deserve you," Ryder said under his breath as he folded the letter. "So, we good?" he asked Gray.

"He didn't have evidence on POTUS's SEAL teams, either. Just Stratos. But it's all here. Everything my dad will need to take them off the map for good," Gray confirmed before closing the laptop.

"We'd assumed Mitch might have intel on the teams because of that lie Beth had originally fed us. Since it wasn't him behind this, looks like the only one who had any evidence on the teams—"

"Already handed it over to us by Beth," I finished for Ryder. And that reminded me, would I still be keeping up my end of the deal by visiting her in person? One thing at a time.

"What do we do now?" Audrey circled her brother to get back to me, looping her arm around my back, pinning herself to my side.

"We take you to Chase, and we put all this behind us," Ryder told her. "And then I pick up the love of my life in New York."

I turned toward Audrey and leaned in to set my mouth to her ear. "And I also tell you what I said to you in Spanish last night."

I ignored the eyes and awkward throat-clears around me, prepared to translate, but she beat me to it.

"I remembered some of it." She pulled back to tilt her chin up at me, smiling. "I looked it up on the way here."

"Oh, did you?"

"Curiosity got the best of me." Hand to my chest, she whispered back what I'd said in Spanish, but added one word at the end: "Crazy or not, I'm falling in love with you, *too*."

CHAPTER FIFTY-NINE

Audrey

Fort Collins, Colorado

"Coffee?"

I looked over at my future sister-in-law, who was nudging an oversize mug my way. I must've been in a daze—and I was also burning the eggs, wasn't I?

Lowering the heat on the stove, I accepted the java with a quiet "Thank you."

Seraphina didn't say anything right away, just took a sip of her own and watched me, the way people do when they're making sure you're still breathing.

We hadn't originally come to this place by choice, but now that we were being told we could leave tomorrow, I found myself not wanting to go.

Secretary Chandler had ordered us to lie low. This was day seven in our temporary hideout, a much bigger home than Wyatt's.

We were tucked away deep in the woods with a security system just as advanced as his—though, sadly, it had no piano. But it was safe, and I'd spent a week surrounded by people I love.

After we flew back to the States last week, Ryder went straight to New York to bring Seraphina here. He refused to spend another day without her. Having her steady presence made this place feel less like a safe house and more like a refuge.

"You okay?" she finally asked.

"Just . . . Is it really *over* over? Because it feels too good to be true."

"You know Ryder wouldn't let us leave tomorrow if he had any doubts or worries. The man puts the word *over* in *overprotective*."

"A man after my own heart," I said with a light, nervous laugh.

"And Chandler's just as stubborn, so he wouldn't give us the green light to leave if every last bad guy wasn't confirmed dead or locked up."

Also true. "I'll still probably need some reminding of that a few more times before it sinks in." I turned off the burner and slid the pan to the side. The eggs were burnt, but Chase liked them overdone anyway.

"Well, I can do that." She gently squeezed my arm. "Too bad Rhett and Beau are still alive," she added, her voice dipping into the factual. "But at least they're in a CIA black site now. They can't hurt anyone again."

I wasn't so sure about Rhett. That man had one too many tricks up his sleeve. I guess that was my issue now. I was worried he wasn't done yet. Maybe not now. But one, two, or even ten years from now . . . no telling.

"And although we found out Rhett didn't start up Helix, only took control from the owners four years ago, at least we know they're officially out of business. *Forever* forever," she continued with reassurance.

"This is all good, I know. Case closed. Time to move on." I set aside my coffee. "So why do I still feel stuck?"

She mirrored my movement, abandoning her mug and fully facing me. "That's a normal feeling. After everything you've been through, it's your brain trying to protect you. You're stepping into a new life with Alex, with your son. And you're scared something from the past might come back and rip it away."

I nodded, my breath hitching as the words hit home. "This week's been perfect. Everyone here. Safe. Together. Now we have to leave the bubble and face the real world again, and that terrifies me."

She pulled me in for a hug, wrapping her arms around me like armor. "Do you want real?" she whispered. "Or do you want the illusion of it?"

Ugh, I was done with illusions forever.

"Because as nice as it's been, this isn't forever. It was never meant to be."

"You're right," I murmured. "I guess I need to let the bubble pop, even if Eden's not ready to go to their lodge yet." A lodge she and Trevor now planned to sell, and I didn't blame them. "And Chase is dreading school." Also didn't blame him. "And as for me? My new house that never really had a chance to become a home . . . I'm not looking forward to returning."

"Have you considered moving to Charleston? We're in a new-construction neighborhood." She stepped back, brushing my hair behind my shoulder. "Move in with Alex. Trevor and Eden could live together for now down the street, too. She needs to be around family after what Beau did to her."

Was she serious?

"Ryder would love it. Chase would freak. You know, in a good way."

She was right about that. "All of us in the same neighborhood? I like how that sounds." And it wasn't out of the realm of possibility, especially not after what had happened last night.

One minute, we'd all been playing a board game together, and the next, Chase had looked back and forth between me and Alex, asking when we were getting married and could he be the best man instead of the ring bearer. He wanted a "cooler role" in our wedding that we were apparently having.

I'd choked on my wine. Alex, his bourbon.

And Ryder had, shockingly, laughed. "Gonna have to fight me on that spot, little man."

As for Trevor? He'd grinned and commented, "Not weird if I come, too, right?"

In the blink of an eye, I'd gone from a woman never wanting to date, to falling in love and having both my son and his father welcoming another man into the family.

Seraphina pointed to the eternity band on my finger. "You haven't taken off that ring, I see."

"It's stuck. I can't get it over my knuckle. Guess my fingers swelled up."

"Or maybe God's trying to tell you something?" She casually winked, then picked up her coffee.

"Tell you what?" Ryder's deep voice filtered through the air, and he walked into the kitchen and over to his fiancée to kiss her. "Everything okay?" he asked after popping a pod in the Nespresso machine and starting it up.

Seraphina shared her neighborhood plan, and his eyes lit up.

"That'd be amazing." He leaned forward and lightly squeezed my shoulder. "Reed could get a place, too. He's a man without a home. Wandering from place to place. Could get a dog to live with," he added with a laugh.

"After spending time with that team dog, Bear, Chase will beg for a pet, too," I said at the memory.

"And hell, Hollis could probably just buy out every house there and it could be our private safe haven," Seraphina teased.

"Don't give that woman any ideas," a new voice cut in. "And did I really just hear you all planning to start a compound?"

I turned to find Reed in the doorway, arms folded. Classic brooding stance. Honestly, the man could scowl in his sleep.

"Should sound like heaven to you. No chance of strangers and small talk. Just people you like," Ryder joked.

"Who says I like you?" he responded with a tight voice while also clearly fighting a smirk.

I waved a finger at him. "We need to find someone for you that'll turn that frown upside down for good."

I focused back on the pan. Eggs were now not just burnt but also cold. *Oh well. Frozen pancakes it is.* I tossed the egg disaster into the trash. "Where's everyone else?"

Reed shrugged. "Trevor and Alex are in the office, talking about something."

Something? That was vague enough to concern me.

"And my nephew is trying to lift Eden's spirits by performing a magic trick for her that Alex taught him," Ryder said with a smile after I retrieved the pancakes. "You raised a good kid. He's going to be okay."

I could hear Chase's muffled laughter down the hall as he performed that trick. He sounded light and free. And I wanted to keep it that way.

"Mind if I steal a word?" Ryder tipped his head to the side, seemingly forgetting about the coffee machine he'd started up.

Seraphina took the pancake box from me. "Here, let me. Go ahead."

"No, no. I'll cook. Don't eat that garbage," Reed grumbled, pushing away from the wall before I followed my brother from the room, curious what kind of sidebar conversation he wanted to have with me.

Any chance it was similar to the one happening between Trevor and Alejandro?

"What's up?" I asked once we were in the library, rolling ladder and all.

Ryder closed the door and slowly faced me.

Was he about to lecture me on the make-out session he'd witnessed in the laundry room? We'd tried to behave. Really, we had. No shared room. No PDA. But we were also human.

And maybe this morning's shared shower wasn't our most innocent moment.

Okay, definitely not innocent. Thankfully, the door had been locked, for no interruptions.

"What are your thoughts on Trevor working with us?"

Talk about a way to pull my head from the shower and back into the room. *"What?"*

"Not active duty. Not all the time. Maybe a job here and there twice a month? Quick in-and-out things. Two, three days, tops, each time. Would pay well enough he'd have free time to be a stay-at-home dad all the other days of the month." He let that idea sink in before continuing, "And that would give you a chance to do something you gave up."

I walked backward, processing, trying to wrap my head around his words, worried this wasn't real. Maybe Seraphina was right and I had a little PTS after what had happened, too. I might need some counseling, along with Chase and Eden.

"Perform again?" I lifted my hands, staring at my fingers, which were aching to touch piano keys again.

"Yeah, that's what I'm suggesting." He stopped in front of me. "If that's what you want, of course."

"First, Seraphina offers me the dream idea of us all living down the street from one another. Now you're suggesting offering Trevor the chance to do something that I know will fulfill him, and . . . *this* too?"

"I'm saying that one thing I've learned since meeting Seraphina is that the sky's the limit on what we can have if we believe it's possible."

He opened his arms, and I accepted the offer and hugged him.

"Well, you're going to make an excellent father one day," I said against his chest.

"And speaking of dads . . ."

My heart flatlined at that. "Yeah?" I lifted my chin to look up at him.

"You're never going to ask me to confront and forgive him, are you?" His brows slanted. "Because if I face that man, I'll probably clock him across the jaw."

I laugh-cried. "I might pay good money to see that." I let the moment sit between us for a second before sighing. "No, I think we leave him in the past, where he wants to stay." I swallowed. "And since you were kind enough to FaceTime my mom this week and virtually meet her and forgive her—motivating me to also forgive her—I think that's enough forgiveness for now."

"You can't forgive someone who doesn't even think they were wrong." He paused. "That goes for Rhett, too." He let go of me. "I don't know how I feel about him continuing to do the whole living thing."

I pulled away, curious where he was going with this.

"Chandler got what he needed from him. Maybe Rhett should do what he had his girlfriend threaten Beth he'd do to her? A slip on wet concrete. A blown fuse. A glitch in the cameras to hide the truth of what happened."

He gave me his back and went over and set his hands on the spines of the books on a shelf, hanging his head.

"Will Hobbs pulled off some wild shit while in a black site himself. Echo Team put him down, but . . . can we really take the risk that someone like Rhett won't do the same?"

"So that's what this is." My eyes drifted to the ceiling. "You're asking me to green-light an execution."

He pushed away from the bookshelf, returning his attention to me.

"I'm asking to send a dead man back to his grave." His jaw clenched, eyes on me. "To protect you. Chase. Protect our future kids." His gaze dropped to my stomach as if he knew one day I might have more, and with his best friend. "That neighborhood dream of ours . . ." His words trailed off, emotion catching in his throat.

The knock on the door yanked me out of the morally gray zone Ryder had just dragged me into. Had he forgotten he was talking to me, not Hollis?

I didn't know whether to feel relieved or the *over* in *overwhelmed* about all this as Alejandro joined us.

He shut the door, eyes sharp on Ryder. "You talk about it yet?"

Just like that, I was being asked to approve both a murder and a move all before breakfast. "Does Trevor know about this?"

"No, he doesn't need this decision on his shoulders." Alejandro approached me. "But I did mention the idea of working with us." He took my hand inside his big one, standing next to us. "POTUS agreed to have a team on standby for us like that. Three other guys, a new unit, and they don't have to be Delta."

This was all moving so fast.

"I'd love for y'all to work together. You did a great job last time." I forced a smile, still uneasy over the other part of this conversation.

"Take your time and think about what else I asked you. Though the sooner, the better. I'd like to get this wrapped up so we can focus on moving you to South Carolina." Ryder lifted his chin Alejandro's way. "Seems to me you have some moving to do yourself." He patted my shoulder. "I'll leave you two to chat." He left without another word and closed the door behind him.

"I don't want you getting blood on your hands." I pulled my hand free of his to rest it on his chest.

"If I promise blood won't literally end up on my hands or Ryder's?"

Yeah, I read between the lines on that one.

"What'd Trevor say about the job offer?"

"On board. He said he already got your okay about operating in Queenstown." He smiled. "You plan on taking that piano out of storage and playing again?"

I brought my hands up to his scruffy jawline and held his face. "Maybeee."

"Any chance you'll play for me again? Just you, the piano, and lace?" he asked before slanting his mouth over mine.

"Mmm," I murmured against his lips. "I think that can be arranged."

CHAPTER SIXTY

Alejandro

CIA black site; undisclosed location

Beth lounged in her chair, no longer in orange, as previously required, thanks to our deal. Her posture was relaxed despite the metal cuffs anchoring her wrists to the table bolted into the concrete floor.

Sitting across from her, in a windowless room in the secure wing, I leaned back, arms crossed, still regarding her as a possible threat. Hard not to do. "You know, you could've saved us all a lot of trouble and just told me the truth on that call. Just asked me not to tell Rhett that I knew he forced you to lie."

"Where would the fun in that be?" She lifted one shoulder. "Doubt you'd have followed through with this meeting if I did."

I studied her, jaw tight. "Some things never change, huh?"

Beth gave me another light shrug. "I knew your team would crack something on that flash drive. I had faith in you. I didn't marry an idiot." She smiled faintly. "But I'm still a work in progress. Trying to change, whether you believe that or not."

I was there.

Trying to.

But damn.

Could people like her really change? I mean, maybe there was something different about her?

Her eyes, which were once a sharp, icy blue, seemed softer now. Maybe I was imagining it? Maybe I needed to believe the evil had bled out of her and she wasn't a threat anymore. That I could walk out of here and not worry that she'd find a way back into my life to try to mess it up again.

"But I guess old habits die hard," she added, with an uneasy smile this time.

"I was hoping you'd say that." My pulse ticked higher. The fluorescent lights above buzzed. I braced my palms on the cold steel table and pushed to stand, not interested in spending another minute longer with her than need be.

"Why are you really here?" Her gaze narrowed slightly, trying to get an accurate read on me.

"Guard," I called over my shoulder. The reinforced door opened with a beep and a metallic groan. "Bring him in."

The guard nodded silently.

I checked the overhead camera in the corner. No blinking red light. Disabled, as requested.

Beth peeked around me. "What's going on?" she asked, voice still calm. Cool and controlled. Much more like the Beth I remembered, and unfortunately, I needed *that* her today.

"You'll see." I flexed my fingers as I waited, knuckles cracking.

A moment later, the guard returned, escorting Rhett in bright prison orange. His hands and ankles were shackled, and his gaze scraped over me as he was shoved down into my previous seat.

"Thank you. You can leave us," I said after the guard attached his cuffs to the table.

He obeyed, leaving the heavy door cracked for my exit.

"What is this?" Rhett gritted out.

Beth glanced at me as I circled the table and moved to her side.

I bent down, unfastened her cuffs with the key I'd been provided, then helped her stand before stepping back. "I'm giving Beth here a chance to do what I wish I could."

"And what's that?" Rhett strained against the cuffs.

"An opportunity to get blood on her hands." I drew the Glock from the back of my jeans and held it at my side. "You blackmailed her. Had your girlfriend threaten and torment her." I looked over at Beth. "Do you really want to be in the same prison as him?"

"Nah, you're too by-the-book. You won't kill me,"' Rhett snapped. "You *can't*."

"Like I said, *I'm* not doing anything." I handed the Glock to Beth. She took it carefully, watching me with something unreadable in her eyes, then rotated the weapon in her palm.

"It's empty," she said flatly. "I can tell."

I pulled the single round from my pocket.

Rhett's face contorted. "You won't let her do it."

I rounded the table and grabbed his chin with my free hand, squeezing until he flinched. "You sure about that?" I leaned in. "Is it really murder if you're already dead?" I let go of him and returned to Beth's side.

I held the round between us like the peace offering I couldn't believe I was giving to her.

"The choice is yours: He lives. Or he dies."

"You really trust she won't shoot you on your way out?" Rhett barked out, yanking at the cuffs.

I looked at Beth, then back at him. "That's a risk I'm willing to take." I placed the round in her open palm. "Just the one. Make it count." I nodded once and turned for the door.

"Alex?" she called out.

I paused in the doorway. A chambering click echoed. "Yeah?"

"You never said if you forgive me."

The question hit harder than I wanted it to. Her voice, just this side of sincere, gave me pause. “I can’t speak for the others you hurt, but don’t shoot me and that’d be a good start.” I stepped into the hall, the heavy door clicking shut behind me.

And a second later, a shot rang out.

EPILOGUE

Audrey

Charleston, South Carolina; ten weeks later

The Charleston breeze drifted through the cracked window, sweet with magnolia and salt from the nearby harbor. Our new neighborhood was quiet and perfect. The kind of place where porches mattered and people actually waved when you walked by. Heck, even Reed, who lived four doors down with a Belgian Malinois puppy, sometimes managed a half smile.

Chase loved it here, especially being within walking distance of everyone he loved and so close to Reed's puppy, who he was charged with dog-sitting when Reed was away on ops.

Trevor had already spun up on his first op with Delta Shield's new secondary unit, which now consisted of two other former operators. Chase couldn't have been prouder, either. His favorite people working together to save the world and catching bad guys.

We'd slipped into a routine here more easily than I'd expected. School, missions, banana bread baking. You know, life.

And tonight, Alejandro and I had something to share with our friends and family. My stomach fluttered with nerves even though I knew we'd be surrounded by love when giving everyone the news.

With Trevor out with Chase for the afternoon so we could get the place ready for the party, I'd decided to steal a few moments to decompress and play the piano first.

I'd put off trying out for an orchestra, choosing instead to play at home. In a house that had quickly become our sanctuary. This was happiness. The very definition of it. Being able to play for someone who really listened. Who truly cared.

"One more." Alejandro gave me prayer hands when I finished what I'd meant to be my last piece.

I smiled, the sunlight filtering across the keys. Natasha had gifted us her Yamaha after the wedding, a major upgrade to the one in storage. I'd tried to argue, but she'd waved me off and said it belonged with me.

"Your mom is early to everything," I reminded him as I glanced at the clock. "And then my mom tries to compete by being earlier than her, which means—"

I dropped my words when he peeled off his black tee, striding toward me. Muscles on display, every inch of him the embodiment of trouble I couldn't resist. My breath caught as he unbuckled his jeans, letting the belt slip free with a flick of his wrist that should've come with a warning label.

"Ah, I see what this is really about."

He gave me that lazy, devastating smile. "My wife's playing jazz wearing only pink lace panties, looking like a dream. What do you expect me to do? Just listen and not want her after?"

"I expected a little restraint," I teased. "My mistake." I smiled and gave in rather easily.

My fingers hovered; then I fell into the familiar rhythm of Ella Fitzgerald's "The Man I Love." This time with no ache in my chest. No ghosts in the music. Just love. Just us.

When the final note faded, he was at my side. Totally naked now, body hard and ready.

He lifted me effortlessly, carrying me from the room and down the hallway. I looked around as we passed the photos on the wall, at the life we'd begun building.

The photos when Chase and I'd first met my brother at Christmas.

The wedding photos from five weeks ago.

More and more happy memories lined the walls with every step he took.

When he set me down on our bed, I reminded him, "Time is precious."

"Don't I know it," he whispered before joining me.

He slanted his mouth over mine, hand between us, shifting the lace aside. He had a thing about taking me while I was still in them. His turn-on turned *me* on.

He bit my lower lip while pushing two fingers inside me. "Drenched," he said after freeing my lip. "What am I going to do with you?"

"It's the hormones—or maybe our baby's father making me all hot like this. Coin toss," I teased, a light laugh passing between our lips, which he caught with his tongue.

"You know what you do to me when you call me a father like that." His voice was rough as he removed his fingers to situate his hard length between our bodies.

"Make you want to get me pregnant all over again?"

He lifted his head, eyes tight on mine. "Over and over and over again, to be exact," he said before thrusting inside me, which had my breath catching, fingertips burying into his biceps. "Hands," he demanded once my body stretched for him.

He lifted our clasped palms alongside our heads. Fingers threaded together, he rotated his hips, moving like a dance. Making love. Making every moment count. Making me . . . "Come too fast," I cried out as he used his pelvic bone to rub against me in just the right spot to cause friction.

"Something about time, *sí?*"

"Not that fast." I laugh-moaned, shifting harder and faster with him, unable to slow down now that the orgasm was building.

This man. My God, this man. We might wind up with five more babies after our child was born. I wouldn't put it past him. I also wouldn't mind.

We came together with sighs and tangled limbs, a rhythm even more natural than my music.

When it was over, he stayed close, brushing his fingers along the curve of my hip. "I didn't think this through, did I?"

"Going to get the covers messy, yeah. Gotta keep your mom and mine out of here. Decoys and diversion tactics," I added with a laugh.

He let go of my hands, bracing his alongside my body without pulling out. His eyes went to my breasts. "You were already big, Mama. Now . . ." He licked his lips. *"Peligroso."*

"It's amazing no one has figured out yet I'm pregnant from my chest size alone." I palmed his cheek, urging his eyes back to mine before the man got horny again. Think I'm kidding? He recovered fast and could go all day and night. *Stamina* was an understatement. "They're going to do the math when we tell them tonight. They'll realize we were pregnant before the wedding."

"Distract. Deflect. That's our mission." He smirked. "It's our only choice, since both of us are lousy liars." He gave me a soft kiss; then we did our best to make the least mess possible and washed up just in time before our mothers arrived, early as expected.

The next several hours blurred by, the party in full swing. The house was packed with guests, laughter, and delicious food.

And once we finally shared the big news about the pregnancy, it was clear most of our family had suspected.

"About time you told us, so we could act like we didn't know. No wine all of a sudden—come on," my mom said with a laugh, then embarrassed me by pointing to my boobs in front of everyone. Including the secretary of defense.

"¡Bebé!" Alejandro's mom was overwhelmed with joy, tears hitting her eyes, which had my husband blinking back a few of his own after she hugged us both. *"Gracias a Dios."*

More hugs and happy tears all around. And then Alejandro's father pulled a cigar out of nowhere like it'd come from a magician's hat.

Sheesh. They really did know why we were having this party tonight.

"I can't wait to be a big brother!" Chase shouted later that night, sitting on top of Alejandro's shoulders, fist pumping. "Daddy has to have more kids, too! We can be one big family. The bestest!"

Trevor smirked. "Let's leave the sibling business to your mom and Alex."

"Too busy saving the world to meet a girl?" Chase grinned, and everyone within earshot laughed.

"Don't forget doting on me every five seconds as if worried I might break," Eden added, resting a hand over her stomach. She was pregnant with Beau's (a.k.a. Zander's) baby. She'd decided to turn something awful Beau had done into a miracle, and it seemed being pregnant was healing her from the inside out.

I admired her so much. She was finding strength in the aftermath of what had happened.

And our babies would be born close together. New beginnings, side by side.

I turned to find Hollis coming back after stepping away for a call from her father. "I actually have to cut out early, I'm sorry."

Reed looked up from where his puppy had curled in his lap. "She's probably off to stab someone with cutlery."

"That's Carter, not me," she shot back, grinning. I had no clue what they were talking about. "Besides, hopefully there'll be no stabbing involved. More of a recovery mission." She leaned in closer. "Remember the artifact I offered to use to get us into the auction? It got lost in the chaos, and my dad finally got a fix on the location, and he wants it back." She stood by Reed and scratched behind his dog's ear.

"Traitor," he grunted in response to Ranger's moaning from her attention.

"Could use an assist. You in, Jason?"

"I told you not to call me that."

"Why don't you like your first name?" She stopped petting Ranger, and Reed shifted the puppy from his lap. He wagged his tail all the way over to his second-favorite human (probably, secretly first), Chase.

I ignored their grumbling back-and-forth while looking on at Chase dropping down to hug Ranger. He was standing with Alejandro, Ryder, and his dad as they talked about something.

Alejandro caught my gaze. "I love you so much," he mouthed.

To which I mouthed back, *"Te amo mucho."*

My Spanish was a work in progress, but I had an excellent teacher, who rewarded my hard studying with orgasms on a nightly basis.

"Well, if you change your mind, you know where to find me." At that comment from Hollis, I turned to face her again, finding Reed scratching his jaw, an agitated stare pointed her way. "Sorry again for bailing early." She pulled me in for a quick hug.

"Can you tell me where you're going?"

"Safer if you don't know."

Of course she'd say that.

Her gaze dropped to my stomach and a flicker of a smile crossed her lips. She leaned in and whispered into my ear, "It was that night, wasn't it? He got you pregnant before the auction."

She lifted her head, shooting a knowing smile my way despite me not confirming she was, in fact, correct.

"Well," she said, gaze bouncing between me and Reed, "off to my next adventure." She shifted her wavy hair to her back while tossing out, "Be seeing you around, Jason."

"Yeah, sure." He mock-saluted. "Don't die or anything."

"That'd give you too much joy. I wouldn't dream of it." She winked, then hugged me one more time before leaving.

Reed dropped back into his seat with an annoyed huff before calling his dog back over.

Alejandro came up behind me a few minutes later, wrapping his arms around me. "What was that all about?"

I tipped my chin up to meet his eyes. "I think it's an open loop?"

He smiled. "Translate."

I looked around the room at everyone. At Eden. Trevor. And lastly, Reed.

"It means," I said, warmth flooding me, "we're surrounded by unfinished stories that need happy endings."

He tightened his arms around me in understanding.

"And thanks to you, mister . . . now I know it only takes one note—one incredible meant-to-be—for everything to come together."

AUTHOR'S NOTE

One of my favorite things to do is to have characters from other series cross over into new books to keep them "alive." Delta Shield Security has quite a few cameos from three different series.

The Costa Family—Italian American "vigilantes" (in private security) who are former military: Enzo (*Let Me Love You*), Alessandro (*Not Mine to Keep*), Hudson / Isabella Costa (*The Art of You*), Constantine (*The Best of Us*).

Stealth Ops—Navy SEALs working covert ops for the president of the United States.

- **Stealth Ops: Bravo Team**
- *Finding His Mark* (Luke, Bravo One)
- *Finding Justice* (Owen, Bravo Two)
- *Finding the Fight* (Asher, Bravo Three, Jessica's husband)
- *Finding Her Chance* (Liam, the Aussie, Bravo Four)
- *Finding the Way Back* (Knox, POTUS's son, Bravo Five)

- **Stealth Ops: Echo Team**
- *Chasing the Knight* (Wyatt, Echo One)—where we first meet his daughter Gwen
- *Chasing Daylight* (A.J., Echo Two)
- *Chasing Fortune* (Chris, Echo Three, K-9 handler for Bear)

- *Chasing Shadows* (Roman, Echo Four)
- *Chasing the Storm* (Finn, Echo Five)—his wife's brother is Michael Maddox from *The Safe Bet*

Falcon Falls Security—features former army operators who work private security. This series is a direct spin-off from the Stealth Ops series. Carter Dominick (*The Fallen One*) co-runs Falcon with Grayson Chandler (*The Taken One*). Book 1 in the series is *The Hunted One.*

Gwen Montgomery is also a main character in the Falcon Falls Security series—she joined in book 3, *The Guarded One*. Her book releases in fall 2026 as a stand-alone spin-off.

ABOUT THE AUTHOR

Brittney Sahin is the *Wall Street Journal* bestselling author of numerous series, including Delta Shield Security, the Costa Family, Falcon Falls Security, Dublin Nights, and many other novels of romantic suspense. She began writing at an early age with the dream to be a published author before the age of eighteen. Although academic pursuits (and later, a teaching career) interrupted her aspirations, she never stopped writing or imagining. It wasn't until her students encouraged her to follow her dreams that Brittney said goodbye to Upstate New York to start a new adventure in the place she was raised: Charlotte, North Carolina. Here, she decided to take her students' advice and begin to write again. When she's not working on upcoming novels, she spends time with her family. She is the proud mother of two boys, and a lover of suspense novels, coffee, and the outdoors. For more information, visit www.brittneysahin.com.